He ran the tips of his fingers down her cheek, along the curve of her jaw. His touch was as hot as the stroke of a brand, yet left a trail of gooseflesh in its wake.

"Ha! 'Tis but conceit on your part, sir. Or wishful thinking." She tried to push past him, to thrust him aside, but he pressed her back against the pillar and held her there. "Are ye saying ye have no feelings for me?" he demanded, tilting her chin, so that she had no choice but to look at him.

She glared at him mutely, painfully aware of their proximity. She swallowed. *Dear God,* this near, she could all but feel the thud of his heart against her own!

"Answer me, firebrand!" he commanded again, ducking his head lower.

"Nay," she whispered fiercely. "You are my husband's brother. Nothing more."

"Nothing?" He was so close, so close his lips were almost brushing her hair, nearly touching her brow. Perversely, longing filled her, even as fear closed her throat. Surely, oh, blessed God, surely he could not mean to kiss her?

But he did.

Cupping her chin, he lowered his dark head and fitted his hungry mouth over hers.

LOOK FOR THESE REGENCY ROMANCES

THE LOVE WITHIN

Penelope Neri

Zebra Books
Kensington Publishing Corp.

http://www.zebrabooks.com

ZEBRA BOOKS are published by

Kensington Publishing Corp.
850 Third Avenue
New York, NY 10022

First Printing: June, 1997
10 9 8 7 6 5 4 3 2 1

Printed in the United States of America

"Employ the silver adder's tongue,
If his imperiled soul you'd win.
With courage, slay the monstrous beast,
Set free the love that lies within!"

—Sven, the Skald

Prologue

"I curse you, sea-wolf!" the old earl whispered. He tried to sit up, but bubbles of red appeared between his lips, and he fell back with a soft groan. His fingers were clamped about the hilt of a dagger. It jutted from between his ribs like a crucifix. When he tried to speak, as he did now, whistling noises escaped him. "A curse upon you—yea, and upon your seed, Torrin the Red! Man-wolves! Unholy curs! Slayer of innocents! You shall rue the day you sailed your dragonships to Waterford!"

In response, the towering Viking threw back his red-gold mane and roared with laughter. Firelight burnished his conical bronze helmet, which was winged like a screaming bird of prey. More light from torches and rushlight gleamed on the wide bands of hammered copper at his wrists, the bronze brooches at his shoulders, the jewelled hilt of the broadsword that clanked noisily at his side.

His giant shadow aping his movements, Torrin Ericksen snatched an apple from a pottery bowl. Sinking strong white teeth into the fruit, he chewed, then idly nudged the earl with the toe of his boot to see if he yet lived.

The old man groaned in agony.

"What's this? *I'll* rue this day? *Nej*, old fool! *I'll* regret nothing!'' he scoffed. He lobbed his apple core at the fallen man, then lewdly sucked on his sticky fingers, one by one. ''I shall be too busy enjoying your daughter! *Canute! Rolf!* Make haste, you whoresons! Bring me the blackhaired witch!''

While he waited for his brothers, Torrin leered down at the dying man. His light-blue eyes grew small and hard with spite.

Thank the gods, he had won! He had taken Waterford Keep, the gateway to Eire, as his own. Within the month, all of Munster would be his. . . .

His gaze narrowed. 'Twas already past moonrise. He must be quick! Before the day waned, he had sworn to secure his victory by taking earl Murragh's daughter, Deirdre, to wife, and planting his heir in her belly. A babe conceived on the night of his father's greatest triumph would surely be a warrior among men!

But meanwhile!—He chuckled. Meanwhile, he would savor the helpless fury that blazed in the old man's eyes, when he saw the girl brought, weeping, before him. . . .

''Did you hear me, old man? *Your daughter,* I said!'' he repeated, looking down in triumph.

But his boast had come too late.

Earl Murragh of Waterford was already dead. His soul had fled to the feast halls of Valhalla—or perhaps to the insipid heaven promised by the Christian priests, somewhere far above the clouds.

Torrin stirred uneasily, as he looked down at the corpse's face. He had seen many dead men in his lifetime, but none who had looked like this. None who'd died in agony, yet wore a smile! Worse, Murragh's lifeless eyes, glassy in the torchlight, seemed to follow him accusingly, as he backed from the bower. Left or right, there was no escaping them!—

A trickle of foreboding sluiced down the warrior's spine as he sped across the bailey to the keep's great hall, instead of waiting for his brothers to bring the maiden. *By Odin's Ravens, what had the old man to smile about as he died?* The towering Viking frowned, trying to remember what words Murragh had uttered with his dying breath:

"A curse upon you—yea, and upon all your seed, Torrin Ericksen!" he had said. *"Man-wolves! Unholy curs! Slayers of innocents! You shall rue the day you sailed your dragonships to Waterford!"*

And from the distant woods, the wolves began to howl.

Chapter One

Raven hair furling behind him, he dug his boot heels into his glossy black horse's flanks. Crouched forward over Conn's arched neck, he raced the eager stallion along the shore, his green and black plaid flapping and twisting on the wind at his back, clods of wet sand churning up behind the horse's flying hooves.

The sea was wild in St. George's Channel this brisk spring morn. She hurled angry plumes of froth high over the crags, edging ever closer to the foot of the standing stones known as the Gray Maidens, the circle of pagan monoliths that had been raised there long ago by the magic of druid priests. And there they would remain till the world ended, he'd decided, when he thought about it at all: keepers of ancient secrets.

Reining Conn in, he twisted in the saddle to look back the way he'd come.

Wulfskeep, built by Jarl Torrin many years ago on the place where earl Murragh's keep had once stood, rose from a lofty mount overlooking the mouth of the River Suir.

Across the small valley—as if erected in defiance of the old gods's power—stood Kerrin's destination, the austere stone convent of St. Brigit. 'Twas to St. Brigit's that his mother,

Deirdre of Waterford, had been exiled over two decades before by her husband, Torrin, for the sin of adultery. His mother's banishment had left him, to all intents and purposes, an orphan, and he had been raised by the old midwife, Myrla.

He scowled. His mother was not expecting him, he knew. Why would she, after all these years? For some reason, though, he had felt compelled to visit her before he left for Britain. He did not know why, unless it was to remind himself of the high cost of trusting a woman—any woman.

Sure, and he'd taken his pleasure of many ripe female bodies since becoming a man, but he had given none a second thought, let alone his heart, once he'd fastened his breeks. In truth, he sorely doubted he had a heart to give! But just in case he was tempted to trust the Saxon princess, who would be his bride, a visit to the woman who'd betrayed his father would serve to remind him. Caring was folly.

"Welcome, my son," his mother exclaimed, when the nun ushered him into her barren cell. Another sister placed a flagon of watered wine and a platter of oatcakes on the table, then left the two of them alone. "Will you not sit with me at table, Padraic?"

"I am known as Kerrin."

"Very well. Kerrin. I—Let us partake of a little refreshment together and mayhap after, you would tell me about your life?" She busied herself breaking the oatcake and pouring the watered-wine into goblets, knowing she was talking too much, but unable to help herself. Her prayers had been answered, at last. Padraic—or Kerrin, as he called himself, had come to see her after all this time! Her lower lip trembled. While only hours old, Kerrin had been torn from her breast, taken away to be raised by others, while her own milk hardened in her breasts. She ached now to hold him, to stroke his fine, dark head, but dared not! His expression was too cold, too filled with hostility, his body was carried too rigidly for embraces. She sighed. He had grown into a cold, hard man who knew nothing of a mother's gentling influence. Or, she feared, of love and tenderness. What manner of husband would such a man become? It would take a rare woman to unlock the softness that was buried within him.

"Padraic, beloved son, it has been so long since I saw you."

His lip had curled with contempt, she saw, but she had been unable to keep from calling him "son." The Good Lord knew, she still thought of him as her son!

In reality, a grown man stood stiffly in her doorway. A strikingly handsome man who'd inherited her father's chiselled Gaelic features and proud bearing, her own hair coloring, and a forgotten ancestor's leaf-green eyes. She had scarce recognized him today, for when last she'd seen him, he'd been an angry, bratling with a shock of ragged black locks. A rude boy who had sought her out for the express purpose of telling her, with tears streaming down his face, that he did not love her—had *never* loved her—*would* never love her, because she had made him a bastard!

Now he was a score and nine years, and the scrawny lad had vanished. The top of his dark head brushed the ceiling of her cell, she noted, a fierce burst of maternal pride swelling her breast, and his broad, manly shoulders filled her doorway. *The height and shoulders of his Viking father.* "When last you came, you were but a stripling, my dear! And now—"

"Now I am a man, aye. But, what is that to you?" he snapped, scowling like a thundercloud.

She shrunk a little at his tone, all hope that they could mend the rift between them shrivelling beneath his contempt. So. Time had done nothing to improve his manners, nor to soften his hatred of her. Surely she had her husband, Torrin, to thank for that! Padraic had been his innocent victim, as had she. *Oh, Torrin, what a blind fool you are! Can you not see yourself in this, your only son? The stamp of your blood is burned upon him as clearly as a brand! Proud, foolish Viking, you cheated yourself of a fine son—and a loyal and loving wife!—when you chose to believe Canute's lies over my sworn word!*

Nevertheless, Deirdre kept her thoughts to herself and forced a hesitant smile, one that illuminated her pale, still lovely face and animated her weary eyes. But alas, no smile warmed her son's hard, handsome features in return. "Edana of Kenley would be eighteen winters by now, yea? Her mother was a great beauty in her youth. As I recall, our *senachies* called her the fairest jewel ever brought to Britain from the sea! Yet rumors claim her daughter is fairer still. You are fortunate your father contracted such a match for you, my son. Your betrothed's father had the ear of Alfred of Britain and is as close to Edward Elder, Alfred's heir. Your marriage will bring Waterford great riches and powerful allies, as well as protection from—''

''Surely you forget yourself, lady? Jarl Torrin is no longer your husband—any more than he was ever my sire!'' he snarled, turning on her with his green eyes blazing, his handsome features twisted into a mask of hatred. ''You are naught but an adulteress—my uncle's whore!''

''How dare you!—'' his mother whispered. Drawing back her hand, she struck him. The blow snapped his head to one side and left a crimson palm print on his face. ''I was untouched when I became Jarl Torrin's bride. My virginity was the prize awarded my father's murderer, along with his keep and his lands!''

''Enough, woman,'' he growled. His eyes had changed from green to molten gold in his fury.

''Nay, Padraic, You *will* hear me!'' Deirdre vowed, rounding on him. Her pallid beauty had a rare fire in her anger. Her cheeks were crimson against the inky blackness of her hair. ''Torrin the Red sailed up the Suir with his dragon-ships to raze and pillage Waterford. He and his foul brothers, Canute and Rolf Ericksen, took everything we had. Our strong young men, the flower of our womanhood—even our little children were loaded like cattle onto their dragonships, and carried off to Norway to become slaves. My churls were left with naught but the crops left rotting in the fields, unharvested—and myself!

''When there was nothing left, Torrin came to my bower. He demanded my maidenhead and my hand in marriage, in return for my people's lives.'' She drew herself up to her full height. ''I am—was!—the lady of Waterford. Your grandfather, God assoil him, had perished by Torrin's hand, as had my two older brothers, Brian and Donovan, both of them slain whilst defending our keep. I was all my people had left. What choice did I have?'' She shook her head, remembering. ''Ten moons later, you pushed yourself into this world from my womb. You, Padraic. Torrin's son.''

''Rolf's son,'' he seethed.

''Nay! You are truly Jarl Torrin's seed. He knows it, too, in his heart of hearts, tho' he's afraid to admit it!''

''Afraid?'' he jeered. ''Of what?!''

''For his immortal soul!'' she whispered hoarsely. ''Don't you see? If Torrin accepts you as his son, then he killed his brother, Rolf for naught!''

''You mean, he slew your lover, do you not?'' Padraic barked. His upper lip was curled in contempt. His tone was savage with anger.

''We became friends, Rolf and I. I do confess it freely. Of the three brothers—Torrin, Canute, and himself, Rolf was the kindest. But, we were never lovers.''

Padraic snorted. ''So you have claimed since the hour Torrin banished you to this convent, Mother. I wonder, what do you here, with so many empty hours to fill?'' he demanded harshly, all the bitterness of his lonely childhood and the cruelties inflicted upon him spewing forth. ''Cast spells to make his women barren?'' He chuckled mirthlessly. ''I wager you'd enjoy seeing Torrin forced to choose between me—his brother's bastard!—and Canute, the brother he hates—for an heir!''

''How can you think me capable of such wickedness?'' Deirdre protested. ''Besides, Torrin knows you must succeed him, Padraic. He has no choice.''

Padraic's chiselled lips curled in a mocking smile. ''If you are given your heart's desire, I doubt it not, Mother. You'd not be the first woman who plotted her return to power from a convent cell. Nor will you be the last. But, mark me well, Deirdre of Wat. You'll not ride to greatness upon my back! Even should Torrin choose me to rule Wulfskeep when he is dead and gone, I shall never free you from this spartan cell!''

''I care not. My life ended the day he tore you from my breast. Now, be gone with you,'' Deirdre cried, overwrought by her son's accusations. ''You, who should have brought me joy, have brought me naught but tears and sorrow. I shall pray each day for God to open your eyes to the truth, Padraic mac Torrin! One day, you shall come to regret your cruelty to me. When you come to me on bended knee, I pray I yet have breath to forgive thee. For now, be gone with you. Oh, be gone—!''

Turning on his heel, he left her.

''Well? What did the old witch say, eh?''

Padraic had found Torrin in his bed in the chieftain's smoky bower, plagued with congestion of the lungs that made his breathing raspy. His eyes were sunken and bloodshot, the whites markedly yellow. And, though it was spring and several braziers had been placed about the chamber at his request, he still complained of the chill.

Did she wish ye well on your bride-quest?'' Torrin sneered.

''She did not. She said only that she would pray for God to open your eyes to the truth, *min jarl,* and hope that one day, you would regret your cruelty to her.''

''Ho! Did she, now? I say 'tis she who'll rue the day she bedded with my brother—may hell devour his soul!''

The closed, stony expression on Padraic's face faltered, softened. ''There . . . there is no truth to her claims, I suppose?''

''Never! She's a clever vixen—that's all! You are my nephew, *ja*—but no son of my loins—aaggh! Aagh!'' He fell to coughing, his face turning livid before he had cleared his throat of spittle. ''By Loki, I warned you not to visit her. She has you wondering, now, eh, that crafty slut?'' Torrin drank from the jewelled beaker of mead that Padraic handed him, wiped his matted red beard upon his fist, then flung the vessel to the rushes. ''Women! They're all the same—hot to mate with any man, no matter their marriage vows! Believe me, lad, their word is not to be trusted!''

He coughed loudly and thickly again, and the scorn faded from his face. Instead of a fierce sea-wolf, a warrior-lord, he became simply a barrel-chested, aging Norseman with frightened eyes and a big belly, one whose thick mane of ragged locks were more gray than red in the gloomy hall, like those streaking his beard.

Struggling to sit up, Torrin was breathing heavily as he waggled his index finger at Padraic and added, "Your fair bride will prove no different from the rest, whelp, albeit the blood of kings runs in her veins! Should ye once turn yer back— *beware!* She'll whelp another's bastard in your bed, as did your mother in mine!"

A dark, angry flush rose up Padraic's throat to darken his cheeks. He had grown to manhood hearing such claims. Indeed, the worthlessness of women had been hammered into his skull with no more thought than had Torrin's clouts. By the time Padraic had reached ten summers, his mother, Deirdre—the "Wanton of Wat," as she'd come to be known—had already been confined to the nunnery of St. Brigit for a decade, while he had been reared by an assortment of slatternly serving wenches and house churls about the keep, well-meaning but harried folk who'd had no time nor love to spare for a lonely, frightened little boy's care.

Only Myrla, the midwife who'd delivered him, had ever shown him an ounce of affection, or a moment's understanding. Consequently, it was to her hovel he'd flee, whenever anger or fear overwhelmed him and when the wildness in his heart grew too great to bear alone.

It had been Myrla, too, who had tried to persuade Padraic of his mother's innocence, when he was of an age to understand. But alas, her efforts proved to no avail.

"Believe me, lad, to the last maid, women are not to be trusted!"

Torrin's words still echoing in his ears, Padraic clenched his fists and jaw, determined to challenge the old sea-wolf's claims.

"There you are wrong, my lord uncle!" he vowed softly. His green eyes were cold, distant, as he gazed into the great fire that crackled on the hearthstones of the hall. "Long before Edana shares my furs, I shall know if she owns the loyal heart of a princess—or the easy virtue of a camp follower. I swear it upon my broadsword, Widow-Maker."

Chapter Two

"Your face betrays ye, Prince Alaric! My brother's message has displeased thee," the lilting voice observed, thick with the brogue of distant Ireland and the peat bogs. "However, there's naught to be done about it now—unless ye would break the betrothal? Jarl Torrin was dying when I left Eire, sir. I'faith, he may already have joined the angels in heaven by now, God rest his soul! Surely you understand that Padraic's place was at his . . . our father's deathbed? To leave at such a time would have been unseemly."

"Indeed it would," Alaric of Kent agreed, though his gray eyes said otherwise. Still, as host to the Irish chieftain's brother and his men, as well as the father of the bride, it seemed prudent he keep his opinions to himself. "It is our earnest hope you will return to Waterford to find Jarl Torrin fully recovered, is it not, my lady?"

Beside him, his wife, the lady Marissa snorted her displeasure. Alaric shot her a warning scowl that persuaded her to clench her teeth and answer in the affirmative, though the spark in her sapphire eyes betrayed her true feelings on the matter. "It is indeed, master Kerrin," she ground out.

The man inclined his head before continuing. "We had, of

course, intended to make the voyage to Kent by ship. However, my vessel was badly damaged in a storm. She ran aground off the west coast of Wales and is undergoing repairs at St. Daffyd's, where we will rejoin the rest of my crew.''

"An unfortunate turn of events, sir. No lives were lost, I trust?''

"Not a one, thank you, sir.''

"Thanks be to God! Tell me, how many men does your escort contain?''

"My brother entrusted the Lady Edana to no less than thirty-six men, including myself, sir. Alas, only a handful of that number rode on with me from St. Daffyd's to Kenley. But never fear, my lord, gracious lady. Your daughter will be safely escorted to her new home. And you may rest assured that Padraic intended no insult to either King Edward or to yourself by sending me to represent him.'' The corners of his mouth twitched but, whether in amusement or mockery, it was hard to tell. He added, "On the contrary. Padraic's wishes are mine.''

"Quite so, quite so. And you must forgive us if we seem somewhat ... taken aback, milord Kerrin. However, even as we speak, there are sides of venison roasting on spits in the kitchens, sir! Swans and geese are being plucked. Great baskets of lampreys and eels were taken fresh from the sea this morn, when your banners were first sighted. What, pray, are we to do with such quantities of food, if there is to be no wedding feast?'' Marissa asked, tapping her foot on the rushes. The thought of such senseless waste, coming on the heels of a long, hard winter across the isle of Britain, infuriated her.

The Irishman's casual announcement that Edan's bridegroom had not sailed with him from Eire had initially been met with considerable relief. *God be thanked!* she'd thought. *This wild-haired ruffian is not my lovely Edan's bridegroom!* Anger had followed quickly upon the heels of relief; anger that this—this thoughtless rogue had sent no rider ahead of him to warn her household of the change in plans! Surely the Irish were a race of ill-mannered peasants!

"There will assuredly be a wedding, madam, never fear. Padraic has made special provisions for that event.''

He spoke in the low, reasonable tone employed when speaking with dimwits, the Lady Marissa observed, her anger mounting. "Oh? How so?" she snapped.

"This document should make everything quite clear, my lord, my lady. Padraic was most anxious to set everything down in his own hand. Your—er—your household cleric could read it to ye . . . ?"

"I can read well enough for myself, sir," Marissa informed him coldly, before Alaric could speak for her. Accepting the rolled parchment from her husband, she broke the red wax seal.

Her tawny brows lifted in surprise. The curling lines of graceful script impressed her, despite her anger. If Padraic of Wulfskeep, County Waterford, had indeed written the document himself, he was hardly the Irish barbarian his brother appeared, in that outlandish green and black plaid. Rather, his penmanship hinted at an educated man, one who—she broke off, her lovely brow knitted. "Why, this document states that you are to stand proxy in your brother's stead, sir!"

"Indeed it does, my lady," he acknowledged.

"Then I suppose the wedding feast may proceed as planned, may it not? The people of Kenley shall enjoy the celebrations they have been awaiting."

"But of course, my lady." He wondered, as he fixed an insolent eye on the imposing lady of Kenley, if the daughter was as striking as her dam?

Marissa of Kenley wore her red-gold hair in a coronet that gave her a regal air. The clean lines of her Scandinavian features were still pure and strong, her figure slenderly curved beneath a kirtle of turquoise wool. In all, she was a woman to draw any man's lustful eye—yea, and her husband's broadsword with it! The Saxon prince was a lucky dog!

Had the daughter her mother's beauty? Did she possess her dam's fiery temper, he wondered? He hoped so, for to his mind, a beautiful woman without spirit was as tasteless as a portion of tender meat eaten without salt—and as quickly forgotten. Still, he supposed he'd find out if the rumors had been true soon enough, he reflected, impatiently slapping his leather gauntlets against his thigh. The lady of Kenley, startled by the sudden sound, jumped, and he hid a sly grin. By his own design, he had become a man few mothers dreamed of their daughters' marrying, even by proxy!

His thick black hair had been unevenly shorn and fell about his shoulders like a ragged mane, courtesy of Niall's blunt dagger. His unshaven cheeks were dark with stubble, having felt no blade in over three weeks. A length of the Murragh plaid completed the look of a barbaric savage he'd cultivated. In truth, he had knelt to drink from a glassy pool that morn and given himself a jolt!

The rare Greenland hawk, perched regally upon his shoulder, added to his exotic, foreign appearance. Uttering throaty little noises, she lovingly rubbed her snowy head against her master's cheek. Her movements made the silver bells attached to her bewits jingle prettily.

The combination of dark, scowling man and pristine bird of prey was a striking one—enough to give little Gayla, her youngest daughter, nightmares, Marissa thought, hiding a shudder. In truth, the rogue was deserving of his name, which, he'd explained upon his arrival, meant "Mysterious" or "Dark One" in the Gaelic tongue. Ha! Surely the towering brute before her was more warlock than warrior?

But she steadfastly resisted the urge to have him removed from her hall. As chatelaine of her husband's keep and lady of Kenley, she had certain obligations to perform, quite regardless of her personal opinions. Being the perfect hostess to their guests was one of them.

"We bid you fond welcome to our hall, sir," she told him at length, making a barely civil flourish with her jewelled hand. "Pray, rest and enjoy Kenley's hospitality, while I summon our daughter. One of my house churls will escort you to a bower, where you may wash away the dust of travel. Anon, we shall discuss the nuptials."

"A bower will not be necessary, my lady. Nor shall I require a body servant. If your churls will bring water to the byre, that is all I require. I will make my bed there."

"Very well, milord," Marissa agreed uncertainly. Ha! What man in his right mind preferred sleeping on a heap of straw, to a pallet filled with goosedown? Or a thin mantle, over warm furs and woolen coverings? It made no sense to her at all! She could not resist asking, "But, will you not be uncomfortable there?"

"Not at all, madam. 'Tis but for the one night, after all."

Her tawny brows shot skyward. "One night? But, why such haste to leave Kenley, milord?"

"I am urgently needed back in Ireland, my lady. My brother will have his hands full, with our father—may God assoil him!—dead. There are neighboring chieftains and Viking invaders who covet the county of Wat for her fertile fields and fine harbor." He did not add that Waterford was the gateway to Munster, nor that through it lay control of southern Eire. Instead, he added, "Warring clans, who would think it a prime time to attack my—Padraic's keep, with so many of Wulfs-keep's garrison gone. As you know, we have many leagues of travel across Britain, before we can take ship for Ireland. Perforce, we have little time to tarry.

"Summon your household priest straightway, madam. The lovely bride and myself shall exchange our—the—vows this very afternoon. Tonight, we shall feast! Then at first light on the morrow, we take horse for Wales."

Marissa bristled. "But what difference can another day or two matter? Such eagerness to wed and be gone will appear unseemly. Why, His Grace, the Bishop of Canterbury, has himself promised to hear the vows!"

"A Bishop?" He snorted. "We have no need of a bishop, madam. For all his fancy garb, a bishop's no more than a—a wealthy priest with a fat belly!"

"It is too late, milord! A messenger was dispatched to his Grace when your banners were first sighted. But even so, that good man is not expected until late on the morrow, sir! Could you not delay?" she implored. Her cajoling tone had never failed to win her husband over, but it had no discernible affect on the Irishman. To her dismay, Kerrin's features remained as coldly implacable as granite.

"Alas, nay, my lady. But never fear, your household cleric will be more than adequate for our simple needs," Kerrin assured her, in his lilting brogue. " 'Tis but an exchange of vows, after all, is it not?"

He grinned evilly, and winked in an infuriating, insolent way that made her itch to pluck his eye out with the sharpened point of her eating knife, then crush it beneath her boot heel like a grape. To her credit, however, she bit back her opinions of the Irish in general, and the Irishman before her in particular, and mustered a graceful curtsey. "As you will, my lord Kerrin."

He nodded in satisfaction. "Then pray bid your cooks continue with their preparations, my good lady. We shall wed, then we shall feast. But on the morrow—prompt at cockcrow—*we shall depart!*" For all its silky quality, his tone brooked no refusal.

Color flooded the lady's cheeks and stained her throat—a warning to those who knew her that she was close to exploding with anger. That insolent whelp! He made no secret of his disrespect for women! "Should my lord husband grant his permission, sir, you and your companions shall indeed depart at cockcrow." She smiled a venomous smile. "For now, gentlemen, I beg your leave to go to my poor—to go to our daughter. In my absence, our bard—one of your own countrymen!—will sing for your pleasure, sir."

Alaric bit back a chuckle, covering it with little success in a noisy show of clearing his throat. Liam's singing a pleasure? That was a good one! "Pray be seated, sir!" he urged the Irish envoy, when he'd recovered. "I would hear more of your country over a goblet of mead. Simon, refreshments for our guest! You, Peter! Rouse Master Liam from his bolt-hole."

Striding past her, Kerrin mounted the dais and—to Marissa's displeasure—took his seat at the lord's high table, selecting her husband's carved chair. He leaned back, his booted feet propped upon the trestle before him.

As he passed her, she gasped out loud and took a hasty step backward. For a fleeting second, she thought she'd glimpsed a shadowy black and silver wolf padding at the Irishman's heels, weaving, like a gray mist, amongst the swirling folds of his mantle. A huge, shadowy creature that cast her a baleful look from slitted golden eyes, before it melted into the shadows. . . .

Fingertips pressed to her temple, she blinked to dispel the unsettling image. Straightway, the wolf vanished. She frowned. Surely what she'd seen had been but a trick of the gloom and smoke in the hall, coupled with her upset? Surreptitiously crossing herself, she left the great hall, but not before she saw the gleam of *amusement* in Kerrin's eyes. . . .

Chapter Three

"Can you see him, Grania? Is he handsome?" Edan's voice was muffled, as she struggled to pull the kirtle down over her head.

"Weeell, nay, my lady," her serving woman supplied, unhelpfully, smothering an impish grin.

A snort of impatience escaped the folds of the kirtle. " 'Nay he's not very handsome,' or 'Nay, you cannot see him?' " Grania's young mistress demanded, worming her damp arms down the garment's unwieldy sleeves.

"No, I *can't* see him—so I can hardly tell if he's handsome or not, can I, my lady?" Grania reasoned.

Edan's dark head appeared through the neckline of her kirtle, like a mole popping up from its burrow. Her long, damp hair was a tangled mane of black curls. Her gray, lavender-ringed eyes dark with apprehension. "He *must* be handsome," she pronounced on a gusty sigh, as if she had not heard the steward's daughter. Smoothing the finely woven folds of the kirtle down over her willowy figure, she snatched up a comb of jewelled elk horn to rake through her freshly washed tresses. "I simply cannot spend the rest of my life with an ugly man!"

"You're in for a disappointment, I warrant, then," Grania

observed slyly, her fresh, comely features mustering a suitably pitying expression. "What I can see through this windeye now is ugly as sin!"

"Oh, surely not?" Edan protested, running to the windeye to see for herself. "I cannot believe Father would betroth me to a boy who—oh, you wretch! You wicked, wicked wench! You cannot see a thing from here, not with the rumps of those plow horses and that wagon standing there! I'll box your ears for this, Grania Tomsdotter," she threatened.

Grania's merry peal of laughter confirmed Edan's suspicions that the wench had been teasing her.

"Lying wretch! I should ask mother for another serving wench," she grumbled, shooting Grania a darkling look. "You, Grania Tomsdotter, are getting above yourself."

The serving girl snorted, unimpressed by her young mistress's threats. She stuck out her tongue. "Your blessed mother, as I recall, my lady, thanks *me* for keeping you on the straight and narrow since you came to womanhood. The lady Marissa says I have a 'calming influence' on you. So there!" she declared, with a smug little smile and a jaunty lift of her shoulders.

"That's only because Mother doesn't know what you're *really* like," Edan said hotly. She glared at the girl, who shrugged and knelt down to open a large wooden chest that stood in one corner of the bower.

"Never mind me. You'd best make ready. They'll be calling for ye soon."

The lid and sides of the chest were carved with mermaids, sea sirens, dragons, shells, and the like, set with cabochon-cut jewels that winked dully in the gloom. From its depths, Grania withdrew a mantle of lavender-blue, bordered with bands of stunning tablet embroidery that Edan's mother, the lady of Kenley keep, had sewn herself in silver, gold, and dark blue silks.

She shook the garment out, then tossed it over Edan's shoulders, smoothing the folds so that it hung gracefully. Lastly, she fastened a girdle of chiming silver links about her mistress's slender waist.

From the last links dangled an eating knife with a heavily jewelled handle, a small silver spoon, likewise elaborately chased, and a little metal box—all symbols of Edan's high rank as the eldest daughter of the powerful household of Alaric, ealdorman of Kent, viceroy to King Edward, *Bretwalda* of Wessex.

Grania sighed. Her handsome lord and master, Prince Alaric, had first met lady Edana's Viking mother when she'd led her Danish crew up the River Thames in a daring raid upon the hamlet of Kenley. The pair had crossed swords, according to the tales the old ones of Kenley told by the fire on long winter's eves. And, only after a fierce battle did the young lord Alaric capture the fiery, red-haired battle maiden. He had ordered her brought—naked, yet still defiant—into his hall. Thirsty for revenge upon her bloodthirsty, warring father, Thorfast of Danehof, who had driven Alaric's mother, Wilone, to madness and slain his father and brothers in an earlier raid, Alaric had made the captive beauty his bower slave. He had sworn to use her cruelly.

But, as always happens in the best of stories, Freya, as she had been called then, had dazzled her master with her beauty and her courage. Against all odds, Alaric had lost his heart to his "jewel from the sea," instead. He had bedded her, freed her, and wed her in quick succession. And, upon abandoning her Norse gods, Freya had taken the Christian name of Marissa, instead.

The pair had been blessed with six children since that happy day.

Firstborn had been the twins: Edana, the Fiery One, and her brother, Beorn "Two-Bloods" Alaricson, both eighteen winters.

Next had come lovely, sweet-faced, inquisitive Danica the Good, who at sixteen winters favored her pagan Viking grandmother, the lady Verdandi, and longed to take holy orders. Lord Alaric had promised to gift the convent of St. Theresia's with a large dowry next year in order for her to do so, though the lady Marissa was secretly hoping that Danica might yet change her mind.

Next came two more male "cubs" for the Bear of Kent and his lovely bride: fifteen-year-old Edward, who was black-haired and gray-eyed like Alaric and Beorn, followed by copper-haired, sapphire-eyed Gareth, who was fourteen and favored his dam.

Lastly, the happy union had been blessed with the darling baby of the family, little Gayla, who at six winters was the apple of everyone's eye, especially her brother Beorn's, Grania reflected with a pang. Hot tears stung behind her eyes. Beorn had spent little time at home of late, since he and Lord Alaric had quarreled. Beorn's frequent absences left all the wenches of Kenley missing him more keenly than a mouth mourned a lost tooth—she more than anyone! Truth was, she floated on air for days, if Beorn so much as smiled in her direction. . . .

"There, my lady! All ready!" Grania declared, forcing herself to sound cheerful, as she stepped away from her mistress to admire her handiwork. "And ye do look wondrous fair, even if I say so myself! That shade of blue suits you, it does. It brings out the heather in your eyes."

"Heather—humph! Don't try to flatter me, 'Nia, not now. I'm far too nervous—and too vexed with you!—to be placated *or* teased," Edan warned. Yet there was a catch in her voice as she spoke. "Oh, how I wish Beorn was here! Why did he have to go hunting today?"

"Amen to that!" Grania muttered with feeling.

"I need his counsel so badly, and he probably won't be back until after I—I am gone to Ireland." Her lower lip quivered.

Grania took her mistress in her arms and hugged her fiercely, offering up a silent prayer that Edan was wrong. She would dearly have liked to bid Beorn farewell herself—aye, and with a kiss! "There, there, now, my lady, don't fret. Men—why, they're just like young stags once they reach a certain age— forever locking antlers and fighting, you mark my words! And Beorn's too much like his lord father to settle for less than being chieftain of his own household, though everyone knows there can only be one stag to any herd, aye?" She squeezed Edan's hand. "Their quarrel will be soon mended and forgotten, you'll see."

She sighed. "I suppose so. But I heard mother talking with Beorn the other day. She suggested Beorn sail to Denmark and do battle for her father's old hall of Danehof."

Grania sighed. "When that day dawns, he'll have Viking wenches to warm his furs each night!" she murmured wistfully, wishing *she* could have been one of those maidens. "Still," she added, "there's nothing lord Beorn could do about your marriage to that barba—the Irishman, even were he here. This day was bound to come, sooner or later, my lady. 'Twas what your lord father had in mind all those years ago, when he betrothed you to Wulfskeep to seal the alliance between Wessex and the Irish Vikings."

Her young mistress nodded in unhappy agreement.

"Just remember that whatever happens, you won't be alone there. *I'll* be with you."

"Promise?"

"Promise! I swore when we were little, remember? A blood oath to remain friends forever!"

"I remember," Edan acknowledged gratefully, hugging Grania back just as hard. She blinked rapidly to dispel the shimmer of tears in her eyes. "And my heartfelt thanks for your kindness, dearest 'Nia. I do not always deserve your understanding, nor your affection, but I am truly grateful for both. However . . ." She grimaced. Apprehension quite distorted her lovely face. The slightly slanted, expressive gray eyes were shadowed beneath their fringing of long, sooty lashes. The finely drawn, ebony brows that arched like two delicate wings above them knitted in a frown. Her small, pretty nose was delicately scrunched up.

"But you're still afraid of what's ahead?" Grania supplied, responding to the flicker of apprehension she'd glimpsed in her mistress's face.

"Ye-ea."

Grania sighed. "Aye, I know. And who can blame you, pet? I'd be afraid, too, were it me marrying some wild Viking-Irish chieftain I'd never even seen, let alone met." She shuddered. "Or were I the one who'd have to share his furs at night!" She forced a reassuring smile and added brightly, "But there's nothing to worry about on that score, truly there isn't. Edythe says—''

"Edythe—ha! She's a fine one to soothe an innocent maiden's fears!'' Despite her sharp words, Edan's tone was fond. Eadie—the woman who had served as nurse to herself and all her brothers and sisters as babes—had a reputation for being a lusty wench. 'Twas said she enjoyed variety in her men and was sampling each and every one of lord Alaric's garrison in turn, from a young and beardless lad of thirteen to a hoary old graybeard of sixty!

"Anyway,'' Grania continued, lowering her voice to a whisper, "Edythe says once a wench's maidenhead has been properly breached, coupling is all pleasure and no pain.''

A chill slid down Edan's spine. She swallowed. She was no mewling faint heart, but nonetheless, the thought of her wedding night filled her with apprehension. She scowled. "Eadie mates as freely as my father's stag hounds, and well you know it,'' she observed. "In truth, 'tis only by virtue of those herbs and vinegar washes she sets such store by that she's never whelped! Still, I fancy her knowledge of such intimacies must be wanting. A tumble in a byre cannot be the same as in the marriage bed.''

Grania sighed at her mistress's naivete, as she turned Edan about. She was still thinking, as she deftly began plaiting a section of her silky black hair. From what she'd gleaned about such matters over the years, coupled with what she'd witnessed for herself in the great hall nights, where privacy was nonexistent, there was precious little difference between being tumbled in a pile of straw, or in a bed amongst heaped furs. Not unless you were truly in love, like the lady Marissa and her lord Alaric, that was. *Those two* seemed to take greater pleasure in their bedsport with every passing year, judging by the merry sounds escaping their bower—and their contented smiles whenever they left it.

Still, it was no use talking to her young mistress, not when she was in this mood—and certainly not when the green silk banners emblazoned with the black wolf's head of lady Edan's betrothed, had been spotted by the look outs in the battlements.

Within the hour, or very soon thereafter, they would at last set eyes upon the man who would rule their future, and wrest them away from Britain forever. . . .

"Hark! I can hear your lady mother's serving woman calling for you. Your betrothed is in the bailey!" Grania exclaimed suddenly, cocking her head to one side to listen. *Aye.* She'd not been mistaken. They were calling for her young mistress! Taking Edan's cold hand between her own, she kissed it, then pressed it to her cheek. "God bless. May every happiness await thee, my lady!"

"Aye, and Amen, Grania. May the good Lord bless us both!" Edan echoed with feeling as she crossed herself.

Then, drawing a deep breath, she led the way from the bower.

Chapter Four

"Wait! Where are you going, Mother?" Edan demanded, almost colliding with her lady mother, who had burst from the hall like a fiery arrow loosed from a bow.

Edan had planned to appear unimpressed by the strange horses and riders milling about, under the fluttering emerald banners of Padraic of Wulfskeep, but her high color and breathlessness betrayed her excitement.

"Do not go in there! I forbid it!" Marissa burst out, suddenly fearful of the dark aura she'd sensed surrounding the Irishman. "Please, *min yndling*," she implored, grasping Edana's hand. "Not—not yet."

As the two noblewomen talked, Grania squirmed in discomfort. They were in the center of the bailey, and consequently the center of attention, thanks to the lady of Kenley's dramatic outburst. She was acutely aware of the looks cast her way by the wretched Irish louts, who had come to escort her mistress and herself to their wild land. And, while 'twas true they were a fierce looking people, gossip and rumor had forgotten to report that they were handsome, too! Grania blushed, far from immune to the men's appreciative nods and loudly whispered compliments, as she waited for her mistress to finish her conversation with her lady mother.

". . . . well, now, and that one's fair as sunshine, is she not, lads? That hair—like a spill of summer wheat down her back, it is, sure! And those eyes—why, they're the blue of a robin's eggs!''

"Or the lough of Comeragh!'' added another, not to be outdone.

"Sapphires,'' insisted another man firmly. "T'be sure, a man could lose his heart t' such a colleen, could he not . . . ?''

"Ah, Hurleigh, lad, 'tis not my heart that aches for her!—'' quipped another, adding more fire to the crimson in Grania's flaming cheeks. "It's my—''

"Enough! Have you wretches naught to do but embarrass decent women?'' demanded another man. His voice had the ring of authority over the others.

Glancing over her shoulder, Grania found herself looking into a pair of dancing brown eyes set in a smiling face that was every bit as puckish and mischievous as Robin Goodfellow's. "Mistress Beauty, your pardon,'' the tall, lean fellow declared, doffing his cap to reveal a mane of light brown hair, as he swept her a gallant bow. "These—louts!—know no better.''

His comment brought him a chorus of groans and good-natured mutters from his companions, most of whom wore lengths of green and black plaid, pinned at the right shoulder.

"Ignore them, mistress, while I introduce myself. My name is —''

"Grania? *Grania! What is wrong with you, girl?''*

"Aa-ye, my lady?'' Grania stammered, flinging about to face the glowering mistress of Kenley.

"I bade you escort your mistress back to her bower. Go!''

"Straightway, my lady. But—begging your pardon, my lady, are we not to meet Lady Edan's betrothed?''

"Anon,'' Marissa snapped. "He is. . . . with his lordship.'' The tightened line of her lips and the high color in her cheeks said there was far more to it. Could the lady of Kenley have quarrelled with the lady Edan's betrothed, Grania wondered?

Unlikely, but 'twas possible. Something had upset her terribly. She had never seen her so agitated!

"Edan?"

"Yea, Mother?"

"I will come to speak you anon. Await me in your bower, pray."

"Aye, Mother," Edan agreed, in a demure tone she was far from feeling. What had gone wrong? Why was her mother so very angry, she would forget herself and snap at poor Grania before these . . . these foreigners? She swallowed. Had something happened to Padraic, was that it? Her stomach lurched with dread. Where, but a short while ago, she had dreaded the marriage taking place, had dreaded leaving Kenley for distant Ireland, now all she could think of was how awful, how very *demeaning* it would be if, for some reason, her bridegroom had decided to break their betrothal. Or had been slain. "Is—is anything wrong?"

"Oh, my poor, dear girl!—Nay, nothing. Nothing at all," Marissa insisted. Then she picked up her skirts and hastened towards her own bower, leaving her two serving women to flutter after her like ungainly herons.

"You heard your lady mother, Edan," Grania murmured, noting the mutinous gleam in Edan's eyes. "Back to the bower with you!"

"But, I've been cooped up in there all day," Edan grumbled. "I think I'll change and go for a gallop on Fayre before Mother remembers she wished to talk to me. Who knows? Mayhap I'll run into Beorn? If Mother comes before I get back, you'll make some excuse for me, won't you, dearest Grania. . . . ?"

Grania snorted. "Nay, not today. Come back, do, Edan! There'll be Hell to pay, should ye disobey your lady mother today!"

"Hmmm," Edan agreed, her expression thoughtful. Blowing Grania a kiss, she sped blithely away to change.

"I care nothing about alliances and pacts, milord husband," Marissa seethed, rounding on the towering, black-haired chieftain-prince in their bower a few hours later. "Proxy or nay, *I will not* send our daughter away with that—that—"

"Man?" Alaric suggested, with a glint of amusement in his smoky gray eyes.

"That—that unkempt brute! That whiskery wretch!—" she ground out, pacing furiously.

"Come, come, now, mistress wife. Be charitable, I pray thee. The man may be a trifle ragged, I agree, but he has endured a difficult journey to reach Kenley." He chuckled. "And even if he hadn't, the poor fellow cannot help his appearance, can he, now? Come, my sea jewel! Where is your Christian pity? Your compassion?"

"Gone, sir. All gone!" his lady muttered, casting him a darkling look. "Both flew out the windeye like sparrows when I first saw that—that lout!"

"Besides," Alaric continued, as if she'd made no comment, quaffing mead from a jewel-encrusted goblet with every evidence of relish, "what do the man's looks matter? Edana is to wed his *older brother*—not him! Just keep in mind that this Kerrin is but an escort, nothing more. You must admit, he seems capable enough for that task, despite his ragged locks?" He grinned, and she glared at him, knowing he was making gentle sport of her. "And by all accounts, he is most skilled with a broadsword—"

"Oh? And how did you come by that knowledge, pray?"

"From Edward. Our son says the Irishmen are well-trained and fiercely loyal to the man. He feels they'd follow him through fire, if need be! Our son is no poor judge of a man's mettle, as well you know, madam. Why, even little Gayla seemed to like him, and sh—"

"Gayla? You allowed him to meet my sweet, innocent baby?—"

"Aye. What of it? My little poppet left her nurse, trotted over to him, and clambered up into his lap!"

Remembering what she thought she'd seen, Marissa crossed herself. Never overly religious—religion and such Christian ideals as turning the other cheek and loving one's enemies had never sat well with her own, somewhat fiercer views—such protective measures were becoming an annoying habit since the Irishman's arrival. *"Christus sanctus!* What were you thinking of, husband? You made no move to stop her?—''

"Should I have?" Alaric shrugged. "I saw no harm in it, none at all. Besides, the Irishman seemed enchanted with our little minx—and she with him and his hawk! Why, your fearsome 'barbarian' but laughed, even when our naughty minx tried to pry the leather hood from its head! Calm yourself, wife. I have every assurance that lord Kerrin will prove a more than capable guardian for our daughter—unkempt or nay!''

Marissa frowned, clearly not a whit placated. She straddled her husband's leg and hauled off his soft kid boot, huffing and puffing as she did so, and scowling horribly. "You spoke with him at some length, *ja?*''

"I did, yea."

"And found naught wrong with him in all that time?" There was a world of accusation and doubt in her tone.

Alaric sighed. Truth was, he'd been impressed with the Irishman—though he had no intention of telling his wife that. Discretion forbade it! Adorable though she was, several years of marriage to Marissa had merely confirmed what their tempestuous courtship had accurately foretold: that his beloved was also possessed of a fiery temper when crossed or gainsaid; one that could result in him spending a long, miserable night upon the bumpy rushes of his great hall with both serfs and hounds, instead of in their bower, nestled comfortably upon goosedown pallets! "Naaay, nothing other than the obvious, my sweet,'' he disclaimed, airily.

"This Kerrin did not seem . . . sly . . . to you? As if he were . . . lying? Or other than what he'd have us believe?''

"Other? What else would he be, wife?" Alaric asked, frowning. "A shape-shifter? A wizard?" He grinned. "One of those magical little folk—what is it the Irish call them?—''

"Leprechauns. Pixies."

"Aye. Is he a leprechaun, my love? Nay, I think not!''

Infuriated by the teasing laughter in his tone, the amused sparkle in her husband's eyes, Marissa snorted. Men! Pah! "I should not have expected otherwise from you. Even the best of your sex is readily taken in by gentle words and charming smiles!''

"We are indeed, *min yndling*. 'Tis why, Lord help us, we fall prey to the wiles of . . . *women!*'' Grinning, he dropped a fond kiss upon his wife's brow and patted her bottom. "Come, now. Don your prettiest kirtle while I bathe. This night, we celebrate our daughter's wedding!''

"I could scrub my lord husband's back, if it would please him? . . .'' Marissa suggested in a smoky voice, her sapphire eyes heavy-lidded with desire. There was more than one way to win her lord husband over, she had learned during the years they'd been married. Mayhap she could persuade him to send some of Kenley's garrison with Edan's escort as far as Wales? *"Would* it please him?'' she repeated breathlessly, running a wet fingernail down the very center of his oaken belly.

He had no need to answer her. The hardness riding against her belly, as he pulled her roughly to him was answer enough. "Vixen! It would indeed, but . . . what of our guest, sweet?'' he asked huskily. "He is waiting, is he not?''

Marissa chuckled. "He refused my offer of a bower and a bath. Let him enjoy Liam's playing and singing a while longer, my lord.''

Alaric winced, yet could not staunch a chuckle of his own. "You are a cruel woman, wife,'' he accused, grinning. Their household bard, though greatly loved, was surely the *worst* harp player in all of Britain. Indeed, 'twas said Liam's singing sounded more like the barking of a lovesick walrus than a dulcet melody to delight the ears!

"*Ja*, I am, sir,'' Marissa agreed on a sigh, as she reached for the lacings of his breeks and freed his aching shaft. *Most* cruel. . . .''

Chapter Five

"*Oh!* Who are you? What do you here?" a startled Edan demanded, pulling up short.

She stared at him, thinking she had never seen such a stirring sight as the stranger before her.

Standing there, his back toward her, he was naked as Adam in the Garden of Eden. The mellow afternoon light filtered through chinks in the byre's wattle-and-daub walls to braze his smooth, hard-muscled body with its golden beams. The diffused light lent a raven's bluish sheen to the long, black hair he wore, scraped back and tied with a leather thong at the nape, like some fierce Mongol lord. His shoulders were broad and straight. His upper arms rippled and shimmied with muscle. The knobs of his spine raised ridges beneath the flesh of his back that led down to his rump. His buttocks—here she smothered a giggle—his buttocks were round and very firm, yet markedly paler than the rest of him, as if he spent much time in the sunshine, clad only in his breeks. His powerful legs were the heavily muscled limbs of a horseman, generously sprinkled with black hair.

As she gaped at him, the reason for his nakedness became apparent. A pottery basin of water had been placed on the manger before him. A linen cloth lay beside it. Ye gods, she had disturbed the fellow at his bath!

"What am I after doing here, ye ask? Why, I might ask the same of you, my lass! Spying, are ye, then?" he came back, with a wicked grin, turning suddenly to face her.

With a shriek, her hands flew up to cover her eyes, but, still grinning, he had flipped the linen cloth over his middle before she could see what she should not.

"I—I came for my horse," she murmured lamely, not knowing where to look. She settled on a small, hairless area of his breastbone.

"Aaah. A horse, is it, now?" Stormy black brows creased above a pair of intelligent dark green eyes. He shot her a challenging grin. "A fetching wench like yourself—ye'll be wanting a stallion then, aye?"

He sounded amused, though why, she did not know. "Nay, sirrah," she retorted crossly, angry more at herself than at him. "The mare. The gray one named Fayre. She's over there."

"Ah. You're a groom, then?" He looked her up and down and grinned.

"Nay, dolt! Of course not."

"Then what are ye after wanting with a nag, colleen? Could it be for your mistress?"

"My mistress?" she stammered, frowning. Belatedly, she realized the simple, homespun garment she'd changed into to go after Beorn had misled him. He'd mistaken her for a house churl! "Oh, my *mistress*," she repeated, pretending she'd misunderstood him.

"Yea, my wee Saxon plum. Your mistress. Now, which one is she?" He winked. "The lovely red-haired vixen who's ripe enough to teach a man a thing or two? Or . . . the blackhaired Hel's cat who hides from m . . . from her bridegroom like a sickly mare?"

Edan bristled. " 'Tis the blackhaired one, sir," she ground out through clenched jaws "But, what's it to you who I serve, I'd like to know?" *How dare this dolt call me a Hel's cat! Or a sickly mare either, come to that?*

"My—er—my master's to wed your mistress, that's what!"

he came back, taking two long strides to close the gap between them. Hands on his hips, he looked her over from head to toe, in a bold, insolent way that made her flesh crawl—but was peculiarly exciting, nonetheless. "God knows how many leagues the poor divil's travelled, yet his cowardly bride hides from him behind her mother's skirts, pouting like a pampered weanling!"

"She *hides,* you say? But . . . 'tis untrue, sir! I—my lady came straightway to the great hall to meet with your master the very moment he rode into the bailey, but was told he was speaking privately with m—Lord Alaric. My—mistress's mother, the lady Marissa, has met with him, though." She smiled sweetly. "My lady said the Irishman—your wretched master!—is surly as a bear with a boil on its rump, and ugly as sin, besides. She said he has the manners of an Irish peasant, too. A loudmouthed, squalling banshee of a peasant, brought straight from the muck of the peat bogs to soil her father's hall!" She tossed her black head, daring him to contradict her, before adding sweetly, "Or so my lady said."

"Oh, she did, did she now? And so, you've come for your mistress's horse," the man purred in a lower, lilting voice. "How so? Vexed, is she? After a good, hard ride to cool the . . . fire. . . . in her blood?"

He stood but a few inches from her now—so very close, she could feel the heat rising from his body. Could see the tiny beads of water that still clung to his skin, the few soapy suds he had forgotten to rinse away. The lusty innuendo in his tone brought heat boiling to her cheeks. "Ye-yea," she answered. She closed her eyes, swaying ever so slightly where she stood, inhaling a mixture of lemongrass, mint, and clean, healthy male, coupled with the earthier scents of horse, cow, grain and straw. 'Twas a scent that teased her nostrils and somehow quickened her senses, so that every—

Oh!

At the sudden warm brush of his fingers on her cheek, she flinched. Her eyes flew open, and she found herself drowning in the stranger's emerald ones.

"And what of you, then? Is her horse all ye're after wantin', mavourneen?'' he asked huskily, running his knuckles down her cheek, in which color bloomed like roses. His lips twisted in a knowing, mocking smile that almost stole her breath away.

"Of course 'tis a horse, sirrah. What . . . what else would I be after in a byre?'' It was difficult to speak. The way he was— Jesu, the way he was *looking* at her, as if he could plumb her very depths—was so unsettling!—

Before she could react, however, he took another step. Splaying his fingers over her slender curves, he caught her about the waist and drew her roughly to him, ducking his head to whisper in her ear. In a lilting voice, he told her exactly what it was he thought she was after, and wickedly promised to supply it, right here and now, upon the sweet straw heaped at their feet. Aye, and what lusty pleasure 'twould be for the two of them, he promised. . . .

"Why, you foul-mouthed rogue!—'' she cried hotly, wrenching herself free. "M—your master shall hear of your impudence, sirrah!'' Bringing up a small clenched fist, she soundly boxed his ears, aimed a reckless knee at his groin— which missed—then picked up her skirts and fled the byre, his scornful laughter ringing in her ears.

She ran all the way back to her bower without stopping. There, she flung herself across her feather pallet, furious that that—*man,* that *animal*—had dared put his dirty hands upon her, let alone speak to her as boldly as he had done. She promised herself she would see that he was punished—yea, the very moment she had recovered her composure, she would see to it that he was soundly whipped for his insolence!

But of course, she did not.

Rather, the meeting in the byre that afternoon remained her little secret, one she carried with her to her proxy wedding.

That same night, in the candlelit stone chapel of Kenley, which had smelled of burning wax, incense, and wild spring flowers, she had been horrified to discover the identity of her substitute bridegroom. Yet, kneeling beside a scowling Kerrin mac Torrin, a wreath of virginal white mayflower crowning her loose black hair, she had somehow found the spirit to speak her vows.

With but a few simple words, she was joined in marriage to Kerrin's absent brother, Padraic, made his bride and the lady of Wulfskeep both by the vows Kerrin uttered in his brother's absence.

And mayhap it was for the best this way, she decided much later, crawling beneath the soft woollen coverlets and silky furs of her bed alone, while the rowdy wedding feast continued without her. Surely it would have been wrong to surrender her maidenhead to Padraic, when the memory of his wicked brother's touch yet lingered? . . .

Chapter Six

"I have been meaning to give you this talisman for many years, my darling," Marissa began in her daughter's bower the following morn. Her voice was choked with tears, as she stroked Edan's bowed head and caressed the long, silky black curls she had loved to caress since Edan was a little babe, carried in her woven basket. "I had always thought there would be time for it, but now!" She sighed. "Well, of a sudden, there is so little time left."

"I know, mother," Edan whispered. Biting her lip, she stared through a misty veil of her own tears at the silver amulet clasped in her hands. A lump had lodged in her throat. She could hardly swallow over it, for in a very short while, she would be leaving her home and her family to live in a foreign isle. 'Twas at Wulfskeep she would make her life, henceforth. And once in that faraway place, who knew if she would ever see her family again?

"It—it looks like the scorpion amulet Beorn wears about his throat," she observed huskily, staring at the round disk. On it were engraved two silver fishes, swimming in opposite directions, mouth to tail and tail to mouth. Within each of those fishy mouths was a huge cabochon amethyst. The purple gemstone had the power to protect its wearer from harm and to promote the swift healing of wounds. "Where . . . where did it come from?" she asked, more as a means to keep from breaking down, than from any real interest.

"Both this and Beorn's amulet were made at my Uncle Sven's bidding, almost fourteen . . . nay, fifteen years ago."

"Uncle Sven? Wasn't he the old Norseman who became a Christian monk? The one gifted with the Sight?"

"Ja. None other. My dear Sven passed on when you and Beorn were yet little children, God bless him. But before he left us, he had a silversmith fashion the scorpion and fish amulets for you and your brother to wear as talismans."

Edan frowned. " 'Tis a pretty trinket, but—why these designs? You gave birth to me in the month of May, when Taurus, the Bull, rules the heavens. This design is the emblem of Pisces, the Fishes, is it not? What does it mean?"

Marissa shrugged her slender shoulders, as she placed a pair of jewelled elk horn combs in her daughter's casket with an air of finality. She closed the lid, then motioned the waiting serf to carry the cask out into the bailey before going on. "Sven said he had been sent dreams that foretold of the man to whom you would give your heart and of the woman who would someday lay claim to Beorn's. He claimed the talismans would help you to find them. To recognize your soul mate when he came for you."

"You mean, the man I will—the man I have—married, surely, do you not, mother? Padraic mac Torrin?"

Marissa sighed. "We can only hope and pray that they are one and the same, my dearest daughter!" she said with feeling, patting her daughter's cheek. "Come. Turn the talisman over, *min yndling.* See, my darling? There are runes etched upon the other side."

Edan held the amulet up to the light and peered at the series of small marks etched in the shining silver, but she could not decipher them, although—unlike most women of Britain—she could read Saxon English and Latin. "What do they say?" she asked her mother, curious.

" 'Tis written in the Norse script of my native Denmark. It says,

> *Employ the silver adder's tongue*
> *If his imperiled soul you'd win.*
> *With courage slay the monstrous beast,*
> *Set free the love that lies within.*

"Strange. What does it mean?" Edan asked, frowning, as she turned the amulet this way and that.

"I cannot imagine, dearling," her mother admitted. "All I can tell you is that Sven felt the runes would guide you in some way."

Edan nodded and let the amulet fall. It swung gently to and fro, suspended from a chain of twisted links that winked dully in the rushlight. However, she had already forgotten both the silver disc and its ominous inscription, as she glanced from her bower windeye. She shivered.

As if in omen, the fine, bright days of spring, which they had been enjoying since winter fled Kent, had vanished this morn.

The sun had risen a short while ago, but had since retired behind a pewter shield of rain clouds. The dawn sky was no rosy pink and saffron this morn, but overcast—as dour and brooding as her aching heart. She swallowed, her lower lip trembling. She caught it between her teeth to still it, for even now, lord Kerrin, the captain of her escort and her lord husband's brother, was impatiently awaiting her in the bailey, eager to be away. . . .

She glanced down at the golden ring encircling her heart-finger. Seeing the ring reminded her. Last night, when he'd uttered the bridegroom's vows in Padraic's place, Kerrin's eyes had seemed to bore deep into her very soul, and she had been struck with the horrible fancy that he could read her mind. That he knew full well what adulterous fantasies had fluttered in her head.

"Oh, *Mother!*" she cried hoarsely, and flung herself into Marissa's arms. Her head cradled upon that familiar, beloved bosom, she sobbed. ''I cannot bear to leave you and Father, nor little Gayla and the boys!—I'll never tease Danica about becoming a nun again, if only you'll let me stay here—please, Mother? Forgive m—my weakness, but I cannot bear to leave you all, now that it is time to go!''

"Hush, dearling, hush. Do not weep, I beg thee. It is no easier for us,'' Marissa murmured, in a choked voice, holding her daughter fiercely to her. "Every one of my children is precious—dearer to me than my own life, but you!—You are my eldest daughter and the first to leave my care. Mayhap it will help if you remind yourself that this is what we were born for, you and I. It is our place to marry and make powerful alliances for our fathers, our kings, our country. 'Tis our place in the scheme of things, you see, for we were not born churls, bound by our humble births to live in one place, serving a master. You and I are noblewomen, Edana. Daughters of princes and lords! And some day, God willing, you will become the *mother* of princes and lords. Your destiny is in Eire, *min yndling.*''

Edan sniffed back a tear. Biting her lip, she nodded bravely. ''*Ja*, Mother. I have always known it.'' She sighed and drew a deep, shuddering breath. "I am composed now. And I will not shame you by weeping before the Irish,'' she promised bravely, a little of her old self-confidence and obstinacy returning, if the stubborn tilt of her jaw was any indication. "Lord Kerrin awaits me in the bailey. Let us go and get it over with quickly, shall we?''

''*Ja*, my brave girl,'' her mother whispered proudly, her own eyes shimmering with unshed tears. ''*Ja. . . .*''

As she had said, her escort awaited her and Grania in the bailey, a half-dozen fierce-looking men mantled in plaid, daggers and swords at their waists, as well as an old woman with a donkey. Horses and heavily laden pack animals milled about, tossing their heads and champing at their bits, eager to be off.

Kerrin disentangled himself from their midst, mounted upon the most beautiful horse she had ever seen: a prancing black stallion taken from the deserts of the east. "My lady, are ye ready to leave? The day's wasting!''

"I am ready, sir Kerrin," she murmured, biting back a scathing retort. The man was surely mad! The pale glimmer of dawn was only now lightening the eastern sky, and the air still held the sharp bite of night.

A strong hand reached out and took her elbow to help her into the saddle. "My lady?" a deep voice murmured.

"Beorn! Oh, Beorn, I thought I must go without bidding you farewell!" she cried, throwing herself in her twin brother's arms.

He hugged her fiercely, then kissed her. "Silly goose! Did you really think I would let you leave without saying goodbye? We've been together since we left our mother's womb, almost eighteen years ago," he reminded her huskily. "I will miss thee, sister mine."

"And I you, dearest brother." She went up on tiptoe and kissed his cheek. "God be with you, Beorn."

"And also with thee, little sister," he murmured, then lifted her up onto her mount. To her escort, he said sternly, "Guard her with your life, Kerrin mac Torrin—else answer to me!"

With a curt nod, the Irishman touched heels to his stallion's sides and led the way from Kenley.

He must be a wizard, Edan decided many hours later, risking a side glance at her escort, Kerrin of Wat, who sat as effortlessly in his saddle, as if he'd been born there, wretched man. He showed no evidence of tiring, either.

For her own part, her backside had grown numb long since. Surely poor little Grania, who, unlike herself, was not accustomed to riding, must be suffering terribly.

They had left Kenley soon after dawn, their departure accompanied by a fine yet constant rain. Several of Kenley's people had braved the weather to run after her horse and press parting gifts upon her: a satchel of herbs from her weeping nurse, Edythe; from Dewy The Welshman, Kenley's master fletcher, she'd received a leather quiver filled with exquisitely shaped arrows, each with notched goose feather flights, as well as a mold for the casting of metal arrowheads; a dagger with an ornate guard of filigree wire had come from old Emmet, the weapon smith.

Once her gifts had been safely laden upon her packhorses, she had kissed Danica, Edward, Gareth, and a sobbing little Gayla farewell and rode quickly on without looking back for several yards. When she had, she'd waved till both her arms were tired, and she could no longer see any of them standing forlornly on the grassy motte, or mound, upon which Kenley had been built.

Now it was late afternoon, and many leagues lay between this place and her home. The bright optimism that always attends the outset of such journeys had long since given way to fatigue and aching muscles. Praise be, the miserable, soaking rain had vanished, though. Now she and her escort of seven men, along with one grizzly haired, sharp-eyed old hag mounted upon a donkey, and the indefatigable Kerrin of Wat, were trotting across rolling green downs, headed west toward the setting sun.

Everything was bathed in the mellow, golden sunlight of a late spring afternoon. The chalk in the dark, fertile soil gleamed like old ivory bones here and there between the blades of coarse turf. The empty, rolling moors were bounded by the broad, gray stripe of the sea on their left and by still more billowing downs on their right.

Despite the lateness of the hour, Kerrin showed no sign of halting, gave no order to make camp for the night, nor seemed in any way inclined to seek out comfortable lodgings for herself and her serving woman at one of the monasteries or convents they had passed that afternoon. He seemed similarly disinclined to lay claim to some flea-ridden blanket by the fire in a shepherd's tumbledown hovel. As the light began to fade, she began to fear they would ride west forever. . . .

Jesu! Her belly was growling horribly. Small wonder. In her nervousness, she had eaten but little at the sumptuous wedding feast her mother had ordered prepared the evening before. She had also been unable to stomach so much as a single bite this morning at the fast-breaking, she'd been so heartsick about leaving her family. Furthermore, her eyes felt so heavy lidded, they could scarce stay open. If they did not soon halt, she might well fall from her saddle.

Still, she refused to show the Irish any sign of weakness, nor would she be the one to ask Kerrin to call a halt. Let him think what he would, she thought proudly, lifting her heavy head and straightening her aching spine. No foreigner would find a Saxon noblewoman lacking, either in courage or in endurance. . . .

Her fierce pride would never let her forget—nor forgive—that the second time he'd set eyes upon her—this time arrayed in her finest yellow kirtle, adorned with her costliest jewels, her long black hair floating like a cloud about her—he'd observed that, while she seemed as lovely as her reputation had promised, he feared she would prove "a pouty, pampered creature, ill-suited to the bearing of a Viking chieftain's sons."

Her cheeks had stung with indignation.

"Appearances are ofttimes deceptive, my lord," her father had warned him with a chuckle, well aware of the fury the Irishman's words had ignited in Edan's smoky eyes. "Daughter? Catch!"

As his deep command rang out, Alaric had tossed a withered apple across the table to Edan, laughing when her hand came up like lightning to spear it on the point of her eating knife.

Alaric grinned. "There! Do you see now what I meant, good Kerrin of Wat? Had that apple been a man's hand, he would be wearing it as a brooch, pinned to his very heart!" he crowed proudly, delighted by his daughter's quick reflexes. "By God, the women of Kenley are wenches to be reckoned with, are they not, wife?" he'd added, planting a kiss upon his lady's lips.

"We are indeed, my lord, *ja*," Marissa had acknowledged coolly, yet she had regarded the Irishman as Edan had often seen her assess an opponent at chess—as though he were a dangerous enemy whose strengths and weaknesses needed to be learned at all costs.

Later, in Edan's bower, Marissa had warned Edan, "I have changed my mind about this Kerrin mac Torrin. He will do well enough for an escort, I fancy, but only if you keep your wits about you. He has a dangerous weakness, you see. One you must guard against, dearling, lest it prove your undoing.''

''What weakness is that?'' she'd asked.

Her mother had sniffed, showing her contempt. ''He doubts himself! He does not have it in him to kill instantly and without thought.''

''But, that is a virtue, surely, not a fault?''

''In a priest 'tis a virtue, *ja*. But in a man who earns his living as a warrior, a bodyguard?—'' She had snorted in disgust. ''An instant's hesitation, a moment of doubt, could easily cause your downfall, my dearling! You must be very careful and never, ever leave yourself open to—''

''Blessed Mary and all the saints preserve us! *I asked if ye're weary, my lady?*'' Kerrin's thunderous voice broke into her reverie.

Edan clenched her teeth and winced. *''Nay!''* she ground out, shooting him a quelling look.

''Well and good, then, Edan—I may call ye Edan, as your brother-in-law, I trust?'' Without waiting for an answer, he continued, ''Moreover, ye've no need to bite off my blessed head! No one's going to force ye to do aught against your will, woman. 'Tis just that—whist! I'd thought your little serving wench might welcome a wee respite? Still, if ye say nay, milady, then nay it is. I'll call a halt later, aye? After sunset.''

With a scowl, he galloped ahead, while his white falcon—Yseult, the Fair One—circled and called piercingly, as she rode the air currents high above the darkening downs.

Edan stared stupidly after Kerrin's retreating back, wishing to God she'd kept her wretched mouth firmly shut. Oh, her cursed backside!—It begged to be removed from this plaguesome saddle, and cushioned by bolsters of goosedown. . . .

''Mistress? Milady Edan?''

''Aye, what is it?'' she answered sulkily, turning in the saddle to find Grania's anguished face glowering up at her.

''What in heaven were ye thinking of, my lady?'' the girl hissed crossly. ''Whilst your backside might not be deadened, of a certainty, *mine* is! Aye, and has been for many a league!

In truth, I know not where my rump ends and my legs begin, 'tis s' blessed numb!''

''Is it, now? And would the wee colleen like me to chafe the feeling back into it for her, then?'' offered Tavish, Kerrin's closest companion. The brown haired Irishman with the merry face had been stealing glances at pretty Grania ever since he'd first set eyes upon her in Kenley's bailey. His brown eyes likewise twinkled mischievously.

Grania snorted and brandished her eating knife with a warning glare. ''Lay a hand upon me, ye Irish barbarian, and you'll lose it!''

''A true Valkyrie maid, by God!'' declared Lachlann, one of Tavish's companions, punching his shoulder. ''Have a care, lad. I think the little she-wolf means it!'' In a patently overloud whisper, he added, ''Ignore her warning, and ye may lose more than your fingers!''

The other men chortled, as Grania blushed an alarming shade of crimson that reached to the roots of her fair hair.

''Have done, all of you!'' Edan snapped, flashing charcoal eyes at the grinning lot of them, for she could tell that Grania was perilously close to tears in her exhaustion, despite her brave threat. ''You, sirrah?—''

''Me? I am named Tavish, my lady.''

''Aye, Tavish. Ride after your master, sir, and bid him turn back. Tell him that my serving woman is unaccustomed to long days in the saddle, and that she can ride no farther. Tell him— tell him that *I* have decided we shall camp here for the night.''

The impish grin faded. ''But, my lady, milord Kerrin has already decided to ride on!''

''Aye. I heard him well enough. But *I* have decided we shall camp here for the night. Ride on, and tell your master so, sirrah!''

''As you will, my lady,'' Tavish said, doubtfully, inclining his head, though it was clear he was not happy that she had countered his master's order. Still, he wheeled his mount after Kerrin without further protest, much to Edan's satisfaction.

''You two, set up my tent, pray. Meanwhile, you, sir?—''

"Me, madam? I am called Niall, madam," supplied a serious-faced older man.

"Niall, would you assign men to draw water for us, pray? There is no need for you to hunt today, gentlemen," she added in a louder voice, so that all of the party could hear her. "My lady mother has sent us on our way with sufficient victuals for an army!"

"Has she now? Then 'tis well and good we have a warlord t' lead us, is it not, lads,—albeit one wearing skirts!" scoffed a now familiar voice.

Edan twisted in the saddle to find that Kerrin had returned. And, judging by his dark expression and clipped tone, he was not pleased to find her giving his men orders in his absence.

"Grania is unwell, sir," she hastened to explain, coloring nonetheless. "Since she is my sole companion, and most dear to me, besides, I would ask your indulgence this once, milord?"

"You would? Then of a certainty you shall have it, sister-wife," Kerrin promised mockingly, his eyes very bright, his stern mouth curved in a thin, mirthless smile. "All of you! Mount up! You, Trevor, take that tent down, man!" When the others were out of earshot, he added, "Next time, I expect ye to do me the courtesy of asking *before* you give an order, madam, not afterwards. Ye see, my men obey only my commands—or shall hereon, if they know what's good for them!" he added, pointedly. In a louder voice, he bellowed, "There's a river half a league to the west. We'll camp there for the night. Ride on!"

Chastened, but by no means cowed, Edan bit back a heated retort and urged her palfrey on, trying to pretend she had not seen the shimmer of tears in Grania's eyes—nor the gleam of triumph in Kerrin's green ones, as he overrode her commands to his men.

It promised to be a long journey, she decided, as she crested a hill, and the gleaming snake of the river he had mentioned came into view. One that would take them to Wales by way of the city of Winchester, where they would ask the high-king, Edward Elder's blessing upon her marriage, before travelling on. But it would not, she was willing to wager, prove a boring journey! She had grown up in the company of strong-minded men and, like her mother, had held her own. She hid a smile. Master Kerrin had a rude awakening ahead of him, if he expected her to meekly come to heel. . . .

She straightened her spine and dug her heels into Fayre's sides. "Faster, my beauty! Let's see if we can outrun that black devil, shall we?" she murmured, leaning over her mare's neck to whisper in her pricked ears.

Only Edan knew if she meant the horse—or its rider.

Chapter Seven

Edan waited until the last man of her escort had rolled himself into his mantle by the fire, before slipping from the tent she shared with Grania.

Carrying a clean shift and a kirtle under her arm, she skirted the sleeping men, edged her way between the picketed horses, and went down to the river.

A full moon glinted off dark water. Windblown ripples sparkled glassily through the shadows, as she wove her way among the bushes. Reeds rustled, as she threw down her bundle, sending small night creatures scurrying for cover. A nighthawk screamed, as it drifted over the downs in search of prey.

Bending, Edan hopped on one leg, while she hauled off her soft suede boots, then wriggled from her soiled kirtle.

A chill breeze lifted her unbound hair and caressed her cheeks. She inhaled. The night scents of grass and damp earth were wonderful, fresh, and exciting. The spring night was a taste on her tongue, a song in her blood, a stirring in her loins— as bracing as her dive into dark water would prove. She set her jaw, shivering in anticipation. Not even icy water could dissuade her from her swim. She was accustomed to bathing almost every day, as was common in her mother's native Denmark. It was a luxury she thoroughly enjoyed, unlike most Saxons, who considered daily bathing a peculiar "Viking vanity, as alien to good Saxons as the daily combing of the hair." Why, even the priests claimed that washing the body was likely to invite the attentions of Satan! For her own part, however, she fancied being unwashed year in and year out was more likely to attract attention from itchy, many legged creatures, than the Devil incarnate!

After leaving Kenley, they'd ridden west for three long days, as if chasing the setting sun over the horizon. They had stopped only for the evening meal and to sleep for a few hours, though never long enough, to her way of thinking. The fast-breaking had been a simple meal of dried meat, bread, roasted capon— foods that were easily consumed in the saddle, then washed down with spring water or swigs of watered wine from leather canteens.

During that time, the sweat had dried upon her body more times than she cared to count, she reflected, wrinkling her nose. She unfastened her ribbon garters, then rolled down her nose. Come Hel or high waters, she would bathe 'ere she found her bed this night!

Standing barefoot in the grass, nude now but for her sheer linen undershift, she ran down the banks toward the reeds, uttering little gasps of pleasure, as coarse grasses became swishy, cold mud between her toes. Aaah, heaven!

But just as she was about to arch forward into the winking blackness of the river, she was brought up short by a low, rumbling growl in the reeds ahead, a sound that raised the hackles on her neck.

"*Jesu!*" She gasped as a shadowy wolf rose from the gleaming water only an armslength length away, materializing from the reeds, as if wrought of shadows and starlight. She hastily crossed herself, the blood draining from her face, as her eyes met the beast's shining golden ones.

Motionless, unblinking, scarce breathing, wolf and woman stared at each other for moments that seemed an eternity. And then, the beast broke the contact as, throwing back its head, it gave throat to a chilling howl.

Its cry was answered from the hills beyond the river, till the distant darkness rang with a chorus of howls. In their wake, silence descended once more over the sleeping downs, dark and all but absolute.

Edan blinked. In that instant, the wolf was gone, the moment's magic dispelled. Instead, on the perimeter of her vision, she saw a man rising from the river's edge, in the place where the wolf had vanished an instant before. Crystal drops sprayed about him like scattered jewels, as he shook himself off, then clambered up the grassy banks. His broad shoulders cut an ebony swathe from the midnight sky that framed him, while the long, raven-black hair he wore, drawn back into a narrow thong at his nape, left his chiselled profile bare.

"You!" she exclaimed.

Following her gasp of recognition, Kerrin abruptly turned and dived. Hardly a splash marked his reentry into the oily black water. Only the everwidening echo of the ripples, rimmed by starlight, and the path of the full moon, betrayed the spot to where he had vanished—or indeed, had he been there at all?

"Mother of God!" Edan whispered faintly. Surely she had seen a shape-shifter, a man with the magical power to turn himself, at will, from mortal to golden-eyed wolf, then back again!

She hastily crossed herself a second time, wanting to run, but frozen to the ground by fear. In truth, although she would gladly have tested her warrior's mettle against any mortal man, the element of . . . of the supernatural, of magic and the Otherworld surrounding what she'd seen had rooted her in the chill mud!

"My lady! Lady Edan!"

Kerrin's deep, commanding voice jerked Edan back to the present. "I—I'm over here, sir!"

Turning, she saw Kerrin emerging from the bushes behind her. He was fully clothed now, swathed chin to heels in a swirling dark mantle. His raven hair spilled about his crooked shoulders, its wet strands framing a stern, unsmiling face. In the moonlight, the expression in his eyes was fierce. He looked every whit as comforting as a marauding Vandal or a Magyar warlord, about to pillage a helpless hamlet. But did he in any way resemble a golden-eyed wolf? Hardly.

"Why come you here alone, lady?" Kerrin demanded in a low, disgruntled tone, casting her a look of censure. "Our camp's back there, on drier ground." He jerked his chin in the direction she'd come and scowled at her with brows like inky thunderheads, jostled together in an ominous dark line.

"I know its whereabouts, *takke*, sir," she ground out, resenting his domineering tone and his belligerent expression. The nerve of the man! Did the river not belong to everyone? Why then should he have exclusive use of it! She scowled. He'd proven such an overbearing brute, from the outset! In truth, she could scarce wait to reach her lord husband's side and be well rid of her ill-tempered, bullying escort.

"So say you," he observed coldly. "But, that being so, what are you doing so far from it, I wonder?"

She shot him a withering glare that had quelled lesser men. It had scant effect on this one. "Do you forget that women, like men, have needs, sir? Like you, I came here to swim in the river."

He snorted in blatant disbelief. "I wonder, princess? Did you really mean to swim—or were you planning to flee? Will ye run back home to your father's keep, the minute my back is turned?" he challenged. He had seen the way it was. Her entire family doted upon her! As for her . . . well, he had seen the tracks of tears, wet on her cheeks, as they rode forth from Kenley. He would not have been surprised, had she tried to run back to them.

Indignation made her bristle like an angry kitten, its fur standing on end. Her gray eyes flashed, cold and pale as ice. She, Edana Alaricsdotter, run from the likes of this Irish bog gnome and his littermates? Ha! She muffled a scornful snort. "Run, sir? Ha! Surely you jest? 'Twill be a cold day in Hades, before I run from aught, once my word is given!"

So saying, she drew herself up to her full height, forgetting entirely that her undershift was of the finest, sheerest linen— and rendered nigh transparent by the silvery light of the moon, as it sailed from behind a cloud.

Kerrin wetted his lips, aroused despite himself. The soft cloth formed rounded hillocks over her breasts, then skimmed the jut of her hipbones, before swathing her long, shapely thighs and legs to her ankles in its sheer folds. Starlight likewise touched her inky hair and the blades of grass at her feet, winking off each strand and leaf with a gilt sheen that reflected the lustre of her eyes. He muffled a curse. If beauty were guarantee of goodness, the wretched woman could have been St. Patricus himself, he thought sourly, glowering at her.

"Do not cast such doubtful eyes upon me, sir!" she snapped, noting the look he cast her. "Edana of Kenley is no oath breaker. Nor does she run from her duties like a frightened serf. Your brother is my lord and husband now. I have sworn vows before God to honor him, and, to my last breath, I shall do so." Her expression softened. " 'Twas just that . . . the river called to me! And once it had, I knew I could not sleep." She gave a helpless shrug, her tone daring him to scoff at her fanciful thoughts. Let him think her fey or foolish, she cared not. It was the truth.

One thick black brow rose dubiously in a show of scorn, but her comment had startled him, if truth were known. More comfortable with wild creatures and the elements himself, he had often imagined the wind calling to him, or the trees whispering his name. That she—that Edana of Kenley—should admit to having the same fey fancies amazed him. "It called you, you say?" he echoed.

To her relief, he sounded more curious than scornful. His mouth—a surprisingly sensual mouth, she noticed for the first time—had actually softened. "Aye," she admitted, a trifle emboldened by his response. Her chin lifted. "It called to—um—to me."

"Did it, now? And what was it after telling ye, then, the river?"

Despite the hint of sarcasm in his tone, she smiled. "It said, Come, Edan! Come and bathe in my cool depths! Wash away the dust of travel, before sweet Morpheus claims thee!"

"Sure, and the river's a *shanachie*, an Irish bard, to be

speaking such blarney to a wench,'' Kerrin declared, with a reluctant grin.

To her surprise, she shared his jest, showing strong, pretty white teeth in the shadows, as she laughed. Then, suddenly embarrassed by her admission, a crescent of long, dark lashes dropped to veil her smoky eyes.

The seductive gesture made Kerrin's groin tighten, dried the spittle in his throat. *God, but she is lovely, Edana of Wulfskeep.* All the rumors about her fell far short of the woman before him. Woman? Nay. His *bride.* She belonged to him, before God and according to the laws of man. There was no reason at all why he should not—

Catching himself in mid-thought, he bit back a snort of self-disgust. Ye gods, what was this? Had he been bewitched by this night-haired sorceress after less than seven days spent in her company? Had he become ensorceled by this ashy-eyed enchantress, who dallied with unshaven strangers in her father's barn, not so much as a serving wench to preserve her honor or good name?

The moment her father had led her to his side in Kenley's great hall, he'd recognised her as the black-haired beauty he'd met in the byre, though her well-worn homespun had been replaced by the finest garments. Though he had said nothing of it, he had been angry that she would dally with a stranger on the eve of her wedding. And now, here she was again, wandering the riverbanks by moonlight, and once again unescorted! Had she truly come here to bathe, as she claimed, or to meet a Saxon lover? Mayhap some lovesick clod had been following their little party over hill and dale, biding his time until he could steal the lady away from her husband's escort?—

His eyes darkened, turning almost black. His lips set in a hard, thin line, he forced himself to look away from the lovely witch. *His vow!* He had sworn he would not let her beauty nor her fiery spirit sway him from his purpose! He had vowed to prove his bride was just like his mother and the remainder of their sex—not to fall under her spell like some callow youth! And he would do so. . . .

But, what of the curse he carried? What of that?

"I must agree, milord."

"Agree? Agree to what?" He frowned. His thoughts had been worlds away.

"To what you said. You know, about the river being Irish?"

"Hmm? Aye. What of it?"

"Nothing," she murmured, disappointed, for it was clear his moment of good humor had already passed. "As I said, I wanted to swim in the river, milord. But, there are wolves abroad this night."

His head jerked up. "Wolves! Surely you are mistaken, my lady? There are no wolves here." So. *She had glimpsed his brief metamorphosis.*

"Indeed there are. I saw one crouched right there, in the reeds." She nodded towards the place. "It probably came out of the forest to drink water. Did you not hear its fellows howling at the moon, sir?"

"Aye, mayhap I did, on second thought." He smiled thinly, a distant light in his eyes now. "But never fear, my lady. I will wait beyond those bushes, my dagger drawn, while ye bathe. You'll have naught to fear from wild beasts, be they two-legged or four. Not with me close by. No hungry wolf will devour thee, nor any man spy upon thee." He sounded scornful. Mocking.

"None but yourself, mayhap," Edan observed softly, her winged brows lifting like inked commas on a sheet of vellum. A mischievous smile tugged the corners of her full-lipped mouth.

"Are you suggesting I would spy upon thee, lady? When I have sworn to defend thee?" he demanded, bristling, as he returned her challenging expression.

She snorted, not persuaded by the wretch's oh-so-innocent tone. After all, he was staring at her now, as if her shift were transparent. "You, spy, sir? Oh, surely not! You would be no more likely to spy upon me than . . . than I would be likely to run back to my father's household, say?"

Against his will, her veiled jibe drew a deep chuckle from the Irishman, surprising even him. By virtue of his past, he was not much given to laughter or jests. Or never had been, till now . . . Irritated that she could so easily make him forget himself, he made her a stiff bow and muttered, "Be quick about your bathing, madam! I'll await ye yonder." With that, he turned and strode off between the bushes.

Shrugging, Edan waded into the river, determined to drive all thoughts of the moody Irishman from her mind.

Ducking, she gasped, as chill water flowed over and about her limbs like icy silk, invading every warm and vital part of her. The current stirred her sluggish winter blood to tingling, shivery life with its frigid caress.

Cupping handfuls of water, she splashed her face, surprised to find her cheeks were still burning from her exchange with Kerrin, despite her wish to forget about him. "Devil take the wretched brute!" she muttered, then leaned back and kicked away from the banks like an otter.

Her long black hair fanned out behind her, floating on the water like skeins of embroidery silks. Her bare limbs gleamed, ivory-pale beneath the water's surface, while the gauzy folds of her shift billowed and swirled about her like flower petals, now caressing her breasts, now swathing the sleek line of her hips, flanks, and belly.

As she swam, she nevertheless found her thoughts straying back to Kerrin as he'd looked, climbing up the banks of the river, a tall, powerful man. His broad shoulders, lean flanks and well-muscled legs had been silhouetted by the full spring moon. Even now, she felt a tiny flutter deep in her belly, when she remembered him that way.

She closed her eyes, recalling their encounter in her father's byre. The gentle brush of his fingers on her cheek. The exciting scent of him. She felt the same stirring in her belly now, as she'd felt then, like fire in her loins.

She sighed as she floated, gazing up at the millions of starry points of light in the indigo sky. If her husband proved as pleasing to her eye as his brother, then she'd share his furs with a smile on her lips and a song in her heart!

I wonder. . . . where are you now, Padraic of Wulfskeep? she asked the full, smiling moon, as it scudded across the indigo sky. *Do you ever wonder about me, as I've wondered about you for over half my lifetime? Do you give any thought*

*to the woman who will soon share your bed and have your
children . . . ?*

The thought of sharing Padraic's bed made her tremble with
fear of the unknown, and—did she but admit it—with desire,
too. Aye, and why should such thoughts not excite her? She
was no longer a child, but a woman, and women were no less
lusty than men, her mother had explained. They were simply
more able to control and conceal their desire. Her body was
ripe, ready to be mated and bear children. She could feel it!
Yet, the marriage bed was not all she dreamed of. She wanted
to share the rest of her husband's life, too. To be privy to his
thoughts and dreams, his ambitions and his fears. And, with
God's good grace!—she hoped someday to hold a place in
Padraic's heart, not just as the mother of his children, but in
her own right.

Silly goose! Like the wolves, she was surely howling at the
moon, yearning for something she would never have: a marriage
enriched by love and friendship. The love her parents had forged
was rare—rarer than hens' teeth or blue moons. She must do
the duty her noble birth demanded of her and never ask for
more. To ask for love, to think that Padraic—chosen as her
husband while they were both still children—could ever be her
soul mate, was courting bitter disappointment.

She shivered. Of a sudden, the river no longer seemed inviting, but bottomless and threatening. Perhaps, like her future,
its dark depths harbored choking weeds and unseen dangers?

Striking out for the muddy banks, she clambered up them,
her chilled hands clawing for tree roots and reeds by which to
pull herself up onto dry land.

On the banks, she hastily squeezed out her dripping hair,
pulled on fresh garments, flung a woolen mantle over her shoulders, and hurriedly scampered back to camp.

As she ran, she glimpsed the huge wolf again, weaving its
way among the willows. It made no move to spring at her
throat, but, instead, kept pace beside her. Its passage was as
silent as smoke, as it wove it way among the grasses. Terrified,
she wondered, angrily, to its warm hollow her wretched escort
had vanished, his promises to protect her notwithstanding? . . .

From the cover of the willows, baleful golden eyes followed Edan to her tent, then watched as she ducked inside.

The wolf's gaze narrowed. Its tongue lolled. Raising its nose, it tasted her female scent upon the wind and, with it, the scent of her fear. Something had panicked her. What had it been, he wondered? A whispery rustle in the grass? A shadow that had seemed somehow threatening and . . . wolf-like? His upper lip peeled back from his fangs in a lupine snarl. Or, had it been that fleeting glimpse of himself, rising from the water, male, mortal, naked, and aroused? Was that what had so unsettled the lady, and put her to flight? . . .

Lifting his muzzle to the milky full moon, he howled again.

The chilling yelp set the horses, picketed beneath the birches, to snorting and stamping restlessly. Again, it stirred a choir of answering howls from the distant hills.

"Wolves, my lady! Do ye hear them?" Grania whispered, stirring nervously in her warm sleeping bag lined with fur.

"I hear them, aye. But we have a long ride ahead of us on the morrow, Grania. Go back to sleep now," she soothed. Drawing her knee harp, Calandra, the Lark, across her lap, she drew her fingers over the taut strings in a sweeping motion.

Straightway, golden chords poured from Calandra's magical throat, filling the night with wonderful rippling song. The melody told of bubbling brooks, as they sang their way to the sea. It told of the wind dancing through the forest, playing catch with the leaves. It told of the soft, gentle rains of spring, pitter-pattering as they fell from the sky, bringing life to all things.

And, crouched deep in the willows, the man-wolf pricked his ears to listen to the harp's song. Little by little, the knot of hatred in its breast was loosened. The wildness was soothed.

Murragh's curse—for the moment—was lifted.

Chapter Eight

"How now? What news, messenger?"

"They come, sir!" the lad cried breathlessly, holding his cramped side. He bowed his head to catch his wind and hung there, shoulders heaving.

Canute's eyes gleamed. "How far, sirrah?"

"Two leagues t'east, sir," the lad panted. "They'll be here within the hour!"

"So soon! They did not see you, boy?"

"Me?" The lad preened like a cockerel. "Nay, lord. I hid meself up in a tree 'til they'd passed by, I did."

"Och, you're a clever wee cock, you are, to be sure! And what of the ealdorman's daughter, Edana Alaricsdotter? She is with them?" The man leaned forward in the saddle, his expression intent.

"Aye, *min jarl.*"

"Aaaah. And is the lady as fair as the bards would have us believe?"

The young messenger grinned. "Fairer, sir! Her hair reaches clear to her arse. 'Tis the color of a raven's wing, while her eyes—why, they're gray as the Irish sea, sir! In truth, she's a fit bride for Padraic mac Torrin, sir. Aye, and a fitting lady for Wulfsk—''

Too late, the youth realized the folly of his words. He bit his tongue. What a brainless dolt he'd been, t'say such things! His master Canute's jealousy of Lord Padraic was no secret. Sure, and old Darby, his father, would fetch him such a wallop when he heard. . . . Blanching, he ducked his flaxen head and stammered, "Forgive me, my lord. Truly, I did not think! *You* will be lord of Wulfskeep, once earl Torrin feeds the worms! Not Padraic, God rot him, but *you,* my lord!''

"Rest easy, boy," his master crooned silkily. "I'll not hold a slip o'the tongue against ye, fair man that I am. Hush, now.''

"Thanks be to God!" the lad whispered fervently, crossing himself.

Canute smiled, a mere baring of his teeth. "Amen. Now, run along and join the others, bratling." He winked. "Tell Olaf you're to have double rations this even'. You've earned them, by Loki, keeping watch all the night long as you did.''

"Double rations, sir? Oh, *takke,* sir!" the boy babbled, almost weeping with relief. The hunters had brought down a young doe in the forest. They'd been butchering it, when he returned to camp. There was little to compare with a hunk of juicy spit-roasted venison, to his mind—and tonight, he would have *double* his portion! His eyes shining like great blue sapphires, he tugged at his forelock, then ran off to join Canute's other retainers. His dirty feet skipped over the grass like a young goat's.

"A handsome lad," Canute observed, in thoughtful fashion, scratching at the chin hidden by his straggly red-gold beard. "A son to make any father proud! What say you, Lothar?" he asked idly.

The giant, mounted upon an enormous warhorse with feathered hooves, gave no answer. Thick-featured, dull-eyed, he sat two feet taller in the saddle than most men and had eyes that were empty of mercy, empty of compassion, lacking so much as the smallest morsel of tenderness, or a tiny flicker of human kindness. On cold winter's nights, the *skalds'* sagas were all of Lothar, and how his monstrous appearance struck terror in the hearts of even the bravest warrior, and turned heroes' bowels to water.

'Twas said that even the fearless bear-men, the berserkers, who became mad with bloodlust before a battle, turned coward and ran when Lothar reared up before them, beating his barrel chest with his fists, or whirling his blood-axe. Not surprisingly, wenches—even the lowliest slatterns who sold their favors in muddy ditches—opened their own veins sooner than share Lothar's furs—or, if forced, went mad at the prospect. Many wondered how Canute could make Lothar obey him.

"You heard what the boy said, Lothar?" Canute repeated softly, when the giant remained silent.

"Aah."

"It appears our little Irish maggot favors my nephew over me, Lothar—aye, and half the county of Wat with him, I'll wager! By Loki, I'll harbor no traitors in my camp—not even snot-nosed bratlings. Remember, Lothar, that from the nit grows the louse. From the wriggling maggot grows the dung-fly. He offended me!" he barked suddenly. "Kill him!"

Lothar smiled, baring crooked yellow teeth in a dreadful grimace. *"Ja, min jarl."*

"You're certain the boy saw you? That he heard Niall's orders to the men?"

"He did, aye—unless he were deaf," Tavish confirmed. "He perched above us in the oak like a blue-eyed owlet, frowning something fierce, as he committed our words to memory. We pretended not to see him there. We talked instead of the road we would travel this morn—how many leagues of our journey yet lay to east or west, or to north or south, 'ere we moved on." Tavish grinned, his puckish face crinkling up in merry humor. "He swallowed it like a fine fat trout takes a fisherman's bait! Then, when he thought our eyes elsewhere, he shinned down the tree and bolted like a frightened hare!" He shook his head. "I don't envy the lad, once Canute learns his directions have taken him leagues in the other direction!"

Kerrin frowned. ''You're certain 'tis my uncle's spies who follow us, then?''

Tavish shrugged. ''Who else would it be? We've made no enemies here in Britain since we landed. Nay, 'tis Canute and his sty fellows! They follow us as homeless fleas hop after a dog!''

Despite his misgivings, Kerrin could not help but chuckle.

Tavish grinned, too, as he leaned low over the riverbank. He cupped icy mountain water in his hands and drank thirstily, before asking, ''How goes it with the lady Edana?''

Kerrin was not deceived by Tavish's bland expression. His companion knew everything there was to know about him, from the curse that had overshadowed his life since he'd come to manhood, to the vow ''Padraic'' had taken to test his young bride's fidelity. Knew, too, exactly *how* his friend had intended to test her! So far, alas, it'd proven impossible to woo her, let alone to seduce her, for surely there was no better tool for gelding a man than a woman's sharp tongue?

''It goes not at all,'' he admitted, scowling, his former good humor fled. ''The maid shies from me like a skittish mare shies from an adder coiled in the grass!''

Tavish snorted. ''Small wonder! You've not said a gentle word to her since we left Kenley!'' Grimacing, he shook his head. ''If you ask me, 'tis a dangerous game you play, my friend! Better you tell her who you really are, before it's too late. Unless, of course, you don't care what happens when she discovers you've lied to her?''

Kerrin grimaced, wishing he cared *less*. '' 'Tis already too late, I fear. She would as soon have nothing to do with me.''

''Of course! Sure, and you're going about this the wrong way, friend Kerrin. The Lady Edan's not some peasant woman you can tumble, toss a penny to, and forget. She's highborn, gently raised. Such women must be wooed, before they may be won.''

''You know me, Tavish. I know little of wooing wenches. Besides, when we speak, she is either angry, or else her thoughts are as flighty as—as Yseult's, say.''

He glanced up, shading dark-sapphire eyes against the bright sunlight to watch the Greenland falcon in flight.

He had stolen the Fair One from her nest as a fledgling, while exploring the rumbling volcanic mountains of The Isle of the Smiths. He had fed her fresh meat from his own hands, lived in an ice cave with her, bathed in the hot springs there, until she had grown and could endure the sea voyage back to Ireland.

Many months in Torrin's mews at Wulfskeep had followed before the falcon had been properly "manned," months that Kerrin had spent in patiently taming Yseult to hunt, to answer his to whistle alone, and to return to the lure, his fist, or her wooden perch, upon command.

Now, watching Yseult ride the wind currents, carving pure white arcs from an azure sky, or stooping from the heavens to strike her prey, filled him with a surge of pleasure—the same inexplicable rush of pleasure he felt whenever Edana was near—curse her!

Edana, the Fiery One. Edana of Wulfskeep. Edan, his secret bride. . . .

By Frey, her very name bespoke Heaven!

Like the she-hawk, she was delicately fashioned, finely boned, exquisitely feminine. Yet he was fast discovering that, like Yseult, a core of tempered steel ran beneath her fine outer plumage. She carried herself alertly, lithe as a sleek Saracen hound, possessed of a swordsman's supple speed and a grace that left even his dainty Yseult wanting. And her face!—By Frey, her face glowed like a jewel, as if lit from within!

Gray-lavender eyes as soft and mysterious as an Irish mist. Skin dewy as the first snowdrop at Candlemas. Lips as red and ripe as wild strawberries. Her exquisite features were framed by a silky mane of curling locks that spiralled to her hips; blue-black, glossy plumage that was in striking contrast to Yseult's white feathers.

Beautiful, she was. As beautiful as the water fairies that rose from lakes and pools and lured enamored mortals down to their watery kingdoms.

In truth, ever since they'd met, 'twas as if he'd entered the

Otherworld: a magical place where time stood still and decades passed in but the twinkling of an eye. Edana was beautiful, bewitching—aye, and dangerous to his plans, by virtue of that loveliness! How could he test her loyalty to "Padraic," when the merest glimpse of her, the faintest whisper of her scent, made him harden like a green lad, and burn to bed her, there and then, his "test" be damned?

A distant light filled his eyes. What pleasure it would be to tame that lady-hawk to his fist alone! To stroke her raven feathers and draw a piercing love-trill from her berry lips, as they climbed the heavens, singeing their wings upon desire's fierce sun! To know that, when she left his mews to ride the winds of the world, her love for him would ensure she always returned to his hand. . . .

Trust. Love. Loyalty.

Could they exist between man and woman? Husband and wife? He snorted. If so, he'd yet to see it. Falcons, on the other hand—aye, falcons were different. Most falcons mated for life, then returned, year after year, to the same nest to raise their young together. Would Edana honor her husband, Padraic mac Torrin, all the days of their life together? Or, like his own mother, Deirdre, who had sported with Rolf Ericksen. Would she sport with Kerrin, the Dark One, the "escort" her husband had entrusted to bring her home?

Only time would tell. . . .

Meanwhile, he feared he was growing bewitched by her charms, ensorceled by her quicksilver moods, her enchanting smiles, her fiery spirit!

This morn, when they'd risen from their beds in a hollow plagued with nettles, she had gathered up a bundle of garments, flashed him an arch look, then vanished into the bushes.

Appearing a short while later, he had been slack-jawed to see that she had abandoned her noblewoman's richly embroidered kirtles and surcoats, her fine fur-lined mantles and jewelled bronze brooches, in favor of *male* garments!

Now she wore a tight-sleeved tunic of the finest creamy linen, worn with a short surcoat of supple doeskin laced over it. The surcoat hugged her slender body almost as sleekly as it had fitted its original owner! It skimmed over breasts and hips, drawing a man's lusty eye to the pert curves of a firm, shapely rump. A wide girdle of knotted leather cinched her tiny waist. From it hung a short scabbard of leather, from which jutted the twisted handle of a jewelled dagger. Suede breeks hid a pair of the longest legs he had ever seen on a woman. The latter were worn encased in knee boots of soft suede, which hugged her shapely calves. She had plaited her ebony tresses into one fat, glossy braid that bounced saucily against her back, as she strode past him, wearing a defiant expression that he was coming to know all too well.

As a finishing touch, a curious round amulet of silver hung to her waist from a thick chain of twisted silver links. On its convex face, two ornate fishes had been engraved in detail. The frilled tail of one touched the mouth of the other, as they swam, elegant fins rippling about them. Within those gaping fishy mouths had been set twin cabuchon amethysts the size of pebbles. Countless times, as she made her way to her horse, the talisman's highly polished surface had caught the morning light and flung a sunburst back at him. The mercurial bolt of lightning had been nigh blinding and had seemed, somehow, to mock him with its silvery brilliance: *Look upon my shining face, Kerrin of Wulfskeep. In it, glimpse your destiny!*

"You appear discomforted, my lord Kerrin?" she had observed saucily, as she led her palfrey toward him by its reins of scarlet leather. He recalled she'd been quite unable to mask the twitching of her lips, the merriment dancing in her gray-lavender eyes, as she did so. "Does my choice of apparel displease you?"

"Nay, my lady." He kept his expression bland, knowing she was testing his authority over her. "I only regret you did not don it sooner."

"How so?" she asked, her smile fled, her suspicions flaring.

"Because astride, you'd have been able to travel from dawn till dusk without tiring, would ye not, madam?—Now, to horse! All of ye wretches, to horse! Think you we've time to waste, sirrahs? To your saddles!" he'd bellowed, with every evidence of enthusiasm. Then, with a quick bow, he'd followed Tavish down to the river, leaving poor old Niall, the captain of his men-at-arms, to see his orders carried out.

Before he'd turned away, however, he'd caught the livid expression on the serving woman's, Grania's, pretty face and had heard her wail, "A curse on your ready tongue, my lady! When will ye learn, pray? You've gone and done it t' me again, ye have—and me with my buttocks still bruised from the last time!—"

"Kerrin?" cut in Tavish's urgent voice, its harsh timbre breaking into his musing. *"Kerrin, hsst!"*

"Hmm? Aye, what is it?" he asked absently, raising his arm aloft and uttering a piercing whistle through his teeth.

The Greenland falcon stooped down from the clouds to land on his gauntleted fist. White wings beating the air a time or two, she settled, uttering little chitters deep in her throat, as she rubbed her white-feathered head against his fingers.

"Over there. Look! Caught among the reeds!"

"Holy Mother of God." Sickened, Kerrin turned away and crossed himself. Though he had seen dead men aplenty in his lifetime, the sight of the youthful corpse bobbing face-down among the bullrushes made the gorge rise up his throat. "Is it the "owlet" you spoke of, man?" He had to ask, although he already knew what Tavish's answer would be.

Tavish swallowed and nodded, his puckish face for once unsmiling and of a greenish hue. "Aye, I fear so, sir. Jesu! Our ruse to mislead Canute proved the lad's undoing!"

"Untrue, my friend." He clenched his teeth, his expression grim. "His *master* proved his undoing, God rot him. Not you nor I. Now, come! To horse, my friend! We must overtake the others, warn them that our enemies have taken our scent. They will soon be snapping at our heels!"

"You think so?"

"I know so. And Canute is no fool. When he's travelled half a league or so with no signs of our passage before him, he will suspect our trick, turn back, and search for us elsewhere. Sooner or later, he will catch up with us. I feel it in my bones."

"Then, what are we to do?"

"We have already tarried too long in England, I fear. This

day, we shall press our horses 'til dusk. We'll ride north, then west, and put our enemies far behind us. Another sennight—mayhap less—and we shall cross into Mercia. Before Lady Moon waxes full again, we'll be deep in the wooded vale of the Severn. Canute will be hard put to find us there, with the mountains and mists to hide us.''

"God willing,'' Tavish reminded him, fervently.

"Aye, if our Lord be willing, and Amen,'' Kerrin returned with equal feeling. "Now, ride!''

"Er . . . a wee bit of advice, if I may, before we go, sir.''

"Aye, friend? What now?'' his lord asked heavily, running his hand over his rough, stubbled jaws. Sweet Christ! The day, though barely born, felt old.

"Ye'll catch more honey bees with nectar than ye will with vinegar, sir. . . .''

Chapter Nine

They made good time that day, covering almost four leagues. They did it by riding hard, with few halts, until the sun had dropped behind the low hills to the west. They supped on dried fish, broken meats, and stale oatcakes as they went, stopping only after the moon had risen.

The following morn, they were up and away, with the first flush of rosy pink in the eastern sky. Indeed, the morning star had yet to fade, when they clambered stiffly astride their horses and set out once again, their mounts' breath making plumes on the chill air to accompany their own.

By sunset of the following day, the rolling green of Sussex had given way to the woods and fields of Wessex and the pretty hamlet of Bishop's Waltham. In exchange for a haunch of fresh venison, one of His Grace's cottagers gave them directions to the old Roman road, which they could follow to Winchester, where Edward had his capital. Then, after Edan had received the king's royal blessing upon her marriage, Kerrin's captain promised, as he trotted his mount alongside Edan's, they would again return to the straight Roman road as far as Uffington. The Romans, mighty though they were, must have feared the power in those standing stones, Niall had added, for the straight

Roman highway skirted the vast horseshoe of towering henges that the druids had raised upon the plains of Old Sarum. Then, in the Vale of the White Horse, close to the hamlet of Uffington, she would see yet another fine sight, Niall promised. Green, rolling hillsides where the turf had been cut away to reveal the chalk beneath in the outline of a vast white horse that could be seen for over a league.

"A horse?" Edan had echoed, frowning. "Cut in the hillsides? But, why? For what purpose was it made?"

Nial had shrugged. "I do not know, my lady. Jarl—hhhrmph—that is to say, lord Kerrin said 'twas made by those who worshipped the horse goddess, Epona, many years ago, when the world was young."

"I see," she observed, vaguely amused that Kerrin, of all people, should have knowledge of such diverse matters. Thus far, the surly brute had not struck her as a scholarly man, let alone one who gave much thought to ancient religions! She muffled a snort. Him, religious? Ha! From what little she'd seen, 'twould be more in character for him to give priests and churches wide berth, as though they were pesthouses!

For the remainder of that day, the leagues fell quickly away behind them. She rode with steadfast, patient Niall at her side, while an unusually quiet Grania and the one called Tavish brought up in the rear. Boastful Lachlann, a short, pugnacious fellow with a shock of auburn hair and a quarrelsome disposition, rode on their left flank with his friend, Brendan, alongside him, while Brendan's brother, Donn, equally dark and of a sullen, sly disposition, guarded their right. The old woman, Myrla, straddling a sweet-faced little donkey, ambled along behind them, chomping on her gums and singing every now and then in a surprisingly wild, sweet voice. Behind her came Trevor and Little Hurleigh, who, though smaller and younger than all the others, had the courage and heart of a lion, Niall had claimed.

Meanwhile, Kerrin ranged far and wide ahead of them on his beautiful black stallion, preferring Conn's silent companionship to anyone else's, except for those times when he rode back to replace Niall at Edan's side, dismissing the poor man with but a scowl.

From what she'd observed about the man, she fancied he took more pleasure in his wild companions—his horse and his hawk—than from the company of people. In truth, that he loved the black stallion was obvious to even the most casual observer. Not an evening passed when he did not rub the beautiful animal down, inspect its hooves for stones, then water and feed it before seeing to his own comforts. And Conn clearly returned his master's love, greeting him each morn with a whicker of recognition and a toss of his elegant Arab head. The stallion's fondness for Kerrin was touching to behold, for the great horse nuzzled his neck like an affectionate puppy.

For herself, Edan was coming to enjoy the simple pleasures of the traveller who has rarely left the place of her birth. She rose eagerly in the stirrups to see what awaited them just over the next hillock, or beyond the next stretch of woodland. She exclaimed over the little things that caught and pleased her eye, before pointing them out to Grania, so that she might enjoy them, too: cairns of stones, half-hidden springs, stone crosses set amidst the weeds along the wayside, small odd-looking stones raised in memory of people long dead.

They followed a long, well-worn track through leafy woods that morning. It wound in and out amongst a pale green tunnel of white hazel and oak trees. More than once, they were forced to duck their heads, or to veer aside to avoid low-hanging boughs of flowering white hawthorn. On one occasion, Kerrin, who had fallen back to ride alongside her, reached across her to pull aside some springy boughs that blocked her path. In doing so, he inadvertently brushed her cheek with his hand.

"Your pardon, lady," he murmured gruffly, yet he did not draw away, as he ought. Rather, he remained leaning forward over his horse's neck and stared at her, as if he'd never truly seen her before. His scrutiny had seemed to last a prodigious amount of time, but in reality must have been a second or two.

In that little eternity, Edan could feel the blood burning in her cheeks, could feel the wild slam of her heart against her rib cage, like the slap of a piece of driftwood against the timbers of a pier when the tide runs full. *Thu-thump! Thu-thump! Thu-thump!* it hammered. Certain he must be able to hear it, too, she blushed, pretending a sudden fascination with the golden daffodils, the snowdrops that looked like icy tears, or the vivid bluebells that carpeted the ground beneath their horses' hooves, when they at last rode on.

Indeed, pastel wildflowers and blossoming trees were on every side and in every hedgerow. The little island of Britain had truly been blessed by the lovely goddess Eostre's fertile fingers this spring. Her green and quickening touch had brought new life and rebirth to every living thing. From bush and briar, meadow-grass and reeds, came the chitter or mewling of mother birds and mother animals, warning their little ones to be still and to hush, as Edan and her escort rode by.

The litter of fox cubs in their den beneath the roots of a great chestnut tree saw their cavalcade pass, as did Mother Brock, the gray and white badger and her brood, who peeked with light-blinded eyes from their dark sett in the rich, black earth. So, too, did the female skylark spy them and take to panicking flight. In fact, she erupted from directly beneath Conn's nose, leaving the ground like an arrow loosened from a bow.

While Kerrin fought to control the startled stallion, the terrified little bird soared skyward, warbling a great burst of song designed expressly to draw Man from her tiny nest in the short, coarse turf.

''Whoa! Hold, sir!'' Kerrin growled, shortening his reins. Yet Conn seemed deaf to his master's commands this morning. Instead of calming, the ebony stallion shot forward, taking the bit fully between its teeth, before streaking away like a glossy black hawk, swooping down from the sky. All four powerful legs pumped furiously, while its ebony mane and tail streamed behind it, like sooty pennants. The ground fell away behind its hooves, eaten up by its great strides.

Edan estimated they'd covered almost a full league before she and her escort finally caught up with Kerrin again.

By the time they happened upon him, he had already dismounted and was walking the animal to cool it down, calming it with crooning words and soothing strokes on Conn's neck and heaving sides. A bloody scratch above one brow and a streak of mud down Kerrin's opposite cheek told the story. Indeed, dirty and bruised, he looked even more disreputable than usual!

"You were thrown, sir?" Edan exclaimed, concerned.

"Aye," Kerrin gritted. He shot her a look that dared her to mock him.

"Ye ask me, ye should give that black demon a taste o' yer whip, sir," Donn suggested sourly and spat in the grass.

"But I did not ask ye, did I, Donn o' Dungarvan?" Kerrin came back witheringly, casting the man a dark look. He had no liking for the fellow, who'd attached himself to their numbers with no invitation back in Eire. He'd let him remain for the sake of his brother, Brendan o' Dungarvan, who was a man to have at your elbow in a fight.

This morn, Donn looked even sourer and more resentful, as he moved away. And, when he happened to pass near the stallion's head, Conn shied away and snorted nervously.

"Easy, my beauty, easy," Kerrin murmured, stroking Conn's glossy, arched neck and wondering what Donn had been up to, on the sly, to make Conn fear him. "Ye know me better than yon surly spalpeen, eh? Ye'll not be punished for obeying your nature," he murmured to no one in particular, though Edan caught his words. It seemed Conn did, too, for the horse tossed its delicate Arabian head and snorted. The falcon, riding high upon Kerrin's other fist, twittered jealously.

"Grania, my herbs!" Edan said crisply, springing down from Fayre's back unaided. Lifting her skirts clear of the sodden grass, she hastened to Kerrin's side.

"Herbs, lady? 'Tis but a scratch—of no import. A wee bump, no more," he insisted, his tone scathing. "Take your powders and spells hence, woman, do."

" 'Tis bleeding a little, is it not?"

"A drop or two, no more. I've had far worse. Have done, will ye, woman?"

She regarded him sternly. "When there's an opening in the skin—however small!—mortification may follow," she declared, sounding for an instant uncannily bossy and pompous, like her country nurse, Kerrin thought, the amorous, buxom Edythe, whom Niall—of middle years and as yet unmarried—had been so taken with at Kenley.

Snatching her satchel of pouches and packets of powdered herbs from Grania, she waved Kerrin down onto a fallen log, then spread a linen cloth over the rough bark beside him.

"Now, what have we here? Ah, yes." Withdrawing a small wooden bowl from her pack, she shook a few leaves into it, then added a few drops of oil from a small corked flask. Delving deeper into her satchel, she withdrew a length of clean linen to bind the compress in place.

But as she made to place the comfrey leaves across his wound, Kerrin reached up and caught her wrist. "There's no need for this, I tell ye, colleen. I'm no babe. I'm a man!"

She looked down at his face, dappled alternately with shade and light by a trick of the sun, slanting between the tossing boughs above them. *A man, indeed.*

This close, she could see the way each inky lash curled up, long and thick, from its bed in his eyelid; see the tiny motes of gold that flecked his forest green iris; the slight flaring of his nostrils; the chiselled lips she ached to—

Her heart seemed to pause in its wild racing. She held her breath. In that moment, with green and growing things all about them, the air alive with the drowsy buzz of insects, it was as if time stood still. The sudden tension between them was so thick and heavily charged, they might have cut it with a knife.

She moistened her lips, wondering what madness possessed her, for a part of her ached to frame his wind-browned face between her palms, to brush the inky curls back from his brow, and fit her lips over his own. But—

"Leave be," he breathed, his voice husky, his tone unsteady. "I'm not accustomed t' such pampering."

" 'Tis not pampering, but commonsense," she insisted softly, scarce able to draw breath, let alone speak, this near to him. She swallowed. Could he not feel the wild thunder of her pulse beneath his steely fingers, locked about her wrist! Did he not wonder at its hectic speed?

"Why?"

"Why?" She licked her lips. "Weeell, if I treat this small wound now, 'tis unlikely it will mortify and become a bigger one later. However, if I leave it!—" she shrugged and rolled her eyes, her gestures saying she would not be held responsible for the horrible—possibly even mortal—outcome. "I—um— I once heard of a maid who—who was darning, and happened to prick herself upon a bodkin. She—er—she died of her small wound, sir." Her gray eyes slid away from his.

"You lie, mavourneen," he breathed, not knowing whether to laugh or scold her for that blatant falsehood.

"Aye. I do," she admitted, meeting his accusing eyes with disarming honesty. "Forgive me, but it could happen, *if* you allow this small wound to go untreated."

"Do you care so much about my welfare, then?" The question was out, before he had time to consider the wisdom of asking it.

"I care about everyone who's important to my lord husband, and all who belong to Wulfskeep, sir. Is that not my duty, brother?"

"Do you mock me, minx? Do you seek to make a fool of me before my father's men?" he hissed, drawing her captured wrist down, so that her face was brought even closer to his.

"Of course not. Truly, I would never do anything to belittle you, milord Kerrin! I but—I but hoped to practice my herbal remedies upon you," she whispered, and it was not wholly a lie. "I thought it would be wiser to practice upon a small injury, before I find myself confronted with a l—larger one." There. Now he knew the truth. Sort of. Her face flamed with the admission. In that moment, she heartily wished the forest floor would open up and swallow her whole, even as Jonah had been swallowed by the whale!

Kerrin stared at her, nonplussed. His knowledge of women was narrow, admittedly so. It had hitherto been restricted to old Myrla, along with sundry rough whores, camp followers while a-viking, and a Wulfskeep's slattern or two. His experience of the fair sex had been further embellished by those jewels of enlightenment and wisdom that his father had told him about his mother, Deirdre. A woman who, by Torrin's reckoning, had surpassed Jezebel, Delilah, and Salome in her iniquity. But this woman . . . he scowled. . . . this woman he could not fathom. She was unlike any woman he had ever met before. She was like a thorn beneath his skin that he could not keep from chaf—

"Sir, you bruise me!"

He had not realized that he had grasped her wrist, nor that he was holding her so tightly. He nodded once, curtly, then released her hand. "Tend me, then," he barked. "You shall have your practice, madam—but, be quick!"

With hands that shook, she carefully bathed and bandaged the small wound, applying comfrey leaves to stop the slow trickle of blood and smoothing a little oil of olive on the torn skin.

Later, she decided she'd rather enjoyed tending him, despite the way he'd growled at her. It had made her feel needed, valuable. However, her pleasure at using her herb skills lasted for only a short while. Her patient, she saw, had cast off his bandage long before they halted to water the horses at midday.

"Don't let that peat-digging Irishman hurt your feelings, my lady," Grania whispered fiercely, shooting a darkling look at Kerrin behind her lady's back. "The other men teased him for your gentle care, ye see?"

Edan nodded. She'd overheard an exchange between the rascally Tavish and Kerrin herself.

"Why, and ye're a lucky cur, mac Torrin, to have the lady Edan care for ye so tenderly! Sure, and I've a splinter in me wretched backside," Tavish had observed thoughtfully, though his blue eyes were filled with wicked merriment.

"No doubt from sitting on it overlong, boyo," Kerrin came back, looking up with a scowl. He'd been digging a small, sharp stone from Conn's hoof with the point of his dagger.

"That's as may be. But are ye after thinkin' that pretty wee Grania would pull it out for me, man? Mayhap even . . . kiss my hurt better, after?" He puckered his lips.

Kerrin had shot him a scowl dark enough and black enough to extinguish the blessed sun itself, and threatened, "Another jest from you, boyo, and I'll remove that dammed splinter meself—aye, and with the sharp point o' this dagger!''

Brandishing the short blade in a threatening fashion, he'd ridden off. His guilty expression said he'd realized only belatedly that Edan must have overheard their exchange, for as Conn passed her, he reached up to touch his hurt and muttered, ''A fine job, my lady. It pains me no more,'' then quickly rode away.

For some reason, his words brought a smile to her lips.

Chapter Ten

"Riders coming up fast behind us, sir!" Niall sang out. He had been their rear guard since dawn that morning and had been ranging far and wide, scouting the countryside at their backs.

His diligence had been rewarded just a few moments ago, when he'd seen a flock of wood pigeons rise from their roosts in a great white covey, half a mile distant. The birds' sudden flight was a sure sign that a party of some size had startled them and was fast approaching.

Standing in the stirrups, Kerrin shaded his eyes against the sunlight. A dozen men, mayhap more, and coming up fast, just as Niall had warned! And there was no mistaking their identity, not with the giant, Lothar, in their midst. Both he and his massive warhorse dwarfed the other riders, including Canute with his winged bronze helmet and red-gold locks.

"Canute and his sty fellows!" Kerrin murmured, "You, Hurleigh, take the three women with all haste. Stop for nothing till ye reach the king's palace at Winchester. Wait for us there."

"As ye will, milord." Scowling, but too well-trained to question an order from his lord, Hurleigh wheeled his mount's head around. He spurred it ahead to where the three women had halted at a small wooden bridge spanning a stream.

"Brendan, Niall, take the left flank with me. Tavish, you Trevor, and Brendan, take the right."

"Aye, mac Torrin. But, what of my brother, sir?" Brendan asked, frowning as he drew a two-bladed axe from his belt.

"Aye, where is Donn?" Kerrin asked, grim-faced, turning in the saddle to look about. "Lachlann? Did ye not share the last watch o' the night with him?

Lachlann looked guilty. "Aye. But I've not seen him since the wee hours, sir. He said then that . . . *by God, look yonder!* That treacherous cur—he lied to me! He said he was going t'find himself a whore back in Bishop Waltham!—" Of a sudden, Lachlann's face and neck had turned deep red, a color not far from the hue of his hair. The reason for his fury was soon apparent, for among the horses thundering towards them was Donn's chestnut, a scarred, ugly-tempered creature with a white blaze down its face. "By Loki, Dungarvan will sing like a wench, when I'm done wi' him, Brendan's kin or nay! *For the gods, and mac Torrin!*" he roared. Long red hair streaming behind him, he raised his blade aloft and spurred his horse up the hill toward Canute and his men.

"Hold back, ye fool! It could be a trap!" Kerrin roared, but Lachlann rode on nonethless, spurring his horse to enjoin the enemy.

"Paggh, that hotheaded lout! He's got bigger balls and more courage than sense!" Brendan said with enormous pride in his friend. He jammed on his bronze helmet. "I'd best go after the spalpeen, before Canute lops off his bloody head! *Odinnnnn!*" With that fierce battle cry, Brendan kicked his chestnut mare into a gallop and streaked across the turf after his companion.

A moment later, Kerrin, Niall and Trevor followed suit, round painted shields raised, their swords or axes drawn, discovering too late that Kerrin's gut instinct had been right. The small advance party had been but bait to draw them into a deeper trap!

As they engaged with the handful of men, other attackers

sprang from bush and briar, or dropped from leafy treetops to surround them, armed to the teeth. They were outnumbered more than three to one!

It was not till they were in the thick of the skirmish that Kerrin took note of the fiercely battling, slender warrior who had sprouted like magic at his right hand. Helmeted in winged bronze, a nose guard hiding his features, he plied his sword with the skill and the tireless arm of a seasoned warrior, dispatching one of Canute's henchman with a wicked thrust beneath the armpit that parted ribs to nick the heart within.

"A worthy thrust, Trevor, lad!" he panted admiringly. He swung his sword in a sweeping arc from right to left that slammed his bearded blond opponent from his shaggy mount and nigh hacked him in two. He turned to offer more encouragement to his brother-in-arms, and was puzzled to discover that Trevor was mounted on Edana's mare. Nay, not mounted—the warrior *was* Edana! "Go back, ye damn fool! Ride!"

"Yeeeeeeaaagh!" Edana howled, deaf to his pleas, as another of Canute's men engaged her—or was he, in truth, no mortal man, but a giant? Fear tasted like bile on the back of her throat, as she slashed at the hulking figure who had suddenly reared up before the two of them, swirling his two-bladed battle-axe over his head by a length of chain and bellowing like an enraged bull.

The giant's snorting warhorse stood a good eighteen or nineteen spans, had long ears, a great Roman head, and enormous red nostrils. His chest was massive, bulging with muscle, its great hooves hidden beneath feathers of shaggy hair. Worse, the enormous beast gnashed twin rows of huge teeth in the air about her head, rearing up on its haunches to lunge at them with wicked hooves, as ferocious in battle as its hulking rider.

Its master, Lothar, wore no helmet, and his flattened features and crooked yellow teeth were horrible to behold. His shoulders and bared chest were broader than any barrel, bulging beneath a jerkin of stained bearskin. His fleshy red lips were peeled back from yellowed fangs in an unholy grin. He leaned down from the saddle, bringing his axe around in a curving sweep that—had he not made Conn execute a nimble sidestep—would have cleaved Kerrin in two. Concentrating his attention on Kerrin, Lothar chose to ignore Edan the same way a bull ignores a pesky bee that tries to sting it.

"Take that, you great slug!" she panted, pricking his beefy upper arm with the tip of her blade and drawing blood. Frustrated, she swung again and sliced off the tip of his ear lobe, deaf to Kerrin's furious commands that she flee, as he put himself and Conn between her horse and Lothar's.

She was fuming, as she was thrust rudely aside. Desert her loyal escort now, as he had ordered, when they were outnumbered more than two to one? Not a chance!

Deprived of the pleasure of dispatching the giant herself, she turned Fayre's head about and streaked after another man who, having brought Brendan to his knees in the grass, was now trying to flee the fight for the cover of the ditches.

She passed red-headed Lachlann, who had crossed swords with red-bearded Canute, as she raced after him—both men having been toppled from their horses early on in the fray. Now they lunged forward, sprang back, or aside, wielding their weighty broadswords in both powerful fists and swinging them to left and to right, or straight down over their heads. The crash and clang of metal upon metal rang out above the grunts, groans and whoops of the fighting men.

Brendan, still kneeling in the turf, dizzily lifted his head to wipe a stream of blood from his eyes. As his vision cleared, he caught the flash of sunlight on metal off to one side and saw his brother, Donn, quietly sitting atop his chestnut horse at the edge of a birch copse, half-hidden by pale green leaves. His longbow was strung, a shaft already nocked and drawn. His target—Brendan followed the direction of his aim—could only be Kerrin! "My lord! Look out! Archers!" he screamed.

His warning came a heartbeat too late. Even as Kerrin heard his cry above the clamor, the arrow found its target in his stallion's withers. With a shrill scream of pain, Conn reared up on his haunches, his front legs galloping on air. The unexpected move spilled his master backwards, toppling him heavily to the dirt. While Kerrin scrambled to his feet, the hilt of his weapon still gripped in his fist, the terrified stallion bolted, galloping across the meadow, before plunging into the distant woods.

"So! We meet again, nephew!" Canute jeered. "Tonight, you shall dine in the feasthalls of Valhalla with your father—whilst I take ship for Wulfskeep!"

"An empty boast, uncle," Kerrin jeered, watching Canute's hooded blue eyes "But then, your boasts have ever been hollow!" he scoffed, bringing up his own bloody blade. "Wulfskeep is my uncle's, if he lives. If he be dead, then she is mine!"

"Insolent pup! I'll lift your head, by Loki!" Canute roared, hefting his sword aloft. " 'Twill hang from my saddle by the hair!"

Kerrin tightened his grip, bracing his legs apart on the turf for the impact of Canute's ringing blow.

It never came.

Hallooo! Hallooo!

The sudden winding of a huntsman's horn rang out, low and mournful, over the countryside. Fear leaped into Canute's eyes. "The high-king comes! Retreat!" he roared to his fellows, whirling away from Kerrin.

Kerrin sprang after him, reaching for a leg, a boot, any handhold by which to drag him back. But with an agility that belied his years, Canute vaulted up into the saddle of a runaway horse and lashed it away to the west.

Those of his men who were still able, despite their wounds, quickly followed suit, catching and flinging themselves astride any riderless mounts they could capture, and racing off.

As they vanished in a cloud of dust over the crest of the next hill, a hunting party and a score of baying staghounds broke from the forest. Grania, old Myrla on her donkey, and Little Hurleigh were with them. The hunters' rich garments and fine mounts indicated they were men of substance.

"Make way for his royal majesty, Edward, high-king of Britain!" a deep voice rang out.

The fine looking man, who rode forward, was dressed simply, yet richly, in a mantle of indigo wool, trimmed with marten at the hems, worn over a black tunic and breeks. A narrow circlet of gold bound his brow, and he was mounted upon a pure white horse. The fine beast boasted a bridle and saddle of scarlet leather, of the sort made by Iberian leatherworkers.

"Kerrin mac Torrin of Waterford, Ireland, your majesty," Kerrin murmured, making a courtly bow. "Escort to—"

Before he could introduce her, Edan tore the helmet from her head, spilling a mantle of damp black ringlets over her shoulders. Her cheeks were flushed, her gray eyes dancing with excitement, as she declared, "Escort to myself, the Lady Edana, sire. I am the daughter of your ealdorman, Alaric, Bear of Kent, and bride to Padraic, earl of Wulfskeep, County Waterford, in Ireland!"

"Greetings, my lady!" Edward exclaimed, eyeing her fondly and with a suggestion of amusement. "You were but a toddling babe when last I saw you! But now—! Egad, madam, you're every inch your mother's daughter!—The Lady Marissa—as I recall my father saying—was also fond of breeks and swordplay!"

Instead of being flattered by his comment, Edan scowled at him, her red lips compressed. "On the contrary, sire. I am my own woman!" she insisted proudly. "And answer to no one but yourself—oh, and my lord husband, of course," she amended, as an afterthought.

"Then I stand corrected, madam," the king said gravely, inclining his head to hide the merry sparkle in his eye. "But come, good people of Eire, make haste and attend to your injured! Surely you are in disarray, thanks to the brigands who attacked you! You shall be our honored guests at court in Winchester, before you continue your journey. By your leave, sir Kerrin, I will order a feast prepared for the refreshment of yourself and your men. My own physician shall tend your wounded."

"I accept your hospitality on behalf of my lady, sire, and on behalf of my men. For myself, however, I ask leave to join your company a little later. My mount was struck by an arrow in the fray, and bolted. I would find him before nightfall."

"Of course," Edward agreed, nodding sagely.

"Of course," Edan echoed, adding, "I will help you."

And despite his sternest efforts, no amount of argument on his part could dissuade her from doing so.

He was fast discovering that she had no equal in obstinacy, except—mayhap—himself.

As it transpired, Edan was the unfortunate one to find Conn.

While searching in a little woodland glade that was carpeted with wild hyacinths and purple violets, she heard strange loud coughing and snorting noises. Drawing her dagger, she crept forward on the balls of her feet, not entirely convinced she wouldn't find a wounded man from that afternoon's battle. What she saw instead was the great black stallion.

The poor beast was down on its side in the long grass between the oaks, its sides heaving. Loud noises escaped its gaping mouth. It was those she had heard: the sounds of a creature fighting for its every breath.

"Over here! I've found Conn!" she called and started forward, only to pull up short, sick to her stomach. *Oh, sweet Jesu, no!* There was an arrow jutting from the area of the withers, behind the poor beast's ribs. Though part of the shaft had been snapped off during the stallion's terrified flight, a goodly portion still remained. She swallowed, close to tears, for by the angle at which the arrow had entered the horse's body, and the whistling sounds the poor creature was making, the lethal metal arrowhead had surely pierced the horse's lungs. There was a ragged hole in the flesh from which the arrow protruded. Great quantities of blood had almost certainly been lost from it, too. Even now, bright red blood was pumping from the wound in a steady stream.

A lump filled her throat. She did not have to be a physician to know that Conn was mortally wounded. The miracle was that he had managed to live this long.

His once glossy, jet-black coat was caked with dried mud and foam. Leaves and twigs were caught in his tangled mane and tail. His expressive brown eyes were no longer bright, but clouded with pain. And yet, the stallion tried valiantly to lift his noble head, to whicker a greeting, as his master thrust past Edan to kneel at his head.

"Conn, me brave boyo," Kerrin crooned, lifting the horse's head onto his lap. His voice broke with emotion, as he continued, "Sure, and what have you done t' yourself now, eh, my handsome lad?"

Tears streaming down her face, Edan hung back at the edge of the clearing, loath to intrude upon the wrenching tableau before her.

The sight of the gravely injured horse, his noble black head cradled gently in Kerrin's arms, whose stern, handsome face was buried in the horse's ebony mane, was more than she could bear. She had no need to go any closer to know that there were tears filling Kerrin's eyes. She could hear them in his voice.

He looked up, then. Their eyes met across the woodland glade in acknowledgement and sorrow. They both knew that Conn was dying. There was nothing anyone could do for the stallion now, but ease his pain and hasten his end.

With a small nod, she turned and ran from the woods, blinded by tears.

She was sitting on the low wooden bridge, dangling her bared feet in the stream that hurried over smooth black stones, when Kerrin came out of the woods a long, long while later.

His face was grim and weary, as he dangled Conn's bridle in one hand and carried the saddle over his opposite shoulder. He reached Edan's side and walked as if all the weight of the world were upon him.

Although she'd found precious little softness about the man thus far, her heart went out to him now. She knew firsthand how strong the bond between horse and rider could become. If anything should ever happen to her pretty Fayre, she could not bear it!

"Is it . . . is it over, sir?" she asked gently.

He exhaled in a deep sigh. "It is."

She twisted her hands in her lap. "I feel for you, milord. Truly. 'Twas no easy thing to do."

A muscle ticked in his jaw. " 'Tis never easy to do what is right, my lady."

She bit her lip. Even in his sorrow, he was as prickly as a hedgehog! "I know, sir. But 'tis especially difficult since you loved the . . . loved Conn so well."

A ghost of a smile played over his lips. "The arrow pierced his lungs. Had he lived, only suffering lay ahead for him. Hours—perhaps even days—of growing gradually weaker, each breath becoming harder to draw. And then one day, he would have looked up to see the carrion crows turning the treetops black, just waiting for him to die." He grimaced and shook his head. *"Because* I loved him, I could not let him reach such a pass."

"But . . . but he is dead!" she whispered, her lower lip quivering. "How can you bear it?"

A distant light filled his eye. "You are yet very young, Edana. Once life has stretched you on her rack a time or two, you will realize there are worse things than dying. Living on, in pain and torment, is but one of them." His face hardened. "I hope and pray that if I'm ever brought to such a pass, a friend will do the same for me, in the name of love."

She nodded and echoed, "In the name of love," before she rose to standing. "Will you come back to camp with me, sir? The men have raised our tents amongst some Roman ruins for the night. Hurleigh has prepared a kettle of stew with some of the venison the king's huntsmen left us. There's also a skin of wine."

"Tell the men they may sup without me. I'll join them anon."

He obviously wanted to be alone. She started to leave, then turned back to him. "Kerrin?—"

"Aye, my lady?"

"I'm truly sorry. About Conn, I mean." Her voice was husky. Her gray eyes were earnest and very bright with tears. "He . . . he was so beautiful—so full of strength and spirit!"

"Aye. He was all that, and more, was he not?" he agreed, softly. On impulse, he took her hand between his own and lifted it to his lips, looking down at her over her knuckles for an instant, before he released her, murmuring, "I thank ye for your concern, Edana. And for calling me by my name, too."

She nodded, flustered by the unusual warmth in his tone and by the lilting way he spoke her own name, with this mood upon him: *Ee-da-nuh.* She had never liked her given name before, much preferring the shortened form of "Edan." But, spoken with Kerrin's musical brogue, it sounded like an endearment—and turned her innards to clabbered cream. "I—um— I had best go now," she said, in a rush, color staining her ivory cheeks like red ink seeping into vellum. "Lachlann's dressings will need changing soon." She wrinkled her nose. "At this very moment, that great baby's probably bellowing that he's dying and trying to pick a fight with Brendan, though 'tis in truth but a small cut. Anon, milord."

With that farewell, she rode back to their camp amongst the Roman ruins of Bignor. There, she and Grania diverted themselves, until daylight faded, by admiring the remains of colorful mosaic walls and tiled floors, fountains and solariums, and by searching for Roman coins amongst the rubble. But, though she waited until nightfall, Kerrin did not return to camp, as he'd promised. She wondered if he had gone after the traitor, Donn, who had fired that fatal arrow, and shuddered. Wherever Donn o'Dungarvan might be hiding this night, she'd not give much for his chances, should Kerrin or his brother, Brendan find him. . . .

She fell asleep beside the red embers of their camp fire, rolled into her mantle, listening to a wolf's mournful howling in the deep woods.

Kerrin rejoined them the following morn, while they were breaking the night's fast. He immediately gave the order to break camp and go on to Edward's palace at Winchester, some leagues to the north.

"Tavish, Niall, and the others will see to everything, milord. Meanwhile, eat this," she told him firmly, thrusting a wooden bowl of the previous night's stew at him.

He shook his head. "In truth, I have no appetite."

"I know. But you cannot ride from dawn to dusk on an empty belly. It—it would please me if you ate a little, sir. A bite . . . two, mayhap?"

He shot her a scowl, but took the steaming bowl from her hands, anyway. It was, he told himself, easier than arguing with the woman. Scooping several huge spoonfuls of the savory mixture into his mouth, he wolfed them down with hardly a chew, then took a swig of watered wine from the cup she offered "There. Now, have done, woman," he growled, and stomped away.

She hid a smile. He was hurting, but he would survive. She was surprised to find it mattered to her that he should.

Chapter Eleven

With Kerrin mounted on Niall's horse, and Niall sharing Hurleigh's game little mare, they left the Roman ruins soon after, passing through a dense forest where herds of shaggy wild ponies roamed. But, despite Edan and Grania's best efforts to tempt the pretty creatures to eat crusts of bread from their hands, they would not come near. In the end, the young women yielded to Kerrin's urging and rode on.

On leaving the forest, they followed the old Roman road that arrowed north, once more, through Salisbury, giving the standing stones that rose from earthen ramparts on the plains of Old Sarum wide berth, just as the Romans had done, when their legions built this road.

Perhaps it was her imagination, but if she closed her eyes and kept very quiet and still, Edan fancied she could hear the cries of the innocents whose blood had soaked the altar stone. With a shudder, she crossed herself, touched heels to Fayre's flanks, and quickly cantered on. By tacit consent, the others followed her lead, though no one volunteered a reason for doing so.

Some things were better not discussed.

They reached Winchester at midday that first day of May,

which was the old pagan feastday of Beltane, to find a Maypole had been raised in the market square. Little maids, with wreaths of pretty white hawthorn blossoms crowning their heads, were skipping about the maypole to the music of tabors and pipes, threading the gaily colored ribands in an intricate braid, as they danced.

A fair was in progress in the meadow. There was a great number of folk coming and going, as well as heavily laden wagons and carts, horses, pigs, and geese. The succulent aromas of spit roasted boar and beef wafted on the breeze, making Edan's mouth water.

She and her escort made their way past St. Mary's Abbey, the nunnery founded by old Queen Ealshswith shortly before her death, riding through the throng of noisy marketgoers, cowherders, goose-girls and their gaggles, to the royal manor where Edward held court.

After being warmly received by the king and his gracious lady, Kerrin requested quarters be found for the injured men, Lachlann and Trevor, in the garrison. When they had been seen to, a smiling servant escorted Edan to a well-appointed bower. The walls were hung with tapestries, the chamber furnished with an intricately carved bed, a chair, and scrivening table, on which stood one of the clever lanthorns that the old king, Alfred had invented. Other servants brought basins of heated water, scented with fragrant herbs, along with fresh linens.

"Their majesties bade me ask you to join their courtiers at the archery butts later, if you are not too wearied, Lady mac Torrin," a serving woman told her, adding by way of explanation, "Queen Aefflaed is the patroness of our archery contest each Mayday, you see, madam? Our dear lady rewards the winner with a purse of gold!"

"You may tell their majesties I would be honored to take part," Edana said warmly. "And my thanks for your assistance, Mistress Eldrida."

"It was my pleasure to serve thee, my lady," the woman rejoined, curtseying respectfully. "Will you have need of a wench to help you with your toilette?"

Edan was about to refuse, when she thought better of it.

Grania had been forgetful and dreamy of late. It would do her good to discover she was not indispensable. Well aware of Grania's indignant expression and dark looks as she did so, she graciously accepted Eldrida's offer.

A short while later, she found herself freshly washed and attired by the serving wench in a kirtle of forest green, over which she threw a mantle of the green and black mac Torrin plaid, pinned at the shoulder with a bronze and enamel brooch. Her loose black hair crowned with a circlet of silver set with olivines and topazes, she sallied out to the archery butts, which had been set up on the river meadow, behind Edward's keep.

Queen Aefflaed and her ladies were already there, seated beneath a silk pavilion, where they might enjoy both the contest and a charming view of the Wey, out of the wind and the sun. In their rich, colorful garments, and wearing costly jewels which flashed like kingfishers' wings in the clear, spring light, they vied with the daffodils and irises blooming in gay profusion along the riverbanks.

Many people were already there—some spectators from the growing hamlet of Winchester, others contestants competing for the Queen's purse. Their fur-trimmed robes and mantles made a bright splash of color against the greensward.

Swans floated serenely past on the nearby river Wey, like miniature snowy dragonships, while ducks, with iridescent, emerald throats, bobbed about, quacking noisily and dabbling, tails up, in the reeds.

King Edward was deep in conversation with Kerrin when Edan crossed the meadow to join them.

". . . as I said, my father, King Alfred, was most interested in the affairs of your countrymen," Edward was saying, "In particular, the religious matters in Ireland, for he was a scholarly man, and deeply religious himself. Throughout his reign, he welcomed Irish pilgrims to his court. Indeed, his beloved friend, Asser, hailed from the Irish stronghold at St. Dyffed's, to the southwest of Wales, friend Kerrin. St. Dyffed's is the port where your dragonship and her crew await you, I believe you said?"

"I did, sire, aye."

"Tell me about your vessel."

"Storm Chaser?" He grinned. "She was my un—my father's dragonship before she became mine. I venture t' say no finer, swifter *drakkar* ever set sail, sire."

"Quite," the king murmured, smiling at the pride in the young man's tone. "My late father, may God assoil him, was very interested in improving our navy, you know? He felt that a fleet modeled upon the superior design of your dragonships would be invincible."

"I agree with him entirely, sire," Kerrin acknowledged with quiet pride. "A dragonship is able to go either forward or backward at will, you see, on account of the mast's position in the exact center of the vessel, and because of the keel. This gives our *drakkars* the maneuverability needed for sea battles and the stability to keep from capsizing. Moreover, the decks are broad enough and the sides high enough t'withstand the swells of even a fierce storm. Take the tempest we were beset with in St. George's channel, during our crossing to Britain, for example. A lesser vessel would have sunk long before her oarsmen could row her to shore!"

Edward nodded, impressed by the Irishman's understanding of his vessel. "Tell me, pray. I had heard that the Norsemen carry their boats overland between rivers. But, surely this cannot be true?" He gestured for a passing servant to bring them refreshment.

Kerrin smiled. "Indeed it is, your majesty. A crew of thirty-five men are able to carry a dragonship a considerable distance. This versatility is what enables the northmen to penetrate inland after raiding coastal hamlets. By portaging their vessels between rivers, they can conquer entire countries at will."

"Mead, your majesty, milord."

Edward drank from the brimming horn the servant handed him, then wiped his moist lips on a linen cloth. "Do you expect to find the channel crossing as turbulent upon your return?

"I pray not, your majesty," Kerrin said fervently, glancing up with an expression of enormous relief as Edan joined them. Having spent most of his life in the company of wild animals or old Myrla, or else amongst sailors and rough fighting men, he did not find himself entirely at ease when at court, either here or in Ireland—a factor only those who knew him very well would realize. He had, however, gone to some lengths to augment his meager learning, while going *a-viking* to the east, and had acquired an excellent education piecemeal, once he had learned to read and write. If not, he would have been counted an Irish barbarian—in more than looks alone—by such noble company as this, he thought, moodily eyeing the cream of Wessex nobility over the rim of his silver goblet. If there was one thing he hated, 'twas to be looked down upon.

Edan made her bow to the king, then another to himself. The impish twinkle in her eyes said that she was aware of his discomfort. That she had read him so easily irked him. "Your majesty. My lord Kerrin," she murmured, prettily inclining her head to each of the men in turn.

"Ah, Lady Edana, there you are—and dressed fittingly in skirts, now, too!" Edward added, grinning at Kerrin. "In truth, your loveliness outshines the sun, my lady! Surely my people will elect you as their May Day Queen!" Edward declared, embellishing his compliment with a fond smile. Alaric and his family had been favorites of the royal family for two generations now. He had seen far less of them than he would have wished, since his father's, King Alfred's passing.

"His Majesty flatters me," Edan denied, blushing prettily. "However, I believe one of the Queen's maids has already been chosen."

Kerrin scowled and rolled his green eyes heavenward in disgust. Such meaningless twitter had no place in his life. "By your leave, your majesty, Lady Edana, I must find a mount to replace my own before we continue our journey on the morrow. With luck, I will find a suitable horse at the market? . . ."

What he really sought was escape. Edan knew, and so she pouted, pleading mischievously. "Oh, do stay, sir, do!"

He shot her a murderous look.

"Aye, mac Torrin, stay," the king commanded. "We would enjoy the pleasure of your company a while longer. And when you are ready to depart, you shall have your pick from the mounts of my own stables. Meanwhile, I challenge you and your countrymen, one and all, to test the talents of your archers against the marksmanship of my courtiers!''

Kerrin brightened and grinned. "I'faith, sire, we can't refuse such a challenge, can we, my lady?'' he asked, turning to Edan.

"Indeed, no!'' she agreed.

He nodded. "Then we accept, sire!''

In honor of the occasion, Edan had her new bow brought to her from her baggage. It was the bow Kenley's master fletcher, Dewey the Welshman, had made just for her. The elegantly curved stock was fashioned from the hardwood of the ash tree; the notched shafts in the doeskin quiver slung over her back were tipped with arrowheads of iron and fitted with goose-feather flights. The bowstring was of strong linen cord, strengthened with beeswax.

She made a comely picture, when it was her turn to step up to the mark, kirtled in hunter's green and mantled by her husband's plaid. Her ink-black hair spilled loose about her shoulders from beneath her jewelled circlet, and her eyes were bright, her cheeks flushed.

It had been several weeks since she had last used her bow, and that had been for hunting, rather than target shooting, she thought, slipping the three-fingered archer's glove of soft suede onto her right hand. But to her relief, the strength of her shoulder muscles and her sharp eye had not abandoned her. Neither had Dewey the Welshman's many hours of patient teaching!

Catching her lower lip between her teeth in concentration, she nocked the arrow against the bowstring and slowly drew it back. Sighting down the shaft at the distant butt, to which a target had been fixed, she took careful aim.

When she loosed it, her arrow sang across the water meadow and thudded strongly home into the center of the target, drawing the approving cheers of both her mac Torrin escort and the crowd.

"By Odin, 'tis the goddess Artemis, come to earth!'' Lachlann, his arm in a linen sling, declared gallantly, grinning.

"The purse! Here, majesty! The purse of gold for the mac

Torrin's Diana!'' quipped little Hurleigh. Though his chin had been nicked, and he'd taken a dagger through the foot, somehow, he was still playing the fool.

Yet the purse was not to be so easily won. Edan's fiercest rivals for it proved not only lord Kerrin himself, but a nobleman named Godfrey, Thane of Cirencester, who had won the Queen's purse in past years.

From a field of over twenty contestants, after the first three rounds, only the three of them, and a half-dozen others, yet remained in the running for the Queen's gold.

A tall, golden-bearded thane with a woodsman's eye—aye, and a roving one!—Godfrey cast Edan a wolfish glance as he swaggered up to the mark for his first shot. Winking at her over his shoulder, he let loose his shaft, chuckling as it took the target cleanly in the center. ''A bull, by God! Nine points, to me!''

Next came Kerrin. With quiet dignity, he stepped up to the mark and selected an arrow from the quiver at his back. As he stood there, adjusting his aim in readiness to let fly his shaft, Godfrey observed in a loud whisper to his second, ''Look at him. He's naught but an Irish peasant!''

Despite the anger that tightened the muscles in his jaw, Kerrin's arrow also found the outer edge of the bull's eye, touching the outer ring in almost the same spot as Edan's, though a little to the right of Thane Godfrey's. The shaft quivered from the powerful impact, long after the arrow had thudded home.

''First round—Thane Godfrey wins. Nine points!'' bellowed the king's bowman, after comparing the points scored by all three arrows.

The crowd roared its approval, well-pleased that the first round had been won by a local favorite.

The next test of their archers' skill was far more difficult. A small wooden disc had been attached to a length of rope, then the rope fastened to the bough of a tree. A yeoman's stout push sent the target swinging smoothly to and fro.

Edan's eyes narrowed, as she paced the moving target. When she fired her arrow, she would have to aim at the place where it *would* be, not where it was. It was no simple challenge. (In order to make the difficult shot, an archer must not only estimate the speed of the shaft, but also the distance it had to travel, and the future position of the swinging target.)

The crowd hushed expectantly, as she raised the long bow, sighted down it, and drew back.

There! A wild roar of approval rose from the mac Torrin men as their lady's arrow took the swinging target firmly in the center.

Giddy with relief, flushed with pride, Edan returned to her place to receive the men's congratulations and to watch while the other contestants took their turns. But, though the other archers managed to hit the target, none had been able to spear the coveted center as she had done. She crossed her fingers for good fortune. Only Thane Godfrey and Kerrin had yet to shoot a second time. Oh, let Dame Fortune be with her! she thought, touching the silver amulet on its long chain for good luck.

Kerrin took up his position. There was a look of grim determination on his handsome face, as he took aim. Having heard Godfrey's loud remark, she knew the reason why. The moving target's path was difficult to estimate. It required the utmost concentration. Could he—still upset over Conn's death and the skirmish with the brigands yesterday—match, or better, her score?

She could tell long before the arrow whizzed to the right of the target that he had aimed wide. With a rueful shake of his head, he made a half-bow to Thane Godfrey, a deeper one to herself, and gallantly conceded the field to the two of them. Despite Godfrey's comment, Kerrin accepted defeat with the good grace and dignity required of any nobleman.

The last round was the most difficult of all. The yeoman would toss a small pouch of sackcloth weighted with grain high into the air. It was the archer's goal to skewer the pouch before it fell to the ground.

She nodded to show that she was ready, but no sooner had her arrow left the bowstring, than Edan knew she had misjudged her target. The yeoman had thrown high and wide, and she had been forced to squint into the sun when she aimed. Consequently, it came as no surprise when the bowman cried, "A miss for the Lady Edana!"

The spectators groaned. Her loyal escort groaned. Hurleigh clutched his heart and fell to the ground. Edana saw him and giggled at his foolish antics.

With a smile, she stepped back, conceding the mark to Thane Godfrey, who strolled to it with exaggerated nonchalance. Shooting her a smug grin, he raised his bow. "Target!" he bellowed.

As she had known it must, his arrow took the missile cleanly through the center, long before it began its fall to earth.

"Thane Godfrey wins!" roared the King's bowman.

His companions and lackeys crowded around to congratulate him. More cheering followed, when Godfrey strode to the Queen's pavilion of fluttering silk hangings, to be presented with the velvet purse of twenty gold mancuses by that gracious lady.

"You are a most deserving champion, Thane Godfrey," Edan told him afterwards.

"And you a most lovely and formidable opponent, my lady," Godfrey murmured, bending low over her hand in courtly fashion. His brown eyes rested on the swell of her breasts against her mantle, then on her lovely face. "I ask a champion's boon of ye, madam! Will ye grant it me?"

"That remains to be seen, sir. You must first tell me what it is?"

"That you grace the seat beside me at the feast this even! Say yes, and I shall serve ye naught but the most tender of morsels with my own hand!"

"You do me honor with your invitation, sir. However, I cannot grant your boon. I am a married woman."

"Married? But, I see no husband at your side, madam," he murmured silkily, his hand closing over her arm.

"Are ye deaf, boyo? The lady told ye, did she not? She is married," growled Kerrin's deep voice on Godfrey's left. "Now. Let go her hand, before I skewer yours to yon tree!" Kerrin's hand closed over the hilt of his dagger. His tone and his darkling look brooked no refusal.

For a moment, the two men glowered at each other like rival stags about to lock antlers, their bodies rigid, their gazes unwinking, the charged atmosphere between them like that which presaged a storm. Godfrey was the first to back down.

"A ferocious watchdog ye have, in truth, madam!" he declared with a smirk, throwing up his hands in mock surrender. Eyeing Kerrin disdainfully, he drew his mantle aside, as if he feared to soil it. "Have a care. If ye persist in consorting with Irish curs, ye'll find yourself plagued by Irish fleas!"

At her side, Edan felt Kerrin's body stiffen anew with anger. He was itching to thrust her aside and force the thane to eat his insults with the help of his fists! Accordingly, she increased the pressure of her hand against his arm, warning him to ignore the man. Godfrey had many friends in this place, and the mac Torrins were few in number.

"Better Irish fleas than a Wessex worm, sir," she said sweetly. The angry color that suffused Godfrey's face said that her barb had struck home. "Lord Kerrin, your arm, pray."

While Godfrey fumed, she inclined her head, lifted her skirts clear of the damp grasses and swept away like a queen to the river's edge, Kerrin's strong hand cupping her elbow as she went.

"Why in the world must ye watch him so, my lady? He gives me nightmares he does, with that brooding scowl," Grania exclaimed at the feast that same evening in the great hall of King Edward's royal manor.

"Him?"

"The Irishman."

She did not need to say *which* Irishman. They both knew who she was speaking of. "You are mistaken, Grania. I do not watch him," Edan denied, forcing herself to look away from Kerrin. Instead, she drew circles with her fingernail on the crisp white tablecloth of Flanders' linen, covering the trestle table before her. Scowling up at the girl, Edan helped herself to a tender morsel of stewed lamprey. A platter of the delicious victuals had been placed between her and Kerrin. They were to be shared, as was the custom.

"I'm just ... surprised ... that he dances so well," she added, knowing her excuse sounded lame, but at a loss to come up with another reason for watching him. Truth was, the way he had defended her honor that afternoon had endeared him to her and made her view him in a far more favorable light than she had hitherto.

Grania snorted and tossed her braids. "By the saints, we both know you lie, my lady!" she crowed softly. And, as Edan's eyes widened, then darkened in her anger, Grania sped quickly away to join the mac Torrrins and the warriors and wenches of Edward's court at the farthest table, fleeing before her mistress could box her ears or pinch her for her impudence.

The feasters were seated on long wooden benches drawn up to huge trestles, which ranged the length and breadth of the smoky banqueting hall. There were two hearths, one at either end of the hall, about which sprawled the king's staghounds and mastiffs, as well as those graybeards whose bones felt the evening chill. The flames feasted on great logs hewn from apple trees. They imparted a pleasing fragrance to the air as they burned.

Faces were made ruddy, eyes made brighter by the fire and candlelight and by the writhing light of the torches stuck in iron sconces along the walls. Sturdy pillars of oak aisled the great hall, creating the impression of a forest planted at intervals with straight, lofty trees. Beautifully embroidered tapestries graced many of the walls, depicting Biblical stories. Adam and Eve in the garden of Eden; The Annunciation of the Virgin.

Here on this Beltane night feasted the flower of Wessex nobility, from King Edward, high-king of Britain, to the lowliest potboy and food taster. The latter—a flaxen-haired lad—was presently gnawing a meaty rib bone beneath the falconers' trestle table, his fingers smeared with grease which he wiped on the hems of the falconers' mantles.

Minstrels raised their voices to be heard above the merry laughter and talk, as they strolled about, strumming harps, playing pipes, or tapping upon little drums, singing the gathering's favorite ballads. Romantic songs of heroes of old and of the beautiful maidens they had won and lost; epic songs of the gods and goddesses who had ruled them all, when the world was young.

Edan shook her head in disgust and annoyance as Grania, her plaits flying, had squirmed out of her reach. *That wretch!* She was becoming quite impossible lately, and she fancied she knew the reason, although the two of them had not spoken of it as yet.

Tavish. Her serving woman fancied herself in love with Kerrin's man-at-arms by that name—the lean, merry-faced one, to be exact. Consequently, Grania had been of precious little service to her on the journey between Kenley and Winchester.

In all honesty, it had come as something of a relief to see the high-king's standards fluttering over the wood and stone towers of his fortress, which was built upon a broad, high motte overlooking the river and surrounded by palisades.

It had seemed of late that, if Edan asked Grania to find a certain ring or a particular brooch to wear, Grania could not find it, no matter where she might look. And even if, by some miracle, she should she find it, moments later it was again mislaid!

The situation had not improved with the passing of the days. The wench stammered, grew pink-cheeked and flummoxed, dropped things and tripped over nothing at all, if Edan should, by some unlucky chance, happen to give her an order in the presence of that wretched Tavish. Moreover, she could not be relied upon to carry out that same order, however simple— even when she claimed to have heard it correctly in the first place!

Indeed, ever since their little party had reached the market cross at East Grinstead, where the old Roman roads crossed, the situation had been trying Edan's patience to the limits. And now, that impudent wench had dared to suggest that *she* was suffering from a similar malady!

Still . . . Kerrin did seem remarkably limber this evening. And it had been no lie she'd told Grania—she *had* been watching him dance. Clothed richly tonight in a dark green tunic and breeks, his green and black plaid mantle pinned at the right shoulder by a snarling wolf's head of bronze, he cut a most dashing, handsome figure in the torchlight. The midnight hair, caught back in a thong once again, gave him the dangerous, rakish cast of a sea raider. Truth was, though she would have given her little finger sooner than admit it, she envied the maid he'd led into the circle of carole dancers!

The tiny fair-haired wench was one of Queen Aefflaed's maidens-in-waiting—the same wench who had been crowned Queen of the Maying, she believed. The girl had seemed reluctant—almost terrified!—when the Irishman first asked her to partner him, Edan had observed with what bordered on malicious pleasure—and mayhap even a twinge of . . . God forbid! . . . jealousy. The foolish twit probably feared he had horns and tails beneath his inky black locks and plaid mantle. She was not entirely sure he didn't, herself.

"Edana? Edana of Wulfskeep?"

Edan glanced up to see the high-king of Britain smiling down at her.

"My liege, forgive me!" She hastily scrambled to her feet and, despite the king's protests that it was unnecessary, swept him a deep, graceful curtsey. "I wished to thank you for giving your royal blessing to my marriage. It means so much to me."

"We were most pleased to do so, child. Your union with the mac Torrins of Wulfskeep is the final step in an important alliance between the people of Wessex and the Irish of Waterford. One that will, God willing, keep the Norsemen of Ireland from ever again plundering our coasts!"

"Amen, sire," she echoed fervently, crossing herself.

"As you know, your betrothal was one arranged many years ago by both our fathers, when the mention of Guthrum the Dane still struck terror in the hearts of Wessex men." He smiled. "Since then, your father has become as vital to me as he was to my father, Edana. I could ask for no wiser counsel than that of my loyal ealdorman, Alaric of Kenley." He paused and took both her hands in his to raise her to standing. "We are loath to bid you farewell, lovely child. To that end, Queen

Aefflaed has requested that you join her ladies-in-waiting, here at court. Will you not stay?''

"Sire, please, do not ask this of me. 'Tis a great honor her majesty has shown me, but—'' She looked down at her feet.

"But you have yet to meet your lord husband. I understand. If you choose to leave Winchester on the morrow, then go with our blessings, child.''

"Thank you, your majesty. My lord's father, Jarl Torrin, was close to death when my escort took ship for Britain. Milord Kerrin fears that, in his absence, rival lords will have attacked his brother's keep. He is most anxious to return to Ireland and add his sword to Padraic's.''

Edward nodded. "Then God be with you on your journey into Wales, Lady Edana. And may your marriage be long, happy—and fruitful,'' he added, bending to place a kiss upon her brow. His blue eyes twinkled.

She blushed. "My thanks, sire. You and your gracious lady have been most kind, both to myself and to my escort.''

He nodded. "Now, tell me. How is it that you sit all alone here, in this shadowed corner, when the other pretty maids of my court are dancing?—Lady Marissa was most fond of dancing, as I recall. Do you not take after your mother in this?''

"I do indeed, sire, but. . . .''

"Milord Kerrin!'' the king commanded.

"Yea, majesty?'' Kerrin responded, making a bow.

"Partner your new sister in the carole,'' the king suggested, resting his hand upon Kerrin's shoulder. "Married or nay, she is far too comely to hide herself here, in the shadows.'' And, to Edan's dismay, he took her hand and placed it firmly in the Irishman's.

And what could Kerrin do, but tell him yea, Edan thought angrily, her cheeks aflame with mortification. To her undying shame, Kerrin took her hand and led her down from the nobles' dais and across the great hall, with all eyes upon them. The rushes and sweet herbs that were strewn over the earthen floor rustled underfoot, as he led her to the circle of dancers.

"In truth, milord, you need not do this!'' she protested, when he found an opening for them. "The king has already forgotten us, do you not you see? Believe me, I was well content to watch.''

'' 'Tis by your king's command that ye're to dance, my lady,'' Kerrin countered, casting her an enigmatic glance she could not read. ''And as for ''forgotten''—? I think not! His majesty is a man who misses little. Come. Step out, colleen! Surely ye'd not refuse the high-king's bidding, lass?'' His tone was light, teasing.

Before she could utter a retort—or a protest, either, come to that—the hornpipes and tabors, flutes, and bells commenced their wild music once again. Smiling men and wenches skipped to the left or to the right, planting their feet solidly upon the rushes in time to the music. Goodwife, goose-girl, nurse, yeoman, noble, and warrior; the direction in which they moved depended entirely upon which circle of the carole dance—the inner or the outer—they belonged. Clasping the hands of those on either side of them, they galloped merrily away, their hair and colored ribands flying out, their kirtles and tunics making a rainbow in the smoky gloom.

''Will ye mind where you're going, sister-wife!'' Kerrin hissed loudly, making no effort to conceal his laughter, as she skipped the wrong way and bumped heavily into a strapping, bearded steward on her left. ''Sure, you'll have these good folk thinking the women of Kent are not elegant swans at all, but waddling marsh ducks!''

''Better a waddling duck than a cross-eyed loon!'' she came back, throwing herself enthusiastically to the right. *''Ooof!''*

Kerrin threw back his head and chortled with laughter, as she stepped on the steward's beefy foot once again, then thudded heavily into that poor fellow's brawny chest, before rebounding off it and slamming heavily into Kerrin's arms. ''What are ye about now, mavourneen?'' he demanded, holding her for what seemed a good while longer and with far greater relish and firmness than was required. Or so she fancied. ''Sure, and this must be a harvest dance, for a lass more like a sack of turnips I've never seen!''

Without hesitation, she kicked him, landing a well-aimed toe squarely on his shin. ''A harvest dance, milord escort?''

she asked sweetly, smiling, as he jiggled about on one foot, looking deeply pained. "Then surely 'tis one for the harvest of the . . . *hops,* nay?"

"Ye blasted she-devil! Can ye not abide a jest?" he muttered, all merriment fled.

"Oh, *I* can, sirrah! The question is, can you?—"

'Twas that part of the carole when each of the dancers turned and wove their way in and out of the other dancers in the ring, moving in a figure-eight fashion. They were forced to pass each other off on their opposite arms, and Kerrin's salty retort was blessedly lost as he moved away from her, around the circle—aye, and good riddance, too!

She had despaired of ever finding him again, when he clasped her hand once more. But, instead of swinging her about, he yanked her from the circle, hauling her after him into the shadows of a massive oaken pillar.

"What now, wretch? I though ye wished to dance?" she reminded him, breathless as he pressed her back against the pillar.

She could feel cold timber pressing solidly against her back—warm, hard male pressing solidly against her front. Her heart skipped a beat, as he braced both palms upon the wood on either side of her head, effectively trapping her between them. He was breathing as heavily as she—and it had naught to do with the dance.

"Dancing's not what I'm after, Edan," he rasped. "Aye, and well you know it!"

His face was so close to hers, she could feel the hot current of his breath, could smell his scent, a mixture of lemon-grass and mint leaves, mingled with the masculine musk and heat of his body. "What do I know?" she whispered, her eyes huge in the shadows.

"Don't play the innocent with me, Edana, mavourneen. 'Tis why ye stare at me." He ran the tips of his fingers down her cheek, along the curve of her jaw. His touch was as hot as the stroke of a brand, yet left a trail of gooseflesh in its wake, as he whispered, "Admit it. Ye want me!"

"Stare? Me? Ha! 'Tis but conceit on your part, sir. Or wishful thinking. And as for wanting *you!*— You must be mad!'' she scoffed. ''Stand aside. Let me pass.'' She tried to push past him, to thrust him aside, but he pressed her back against the pillar and held her there.

''Not so fast, my flighty wren. Are ye saying ye have no feelings for me?'' he demanded, tilting her chin so that she had no choice but to look at him.

She glared at him mutely, painfully aware of their proximity. She swallowed. Dear God, this near, she could all but feel the thud of his heart against her own!

''Answer me, firebrand!'' he commanded again, ducking his head lower, as if he thought perhaps she had not heard him over the wild, sweet clamor of the music.

''Nay,'' she hissed fiercely. ''You are my husband's brother. Nothing more.''

''Nothing?''

''Nothing!'' He was so close ... so close, his lips were almost brushing her hair, nearly touching her brow. Perversely, longing filled her, even as fear closed her throat. Surely, oh, blessed God, surely he could not mean to kiss her?

But he did.

Cupping her chin, he lowered his dark head and fitted his hungry mouth over hers.

Shaken, she brought her hands up between them, pressed them against his chest, yet he continued to kiss her, to deepen and secure his masterful possession of her mouth. The heat and hunger of his lips ignited the embers of her own desire, till she trembled like an aspen. *''Kerrin! Oh, Kerrin, we should not!''*

Her name broke against his lips like surf breaking upon a shore. Again, she tried to thrust him away, but need not have bothered. 'Twas akin to pushing against a weighty door that was barred from within. He did not yield by so much as one part of an inch. Nor did he relinquish his deep, hungry exploration of her mouth. Rather, he slipped his arms around her and dragged her firmly against him.

Little by little, her hands fell away, and, instead, slid up his chest to lose themselves in the crisp silk waves of his hair. Her lips ceased their protests and parted beneath his, matching the heat and hungry ardor of his own.

His green eyes gleamed, reflecting the golden flames of the open hearth, as he broke their kiss and demanded hoarsely, "Admit it, woman. Admit that you want me!"

"Aye. Aye, I want you!" she cried, panting and wide-eyed, like a frightened doe run to ground. "But I am your brother's wife, and because of that, this must cease. I beg thee, sir. Kerrin, brother—do not dishonor me!—"

Shamed by her impassioned pleas, Kerrin's hands fell away. Abruptly, he stepped back. In that moment, she sprang forward and past him, leaving the hall and the merrymakers behind her, as she fled.

He let her go, unsure who'd been the most startled by her admission—Edana or himself.

"An Irish custom, is it, boyo?" demanded a mocking voice.

Kerrin's head came around, as if jerked by a string. Lounging against a nearby wall was Thane Godfrey, a goblet in his hand. "What?" he demanded in a growl.

"Two brothers sharing a . . . whore."

Godfrey received his answer in the form of a fist. It came out of the gloom and slammed itself squarely into his supercilious nose. Bone crunched. Blood spurted. Godfrey whimpered. "God damme ye, mac Torrin! You've bwoken my node!"

"Count yourself lucky it wasn't yer damned neck," Kerrin gritted.

Wiping his lips on the back of his stinging knuckles, he reached out and helped himself to a goblet of wine. His fierce scowl drew a frightened glance from the fresh-cheeked serving lad with the tray.

As he left the hall, he fancied he could yet feel the subtle press of Edan's warm curves against him, and his loins filled with fire. A part of him wanted to go after her, to reveal his true identity, and take her to his bed, but . . . he found he could not. He was not as other men. Even were she to love him— even if she proved as faithful to him as the day is long, their marriage could never be, no matter what transpired.

Because of him.

Because of the curse that overshadowed his life.

Since coming to manhood, he had told himself that Torrin was right: No woman was be trusted. Accordingly, he had set out to prove Edana faithless, to seduce her in the guise of Kerrin, Padraic's brother, and, by so doing, prove his fears founded. Afraid to enter into marriage, so long as he remained cursed, he had planned this in order to give himself a way out. It would not be Murragh's curse that came between them, he had vowed, but his wife's infidelity.

But, somewhere on the road betwixt Kenley and Winchester, he had done the unforgivable: He had fallen in love with his bride.

All at once, the lonely rage, the soulless emptiness that had underscored his existence, came bubbling up like bile to overwhelm him. In his mind's eye, he saw the years of his life unravelling before him like an empty highway, a stony, thorny track that led to nowhere. He would never be free to love a woman, as other men loved, nor to know the love of a woman in return. He would never sire children, as did other men, for he had sworn to take his own life, sooner than see his curse reborn in them.

In that moment, he understood that therein lay the true curse. 'Twas in the loneliness, in the futile longing for what could never be, not in the shape-shifting of itself.

And with that knowledge came unbearable pain.

Throwing back his head, he gave throat to a howl of anguish. And—while those nearby muttered of hellhounds, and crossed themselves, Kerrin bounded from the hall and sought solace in the dark of night, roaming the Chiltern hills with the wild things who'd become his brothers.

Chapter Twelve

A sennight—and some twenty leagues later—found them riding through the green and lovely Vale of the Horse in the Cotswold hills. There, Edan saw for herself the wonder Niall had told her of: the great white horse of chalk that pagan worshippers of the horse-goddess, Epona, had carved from the turf of the hillsides.

The following day, they crossed into Mercia at last, and entered the Severn's lovely valley. There, elegant gray herons stalked the riverbanks in search of fish and freshwater shrimp, oblivious to the fishermen bobbing about like corks in their rawhide coracles. Fishing villages were much in evidence in those days of hard riding, too, wattle and daub huts huddled together along the river inlet like outrageous nests of huge and ungainly water fowl.

Stony-faced fishermen and their dark-eyed women came out to watch the cavalcade ride past, the hostility and suspicion marked in their faces. Their little ones, Edan noticed curiously, were nowhere in evidence.

"What is wrong with us, that they watch us so?" she softly asked Kerrin, discomforted by the watchful, wary dark eyes upon her. "Why do they stare, as if we have horns and tails?"

"Can't ye guess, my lady?" he asked, leaning forward over the saddle to stroke the dappled gray gelding, Orion's neck. "Look at your brooches, the way you plait your hair, the green cross-gaiters favored by myself and my men. Even our weapons and horse trappings!"

She frowned. "What of them?"

"These people recognize in them what they fear most: our kinship with the Norsemen! Till recent years, my forebears— yea, and your mother's own!—were wont to sail up such inlets as this, to plunder and burn the hamlets and churches at their heads. The wariness of these folk is healthy, Edana. 'Tis what keeps them alive!"

"But the children! Where are they?"

"Well-hidden, I'd wager—sent to their bolt-holes the moment we were sighted. A peek under those heaps of sea kelp will find ye a babe or two, I fancy." He grinned. "Shall we have a wee look, then?"

Somehow, his tone and the wicked sparkle in his eyes made her cheeks burn. "Naay, I believe you. But ... surely the Norsemen's raids are of the past? Saxons now live side by side with both Danes and Norwegians. 'Tis the peace that Alfred and my father labored long to bring about—and what Edward strives to maintain."

"Yea, my lady, it is. But of late, that hard-won peace has been uneasy," he explained. "Before we took ship for Britain, I had word that Norsemen had attacked several hamlets along the Seine and the Loire in Gaul." He shrugged. "And 'tis well-known that such news travels the trade routes like wildfire! Who can blame these folk for fearing they'll be next?"

She gave no reply, as they rode on, deeply troubled by his words. *What of Kenley?* she wondered. Her father's powerful fortress and fertile lands lay on an inland river mouth, too. Indeed, Kenley had already fallen victim to Viking attacks more than once! The first time a raiding party of Black Danes had come from Denmark, led by her maternal grandfather, bloody Jarl Thorfast. The second attack had been by a fierce band of Norsemen led by her mother, Freya Frozen Heart. Might Kenley be raided again?

Catching the concern in her expression, Kerrin chuckled. "Come, now. I know what you're thinking. Sure, and you've little to fear for your own family, my lady. 'Twould be a rare Viking who'd attack the lair of the Bear and his Valkyrie bride! Why, back in Ireland, us whelps were weaned on *sagas* about your mother! Our *skald,* Teague, sang ballads about her red hair, and how it sprayed about her as she fought, till she looked like a whirling pillar of fire! Nor is your lord father lacking his share of legends!—Believe me, no Norsemen is so eager to feast in Valhalla before his time—or to anger the allies of Padraic, Jarl of Wulfskeep! Trust me. Raiders will give Kenley wide berth.''

To her surprise, she found his words strangely comforting. And, for the first time since that unsettling moment in Edward's hall when he had kissed her, she was able to look him fully in the eye. "Thank you," she murmured gratefully.

"Aye." He grunted and looked away, clearly embarrassed, but before he turned, she saw the corners of his mouth lift, and knew that he was smiling.

On one side of the track they pursued in the following days lay a dyke: a long, lofty barrier of hard-packed earth that had been raised by King Offa of Mercia. Offa had built the dyke to keep the quarrelsome Welsh to the west from spilling over the boundaries of their kingdom into his own Mercian marches.

On their other flank, either lofty cliffs or reedy riverbanks fringed the Severn inlet, then curved up and around the beautiful coast of Morgannwg, where they were lapped by the gray waters of the Bristol Channel.

Choppy waves marred the channel's glassy surface, and seabirds wheeled and dipped over the murky water, uttering their shrill, sad cries. Edan shaded her eyes and watched them carve white arcs from the soft blue sky, remembering what her mother had once told her: She'd claimed the souls of sailors who were lost at sea became seabirds after their deaths. It had always saddened her to hear their keening.

Once they had reached Morgannwg, three weeks and over

fifty leagues from Winchester, Kerrin at last allowed them to slacken the pace. By his reckoning, they had now put a safe distance between themselves and any would-be pursuers from Canute's camp, for they had reached the southeastern fringes of that mysterious, mountainous land of Wales, which in the Saxon tongue meant "Land of Strangers." So were the Welsh considered, even by their closest neighbors. But for their own part, the people of Wales preferred to call themselves the Cymru, the Countrymen.

In the land of the Cymru, it was rumored, fairies dwelled, living close to the short, dark mortals who communed with them. Indeed, music and the fairy folk and the other peoples of the Otherworld were part of the fabric of their lives.

Here, also, dwelled Hywell the Good, giver of laws, who was high-king of the Cymru. And here—some three centuries before—had dwelt Dewi Ddyfrwr, Saint David the Water Drinker, who had preached the word of the White Christ while travelling the length and breadth of the land.

It was Dewi Ddyfrwr who had brought Christianity's light to ice capped Eryri's mountainous heights, where pagan shepherds grazed their woolly flocks and made sacrifices of lambs to the ancient gods of nature; old Thunor, dark and bloody Twig, and savage Woden, and kept the Beltane and the Samhain rites with bonfires of oak and couplings in the mountain meadows by the goddess's light.

Likewise, Saint David had spread the Word amongst the folk of the deep gorges, the waterfalls, and caves tucked in the valley walls. Yet there were still places where, till this very day—despite stone crosses and small churches and monasteries having sprung up everywhere—many yet worshipped the old gods of fire and earth. Others offered silver in sacrifice to the Lady of the Moon, at cairns erected by the springs to which she gave her blessing.

Kerrin called a halt early that afternoon, choosing for their camp a small, pretty clearing not far from the water. While old Myrla wandered off with a sack to gather herbs to replace her stores, some of the men cast lines in the waters of the channel. Before the light had faded, they had caught enough fish for the evening meal, and Myrla's sack was bulging. When Kerrin returned from scouting the surrounding countryside, the men's catch had been roasted on sharpened sticks over the glowing logs of the campfire, but they were grumbling that Niall had burned the night's bread.

"Ungrateful slugs! By Loki, ye'll cook your own suppers from now on—I'll be dammed if I'll see to it!" he growled, stamping off to meet Kerrin and take his horse. "Did ye see anything unusual, sir?"

"There's a little hamlet a half league west of here. A dozen cottages and a small keep. The lord's name is Tristan, but he was gone from his manor. There's an abandoned cottage through those trees. The walls are still fairly sound. If the weather turns during the night, the women can sleep there."

Niall nodded, a sly expression creeping over his broad-featured, bearded face. His blue eyes twinkled merrily. In a loud voice, he said, "What's that you say, my lord? That you've never seen so many comely wenches? Well, now, and where was this, sir? A half league t'the west, ye say? By the gods, if only I were younger!—"

Sure enough, shortly after supper, little Hurleigh, looking fidgety and unable to keep from grinning, left camp in the company of Tavish, Trevor, and Brendan. They were headed—or so a pouty Grania claimed to have overheard—to a nearby hamlet in search of the "comely wenches" Kerrin had supposedly seen.

This tidbit pleased Niall no end. He slapped his thighs and threw his shaggy head back, laughing uproariously. "That'll teach those timber worms t'complain about my bread! With any luck, 'tis a wet night they'll be after having, instead of a lusty one!"

The men's departure left Edan alone with Grania, who was very put out that her favorite, Tavish, had joined his fellows in their carousing and wenching.

Leaving Grania to sulk in the tent they shared, Edan escaped to the fire, where Kerrin already sat, staring moodily into the flames, his chin resting on his fist. Niall and Lachlann, who was still healing from his injuries, had elected to remain behind, but the two had already rolled themselves into their mantles and were both, to all intents and purposes, fast asleep, thanks to the relaxing draft that Edan had prepared for them with old Myrla's help.

Tossing a velvet cushion to the grass, she took her seat on the opposite side of the fire to Kerrin. Finding a long, slender twig, she occupied herself in jabbing it at the burning logs. Little showers of bright-orange sparks whirled up and were scattered on the nightwind.

"Lady?"

"Sir?"

"You are restless tonight. Have a care with that brand, lest ye burn us all to cinders."

"Your pardon, sir." She sighed. "But you're right. I am restless."

"How so?"

She shrugged. "We have been riding for so long—to the end of the world, it seems! I grow impatient to meet my lord."

He nodded, casting her an enigmatic look. "Edana, I—"

"How now, my fine sir? And a good evening to you, my pretty lady! Might a poor old woman share your fire?" Myrla wheedled, cutting off whatever Kerrin was about to say. "These old bones, they do feel the chill, my chicks—even in these months of spring!"

Edan smiled. "Of course. Ye may warm yourself here, and welcome, Grandmother." Drawing her mantle aside, she shifted her pillow to make room for the old woman, who seemed all angles beneath hooded gray mantle. She cast a dubious eye on the long-eared donkey, which trotted at the old crone's heels, however.

As if aware of her misgivings, the beast suddenly turned and peered down his nose at her. His liquid brown eyes were large and gentle in the firelight—yet somehow disapproving. Irish donkeys, it seemed, had little respect for their Saxon mistresses!

"And who might you be?" Edan asked, reaching up to scratch the donkey's flat, furry forehead.

"This rogue—Ahearn, he calls hisself, meaning Lord o' the Horses—he bids ye good health and good even', my pretty mistress!'' Myrla explained, grinning toothily. ''Go on, then, ye long-eared divil! Make your wee bow!''

She slapped her scrawny thighs at the delighted expression on Edan's face, as the donkey nodded his large head, then bent a foreleg in fair imitation of a bow.

Enchanted, Edan petted the animal's soft nose, then ran her hand down his short, bristly mane. ''Good master donkey— er—Master Ahearn?—I bid ye welcome to our fire. You are in truth a courteous fellow.''

As if returning her greeting, the donkey dropped his head to where the folds of her favorite woollen mantle pooled upon the lush turf. He nuzzled the fabric and Edan laughed again, charmed by what seemed an affectionate kiss on the donkey's part.

Myrla, however, knew the beast too well to trust it!

''Whist, ye great brute! Hisst! Get away from our lady's mantle, Ahearn, ye great spalpeen! Ye long-eared whelp of Satan, hissst! Be gone!'' the crone hissed, flapping her skirts at the animal. ''My lady! He's after chomping on yer skirts, the wicked divil!'' she panted, yanking on the creature's long, velvety ears, then springing up to tug at its tail in turn.

Indignant, the donkey jerked up his head, flattened its ears and brayed in protest. ''Hee-*haww!* Hee-*haww!*''

''Do not quarrel with me, ye were, too, eating it, ye bloody banshee!—Now, be gone, I say!'' screeched Myrla, for all the world, as if she were answering the animal.

Ears laid back, the donkey trotted away, still braying piteously and kicking up his rear heels in indignation every few feet.

''Oh, Grandmother, look at him! Surely you were too harsh with the poor little beast?'' Edan chided the old crone. Finding the corner of her mantle damp where the donkey had nuzzled it, she held it out to the fire to dry—and saw the huge, ragged hole Ahearn's teeth had left in the cloth. ''Oh! 'Tis no donkey, surely, but a long-eared *goat!*'' she screeched.

''Hee-*haw!*'' Ahearn brayed yet again from the shadows, as if outraged by the comparison. Kicking up his hooves in disgust, the donkey trotted off. He halted when he reached the trees at the edge of the forest, where the horses had been picketed, but still complained loudly from time to time.

"Paagh! That long-eared demon! Sure, and he's the Devil's own ass, he is! Enough, Ahearn! Away . . . there! He's gone now. We've seen his last till morning." She slapped her bony shanks. "Weell, now, what shall it be, my lambs? Would ye have me cast the runes for ye, little mistress?" she suggested, eyeing Edan slyly.

Without waiting for a response, she suddenly raised her hands aloft, closed her eyes, and prayed:

"Oh, Mighty Odin!—Giver of Omens and Portents! Master of Runes and of Ravens! Lord Magician Most High of Asgard! Reveal this woman's destiny, I pray thee!" So saying, she emptied the contents of a drawstring pouch onto the grass.

The runes were wafer-thin rectangles of yellowed walrus ivory, etched with the magical symbols of the *futhark*, the runic "alphabet." They clattered to the grass with a dry rattle, like dice of bone. At once, Myrla began poring over them, rubbing the runes between her fingers, while she sucked on her toothless gums and gently rocked back and forth.

Her eyes were wet and shadowed with foreboding when she looked up again. "Ah, my poor little mistress. If only I could promise ye good fortune!—Alas, I cannot." Shaking her head, she sighed. "The runes whisper that the winds of misfortune will use thee cruelly, 'ere ye find happiness! Heed me, daughter! The time is coming wherein ye'll be forced t'take a life, if ye would give a life. When that time comes, ye must not hesitate! Ye must—"

"Enough, Grandmother!" Kerrin growled. Springing to his feet, he cast the old hag a quelling glance. "Enough of your omens and portents!"

A sudden damp, chilly breeze off the sea had blown inland. It stirred along the riverbanks, shivered through the reeds, soughing amongst the leafy boughs of the trees, like a lost and troubled soul. The flames danced in its current. An owl screeched in the distance. And Edan shivered.

"Look! Your prophecies of doom have frightened your mistress! Be gone to your bed, Grandmother. Sleep the while and dream of happier portents.''

"At least let me end the telling, master," Myrla coaxed, darting Kerrin a beseeching glance.

"Nay. Be gone."

With a mutinous shrug of her shoulders, Myrla pulled the cowl of her mantle over her stringy gray hair and hobbled off after her donkey.

"Has she the Sight?" Edan asked anxiously, when Myrla was gone. She looked pale, even in the fire's ruddy glow, and her eyes were huge and luminous, like a cat's.

He hesitated, then decided to lie. What sense was there in frightening her? "If she has the Gift, my lady, I have yet to see it."

Reassured, she nodded. "Milord—"

"Yea?"

"If you recall, sir, while in Winchester, I asked you to tell me about the man who attacked us. Canute?" Edan reminded him. "You bade me wait for my answer till we had put distance between Canute and ourselves. That time is now, surely?"

"I suppose it is, aye."

Then tell me, sir, what is this Canute to Padraic, exactly? And why would he ambush us?" she asked with every appearance of interest.

Alas, such outward appearances were deceptive. While her escort struggled to formulate an answer that would satisfy her, Edan had forgotten what she'd asked him! Rather, she found herself watching her escort from beneath the sooty fringing of her lashes for quite another reason. She could not draw her eyes from him!—Moreover, his honeyed brogue, rising and falling on the firelit shadows as he spoke, was as seductive as kisses.

What could be wrong with her? Despite the danger in the situation Kerrin was describing—the bloodthirsty ambitions of his jealous uncle, who would stop at nothing to wrest both keep and title from his brother, Padraic—she could not concentrate on his warnings. Alas, no!

Her thoughts were all for her wretched, brooding, moody

yet undeniably *fascinating* brother-in-law!—Not for her dutiful bridegroom, attending his father's deathbed in Ireland. Ah, dear me, no! For the infuriating, impossible rogue who was her escort!

If anything, he appeared doubly fascinating this even, with the firelight staining his sunbrowned face, the ruddy hue of polished woods, its flare throwing his black mane and flowing garments into inky pools of shadow. She sighed.

Wizard!—Warlock!—Man of Darkness and of Mystery— what is it about you that draws me, like metal drawn to the magic drawing-stone? What . . . what demon tempts me to forgo the solemn vows I swore thy brother? To abandon honor, heart, and soul, for the forbidden taste of your lips, the sinful promise of your kiss?

Yet, tempted she was.

Aye. Sorely tempted.

Tonight, the only parts of Kerrin that seemed alive, as he sat across from her, were the forest-green eyes he fixed upon her with such burning intensity, the flames mirrored in their depths. In truth, 'twas as if he meant to plumb her soul with those eyes! To drag her secret longings forth into merciless light!

Secrets.

Secret feelings.

Secret . . . sensual . . . sinful yearnings!—

She shivered, but it was a frisson of excitement, not fear, that shimmied down her spine. Desire, not shame or guilt, that spread its heat through her belly.

It made no difference that the brute was Padraic's brother, nor that adultery was a sin. In truth, in that moment, it would not have mattered to her if he'd horns and tail, or if he walked on cloven hooves and reeked of brimstone and sulfur! There was that powerful *something* about him which drew her like a lodestone.

Was it . . . could it be . . . *love?* Had she fallen in love with her escort, was that her answer? Her mouth was suddenly dry, her palms felt moist, for the thought had the ring of truth to it.

"Canute is my uncle. Younger brother to my—my father, Torrin Erickson," he answered her question softly.

His voice seemed to come from very far away. She heard it as if in the depths of a fevered dream. "What, sir? Forgive me, pray! The crackle of the fire . . . the sigh of the wind . . . alas, I did not hear you. Canute *who,* pray?"

He scowled. "Did ye forget your own question?"

"Of course, my question! Then Canute is your . . . cousin, you said?" she guessed.

The scowl deepened. "He is my *uncle.*"

"Uncle. Quite. I thought as much. Pray—er—pray go on, sir." Ye Gods. *Love!* She badly needed a little time alone, in which to think about this revelation and what she would do about it.

Kerrin shot her a scornful glance before carrying on, telling himself he would not to be swayed by the way the fire struck bluish lights in her tumbling black tresses, or lent a lustrous sheen to her gray-lavender eyes. "Years ago, the two of them— Torrin and Canute, that is—quarrelled bitterly over the keep and lands Torrin had taken in his raid upon the hamlet of Waterford . . ."

Chin on fist, she leaned forward and tried very hard to concentrate. But she could no more draw her thoughts from his wretched, handsome face than she could cut off her own hand!

Instead of concentrating on what he was saying, she concentrated on his sensual mouth. On how firm his lips appeared, and how they glistened along their inner margins when he spoke. And what a pleasing smile parted his beard shadow when he grinned—beard shadow that made him look . . . dangerous, wild, a wicked outlaw of the forests. . . .

She swayed slightly where she sat, her nerve endings jumping and alive, desire pouring through her veins like the sap rising through the trees in the fullness of spring. Jesu, what was happening to her? Was it the quantity of potent mead she had gulped down to rid her mouth of the taste of burned bread? Or . . . had the spring madness that had afflicted Grania come upon her, too?

"Canute has coveted Wulfskeep and the county of Wat for

many years, you understand," Kerrin continued, breaking into her thoughts, "although both have belonged to Torrin since he slew my grandfather, Murragh of Waterford."

"Waterford, you say, sir?"

He nodded, exasperated. Was the wench so simple that she must echo his every word, like a vast cavern that threw them back at him? "Aye, aye, Waterford," he snapped. "Yet, from the day he set foot within the keep, Torrin knew only misfortune in his life. Some say . . ."

"Aye?" she asked breathlessly, her lips moist and parted.

He swore under his breath, torn between wanting to kiss and kill the woman. ". . . Some say the old earl placed a curse upon Torrin with his dying breath, in revenge for the slaying of his sons, Brian and Donovan mac Murragh, and for his own murder."

"And did he?"

Kerrin shrugged evasively. "Who knows? Whatever happened, he was no longer the same Torrin Ericksen of Trondheim henceforth. He began drinking heavily. He slept poorly, too. And—when he was able to sleep at all—he dreamed strange, bloody dreams. Before long, he began roaming the woods after moonrise," he added, watching her face intently, "and muttering gibberish to himself. Always fastidious about his locks and beard, he let them grow matted, neither combing them nor plucking the leaves and twigs from them. Some superstitious folk claimed that Torrin was no longer a mortal at all. They whispered that, when the moon waxed full, he had the power to shift his shape, and become . . ." here he paused before murmuring, "a man-wolf."

"An ogre, in truth!" Edan exclaimed, with a shudder, resisting the urge to cross herself. The spell he had woven was a potent one. The vivid memory of the wolf she'd seen by the river shortly after leaving Kenley returned. A question began to form in her thoughts, yet was abandoned when Kerrin continued.

"An ogre, aye. Or . . . something like," he agreed darkly, and smiled a thin-lipped smile. "Little children ran screaming from him if they met him in the woods, fearful that Torrin would gobble them up. 'Be good, bratlings!' their spiteful mothers threatened, 'else the Beast will get ye!' "

"In the end, it happened, just as earl Murragh had promised. Torrin had his keep. He had his lands, and he had earl Murragh's daughter, the faithless Deirdre, in his bed. But, instead of enjoying his prizes, he lived to rue the day he'd sailed his *drakkar* up the Suir to conquer Waterford!"

"And over the years, Canute has continued to challenge Torrin's claims?"

He nodded. "Aye." Aware that her gaze had come to rest unblinkingly upon him, Kerrin raised his horn of mead to the raven-haired beauty in salute. "A salute, my lady! Let us drink to loyal wives, such as yerself!" he proposed softly. "Long life, good health, and kind fortune to ye, lady—Myrla's prophecies not withstanding!"

"To loyal wives!—Amen!" she rejoined. Her voice sounded overly loud, overly hearty.

His emerald eyes were piercing, as they bored into her own, like tanner's hot awls boring into leather. A lazy half-smile curved his beautiful, manly mouth. One she felt as a sudden, hot quiver that struck like a dart, deep in her belly. 'Twas as if something dormant had been awakened and was stirring there.

Wakened by him. Stirred by him, came the treacherous thought. Oh, 'twas dangerous, wicked, to be harboring such feelings for her husband's brother! Yet ... how was she to exorcise them?—

With prayer! her pious conscience bade her. *Counter them with prayer! Better yet,* sound commonsense argued, *put distance between you! Do not find yourself alone with this man, nor let your eyes linger on him with this secret delight—!*

Paagh! A plague on Kerrin, with his toast to loyal wives! 'Twas as if he'd plucked her guilty thoughts from her mind! A horrible thought suddenly occurred to her. Mayhap, like her Uncle Robin, he really *did* know what she was thinking, truly was able to read her mind? For, although he drained the drinking horn in a single, long quaff, he never once lifted those damned, all-seeing green eyes from her. And what God-fearing man stared at his brother's wife with such unholy intensity—unless he knew what she was thinking?

Summoning her willpower, she forced her attention away from the bob of the Adam's apple in Kerrin's brown throat to ask, in a husky whisper, "But, if what you say is true, sir, then why does Canute not attack Wulfskeep? For what purpose is he here, in Britain? What does he hope to gain by attacking *us?*"

"An astute question, lady," Kerrin commended her with a curt nod, scrambling for an answer that would not entail revealing his true identity! "Surely you are as . . . er . . . as clever as you are—er—skilled with a sword, sister-wife," he added. He had intended to say, "as you are fair", but had thought better of it.

His rueful smile melted her very bones and turned her innards to seething broth. *God's Blood! 'Tis not working!* she thought in a panic. Although she'd steeled herself against his warlock's charms, she'd felt that wry smile to the very center of her being!

"Enough of your flattery, sirrah!" she snapped. "Pray answer me, instead. What is it Canute *really* wants with us? My—my dowry?"

"Your *dowry!*—" He slapped his palm against his brow. "Ah, yea, 'tis your *dowry* he's after! Just so, my lady!" he declared, relieved that she had supplied him with a plausibleexplanation herself, for his own wits deserted him whenever he gazed at her. Sometimes, he'd find himself lost in the lavender-gray mist of her bewitching eyes, transfixed by the berry-ripe sheen of her mouth, both of which tightened his groin with lust. "T' be sure," he said too loudly, "the bloody bastard's after yer father's gold—and you with them, I fear."

"Me! But, what have I to do with it, pray? Abducting me makes no sense at all!" she cried.

"Be that as it may, I'd wager he's planning to try again. Even now, he could be hot on our heels." That much was no lie.

"Then I ask again: what does he here, in Britain, sir?" She straightened imperiously, every inch Marissa of Kenley's daughter. Her brows rose, inky crescent moons that found their setting in an unlined, ivory brow. Her magnificent eyes, narrowed now in anger, were the sparkling stars in pale sky. "Why would he not bide his time 'til I am less heavily guarded? And why, sir, would your uncle want *me* in the first place?"

"Can you not guess, Edana of Wulfskeep?" He shot her a grin, secretly enchanted by the combination of warrior-maid and naive female she presented in her men's breeks and mantle tonight, glowering at him from beyond the lapping curtain of the campfire's flames.

"If I could guess, I would not ask, sir!" she cried, and looked close to stamping an imperious foot.

"Then I would suggest you consult your looking glass, damosel, for by certes, you will find an answer there," he explained very softly.

"Will I, my lord?" she asked casually, as if his answer mattered little—then held her breath till her lungs felt near to bursting, while she waited for his answer.

"Aye," he allowed, equally casual. "Surely it comes as no surprise that a man would want you?"

She stared at him, then flicked her head and gave an impatient snort. "Come, come, milord Kerrin! I am not so beautiful that men would sail across poisonous seas fraught with all manner of serpents and dragons simply to have me!"

"Of course not, my lady," he amended, his scornful tone withering her pride. "I was not referring to your beauty, but to your . . . rank," he lied. "You are, after all, the eldest daughter of the high-king of Britain's ealdorman. Mayhap Canute has ambitions to wed you himself and thus cement his claim to Wulfskeep and an alliance to Britain in one fell swoop? Or he may be planning to use you as a pawn in some other alliance. Your family's friendship with the king, along with your dowry, would make you a tempting prize."

"Possibly, aye. But my question yet remains. Why does this wretched Canute pursue *us,* when 'tis Padraic—not I !—who bars his way to Wulfskeep? Canute was far closer to his goals at Jarl Torrin's deathbed than he would ever be here, was he not? Unless, of course, Padraic is not in Ireland at all . . . ?"

She halted in mid-sentence and stared at him, seeing guilt flood his face, even as her thoughts scrambled to make sense of what she suddenly knew, with absolute, crystalline clarity, was true.

The handsome stranger in the byre at Kenley—her impossible escort—the husband she had never met—they were not two different men. They were one and the same!

Padraic was not in Ireland. Padraic was not at his father's deathbed. Ye gods, no. Padraic was right there, sitting across the fire from her!—

Padraic was Kerrin. Kerrin was Padraic. Proxy be damned!

He had lied to her from the very first. He had played her, her family, the Bishop, even the King—all of them!—for fools!

"Why?" she demanded, springing to her feet. "Why did you lie to me? Why have you done this thing? For what dark purpose have you played such a cruel jest upon me?"

He came around the fire and reached out to take her elbow and turn her to face him.

"Do not touch me!"

"Look at me then, woman. Let me explain. 'Tis not what ye're thinking."

She whirled on him, gray eyes blazing. "How do ye know what I'm thinking!"

"You're right. I don't," he acknowledged. "But, I *do* know what it's like to feel betrayed. To feel that ye can trust no one. Edan, mavourneen, let me explain!"

"There's nothing ye could say that I'd want to hear," she whispered brokenly. And, springing to her feet, she fled from him.

Chapter Thirteen

"Edana. Look at me."

His voice, though low, brooked no refusal.

Fingers curled into fists at her sides, she slowly turned to face him, seeing him through a veil of tears. "You are my husband, are you not, sir? Padraic mac Torrin?"

"Aye," he admitted heavily. "Kerrin was the name Myrla gave me as a weanling. 'Twas she who raised me after my—after my mother went away."

"How you must have laughed at me all these days!" she whispered, her voice breaking.

"Never," he denied, crossing the grass to stand before her. "I would never laugh at ye, Edan," he added more softly, his hands closing over her upper arms. "God forgive me, I've been too busy *wanting* ye!" He pulled her against him, crushing his mouth down over hers. He felt her stiffen—felt her try to pull free—felt her small fists come up and pummel at his chest, once, twice, thrice. Then, miraculously, the fight went out of her. Instead of fighting him, she melted into his arms.

Her weight braced against him, she curled her arms around his neck and kissed him back, responding with a hunger and innocent, eager *sweetness,* he had only dreamed of.

Gathering her into his arms, he carried her from the water's edge to the abandoned cottage he had found earlier, while scouting. Ducking his head under the low lintel, he carried her inside, leaving the broken door ajar.

Garlanded with cobwebs, littered with lobster pots and torn nets in the meager light, it lacked the comforts of both a fire and a feather pallet. The hovel was not the flower-strewn bower he would have chosen for his princess-bride. Still, it must serve. He had a gut feeling that, should he hesitate in this, he might lose her forever, in spirit, if not in fact.

As he unpinned the brooch at his shoulder, he prayed that he—who had known precious little of either tenderness or gentleness in his lifetime—could be both tender and gentle with his virgin bride tonight.

Gently setting her down, he spread his plaid across the hard-packed earthen floor. Before he could bid her do likewise, she had unpinned her own mantle and shyly added its softness to his.

"My bride," he murmured, a catch in his husky voice.

"My husband," she whispered, and her lower lip quivered.

Framing her pale face between his hands, he took her lips in a lingering kiss, tasting her tears on his tongue, as they parted beneath his own.

As they kissed, he unfastened the knotted cord at her waist and let it fall, sliding his hands up, beneath the folds of her tunic, to cup both small, hard breasts.

No one had ever touched her so intimately—nor so gently. She gasped against his lips, her sighs becoming moans of pleasure, as he stroked her breasts, showered kisses over her throat, her ears, her closed eyelids, everywhere. Her small nipples had hardened at the first feathery brush of his fingers. Now they stood up, tightly furled buds that crowned each firm mound, exquisitely sensitive to his slightest touch.

Thrusting up the folds of her tunic, he ducked his head. Taking each aching, tiny nubbin in his mouth in turn, he suckled upon them, first gently, then with increasing ardor.

She swayed where she stood, her knees close to buckling, her fingers clenching in his crisp dark waves. *Oh, such exquisite*

sensation! Surely she would swoon ere long? Silvery darts of
pleasure sizzled like wildfire from her breasts to her belly,
becoming molten fire when they reached the silken folds
between her thighs. So fierce was her pleasure, she could scarce
stand by the time Kerrin dropped to his knees before her.
Looking up at her, he unfastened the laces of her men's breeks
and slid them down, over her hips, stroking her long, sleek
thighs, her calves, her dainty ankles, as he drew the breeks
from her.

When she was free of her breeks, he grasped the hem of her
tunic and pulled it up, over her head. She was quite bare now,
except for the midnight glory of her hair, which spilled in dark
torrents about her ivory body, and the shining silver talisman
on its long chain, swinging gently to and fro in the gloom.

"In truth, you are fair, mavourneen," he whispered. His
voice sounded husky, hoarse, like rough silk on the musty hush.
Rough with lust—nay, with *desire*. "Sure, and ye make this
humble hut a palace!"

"I am skilled with a sword, too," she came back defiantly,
reminding him of his own mocking comment earlier. She
proudly tossed her head and gave him a challenging look.
Though the light was poor, her eyes still flashed.

A husky rumble of laughter escaped him. "Aye, mavourneen,
that you are! Now, come here to your lord." He caught her to
him and kissed her again, at first gently, a little teasingly, then
with increasing heat and ardor, as his passion became all but
ungovernable.

She returned the pressure of his lips, met the sensual probing
of his tongue with her own small tongue, till the cottage was
filled with their heavy breathing, the gasps and soft moans of
desire. They were pressed so tightly to each other now, 'twas
hard to tell where one left off and the other began.

As he kissed her, he caressed the creamy curves of her body,
encouraging her to explore him in return. He gritted his teeth,
as her trembling fingers followed the muscular curves of his
shoulders, then traced the dark mat of his chest hair. After a
moment's hesitation, her hand moved lower, fingertips skim-

ming the flat, oaken ridges of his belly. They circled the well of his navel, then halted at the ridge of his belt.

Without taking his mouth from hers, he unfastened both belt and breeks and let them fall. Stepping from them, he swept her off her feet and bore her to the ground, still cradled in his arms.

Edan was trembling, as he lifted himself onto her. The moment of truth was at hand. In but moments, he would take her maidenhead, claim her as his bride—and, brave though she might be, she knew a moment's fear.

She stiffened as she felt the pressure of his knee where her thighs pressed tightly together. She closed her eyes, and her head swam, as panic engulfed her. Surely he would crush her— oh, she could not breathe! He had to let her up!

But instead, he braced himself upon his palms, leaned forward and kissed her again, his tongue warring with her own. Deep within her, a slow, hot, honeyed pulse began to beat, as he whispered, "Yield, proud one. Yield, and 'twill be but a moment's pain, I swear it. Then, naught but pleasure awaits ye. . . ."

She obeyed him, though her limbs trembled uncontrollably. But instead of lunging forward and cruelly rending her maidenhead, as she had feared, he instead covered the curly pelt of her mons with his hand.

She clung to him. A low moan escaped her, as his finger slipped lower, gently probing, moving rhythmically inside her at first slowly, then faster, deeper.

He felt her nipples harden, felt her body grow flushed with desire, then wet with his touch—and his joy knew no bounds. No cold wench this, thank the gods, to shrink from his intimate touch! Though yet a maid, his bride was a giving, sensual woman, a woman who would warm her man's furs, give him strong babes, and share the pleasures to be found in their marriage bed for as long as they both lived.

Aroused, she instinctively arched her hips upwards, uttering his name over and over, like a prayer. Pushed to the limit, he drew back, and she felt his finger replaced by something harder, something far larger, that threatened to rend her in two—yet torched an explosion inside her! In the same instant she would have cried out in wonder and protest, he raised her hips and thrust forward.

A hot, searing pain, and 'twas done with. She almost laughed. Was this what she had feared? She had braced herself for a painful onslaught that never came!

Instead, wondrously, he began to move inside her, to withdraw then deepen his possession of her body, again and again. The slow, hot pulsing in her belly built as he rode her, till she could bear it no more. In an instant, it exploded, hurling fragments of colored light against her closed eyelids.

With an impassioned cry, she arched up to meet his thrusts, growing rigid as a bow bent in the hands of a master archer, as waves of delight broke over her. *"Kerrin!——Ah, Kerriiin!"*

A blinding flash of white light suddenly filled the gloom, followed straightway by a deafening peal of thunder. Startled, she looked up and saw Kerrin's stern, handsome face looming over her, framed by long, midnight locks. His jaw was hard, his green eyes dark and unfathomable, as he sought his own release. And, for a fleeting instant, she had the eerie sensation that their mating had not been of this world at all. . . .

"Don't be afraid. 'Tis but the storm, my sweet," he soothed, stroking her hair back from her face.

His tone—the same tone he used with his animals—comforted her, as did his gentle touch. She clung to him till, with a roar that rivalled the crash of the thunder, he found his own release, spilling the hot flood of his seed deep into her womb.

Afterwards, as they lay side by side, the rain began falling, pattering lightly at first, like elfin feet, then teeming down in a roaring deluge that promised to flood the small hut and carry it off like Noah's Ark. There would be no sleep for them tonight, not in this fierce storm, Edan thought—and she was secretly glad! There were many glorious hours yet remaining till dawn, and many glorious things she had yet to learn about being a woman with which to fill them. . . .

"Shall we watch the storm, Edan?" Kerrin suggested later, when their breathing had returned to normal for a third time.

Running a fingertip down her cheek, he thought how very lovely she looked, lit by the lightning, as she shyly smiled and nodded.

As he drew his mantle about their shoulders, he wondered, stunned, what he had done to deserve such a prize as Edan as his bride, and—now that he had won her, if the fates would conspire to wrest her from him?

It was only then that he remembered Murragh's curse, forgotten in the heat of his lust, and the blood turned icy in his veins. Love and loving had their own terrible price, he realized. The fear of losing one's beloved. . . .

In silence, each wrestling with their own thoughts, they sat in the doorway of the hut, watching the dripping woods and the distant channel through silvery curtains of rain.

The night was bright as day each time the lightning arrowed glittering white paths across the bruised belly of the sky. Seconds later, thunder clattered from Mjollnir, the mighty hammer of Thor, as the thunder god raced his goat-drawn chariot across the heavens.

The bright light also flashed off Edan's silver talisman, prompting her to ask shyly, "My lord? Are you awake?"

"My name is Kerrin, sweet. Or Padraic, if ye prefer."

"All right. Kerrin, then. Do ye know on what day you were born, my lord—er—Kerrin?"

He frowned. "The day, nay, but the month, aye. 'Twas February. The end of the month, or so, Myrla said."

Edan looked down at the silver talisman as the lightning lit the heavens once again. On its face were two fishes, swimming in opposite directions, a cabochon amethyst gripped in each of their mouths. She smiled to herself. The night sky in the latter weeks of February was ruled by the constellation of Pisces, the Fishes, the twelfth sign of the zodiac.

Even from the grave, her mother's uncle, Sven, had reached out to guide her, had somehow *known*. . . .

Chapter Fourteen

It was close to the Welsh coastal hamlet of Kidwelly, several days later, that Kerrin signalled their next halt of any duration.

After lengthy discussion in private with Niall and Tavish, who had ridden ahead of the rest of them to scout the countryside, he ordered Niall to make camp, then signalled Edan and Grania to follow him on horseback.

"Edana, you and Grania shall seek lodging in the guest cells of yonder monastery for a night or two," he informed her, reining in his horse and nodding across the river inlet to where the stone walls of an abbey rose from amidst spreading trees of no little size and antiquity.

"But why?" she exclaimed. Rose colored her cheeks, as she confessed in a lower tone, "Sir, I would rather stay with you."

"And I with you, love," he echoed, reaching out to caress her cheek. "But humor me in this, pray?" He cleared his throat and added, "I could not give ye a wedding night in a scented bower! At least ye'll sleep on down pallets at Kidwelly Abbey! 'Twill be your last chance for a bit o'comfort, till we reach Wulfskeep." He was careful not to look her full in the face, knowing her sharp eyes would read something amiss in his expression, even if she detected nothing in his voice.

"How so, sir?"

"In two days, we shall reach the port of St. Daffyd's, where my *drakkar*, Storm Chaser, has been undergoing repairs. She waits to carry us home."

Home. A thrill ran down her spine. *His* home. And soon, God willing, 'twould be *their* home. "So soon! I'd thought it would take much longer. Kerrin—" Hesitating, she bit her lower lip, wondering how best to broach the subject she wished to discuss. Deciding on a straightforward approach, she plunged in head first with, "My lord, before we reach Wulfskeep, would you tell me why you . . . why you kept your identity from me? What was the purpose of your masquerade?"

He gave no answer, as they clattered over the wooden bridge that spanned the river. On the far side, he reined in his horse. Edan did likewise, waiting for him to answer her question.

The abbey buildings were encircled completely by protective stone walls. But through the open gates, she could see the abbey itself, and at each end, a tall stone tower that afforded a view, some half a league down the inlet, to the Bristol channel beyond. Other buildings—the refectory, the dormitory, the scriptorium, the library, the kitchens and so on—clustered nearby, joined by cloisters lined with pillars that surrounded grassy quadrangles.

Vegetable and herb gardens were set apart from the main building behind a thick holly hedge, as was a terraced area where grape vines rambled over rows of wooden trellises. Small flocks of geese, ducks, and chickens foraged between the rows, while on the sloping water meadow leading down to the inlet, grazed goats, sheep, and a pair of enormous plough horses, tended by herders in the gray robes of the abbey's order.

There was a scattering of wattle and daub buildings off to another side—probably where the monks did the work of coopers making barrels, or of blacksmiths shoeing horses and forging tools, or else pressing grapes or brewing the abbey's beer.

Beyond the abbey gates, on what was also abbey lands, roamed a herd of swine that had been set loose by the monks to fatten on beechmast from the woods. Some of them were wallowing in the mud of the little inlet.

Nearer still, young novitiate monks were wading thigh-deep

in the river, their robes hitched up to expose white buttocks. The lads were scooping up water in broad withy baskets, hoping to net the unwary fish that swam in the inlet's green depths.

"Cover your ugly face, Brother Matthew—you're scaring off my fish!"

"By certes, Brother Alfred, 'tis not my face that's scaring them, but your boil-ridden arse!"

Judging by their banter and noisy laughter, fishing was a popular task!

Their roughhousing startled a flotilla of lovely, white-feathered swans, who were dabbling about in the weedy shade of the wooden bridge. The swans cast the noisy young monks looks of beady-eyed disapproval, before paddling elegantly away. Several muddy brown cygnets bobbed after them.

Edan shaded her eyes and watched the swans sail away like miniature dragonships, before reminding her escort of her question with a gentle, "Kerrin? Husband?"

Despite what she surely thought, he had heard her, but was at a loss how best to answer. Should he tell her the truth: that he had disguised himself, because he intended to test her faithfulness, without first giving her the chance to prove herself? He scowled. Weeks ago, Tavish had warned him what to expect, if he were to admit he'd ever doubted his bride. Edana, his friend had taken pains to remind him, was quite unlike the lusty serving wenches and farmers' daughters they'd shared in the past. His bride was a Saxon princess, a woman of honor, lofty morals, strong principles—and she was very proud, besides. He winced. The thought of those cool gray eyes fixed unwaveringly upon his face, as he mumbled an explanation, was not a pleasant prospect at all. Nor was the furious outburst that would no doubt follow it! And, in the past few days, he'd begun to enjoy the sweet smiles and secret glances that were for him alone—affectionate gestures that had been all too rare in his rough-and-ready upbringing.

And so, he swallowed the hurried excuses he'd been about to offer, deciding he needed more time to make them . . . palatable. Perhaps as much as a lifetime! Egad, he would sooner face his uncle Canute's berserkers, with the bloodlust upon them, than his fiery bride, when she learned the truth! Far better, he decided at length, to feed her the truth in small, vague bites, a little at a time. It would not hurt his cause to soften her little heart first, either. . . .

"Before I explain," he began, "you should know that I have been alone all my life. For many years, I was denied my birthright and, with it, my rightful place as heir to Wulfskeep. Accordingly, over the years I have learned to depend upon myself. To be my own master, and need naught from anyone," he declared, with bitter pride. "Do you take my meaning, lady?"

He cast her a quick glance to see if she'd understood.

He had pulled himself up from nothing by the scruff of his neck. He'd learned the warrior's arts the hard way—by defending himself against those who would have separated his head from his shoulders, just for the way he'd looked at them. He'd wrung himself an education and a knowledge of the world from travel and from Wulfskeep's house slaves—mostly learned monks brought in chains from Gaul and Britain—who'd been glad of his strong back or helping hand with their heavier duties, in return for their tutoring skills. But, to his chagrin, he saw that Edan had understood nothing.

Rather, her face had crumpled. Tears trembled on the tips of her lashes, clung there for what seemed an eternity, then fell, splashing across the back of her hand. "I believe I know what you are trying to tell me, aye," she said huskily. "That a bride was both unneeded and unwanted in your life. That you have little use for me or any other woman, except in your furs."

He could not bear the desolation in her voice. "*Had,* Edana. Not *have,* but *had.* Jesu! I have not a bard's clever way with words! How can I explain it? What I'm trying to say—aye, and poorly so!—is that I knew nothing of affection or—of needing another in my life—till I met thee." The admission was pried from him. In its silent wake, he instinctively flinched, expecting a blow, a torrent of curses, perhaps a peal of vicious laughter in response to his soul baring. *By Odin!* Never in all his years had he felt so naked, so vulnerable and exposed, as

he did here and now! 'Twas akin to baring his neck and bidding
Canute take a swing at it with his blood-axe, he thought ruefully.

"Truly?" she asked, an uncertain smile tugging at her lips.

"On my honor as both warrior, man—and husband."

Astonished, he saw a glow begin in her eyes; a rosy flush
of pleasure that filled her cheeks and spread to her lips. An
answering warmth flowed through his own body. She had not
laughed at him! And she was his equal in courage, in passion,
and fire. All his life, he had disliked and mistrusted women,
but Edan was different. A woman who would draw metal and
fight at his side in one breath, race her horse neck and neck
with his in another, then match his passion, measure for measure, between the furs.

Yet . . . for all her Valkyrie courage, she made him want to
protect her. To keep her safe from harm and to do hurt to those
who would hurt her. She made him want to share all that he
was and all that he could ever be with her. And then, when
their youth was spent, and the fires no longer burned within
them quite so brightly, he wanted to grow old with her. To
look up at her across the hearthstones and see her smile at him,
just as she was smiling now. . . .

He wetted dry lips on his tongue. Was that love? If so, 'twas
an unexpected and totally new sensation—one that made his
heart feel huge and alien in his chest. The sudden urge to lean
down from his horse, lift her astride his own, and tell her
everything was nigh overwhelming.

He opened his mouth to do just that, then thought better of
it. She was many things—all of them wonderful—but . . . was
she also the woman he could trust with his innermost secrets,
no matter how dark or terrible they might prove? He scowled.
His fists tightened on the reins. *Not yet. He would not confide
that much of himself yet. 'Twas too much too soon.*

She would not speak so naively of loving him if she knew
of the terrible curse he carried. A curse that went far beyond
bastardy and a loveless childhood. He dare not risk telling her
that. . . .

"Sure, and will ye look over there, now? The Abbot himself
is coming to greet ye, my lady," he said, harshly, in an effort

to change the subject. "Go on now. Seek his Grace's hospitality for yourself and Grania. We'll speak more of this anon."

"But, what of you, my lord? Have you no fondness for goose-down pallets, after the hard floor of our hut?" she teased gently. "Nor need of absolution for your . . . sins?" Her eyes twinkled naughtily, yet he did not share her bawdy jest.

Rather, a shadow crossed his face. He looked beyond her, staring at the abbey walls that rose above the treetops with an expression of apprehension. Then he blinked, shuddered, and looked away. "Nay, I think not. My men and I shall fare well enough in our sleeping bags for another night or so, anon, my lady wife."

Edan turned in the saddle to watch him go, beset by the sudden, overwhelming urge to ride after him, to beg him not to leave her. Goosebumps rose in prickly, chilly waves down her arms, as if the sun had sailed behind a dark cloud and taken its warmth away. *An omen?* she wondered. On impulse, she clicked her teeth, urging Fayre after Kerrin's horse.

She would have raced past him and on, back to camp, but he caught her mare's bridle and held fast to it.

"Not so fast, firebrand! You were told to stay here—and stay ye will. You'll obey my orders, like them or nay, as you are sworn to do."

"Unhand my horse, sir! I was never so sworn!"

"Yea, madam, you were. Am I not your husband?—Did ye not take vows to honor *and* obey me?" With that, he suddenly hauled her from her saddle and across his own, crushing his lips down, over hers. He kissed her so fiercely, her lips were gnashed against his teeth.

"Brute! Do not think to sway me with your kisses. I will go back with you!" she cried, her bosom heaving.

"Nay," he breathed, as he released her.

She slid from his saddle to stand on the grass beside his horse, her black hair tousled, her lips swollen and red, her expression mutinous, defiant.

The sense of impending disaster was strong in his gut. *Ye Gods, if he should lose her now!—*

Looking up, she saw his green eyes take on an almost golden

hue, as he glared down at her, warning: ''Never think to disobey me, minx, for I swear—by all the gods in Asgard and in Heaven!—you'll regret it!'' he threatened.

His face was dark, hard, closed. And, despite the passionate nights they'd shared, the intimacies they'd known these past few days, he seemed a stranger to her all over again, transformed by the broth of powerful emotions bubbling beneath his skin.

She swallowed, disturbed by something . . . something almost *frightening* which she glimpsed in both his expression and in the depths of his eyes. Something she feared her love, however deep and true, could never reach.

Fixing her with a quelling glare, he growled, ''Stand back, my lady.''

So saying, he cast the abbey a last, almost apprehensive, glance, then pushed her gently from him and dug heels into Orion's sides.

The horse's nostrils flared. Then it threw its head back and screamed, as if he had roweled its flanks, and plunged into the forest's dark emerald shadows.

Leading Fayre by the reins, Edan was scowling as she turned heel and went to meet the beaming abbot on foot, with Grania trailing in her wake. Having a husband, she was fast coming to learn, could be both a blessing *and* a curse!

At stout Abbot Gwyllum's invitation, she and Grania passed the next two nights as the abbey's guests, sharing a narrow wooden bed in a spartan cell with not a feather pallet in sight!

To poor Grania's annoyance, though the amounts of fresh bread, cheese, butter, and milk served them from the dairy were generous—and a considerable improvement over Niall's chunks of charred venison—their fur-lined sleeping bags in camp proved softer than their thin pallets of soft straw here!

'' 'Tis penance enough t'sleep here, my lady,'' Grania grumbled. ''We'll need no confession!''

Still, despite certain drawbacks, their two days at the abbey proved a tiny island of calm in their hectic journey across Britain.

Their mornings were spent in prayer or in quiet contemplation, either in the shady cloisters or in the abbey's chapel. In the afternoons, they made badly needed repairs to their garments, or else admired the beautifully illuminated manuscripts in the scriptorium.

But, calm or nay, it was with little regret that they informed Abbot Gwyllum of Kerrin's decision to ride on the following morning.

Of the two of them, Grania had been especially delighted when Tavish came to deliver this welcome news, for it had been two whole days since she had last seen him.

When he departed, the girl went into raptures about how handsome he'd looked and how very much she'd missed him. Edan, who fancied she'd missed her husband far more than Grania could possibly have missed Tavish, had little patience for her magpie chattering.

"Come, come. Two days are hardly a lifetime, are they?" she scolded, shaking her head, as she neatly folded her kirtles and mantles and tucked them into her saddle packs. "Oh, Grania, not in there, please! The mantle brooches and my silver talisman go in the larger casket, remember?"

"I think he likes me. And I like him, too," Grania rambled on, obediently transferring the items Edan had mentioned into the other casket. "Mayhap even more than 'like'!" she added with a wistful sigh.

She was besotted by the man, Edan thought, shaking her head. Small wonder she'd been so scatterbrained of late! "Do you truly think you love him?"

There was no answer. Edan looked up.

"Why, Grania, you're blushing!" she exclaimed, seeing the pink fill her serving woman's cheeks. "Have you grown so fond of the fellow, then?"

Shyly, Grania nodded. "Yea, my lady. Oh, I know he's not as comely as some, but he makes me laugh! When he rides at my side, why, I'm so busy laughing, the leagues just fly by. I scarce even notice them anymore!"

"You mean to encourage his courtship, then?" Edan inquired.

"Oh, aye!" Grania admitted, her attention readily diverted from the subject of packing her mistress's baggage to the far more exciting subject of Kerrin's man at arms—her handsome Tavish—more exciting, for that matter, than Edan's own startling revelation that Kerrin was, in fact, her mistress's husband, lord Padraic of Wulfskeep.

"Have a care, then, and do not give your heart too soon," Edan advised. "We know very little of the man as yet, after all. It could well be he seeks a woman only to warm his furs."

Grania giggled and hugged herself about the arms. "Mayhap he's found himself one, then."

"Grania! You sound like that wicked Edythe! For shame!"

"I know 'tis wickedness to have such thoughts, but . . . I can't seem to help it, my lady," Grania wailed, clasping her hands to her heart. "Just one look, and he makes me feel all flummoxed, he does. In here," she added slyly, pointing to the pit of her belly. "Ye know how it is, do ye not, my lady?"

"Of—of course not," Edan lied, but her cheeks burned under Grania's sly gaze. Truth was, she knew all too well! Kerrin's voice alone could play skittles with her composure. Likewise, the simple touch of his hands spanning her waist, when he lifted her onto her palfrey, could enflame her desire and make her long for the night ahead, when she could lay beside him. In truth, ever since the night of the storm, she'd become an insatiable wanton! The past two nights they'd slept apart had been a little purgatory on earth! "After all, I'm a married woman," she reminded Grania primly. " 'Tis different for us." She crossed her fingers beneath her mantle, so the falsehood would not count as a sin.

"But ye won't stop me from encouraging Tavish, will ye, my lady?" Grania asked anxiously.

"Not if you're set on him, nay, of course not." She took Grania by the upper arms and turned her about. "I know we've not seen eye to eye of late, dearest Grania, but I truly want you to be happy at Wulfskeep. For *both* of us to be happy! If you've found a man you can love—one who'll love you and honor you as his wife and lady—then I am truly happy for you both."

Grania's pretty face glowed. "Oh, my lady, before he left the abbey, he whispered that he enjoyed watching the moonlight on the water. 'Do you?' he asked me. Well, I told him that I was a good Christian girl, and that I'd be afeared to go wandering by the water after dark, in case the water fairies were waitin' to carry me down to their world. Then he asked if I'd be frightened with him t' protect me," she ended triumphantly.

"And? How did you answer him?"

"I said I wouldn't fear Satan himself with such a warrior beside me," Grania dimpled. "He looked—he looked right pleased, he did. All puffed up, like a rooster!"

"I wouldn't wonder," Edan observed dryly, hiding a smile. Having brothers herself, she knew how gullible men were to a little female flattery. They swallowed every morsel, true or false, like salmon swallowed a fisherman's fly—and believed it!

Grania nodded. "Then he said since the moon would wax full tonight, I must be sure to see it, and rode off. What do you think he meant by that, my lady?"

"That he'll be waiting down by the inlet at moonrise tonight."

"Do you truly think so, my lady?" Grania's blue eyes were round as millstones—and almost as large!

"What else could he have meant, you silly goose? Here! You may borrow my woolen mantle and that bear brooch you covet for your tryst, if you wish. The color becomes you well."

"Can I really? Oh, thank you!" Grania exclaimed. Retrieving the coveted items from her mistress's coffer, she gathered up brooch, linens, and kirtle, bobbed a hasty curtsy, then ran off to find a private place where she could primp and pretty herself for the evening to come.

Left alone in the grassy quadrangle, Edan leaned back on the stone bench. Closing her eyes, she enjoyed the feel of warm sunshine on her face and the restful cooing of the doves under the eaves. She silently offered up a prayer for Grania's and her happiness. She had Kerrin to love, and he had as good as said that he was growing to love her in return. Her future was filled with the promise of happiness! And, very soon, unless she was very much mistaken, her dear friend would have Tavish to love. She had so much to be thankful for!

Lady Moon had risen, when Grania, decked out in her mistress's kirtle and mantle, her long fair hair brushed until it gleamed like golden coins, slipped from the abbey gates.

As her mistress had suspected, Tavish was waiting there. He dismounted and, leading his horse behind them, he silently took her hand and led her down the sloping water meadow to the inlet.

He was right, Grania thought, her heart pounding wildly, as she looked out across the dark inlet. The full moon's silvery reflection swimming in inky water, and her light glinting off the crest of each lapping wavelet, made a pretty sight. . . .

"Grania," Tavish whispered, his face serious for once in the shadows.

"Sir?"

"When I went with Hurleigh and the others—you know, to find the wenches?"

I remember, "Grania said, tightly.

"There were no wenches t'be found, and I was glad. Ye see, lass, all I could think of was you!"

"Truly?"

"On my honor, I swear it."

Both moon and mistress were forgotten as Tavish took Grania by the hands and kissed her. . . .

Chapter Fifteen

Edan tried to stay awake, busying herself in patching the large hole old Myrla's donkey, Ahearn, had chewed in her woolen mantle. Before too long, however, she was smothering yawns and arching her back to rid it of kinks. She'd promised to stay up till Grania returned to the cold monk's cell they shared. But it was growing harder to keep her promise with every passing minute!

She yawned hugely and rubbed her eyes with her knuckles, casting a look of longing at the hard wooden bed. She had donned breeks, tunic, mantle, and boots in an effort to keep warm while she sewed, but it was still chilly within those thick walls of stone. Her fingers were numb on her needle. She sighed. The bed, though hard, would be warm at least, supplemented by her own fur pelts pulled over the one scratchy blanket they'd been allotted by the abbey's almoner. But then, there was her promise to Grania. . . .

An hour or two past moonrise, her eyes began to itch. Her vision blurred. The tiny flame of tallow, which cast her own giantess's shadow on the stone walls behind her, guttered, hissed, and died. Her head drooped on her chest, and she slept. And straightway, a dream unfolded. . . .

She dreamed she was down by the inlet with Grania, watching three beautiful, snow-white swans bobbing towards her over the deep green water. As she watched, the necks of the swans began to grow longer and longer. Their bodies grew larger, until they were no longer swans at all, but fierce Viking dragon-ships, their figureheads of carved wood rearing up from long, swanlike necks, their striped red and white sails bellying in the breeze! Worse still, helmeted Vikings were pouring from their decks, armed to the teeth with blood-axe and with sword, with shield and with spear. They rallied to the raven standard raised aloft by one of their number, unfurling proudly with the promise of victory.

She had to find Grania and warn her!

"Grania! Where are you?" she called softly, yet urgently, searching the reeds and bushes along the inlet's banks. "Grania, stop hiding from me this instant. Show yourself!"

"Mistress! Help me!" she heard a cry.

To her horror, she saw Grania across the inlet, struggling to escape one of the Danes who had waded ashore! She tried to run to her aid, yet it was as if she were running through a river of honey which sucked and dragged at her feet, so agonizingly slow was her progress.

"I'm coming! Hold on! I'm coming!" she screamed.

But, before Edan could reach Grania—or indeed, do anything to help her—the brute had knocked her senseless, flung her over his shoulder like a mannikin, and carried her away.

"Naaaay!" she screamed, as the Dane and his lifeless burden dissolved into mist. "Dear God, nay!"

She jerked awake, her heart pounding, to find herself in utter darkness, shivering with cold and damp—yet still alone.

Like shadows, Thorvald the Black and his men slipped over the sides of their dragonships and waded ashore through glinting dark shallows. As Lady Moon drifted behind a cloud, they crept stealthily up the reedy banks of the inlet to the abbey.

They found the sturdy plank gates barred, yet miraculously—to their way of thinking—unmanned. No sentry called out to challenge them. Neither sword nor axe rattled to warn that armed men lay in waiting beyond, nor would bar their entry. They found the walls of gray limestone similarly unprotected, and their glee knew no bounds! Was there no end to the foolishness of these soft priests of the White Christ? They were ballless cowards, yellow cravens who would sooner kneel and beg for mercy, than fight like men of honor and glory!

A stout tree was swiftly chopped down to serve as a battering ram. In the hands of six sturdy *berserkers,* the ram made short work of the gates. They crashed inward, their timbers splintered, their iron hinges twisted and broken, allowing the invaders to swarm into the abbey's cloisters like bronze-helmeted bees swarming around a hive of honey.

Brother Anselm was the first to encounter them, on his way to toll the vespers bell. He scarcely had time to call upon his Maker for deliverance, before Thorvald the Black cleaved him in two with one mighty sweep of his broadsword. Wound-dew splashed over the flagstones in a great crimson flood.

From his hiding place behind a pillar, twelve-year-old Matthew, a homesick and sleepless novitiate, swallowed the gorge that rose up his throat and shrank back into the shadows.

When the Danes had passed by him, he sprang from his hiding place and raced through the cloisters and down the passageway to the watchtower steps.

There, he urgently sounded the warning bell. *God in Heaven, deliver them!* The moment his mother had always dreaded had finally come to pass. The Danes had attacked Kidwelly!

"My lord!" Niall's deep voice, loud with alarm, rang out on the hush.

"Here, man!" Kerrin cried, rising from his mantle by the fire and drawing metal in the same move.

A horse crashed heavily through the underbrush backing their camp. Its rider reined in the animal so sharply, it reared up on its massive haunches, hooves pawing air, despite its double burden. "Sir!"

"Speak out, man!"

"Sea-raiders, sir! They've attacked the abbey! This young fool sneaked off t'meet your lady's wench," he explained, springing down from his horse with Tavish draped over his arms. "I was scouting for Canute, as ye said, when I saw the two of them walking down by the inlet. Then Danes sprang up from the reeds and took the girl, sir!"

"Is he dead?"

"*Nej.* Unconscious, but not badly wounded. I tried to help the wench, but there were too many, so I rode back for help!"

"That fool! I'd given my orders!" Kerrin growled, slamming a fist into his palm. "Tavish knew better than to leave camp!" he exploded. "Myrla, see to him!" Despite his anger, the blood ran cold in his veins, as Niall carried Tavish's limp body, his arms swinging limply past him to Myrla. He laid him gently on the grass at the old woman's feet. He did not wager much for the serving wench's chances. If the Danes didn't kill her, they would surely rape her, then carry her off. *And what of Edan?* a voice screamed in his head. *What of your love?* But he deafened his ears to its questions. Her fate at the hands of the Danes was one he would not—dare not!—contemplate as yet, for it would leave him helpless and too paralyzed by fear to act.

"To arms, ye lazy curs! All of ye spalpeens, to arms!" he roared, flinging himself astride his horse.

Men sprang up all about the camp. Hastily strapping on weapons and shields, they followed their jarl's suit and mounted up.

"Who are these whoresons?" Kerrin snarled, reining in the gray gelding, which was straining to run and fighting the bit.

"Vikings out of Denmark, judging by their *karfi.* But, does it make any difference, sir?" Niall asked softly. "Dead is dead. By whose blade it matters little, by my reckoning."

His words all but froze the marrow in Kerrin's bones, as he gave the gelding its head.

"May the gods attend ye, my dark young lord!" Myrla cried after him. "Godspeed and fare-ye-well. Your destiny waits! *Go on,* I say!"

The gray gelding leaped past her. Nimble as a cat, it plunged into the forest.

In a breath, in a heartbeat, both horse and rider had been swallowed up, as if they'd never been.

On the night air rose the sudden, plangent clanging of the abbey bell from one of the watchtowers. Its compelling notes confirmed what Niall had said: *Norseman had attacked the abbey!*

Kerrin reached the abbey shortly after the raiders had poured through its walls. Slithering from Orion's back, he took the path the Danes had taken over the fallen, splintered gates.

In the shadowed cloisters, he went from pillar to pillar, hugging the shadows, as he followed the Vikings cutting a swath of carnage and destruction through the abbey and its outbuildings. He found no trace of Edan anywhere, and his guts knotted in fear for her safety. He had done this—*he,* no other, had insisted she stay here! And, in his desire to keep her safe from Canute, who'd been spotted due east of them, he had sent her to her death!

Some of the Danes carried blazing torches of pitch aloft. The grotesque shadows they cast were those of helmeted giants, the Frost Giants of Norse legend.

"Come out, little worms!" bellowed one drunken Dane. "My blade is thirsty for wound-dew!"

"You cannot hide from us, eunuchs of the White Christ! We can smell you!" roared another.

He left them to their cruel sport, knowing, when he heard the old monk's scream brutally cut short, that he could do nothing to stop them. Rather than let Brother Anselm's death stand for naught, he used the distraction to slip away to the dormitory, where he roused all the other monks in their cells.

He found the fat abbot snoring in his own quarters, which were far more luxuriously appointed than the monks, a skin of wine still clasped to his breast. Gripping the tonsured monk by his plump neck, he demanded, "My wife! Where is she?"

"Who?" the abbot asked groggily, still half asleep.

"My wife, the Lady Edana! Wake, and answer me, damn ye!" he rasped, roughly shaking the stout fellow till his teeth rattled.

"Both . . . both ladies are in the guest cells, down the passage to the left. But what do you here at this—"

"Vikings!" Kerrin cut him off with that single word.

Abbot Gwyllum paled. "Brother Roderick, quickly! The communion chalices! Brother Cadell, the crucifixes! Hurry! Hurry!" he cried, running up and down the darkened passageways like a chicken that has lost its head, but has yet to know it. "Brother Bryce, to the scriptorium! The rest of you, to the library! We must save the manuscripts!"

"There's no time for books! If you would save your lives, abandon the abbey! Run for your lives!" Kerrin roared.

"Never! I will not leave God's house to those heathen devils!" Gwyllum vowed, his eyes ablaze.

Kerrin gave him one long look, then dismissed him. His time was better spent on those who wished to live. Instead, he flung the other brothers headlong down the passageway to the quadrangles, and freedom. "Stay then, and burn, Abbot, if you're so eager to see Heaven. The rest of you, *run!"*

They fled in one direction, like lemmings, their cries mingling now with the crackling and popping of burning timber, as parts of the abbey succumbed to the fires started by the ravaging Norsemen. Screams and cries were coming from every direction now, while above the clamor and the smoke rose the frantic tolling of the watchtower bell.

Whoever had found the sense and courage to sound the alarm that would rouse nearby hamlets would soon be in danger himself, Kerrin realized.

The fire had caught and taken. Tapestries and hangings, manuscripts, trestles, benches, wooden beams—all would feed the greedy flames. It was but a matter of time now. Soon the abbey would be reduced to ashes.

He raced down the passage, the torch which he had torn from a sconce held aloft. By its light, he searched the library, the guest cells. In one, he found Edan's saddlebags, bulging with her belongings, but there was no sign of her—or of his lady's sword and helmet, he realized, with a sinking feeling.

"Beloved fool!" he growled. His relief that he'd not found her corpse was now mixed with dread. There was no telling in what direction his bride's reckless courage might have led her. Unless—could it be Edan who'd sounded the alarm?—

Whirling about, he ran down the passageway and took the spiral steps up to the watchtower two at a time.

A terrified scream greeted him when he flung himself into the watchtower, sword drawn.

'Twas not Edan who had sounded the alarm but a small monk—nay, a little lad of perhaps twelve winters. He recoiled and shrank back against the wall, his eyes huge and glassy with terror in the torchlight. "Please, sir, don't kill me! I'll serve ye—I'll do anything ye ask of me, anything! Only, I don't want to die!" he whispered hoarsely.

Kerrin's hard expression softened. "Come on, then. Follow me!"

Some time passed before Edan would admit that she had lost her way in the dark. Muffled shouts and screams reached her, along with the acrid smell of smoke, but she could not seem to find where either were coming from. There were so many passages, and all felt alike in the gloom. She swallowed. 'Twas no use denying it: Something was badly wrong. Nervous, she wetted dry lips. Could her dream have been true?

She was frightened, but she refused to go back now, refused to cower and wait. The thought of poor Grania at the mercy of a band of Danes stiffened her spine and kept her moving resolutely forward, despite her fear. Poor, dear Grania. Where was she now? Had they hurt her? Was she already dead? Ravished? If so, they would pay, aye, and pay royally! she vowed. She was no coward, to flee from empty shadows like a craven, no matter what witchy or monstrous shape those shadows might employ, she reminded herself. She veered away from yet another shadow goblin, which proved to be the statue of a saint!

Armed with her sword and clutching her helmet to her breast, she crept on. She would find and free Grania, she promised herself. And in the process, she would prove to that wretched, doubting Kerrin that he'd married a Saxon lioness, a true she-wolf among women! Their sons would be warrior-gods, their daughters beautiful mirrors of their brothers—children of fire and courage who would follow in their parents' stead. He would learn she was not the pampered princess he'd made sport of in the byre, when first they met. . . .

She pulled up short. Silvery-white moonlight flooded the huge, open quadrangle before her, so that each blade of grass seemed painted with glittering frost, as bright as day. Which way should she go? She could not determine in which direction the front gates lay, nor from which direction the muffled shouts and yells were coming. There was no overt sign of any invaders here, but . . . what if they were hiding behind the pillars, waiting for her to show herself? No matter. She must take the chance and run for it, if she wanted to get outside and find Grania. . . .

Drawing a deep breath, she suddenly broke from cover and raced across the moonlit quadrangle, diving head first into the concealing shadows on the far side. She lay there, breathing heavily, waiting for a shout, a cry, some sign that she'd been spotted. Thank God, there was none. And, after a few moments, she stood and hastened on, ducking from pillar to pillar till— miracle of miracles—she found herself at the abbey gates.

Outside, she drew up short, staring in disbelief at the inlet, where she could see the rearing, serpentine prows of two dragon-ships, rocking at anchor. Behind her, in the western wing, flames were leaping up from the abbey library and scriptorium. 'Twas from there the sound of screams and cries and the crash of steel upon steel had been carried to her on the night wind.

She bit her lip. Not far away, men were dying, others were killing—what should she do? Where should she go? Was Grania out here somewhere with Tavish? Was she safe, or in danger? Had she—dear God, no!—had she come back inside and run afoul of the Norsemen? Or had they found her out here somewhere and carried her off, as her dream had foretold?

Just then, she heard deep, guttural voices speaking her mother's native Danish. She ducked down behind the gatehouse and waited, holding her breath, till the speakers drew level with her hiding place. When they did, she almost cried out in relief. One of them was leading Kerrin's horse!

Thank God! Her husband and his men had come to help the monks!

She opened her mouth to greet them, but, at the last moment, fell abruptly silent. These men were not of her escort, but Danish raiders, like those she had dreamed of! Although they led Kerrin's horse by the bridle, they wore conical bronze-helmets with noseguards that hid their features and boasted flowing moustaches and beards. Their massive chests and legs were wrapped in fur jerkins or bound with cross-gaiters, which made them appear even bigger than Saxon men. *Black Danes.*

Sick to her belly, she saw that Grania was slung across a third invader's shoulders like a dead doe, her long, fair hair almost sweeping the dirt at the sea-wolf's heels, as he ran with her. She was far from dead as yet, thank God, for she was struggling wildly to escape, screaming and pummelling the Dane's back with all her strength.

God in heaven, what was she to do? How in the world could she hope to free Grania from such a giant?—

As if by magic, the years fell away.

" 'Tis true that women lack the size and strength of men, dearling,'' she seemed to hear her mother say in her lilting voice. "However, God Almighty has given us something almost as good to make up for it.''

"And what is that, pray, Mama?'' she had answered, pouting and unconvinced, hot tears still running down her cheeks. Her ribs had yet ached from the sideswipe of her twin brother, Beorn's wooden sword.

"Speed, grace, ingenuity—guile! Unless a man's sword can find its target in enemy flesh, it can spill no blood. And what good is brute strength then, pray? What price, height, or breadth, or power? You will be invincible!''

She had brightened at this. "Truly, Mother?'' she'd asked. "You swear?''

"I swear! Can a gossamer fairy be caught within a mortal's

clumsy grasp? Can a moonbeam be pierced by a dagger point? On my crossed heart do I swear it, min yndling,'' Marissa had promised solemnly, making the sign over her breast.

Stuffing her long hair beneath her weighty helmet, she gritted her teeth, tamped down the tiny asp of fear that reared up in the pit of her belly. For Grania's sake, she must do something, or they would carry her off to their icy strongholds and she would never see her again.

"For God and Wulfskeep!" she yelled, brandishing her sword aloft.

Howling like a banshee, she charged!

Chapter Sixteen

'Twas as if he was a fly, trapped in the sticky web of a nightmare—one from which there would be no awakening, Kerrin thought, as he and Matthew raced from the blazing abbey.

The night was bright as day. The first person he saw, bathed in the ruddy light of the flames, was Edan, battling a towering, black-bearded Dane easily twice her size.

The Dane was wielding a hefty broadsword with both hands clamped around its roughened hilt, making sweeping cuts from left to right, then right to left, that kept her constantly moving. Although the Viking had done her no real damage as yet, it was inevitable that she would tire eventually. When that moment came, she would be unable to dance out of reach of his sword, and would die.

The sly old sea-wolf knew this full well. He was but taunting her, treating their swordplay as a fine game of cat and mouse—with Edan as the mouse.

"Come, come, my beardless Saxon!" he taunted, beckoning Edan on. "Come on! Prick me with your little bodkin, _ja?_" He grinned, his lips fleshy, red, and wet against the curly black of his beard. "By Odin, I've eaten chickens with more meat on their bones than you have, skinny sprout! *Here!* Dance little man! And *here!*—Skip! Skip!'' he roared, laughing as the ''warrior'' nimbly sidestepped, or whirled, out of his reach with each thrust, prod, or sweep of his blade. ''By Loki, if he can spin wool as well as he dances, I'll wed the whoreson!'' Thorvald the Black threw back his head and rocked with hearty laughter.

While he was preoccupied, Edan suddenly darted forward and jabbed at his shoulder. Like lightning, his sword arm came up to deflect her blade. Instead of hacking his shoulder wide open, the tip of her blade nicked his cheek instead, opening a long, deep gash that poured a gush of wound-dew over his beard.

''Why, you little worm, you cut me! Skinny maggot!— Spoil Thorvald's pretty face, would ye? Get ready to kiss the Valkyries, boy! You shall dine in Valhalla this night!'' The sly old sea-wolf stuck out his foot.

And Edan, visibly tiring now—for she had swung, whirled, and hacked like a lioness—tripped over it. She did not fall flat on her face, as the Dane had hoped, however, but instead slumped forward onto one knee, breathing heavily. Her head was bowed as if in prayer, as she tried to catch her wind.

Grinning, Thorvald swung his blade aloft, intending to lop her head from her neck with one mighty blow.

''Min jarl, wait!'' Kerrin shouted in his uncle's tongue, knowing he could never hope to close the distance in time to deflect Thorvald's blow. His only hope was to distract the Norsemen from his purpose. '' *'Tis a woman!''*

''What's this? A wench?'' His curiosity tweaked, Thorvald halted the terrible, death-dealing arc of his singing blade in mid-swing. And, instead of lifting Edan's head, he playfully tipped off her helmet with his sword tip, instead.

As the helmet clanked to the turf, her ebony curls streamed down over her shoulders to frame her lovely face. Flinging the inky mane out of her face, she drew herself up proudly, gray eyes flashing, cheeks flushed, lips red as roses. ''Hell take thee, Norseman!''

''Aha! Look, my brothers! I have caught me a Valkyrie, by

the gods! Mayhap you are right. Mayhap the old hag will take me, little warrior wench—but first, *I'll* take *thee!*" Apparently unafraid, for all that she was still holding her sword, the Viking stepped forward. Hands reaching with a suddenness and speed that his great size belied, he insolently kneaded her breasts, savoring the loathing that curled her lip and blazed in her eyes. "A woman, in truth!" he crowed.

Before he could step back, out of reach, she jabbed the point of her blade downwards, into his booted foot and hissed in his face, "Paw me again, you old goat, and I'll sever your heathen hand from your pagan arm, by God!"

Everything happened very swiftly after that.

Enraged, Thorvald's arm swung high and wide. She saw his broadsword lifted above her, saw its broad blade stained a shining ruby-red that reflected the burning abbey. Then a sickening pain exploded in her skull, one that torched a shower of white-bright stars.

Surely I am dying? came the thought.

In the same instant, Kerrin's white face filled her vision. She saw his eyes change from blazing green to molten gold, as he sprang at Thorvald's throat. Saw his mouth open in a snarl that was no longer human.

"*What are you?*" she heard the Dane's hoarse, strangled cry.

Then the stars went out like pinched candle flames, and she was floating in an endless darkness. . . .

"You! Wake up!"

"Leave me be, wretch."

"Wretch is it, bitch? We'll see who's calling who a wretch, when my chieftain's done with ye!" scoffed the same rough voice. "Aye, and after he's plowed your pretty furrow a time or ten, happen me and me fellows will have a turn at plowing, too, *ja.*"

Groaning, she struggled to sit up, vaguely aware that her hands were joined together at the wrists. She opened one eye and saw a stranger's face leering down at her. A very red, windburned face with golden-blond moustaches that scratched her cheek, as he hefted her, none too gently, to standing. He was none too particular about where his hands strayed as he was doing so, either.

Her head reeled. All that had happened at the abbey rushed back to her in a sickening jolt. *Thorvald. The flames. Kerrin throwing himself on the Dane's blade. . . .*

He had given his own life in a desperate bid to save her.

"Happen the moon will turn blue, but you'll still never have me, you stinking bucket of pig swill!" Snarling, she raked her nails down the man's cheek, forcing him to let go of her.

"Ho! Ho! My little panther has claws, too, does she?" Thorvald chuckled, coming up behind them. He looked even bigger than she remembered. The sword nick on his cheek had ceased to bleed, yet was still raw looking. It gave her enormous satisfaction to see her mark upon him. It was not much by way of vengeance for Kerrin's murder, but it was something.

"I wonder?" Thorvald added, scratching his chin, as he walked slowly around her, grinning at the snug fit of her breeks and the way the supple doeskin jerkin clothed her like a second skin. "Will this black-haired fury fight like a she-cat in my furs?"

"I'll open my wrists before I share your furs, Viking dog!" Flinging her hair over her shoulders, Edan drew herself up to her full height and spat in his face. Her gray eyes were molten silver in the predawn, the dying flames of the burning abbey mirrored in their depths. There was nowhere to run, even had she been so inclined. For while unconscious, she'd been carried aboard one of their *drakkars,* along with other captives. Besides, her wrists were chained together. And so, she forced herself to glower defiantly back at the foul Dane without so much as blinking, while her spittle ran slowly down his ruddy, furious face. *Let him kill her now! She did not care what happened to her, not any more, not with Kerrin dead—and dead he must surely be. How else would Thorvald yet live?*

"You say you will open your wrists, *ja?* Then maybe I help

you die, *nej?*'' Gripping her by the neck with just one massive hand, he squeezed so cruelly, a high-pitched humming began in her ears that went on and on. Blackness hovered on the edges of consciousness. He increased the pressure of his thumb, digging inward. Before long, she could feel neither her arms nor her legs. Her vision began to blur and dim, as the brute dragged her up against him and smeared a wet-lipped kiss over her mouth, roughly fondling her breasts with a paw the size of a small ham. "*Nej,* I think not. You are too comely to die, my warrior-queen,'' Thorvald murmured, and she almost gagged at the sour smell of beer and milk curds on his breath.

She thought for certes she'd swoon, if he did not loosen his grip, but by some miracle, she hung on to her fading senses. When he ducked his shaggy head to kiss her again, she sank her teeth deep into his lips, tasting his blood, before she slammed her knee up into his groin.

Before her knee could connect, the Viking cursed foully and shoved her backwards to the deck with all the force he could summon. "Hell take thee, scrawny Saxon bitch!'' he cursed, wiping the blood from his mouth on the back of his hand. "I've no liking for cold wenches in my bed—nor foul tempered ones. If you'll not purr for Thorvald the Black, then by the gods, he will sell you!—*Ja,* and find a slut who *will* purr for him!''

His crew snickered.

His point made, Thorvald yanked another woman to standing by her long red hair. He tossed the buxom beauty over his shoulder, then carried her for'ard, leaving Edan, clammy with shock, huddled on the damp deck with the other female captives.

"Proud fool!'' the woman beside her muttered. "For the price of a tupping or two, 'twould have gone gently for ye.''

"I whore for no man.''

The woman snorted her disbelief. "Dearie, we're all whores, one way or another. The only difference is our price. Some of us ask for a wedding vow. Others ask for just a bit of bread, or even a little wool.'' She shrugged. "This time, the price is our lives. Pride's a fine thing—but what good is it, once you're dead and buried, tell me that? What good is anything then?'' Her face crumpled. ''If only he'd chosen me!''

When Edan offered no comment, but continued to stare stonily across the inlet to the riverbanks, the sorry wench abandoned all attempts at conversation and fell to muffled weeping like the others.

Soon after she came to, the dawn broke, spilling glorious pearly light over a changed world—one in which palls of smoke rose skyward from the blackened shell of the abbey. More smoke rose in the distance from a small keep and a dozen or so cottages that had been razed and plundered on the far side of the woods.

With the dawning, Edan could also make out the bodies of the monks, scattered over the banks of the inlet, each one sprawled in the obscene, unnatural postures of death. *His body was back there, too, somewhere, denied the dignity of either burial or of prayer, left to feed the dark-winged ghouls that perched, waiting, in the trees.*

A shudder ran through her. Why could she not weep for him? Why did she feel only this emptiness . . . this icy void? Dear God, even the gulls seemed to be singing him a dirge. *Kerr*-in! *Kerr*-rin! *Kerr*-in! But, where were *her* tears? Had she no heart? What was wrong with her? *What?*

Within the hour, the booty and the last of the captives had been loaded or brought aboard. Soon after, Thorvald gave his captains the order to set sail with the morning tide.

The two dragon-ships raised their anchors, moving down the river inlet to the mouth of the Bristol Channel, propelled by the oar power of their crews. Beyond lay St. George's Channel and, beyond that, the Irish Sea.

This was wrong, all wrong!—Edan thought numbly. Instead of speeding her to her husband's home, a Viking vessel was carrying her far from the isles of Britain and Ireland, toward a future she was too heartsick even to contemplate. . . .

As the two vessels sailed past Worm's Head, the winds lifted. They bellied the red and white striped sails of *wadmal* with a loud snapping sound, like the crack of a slaver's lash. The brace of dragon-ships skimmed like smooth, round stones over the gray water.

Soon St. Daffyd's and the west coast of Wales fell away behind the stern, and the fierce *drakkars* were swallowed up by the mist and the spray of St. George's channel, like vanishing beasts of legend.

Chapter Seventeen

"Here. Eat this."

"I'm not hungry."

"Eat it anyway. Lord knows when we'll get another chance."

"It does not matter if I eat or nay."

"It does to me, my lady."

Her brows rose. "Do I know you?"

"I think not. But I've heard of you! You are the Kentish princess who married the Irish Viking. You were a guest of the holy brothers at the abbey, were you not? Now, eat!"

Edan took the crust of stale bread the woman thrust into her hands. But rather than eat it—instead she looked at the woman.

She seemed a little older than the other captives, a score and ten years, mayhap. She had lovely brown eyes and thick, wavy hair the color of cornsilk. Her skin was her finest feature, though, as smooth and flawless as clotted cream, tinged with rose at the cheeks. Her hair had escaped its thick braids and short tendrils framed her face like a wispy golden halo beneath her head-veil of embroidered linen. Her figure was rounded, womanly but firm, and her mantle and night kirtle, though torn and dirty now, were clearly of fine quality. She had been a woman of some substance, before being dragged from her bed by the Danish invaders.

"I am called Maida," the woman whispered, darting a furtive glance in the direction of the crew, who were crawling all over the ship, either tying down cargo or adjusting lines. She sat down next to Edan. "My husband, Hugh, God rest his soul, was steward to lord Tristan of Kidwelly, whose keep lay a half league from the abbey. Our youngest son, Matthew, is a novitiate there," she said proudly, then her composure crumpled. "Or *was,* my poor wee *bach....*" She glanced away, her lower lip trembling. "I fear he is dead, now, and gone to heaven."

Edan, usually so tenderhearted, neither smiled nor made any gesture of sympathy toward the poor woman. She could not, for she was numb, unable to feel the pain of her own loss, or to care about her capture, let alone feel for others.

"Do you know where they are taking us?" Maida asked. There was no answer from Edan. "Someone said these heathen savages are from Jutland, wherever that may be. Their chieftain—the old bull-walrus who brought you aboard—is known as Thorvald the Black. Could we escape if they took us back to their homelands, think you, my lady? . . . My lady?"

"Mayhap." Edan said heavily at length, annoyed by the woman's persistence. She shrugged. "I do not know." Her tone said she did not care, much, either.

Maida placed her hand over Edan's and squeezed. "You have lost someone, too, have you not? Was it your father?"

Edan looked up, her expression blank, emotionless.

Maida clucked. "Poor child! Forgive me for doing this, but— someone must!" So saying, she smacked Edan hard across the cheek.

The blow stung. Its force snapped her head to one side. She sucked in a shocked, pained breath, like someone surfacing after a dive.

When she next looked up at Maida, her gray eyes were no longer vacant, but dark with grief. With a sob, she threw herself into the other woman's arms and wept. "We were wed such a short while, and already he is gone! I have lost him before we were truly man and wife! I never had the chance to tell him . . . to tell him I loved him!''

"There, there, lovie," Maida crooned, rocking her as if she were a child "He knew, lovie. I'm sure he knew. Aye, let the tears flow. Let them all come out. Tell Maida how it was, look you, my angel . . .''

The two *drakkars* sailed due north for the remainder of that day, their red and white sails bellying with the wind, their swan-like prows rising and falling in graceful curves over the rolling gray-green waves. The carved dragonheads that surmounted them screamed defiance at the serpents and spirits of sea and winds, who might try to keep the vessels from their destination.

There was no protection against the elements for anyone aboard the *Thor's Tempest*. The captives—a score in all, all female, the males having been loaded onto the other vessel— huddled on the hard, slippery wooden decks all that day, at the mercy of sun, winds, salt spray and rain, by turns.

Some had suffered small wounds and busied themselves day in and day out in trying to tend them. Others hummed monotonous little tunes, picked constantly at imaginary spots of blood on their kirtles, or else twiddled their thumbs over and over. 'Twas an even bet they would never be right in the head again. Still others remained locked in the grip of shock and simply sat there, staring off into space, as Edan had done. And there was no Maida to break the hold that horror had on them, poor souls.

It came as no surprise to Edan at all when, after several nights of sharing Thorvald's furs, Una—the comely red-haired captive he'd favored—simply stood up one morning, walked to the rail, and threw herself into the sea, preferring death to Thorvald's attentions. And though Maida muttered that survival was what counted and that Una had chosen the coward's way out, Edan privately envied the woman her courage.

Still, to give the Danes their due, the thirty-five crew members lived little better than their captives, during their time on board the *Tempest*. The sailors ate the same fare that their prisoners ate: dried or salted fish with hunks of black bread, the whole washed down with watered beer while at sea; or hot porridge, a little dried meat and cabbage, washed down with still more beer. They ate at those times when headwinds slowed the *drakkar's* progress, and the passengers were able to spend a night or two on land.

They dozed between watches, either huddling beneath an awning erected over the deck, when rain swept across the sea, or else rolling themselves into their mantles on the open deck, when the weather was fine.

When they put into some of the little sheep-islands scattered off the northernmost coast of Scotland, hardy blond or auburn-haired fisher-wenches with babes in arms, and rosy-cheeked toddlers clinging to their skirts, would come running down to the shore to greet Thorvald's crew, laughing in delight, as they were swung high in the sailors' arms and soundly kissed.

Maida noticed that many of the men had wives and children in each of the isolated little islands they put into, and that—although murderous raiders to those they preyed upon—they seemed doting fathers and loving husbands to their own.

Edan had to agree. Her mother herself had once gone a-viking to win fertile new lands and riches for her people, and had instead won herself a Saxon prince. Few had been blessed with a better mother than Marissa of Kenley, for all that she was a former sea-raider.

On the fifteenth morning, Alaine, who had replaced Una in Thorvald's furs, returned from the canvas awning under which she'd passed the night with the chieftain, bearing the news that they would soon reach their destination—the great Viking seaport, market, and trading center of Hedeby, on the neck of the Jutland peninsula of Denmark.

There, Alaine said, Jarl Thorvald planned to trade the silver, gold, and other plunder his sea-wolves had looted from the abbey and Earl Tristan's keep. The captive women on Thorvald's vessel, and the men and boys who had been loaded onto the second dragon-ship—captained by two of Thorvald's sons—were to be sold off as slaves. Alaine promised to find out what more she could, if Maida and Edan would include her in any plans they made to escape.

They promised they would. They had already come to the conclusion that if there was to be an escape, only the three of them would have the determination to carry it out. The other women were an apathetic lot: either still dazed by the horrors they'd seen, or as accepting of their fate as sheep led to the slaughter. In an escape bid, such women could prove dangerous to the rest of them.

"My mother came from Jutland," Edan confided to Maida. "My grandfather's hall there was called Danehof."

"Your mother is a Norsewoman, then?"

Edan nodded. "Was. She married my father, a prince of Kent, and accepted Christianity many years ago." Remembering this, she smiled wanly. "She says she is quite tamed now, and no longer the firebrand my father wed."

"Have you blood kinsmen in Denmark still, my lady?"

"Alas, no. After my mother sailed away to Britain, her father grew feebleminded. Stronger men overran his hall and replaced him as its Jarl. My twin brother, Beorn, is planning to retake my grandfather's hall some day, though. God willing, he will also reclaim the chieftaincy." She pursed her lips thoughtfully, "If we could escape Hedeby, mayhap my grandfather's name— along with my knowledge of the Danish tongue—would give us safe passage across Denmark? . . ."

She had no need to finish the thought. Maida was already ahead of her, nodding vigorously and squeezing her hand. Somehow, her bright brown eyes promised, they would find a way to escape. And—as an added bonus—Edan might even find her mother's kindred.

Chapter Eighteen

As Alaine had told them, the dragon-ships' destination was the Viking trading center of Hedeby.

Before the sun had reached its zenith, *Thor's Tempest* sailed into a shallow harbor formed by a long, man-made breakwater of stone, which curved around the land like a broad arm, protecting the market town from rough seas.

After a hawser had been lashed to one of the metal bollards, the crew jostled the captives to their feet, and they were forced to clamber ashore.

Edan and the other women were all stiff from lack of exercise and had difficulty in standing upright, let alone walking down the gangplank to solid, dry land. Their legs trembled after spending so many days at sea on the pitching decks of the *Tempest*. Still, they stumbled along as best they could, reluctant to show their discomfort, or to fall behind and draw the notice of their captors. Who could tell when a wrong word, a defiant glance, would merit a blow—or worse? Life was cheap to these men.

The *Tempest*'s cargo—great quantities of silver chalices, silver and golden platters, jewelled reliquaries, golden crucifixes, gem-studded caskets, weapons, and so on—were loaded onto waiting horse-drawn carts. The carts followed them as, with guards on all sides of them, the female captives were marched into the walled market town. Chivvied along by two men who were, it transpired, two of Thorvald's sons, captains Arne and Oleg, came the captured men and boys, their wrists in chains. Obviously the Vikings considered males more likely to attempt escape than females—a point Edan hoped to use to their advantage.

"Keep a sharp eye out as we enter the town, Maida," she urged. "We need to know what we'll be up against later, if we escape."

"I will, my lady. But, will ye look at this! The town is surrounded by ramparts as thick as a man's two arms! And beyond that, a moat filled with water! I cannot see any way in or out, except by those tunnels cut in the walls, can you?"

Maida was right, she saw, with a sinking heart. There appeared to be few gates. What there were had been cut into the earthen ramparts, then paved over with smooth stone. Heavy gates and armed lookouts manning the towers, which were set at intervals along the walls, would prevent any runaways from escaping the market city by the gates, just as it would keep sea-raiders from gaining easy entrance. If they were to get away from here, it would surely have to be in disguise, hidden in the back of a wagon, or buried under a load of pelts or kindling, or else from that side of the market town that was bordered by the sea.

After they had gone through the short tunnel, they came out into a bustling city. There were many, many buildings, most of them reed-thatched Viking longhouses with walls of either logs, or wattle and daub, built in tidy rows divided by palisades. To Edan's surprise, there were one or two Christian churches, as well, built of stone and wood. Could they claim sanctuary within them?

In some of the doorways sat women or girls, enjoying the late spring sunshine, while spinning wool, their distaffs merrily twirling. Other women were weaving at their looms, while before some doorways sat old men, carving horn or wood into combs or brooch pins. Though their hands were gnarled and spotted with age, and trembling with palsy, they were skilled at their craft, nonetheless.

Behind the gabled longhouses were outhouses, bathhouses, storehouses, byres, and stables, with horses and milk cows grazing on the pasture surrounding them. And, of course, there were people, people everywhere, people of every description, from swaggering Rus merchants wearing baggy breeks tucked into boots of supple suede, to dashing Russians wearing tall hats of exquisite sable and mantles with trims of costly marten. There were bearded, hook-nosed Arabs from the sun-baked deserts that lay far to the east, wearing flowing burnooses and embroidered silk caftans. There were also Lapps from the far north—so many people, in fact, that poor Maida—who had never been to the teeming city of London, and so had seen nothing to equal Hedeby's crowds or her streets lined with gabled houses—pulled up short and gaped. So amazed was she, in fact, she had to be given a shove by their guard to get her moving again!

On their way to wherever it was they were going, they passed through streets where artisans and smiths had their workshops. There were stalls in front of them from which they sold their wares. All manner of items were being crafted there, from beautifully damascened swords—their polished blades inset with golden dragons, wolves, or serpents—to heavily jewelled sword hilts, bronze helmets, or chain mail coats. There was pottery, painted and gilt-trimmed horse trappings, as well as Arabian and Spanish horses, trained falcons of every kind— even a pair of snarling golden cats with black rosette-spotted coats—held in check by chains of golden links attached to collars of solid gold, studded with rubies. And much, much more. . . .

From the street of the artisans, they continued on past a bigger building which was obviously the town's garrison, for it housed many young men. The warriors—some of them bare-chested to show off their powerfully muscled arms, broad chests, and hard bellies—came jostling each other through low doorways, or else halted their wrestling or swordplay outside the barracks to watch the women pass and to whistle and catcall after them. Slave-watching was clearly a popular sport in Hedeby—more popular, mayhap, than skating and sledding across the lake in deep of winter!

"A fine batch you have there, Jarl Thorvald. My compliments, sir! Those beauties will fetch you a fortune in gold from the Moorish slavers!"

"Good morning, *min jarl* Thorvald, sir! May I offer a freshened cow and a brace of piglets for the ripe one with the golden hair and the big teats?" roared one golden-bearded rogue, holding both hands out before him, as if cupping enormous breasts of his own. "Come now, what say you, good sir? Would you accept a cow and *three* piglets? Four?"

Another leered at Maida as they passed, and pursed his lips, imploring, "Come to me, beautiful Brunhilde! Would you not like to be Gunther's woman?"

"Whatever ye said, I hope your cursed manhood shrivels up and drops off!" Maida hissed back, in the Welsh tongue of the Cymru. "Aye, and I hope your balls turn to stone, too, *bach!*"

For the first time since her capture, Edan snorted and laughed aloud in genuine amusement, for one of the shouter's companions—clearly mistaking Maida's malicious grin for an inviting smile—punched his friend's shoulder and hissed at him in Danish, "By Frey, Gunther, buy the blond one! She fancies you!"

"You there, my dark beauty!" called another man, reaching past the guard to tweak a strand of Edan's hair. She yelped and swung around to glare at him, gray eyes paling to the color of smoke. Unabashed, he winked and cocked his head to one side. "I like the way you fill out those lad's breeks!"

"I'm relieved to hear it, Harald Ragnarson! The last plump arse you praised in breeks *was* a lad's!" quipped another wag.

"Why, you foulmouthed dog turd! I'm no simpering sodomite!" Harald denied, outraged. "Take back your insult—or you'll regret it!"

The other soldiers roared with laughter, as the joker received a hefty thwack across the skull for his pains, with the flat of

Harald's sword. He dropped like a stone to the rutted street, out cold, and remained there, face down in the mud.

While the male slaves were taken straightway to the market place, the female captives were led to a gabled longhouse, roofed with reeds, that belonged to Thorvald the Black. Within moments of their arrival, however, there was little doubt in any of the women's minds that, while Thorvald was captain aboard his ship and chieftain of his men, the household was run by his formidable wife, Marta the Tall.

A handsome woman of considerable height, with a forbidding, steely gaze, Marta wore her graying hair braided and wound about her head like a helmet. She treated her four daughters as sternly as she treated her husband's new shipment of slaves—as though they were lazy, immoral wenches who were both too idle and too lascivious to be left without her own hawkeyed supervision.

By the same token, it was immediately obvious that she doted on her three strapping sons: Arne, Gorm, and Oleg, who were blond giants like herself, but seemed to have inherited none of their mother's shrewdness or their father's lupine cunning. Unlike her husband, however, Marta seemed blind to her sons' faults.

"The slaves look dirty," she announced, disdainfully, wrinkling her nose as she inspected her husband's latest acquisitions.

"That's what you always say, *min yndling*," Thorvald grumbled, throwing himself down, furs and all, across a carved wooden couch spread with reindeer and seal skins. "But they have been at sea for almost a moon since we raided Walas. What did you expect, eh, my big, beautiful wife? They will clean up well enough to fetch a fine price, as always. Now, come here. Forget the cursed slaves and give your Thorvy a little kiss. Then he will give his Marta the present he has brought for her, *ja?*"

Scowling, Marta gave her husband a none too eager peck on the cheek. But her sour expression vanished completely when the crafty old wretch produced a costly white squirrel mantle from behind his back.

"Oh, Thorvald! For me?"

"Who else would it be for, foolish little one!" he bellowed.

Marta simpered and blushed like a coquette, for all that she stood eye to eye with her enormous mate, and could probably have arm wrestled him to the straw, had she a mind to. "Oh, but you should not have done this! 'Tis too costly, too costly by far! Come, husband! Sit! Sit, my Big Bear! Your Marta will serve her Thorvy his beer with her own little hands!"

Chuckling, Thorvald—now undisputed king of his domain— retired to his comfortable couch to down a beaker of suds and to discuss with his steward how business had fared in his absence.

Meanwhile, Marta—all simpering done with—briskly ordered the captives outside to a grassy area behind the hall. Arne, Gorm, and Oleg followed her out, exchanging expectant glances and leers behind their mother's back.

Under Marta's supervision, the house thralls hefted wooden buckets and half-barrels of fresh water from the well, along with slivers of soap and coarse cloths for drying. Clapping her hands together, Marta ordered the captive women to strip off their soiled garments, soap themselves thoroughly, then enter the sweathouse for a steam bath that would rid their bodies of impurities. Clean tunics would be provided when they were finished, she promised, adding, "And remember, the prettiest and cleanest among you will get the richest master, *ja?*"

As if a master of any sort was to be coveted!

"You can go back to your weaving, Mama. We'll make sure Papa's shipment don't run away, *ja?*" Arne promised his mother slyly, winking at Gorm.

"*Ja.* These slippery little sluts won't get past us, Mutter," Oleg promised, all too innocently, nudging Arne in the ribs, as he leered at the bevy of frightened beauties milling about on the grass. "We will take excellent care of Father's merchandise," he promised, grinning. His expression said he'd decided it was high time he and Arne sampled some of the women that their father had selfishly taken aboard his own ship.

Beaming, Marta patted their cheeks. "You are such good sons—and what fine merchants you will be some day! Already you make your mother proud!"

With that, she stalked off to oversee the preparation of a lavish welcome-home feast for her darling sons and her Big Bear, as she called Thorvald the Black, leaving the mustached trio to ogle and leer at the naked slave girls, who were vainly trying to cover themselves.

"I wonder what the old dragon would think of her blessed 'Thorvy,' if she'd seen him cavorting with Una and Alaine," Maida observed. She unpinned her ragged mantle, then stripped off her torn night kirtle, scrubbing at her lush body, till her skin was a glowing, rosy pink.

"I warrant, she knows what Thorvy does when he is gone from his hall," Edan remarked. "In fact, she probably has several chests of such gifts from her 'Big Bear'—one for every poor wench he's ravished!"

Alaine snorted in disgust. "Happen some fine day, old beaky nose will have her own market stall, then!"

They were still laughing among themselves, as they entered the bathhouse.

Pine-scented steam filled the small wooden hut, rising in warm billows from heated rocks, which were tended by a female house thrall. An olive-skinned slave was ladling cool water over the hot stones, so that they hissed and gave off cleansing steam.

"You, girl! Where were the male captives taken?" Maida asked her.

The girl looked at her blankly and shrugged, indicating she did not understand her tongue.

Edan put the same question in Danish, pleased when the girl nodded to show she understood most of her words. She rattled off her reply in the fractured Danish she'd learned since her capture.

"Her name is Leya, and she was stolen from Seville last year. She says the men are being taken directly to the market stalls. Male slaves only have to be strong, you see? Thorvald gets a better price for the females when they are rested and bathed and have been well-fed for a day or two."

"Ask her if she can find out if a lad named Matthew was

among today's new arrivals—Matthew Stewardson," Maida asked anxiously.

Edan did so. "She says some of the more trusted, older thralls run errands between the longhouse and the market. If you like, she'll ask one of the men to find out for you?"

"Tell her I would be most grateful. Alas, I have nothing to give for her help."

Leya smiled shyly, said she had no need of payment, but would let Maida know what she discovered.

When they left the bathhouse a short while later, they saw that Arne and Oleg, the more impatient of Marta's three sons, had wearied of being onlookers. Aroused by the sight of so many nude women, they had decided to sample their father's wares for themselves. To that end, they had each selected a naked girl, slung them over their shoulders, and carried them, screaming, into the hall, leaving their younger brother, Gorm to guard the women.

Terrified that they would be next, Maida, Edan, and Alaine kept their heads down and their eyes averted, as they left the bathhouse. They contrived a means to shield each other from Gorm's hot blue eyes. One held up a soiled mantle as a screen, while the others hurriedly dressed themselves. Their teeth chattered in the cool air, after the hot, steamy atmosphere of the sauna.

Despite everything, Edan had to admit it felt wonderful to be clean again, after so many days without bathing or combing her hair. Wonderful, that was, till Gorm caught her by her wrist, as they were being herded back into the hall by the kitchen entrance.

Jerking her against him, he rasped, " 'Tis not as easy to hide from me as you thought, is it, my beauty? Tonight, you will lay beneath me in my furs. Then I shall take what you hid from me today! You've not had a man in your belly till you've had Gorm Thorvaldson!"

As his hot eyes raked her, Edan's flesh crawled. A sick chill settled in the pit of her belly. Wrenching herself free, she hurried after the others.

"The escape we spoke of, Maida? 'Twill have to be soon,"

she murmured, as they were herded into the kitchens and put to work chopping and cleaning fish and vegetables by the cook. She rubbed her bruised wrist. She could still feel the pressure of Gorm's cruel fingers there, but his threat had left an even deeper wound.

"Aye, I heard him, the bastard," Maida acknowledged, rolling her eyes sympathetically. "Do you have a plan, my lady?"

"I do," she admitted. "But to carry it out, perforce handsome Gorm Thorvaldson must share his furs with *two* wenches, not one."

"Two? Then why not three?" Alaine chimed in, her dark eyes, usually so far away, brightening.

Though she had submitted to Thorvald for reasons of her own, she seemed determined to escape and, was far from being cowed by her capture, Edan thought, and frowned. It was as if Alaine had some secret, burning reason to survive that the others did not.

"Dear Alaine, three's even better! So, are ye game to join me?" She tried to keep the anxiety from her voice. It was a great deal to ask of anyone. Gorm might ravish them all, perhaps even kill them! She could not fault Maida or Alaine, if they refused.

But to her relief, Maida grinned. "My lady, the pleasure will be . . . ours!"

"Aye—and ours alone, God willing!" Alaine agreed, with a naughty smile of her own.

Chapter Nineteen

That night, the rafters in Thorvald's hall rang with the well-wishes of his companions and crew. They drank to their successful raid, and to the fine cargo that would make them all as rich as Byzantine kings on the morrow. The *skalds* sang *sagas* of their bravery, likening their deeds to those of the old Norse gods.

Wine, mead, and beer flowed like water. Before long, those who had imbibed too freely were sprawled on the rushes under the tables with the hunting hounds, or else slumped over the earthen benches that lined the walls, snoring loudly.

As the night grew older, the boasts and the challenges grew more outrageous, more dangerous. Each of the young men tried to outdo the other in feats of bravery or skill.

An axe-throwing contest came and went. Two fingers, an ear, and many bets were lost, before a blind man—nicknamed Hod, after the blind man who had slain the god, Balder the Beautiful—was declared the victor.

Amidst much laughter, bawdy jests, and drunken cheering, poor, bewildered Hod was led to Thorvald, who awarded him a golden amulet cast in the likeness of Mjollnir, Thor's hammer.

''You, wench, over here! Feel the hammer between my legs,

by Loki! 'Tis even bigger and harder than Mjollnir!'' a man named Nils boasted, reaching out to pinch her buttocks.

Edan's temper snapped. Each time she'd scooped a foaming measure of beer from the beer vat, and carried it—slopping suds—to a feaster this evening, he had taken it without so much as a grunt of thanks, then fondled or pinched her breasts and buttocks, as if she had less dignity than a dumb beast. Something inside her snapped, as Nils's fingers closed painfully over her flesh. Being forced to wait on Thorvald's guests, and to serve them whatever they desired—even if what they desired was herself!—was the final humiliation. She was no thrall, but a princess of Britain! She would tolerate this no longer!

Just then, the same huge Dane, draped in smelly bearskins, reached beneath her homespun tunic and gave her another cruel pinch on the buttocks. His fingers hurt so, the blood drained from her face.

"Take your hands off me, you filthy old goat. Touch me again, I'll scratch your cursed eyes out!" she spat, rounding on him. Although dressed in the white tunic of a thrall, which reached only to mid-calf, and stripped of all costly ornaments, she was every inch a Saxon princess at that moment, proud of bearing, her chin carried high, her gray eyes flashing.

Chuckling, the man leered and threatened, "Goat, you say? Well, goat or nay, you will do as I say, slave! Down on your knees!" he bellowed, heaving himself to standing and unfastening his breeks. "Up with your skirts, wench!"

But, before he could free himself, she flung the foaming beer into his face and whirled away, hoping to lose herself in the crowded hall, while he wiped his stinging eyes. He was deeply in his cups. There was a slim chance he might forget her.

"Come back here, you insolent slut. I'll teach you your place! By Loki, you'll not throw beer in Nils's eyes and get away with it! Stop that thrall, you fools!"

The noisy hall suddenly fell silent, as Nils overturned the trestle before him with a resounding crash, hurling bowl and platter, flagon and beaker to the straw-covered floor. With a great roar, he heaved himself to his feet and stood there, swaying from side to side, like one of the great white bears from the far reaches of the snowbound north.

As he took a lumbering step forward, then another, the wenches and young men, who'd been dancing to the music of drums and horns, parted, giving Nils an uncluttered view of his quarry. She was standing at the far end of the smoky hall with her back pressed to a wooden post, one of two rows of such posts that supported the roof of the longhouse.

"Come here, slut!" Nils commanded again, beckoning her with a long, thick finger.

"Hel take thee, sirrah! My dam was of the noble house of Danehof. My sire is a prince of Britain and has the ear of the high-king himself. My lord-husband is . . . *was* . . . a prince of Ireland," she said proudly, her voice breaking. She tossed her hair over her shoulder. "I will die, before I serve his murderers aught but the bitter dregs of my vengeance!"

A murmur of approval rippled through the crowd. The Vikings admired courage, wherever it might be found. And the female thrall was brave, indeed, to defy a longhouse filled to the rafters with her captors! Still, it was not hard to believe the slender beauty, who held herself so proudly before them, had the blood of princes in her veins. Even in her thrall's tunic, she possessed a queenly air, one that Thorvald, eyes narrowing, took note of.

"Princess or peasant, you'll serve me on your back!" Nils threatened, leering as he took a step toward her.

"*Ja?* Well, ye'll have to catch me first, old man," Edan taunted, fists on hips like a fishwife now. "Come on! What are you waiting for? Yuletide?"

With a bearlike cough of rage, Nils charged.

She stood her ground till the last second, then nimbly side stepped him.

Unable to swerve in his momentum, Nils barrelled headfirst into the wooden post and cracked his forehead.

The Danes, who enjoyed nothing better than a good jest, roared with laughter as their countryman—cross-eyed and dazed—staggered about in circles, looking for his agile quarry, who had scampered to the far end of the hall.

Edan let them think that she was only trying to put distance between herself and the Dane, but if there had been a way out that was not blocked by feasters, she would have taken it and fled into the night. As it was, the longhouse had but one door, and that was at the far end. She had little choice but to turn and face Nils.

"Ah ha! I see you there!" he bellowed. Clearly, he had learned nothing from his first mistake, for he put his head down and charged the length of the hall toward her once again, like a bull charging a red mantle.

A heartbeat before he reached her, she hopped up onto the nearest trestle and, running past him, went down it to the farthest end, skipping between flagons and platters as she went.

Not to be outdone, Nils also heaved himself up, onto the trestle. He lumbered after her like an angry bear, taking great strides that were twice the length of her own, and clumsily squashing bread loaves, fruits, and fingers underfoot as he went. Several other small fights arose between him and those who did not care to have his hairy boots in their supper, *takke,* and protested loudly!

The onlookers howled with delight at this fine entertainment and made bets as to the outcome.

When Edan reached the end of the trestle, she sprang lightly to the ground, thankful for the freedom of a short tunic and bare feet. Breathing heavily, she cast about her, not knowing where to run next.

Maida's familiar voice hissed from the shadows, "My lady, this way! Quickly!"

Grateful, Edan dived into the shadows after Maida. She hurried after her down the long, narrow passage that led from the feast hall to the paved porch of the longhouse. They could hear Nils puffing and blowing at their backs, as he tried to catch up with them.

"Quickly, quickly!" Maida rasped. "He's coming!"

"The horses!" Edan panted. "Once we're outside, make a run for the horses!—"

But, it was not to be. As they burst from the hall into the starlit night, they ran headfirst into the arms of none other than

Gorm, Thorvald and Marta's youngest son, returning from a visit to the outhouse.

"Well, well, my dark beauty," he taunted, catching Edan about the waist with one arm and Maida with the other. "And you, too, my golden peach! Looking for Gorm, were you?" He grinned, as their faces paled. "Never fear, my hot little bitches. I was about to come and find you. You will both share my furs soon enough!"

"Let go of her, whelp! Take the golden one, if ye will— but the black-haired bitch is mine!" roared Nils, exploding from the longhouse behind them.

"*Nej.* She belongs to my father," Gorm denied, with a disdainful smirk. "A special purchase for a *very* special customer! He'd sooner give her to his hounds before he gave her to you, old man, so—go drown your sorrows in beer! Tonight, she'll have a young and lusty stallion riding her, not an impotent old walrus!"

Nils snorted in contempt. "Breach her maidenhead and she's ruined for a Moor's harem, if that's what you're thinking!"

Gorm's upper lip curled in a sneer. He grinned. Nils was more clever than he appeared. "Let me worry about that, eh, old man? As for you two!—" He grinned and licked fleshy red lips in anticipation. "You come along with me, my lovely bitches! Tell me, which of ye will be first, eh?" Gripping Edan's wrist in one hand and Maida's in the other, he dragged the struggling women back into the hall.

The bower he led them into adjoined the great hall and was apparently Gorm's own quarters. As one of Thorvald's grown sons, he no longer slept in the hall with the other men of the household.

A carved wooden box bed dominated the chamber, strewn with fur pelts and cushions of satin from the markets of the east. Wide enough for two, such a magnificent piece of furniture usually belonged to a lord and his lady.

Beeswax candles, set in heavy bronze candlesticks, burned in every corner, casting their soft golden glow over the bower. A brace of chests stood in one corner, garments spilling untidily from them.

Leering, Gorm yanked off his tunic and breeches, revealing a broad chest matted with curly ginger hair, hairy muscular arms, a hairy back, a hairier white backside, huge hairy thighs like hams, and an erection the size of a small spear jutting out from muscular, hairy loins.

Chuckling at the way the women's eyes widened in alarm, as he strutted across the room, he threw himself down across the couch and boasted, "So. Is your master not a stallion? When I am done, you will know ye've had a man, by Loki. Both of you, make haste! Strip, then come here!"

Edan and Maida exchanged glances. Maida gave a barely perceptible nod, then Edan lifted her short tunic up, over her head.

Beneath it, she was unclothed. Inky rivers of curling hair spilled to her waist over skin the color of rose petals and snow. Her creamy breasts were surmounted with buds like luscious raspberries.

Gorm was fairly drooling, as he gaped at her—and she gave him every opportunity to gape.

Maida's fairness was the perfect contrast to Edan's raven-haired beauty. Her thick hair was almost as long as Edan's, but fell straight to her buttocks. Its color was the reddish-gold of silky corn tassels, and gleamed in the mellow light. While Edan's breasts were small and firm as peaches, Maida's were the lush, ripe globes of cantaloupes, with nipples as large and as round as grapes. Her hips were broad and lush, made for the joys of passion and for the bearing of many children. A red-gold triangle surmounted her mons, in sharp contrast to the milky pallor of her skin.

The sight of this magnificent pair parading, naked yet proud, before him, shielding neither their pretty breasts nor their curly little mounds with their hands, fuelled Gorm's lust. His man-hood bucked amidst the golden thatch at his groin, throbbing with his desire. "You, wench! You first," he commanded hoarsely, beckoning to Edan. "Come here!"

Another intense glance flashed between her and Maida, then Edan obediently padded to the bed and sat down beside Gorm. Straightway, he grasped her neck, then ground his mouth down over hers, squeezing her breast in one huge hand as he did so. He tore his wet lips from Edan's just long enough to tell Maida, "Watch, my peach. Watching will heat your blood and make you ready for me."

Pressing Edan onto her back, he flung himself across her, his weight pinning her to the pallet. With a grunt, he forced her thighs apart with his knee, then roughly lodged himself between them. Gripping her wrists, he held them above her head in one huge paw, admiring the thrust of her breasts as he drew back, and prepared to enter her in one hard thrust.

"Oh, *master!*—" Maida cried suddenly, her voice shrill with alarm. "Master, *behind you!*—"

Chapter Twenty

Even knowing it was the oldest ploy in the world, Gorm could not resist the impulse to look!

As he turned his head, he saw not one other wench, but *two*—a swirl of brown hair, a glimpse of a shapely breast— then something heavy crashed across the back of his skull.

That "something heavy" was one of the weighty bronze candlesticks, deftly wielded by Alaine! A second thwack from another, wielded by Maida, and with a grunt, Gorm slumped forward across Edan, out cold.

"Not a moment too soon! My thanks, both of you!" Edan muttered with feeling, as she squirmed from beneath Gorm's senseless body and slipped her tunic back on. "Now, let's go!"

"Not so fast, my lady!" Maida protested. "If we leave that lout here like this, he'll raise the alarm, once he comes to. What shall we do?"

"Kill him?" Alaine suggested, with a bloodthirsty grin.

"I say we tie him up and gag him," Edan suggested, casting Alaine an admonishing look. To kill an enemy in the heat of combat was one thing. Cold-blooded murder was quite another.

Between the three of them, it was no sooner said than done. Gorm was quickly trussed like a boar, his wrists and ankles lashed firmly with strips of sealskin to the four wooden bed-posts, his mouth stuffed with one of his own—somewhat aromatic—woolen hose.

"There! That should hold him. And if it doesn't, the smell will surely kill him! Come. Let's be away, before someone comes!"

"Wait! We won't get far in these white tunics. Let's take some of Gorm's clothes."

"Good idea!"

"You two go ahead. 'Twould be impossible for me to pass for a man," Maida said, ruefully indicating her lush bosom, as the other two women dragged garments from the overflowing wooden chests in the corner and quickly pulled them on.

"Very well. Throw on this mantle, and you can be our thrall," Edan suggested, twisting her hair up and pulling the hood of a russet mantle down, to hide it. "How do I look, wench?" she demanded in a gruff tone, affecting an arrogant, hands-on-hips male swagger.

"Comely as any woman, master," Maida approved, with a grin. "As do you, Alaine."

" 'Tis Master Alan to you, wench. Or 'sir'. *Not* Alaine," Alaine growled, casting a dark scowl at Maida.

Just then, their prisoner stirred. Discovering himself bound and gagged, he screamed impotently through his stocking gag, his furious eyes promising Hel to pay, should he ever get loose, as he strained against the sealskin ropes to free himself. Indeed, so furious were his efforts, his face turned a livid purple. His large ginger-furred body arched up from the bed, then went rigid, as his jaws clenched with his efforts to break his bonds, before going slack again.

"Ye gods! What I would give for a harpoon!" Alaine declared, prodding Gorm's belly with the tip of his own sword.

Hands clamped over their mouths, the three women giggled.

"Come on, you two! Enough play. We'll lose our chance to escape if we linger," Edan urged, leading the way from the bower.

Swallowing nervous laughter, the other two followed her out.

To their relief, the passage proved empty, the only sentinel being an ancient graybeard, dozing up against a wall of the porch, with a gnarled wooden staff propped in his slackened fingers. Sour beer fumes surrounded him.

They tiptoed past him and came out again into the starlit cool of the night. Edan turned to the right.

"Not that way, lovie! Like as not, we'll meet some beer-sodden lout on his way back from pissing, like Gorm!" hissed Maida. "This way!"

They headed left, circling the longhouse where the horses were pastured. They had not gone far, however, when an outraged roar arose from the main building, splintering the night asunder:

"Those daughters of Hel! After them, you spleenless whelps!"

That was Thorvald's voice.

Then, *"Find them, you lily-livered sons of Loki!"*

Surely that was Thorvald, too?

Then, *"By Odin, I'll sell the lot of them to the filthiest brothel in Constantinople!"*

Now, that was definitely Thorvald!

They did not wait to see who came searching for them. On the contrary, they had a feeling they already knew!

"Run!" hissed Edan.

And run they did, taking to their heels and pouring out into the darkened streets, scampering toward the forest of masts that indicated that part of the town which faced the stone breakwater and the lading wharves.

When they reached the point where they had turned left that morning, they saw sentries at the tunnel gates. They were squatting in a puddle of torchlight, laughing as they threw bone dice and wagered on the outcome of their throws. There was no way past them without being spotted.

The three women hastily pulled up short and turned right, instead, running till the stone-paved roads and the thick wall both miraculously gave out. There were no longhouses here—nor, come to that, any buildings at all! Rather, there was a broad, flat field of sere, bleached sea grasses from which low mounds rose, one after the other, each roughly boat-shaped in the moonlight. The illusion of beached boats was added to by the washing sounds of the restless sea close by—the only sounds that broke the hush.

"Blessed God in Heaven, where are we?" Maida asked, looking apprehensively around her. She crossed herself. "In truth, I care not for this place!"

" 'Tis a cemetery," Alaine murmured calmly, sitting down with her back against a twisted tree trunk.

"Good enough," Edan decided, also finding herself a comfortable place to sit. "We can halt for a while and decide what to do next. One thing is for certain. That superstitious lot will not come looking for us here till daylight!"

"Do you not fear ghosts?" Maida whispered, looking nervously about, as if she expected one to materialize in broad daylight.

She shook her head. "My mother says 'tis the living we must fear, not the dead. They, poor souls, have gone beyond harming anyone. And she should know, if anyone!"

"Why do you say that?"

"Because she saw the ghost of my Danish grandmother, the Lady Verdandi, when my brother and I were yet babes. It spoke to her and rocked our cradles."

Maida crossed herself, horrified but curious. "What did it say?"

"It warned her that a dear friend had been chosen by the Valkyries to die in battle."

"And did he?"

"Yea."

"Paggh! It said nothing of the sort," Alaine argued goodnaturedly. "It said 'Get some sleep, for but in a short while, you must move on!' " she declared.

They slept for a while then, huddled on the damp ground amongst the grave mounds, with only their mantles to keep them warm.

Soon after she fell asleep, Edan slipped into a dream. In it, she saw Kerrin. He was standing on the banks of a river, black hair furling on the wind, beckoning her to come to him. Her heart swelled with joy. A great shout broke from her lips. He had not been killed, after all! He was alive!

Eagerly, she ran down to the river and leaped into the water, only to find she was in over her head.

The river was broad, its current was swift, its flow was icy and treacherous. Moreover, weeds and mud sucked at her limbs, threatening to drag her beneath the surface, as she fought her way to the far banks.

She was exhausted by the time she struggled out onto the other side, her arms outstretched to Kerrin, yearning to hold him, to kiss him. But—in the instant before her hand grazed his cheek—he dissolved, like a reflection in a pool vanishes when the water's surface is disturbed by a pebble.

"*Kerrin, my love!*" she cried. "*Come back!*"

It was then that she sensed movement in the forest before her and glimpsed the figure of a man flitting between the trees, lean gray shadows slipping after him.

The man was Kerrin—she knew it!

Still cold and shivering from her swim, she summoned her flagging strength and started after him, weaving her way in and out of a seemingly endless forest of lofty trees, whose branches met above her in a tangled tapestry that blotted out the sky. As she went, she had to fight twigs and thorns that scored her face and caught in her hair. A weird, greenish-gray light leeched everything of color. It was neither full day nor true night here, but somewhere eerily in between. . . .

"*Kerrin!*" Catching sight of him between the trees, she ran after him, ran as hard and as fast as she could, twisting and turning through the maze of trees, not caring when branches snagged her kirtle and tore pieces from it.

At last, to her delight, she caught up with him and knotted her fingers in his mantle, holding fast to it, while he struggled desperately to escape her. But—as he had done the last time— he began to change form in her hands. The cloth of his mantle roughened, becoming a silky black pelt, a magnificent ruff. And, as he turned to face her, she saw the baleful sulfur sheen of his eyes and recoiled, crossing herself.

"*God in Heaven, what are you?*" she heard herself cry, just as Thorvald had demanded in that instant before he killed Kerrin:

"*What are you?*—"

"*What are you?*—"

Then she heard a scream—a high-pitched, furious squall that she thought was her own: one that echoed over and over through the labyrinth of her mind, as she fought her way up from the realm of dreams, to waking. . . .

"What was that?" Maida whispered, hastily sitting up. She seemed not to notice that Edan was pale and shivering beside her.

The cry rose again, wailing above the sea sounds. She swallowed, still shaken. The cry had not been a part of her dream, after all, she thought. It was quite real—and frantic. "Mating cats?" she suggested, rubbing her hands together to warm them. She pulled the stolen mantle close about her shoulders, troubled by the contents of her frightening dream. What did it foretell? Was this more of the misfortune Mother Myrla had foreseen in the runes? If only Kerrin had let the old woman finish her prophesies that night!—

"Edan?"

"What is it?"

"That sound! I cannot believe it was cats."

"A wounded seal, then?"

Alaine shook her head dreamily. "Neither, my friends. 'Tis a babe!"

"A baby! What would a baby be doing out here?"

"I know I'm right." There was a closed, stubborn expression on her face that they had never seen before. "See? 'Tis Galen! His cry made the milk flow from my breasts, bless him!"

Stunned and confused, they both saw a spreading wet circle on the front of Alaine's tunic as she stood, brushed herself off, then began running across the cemetery towards the beach, which lay beyond a ridge of dunes.

"Come back! You don't know what's down there, little fool!" Edan called after her, but Alaine ignored her calls.

Resigned, she and Maida followed her at a more cautious pace.

As they crested the rise, they saw Alaine standing on the sand, ankle-deep in lapping gray water. The rising sun was painting the sky with saffron, pink, and lavender, and touching her brown hair with glints of gold. Alaine was smiling, her face radiant, as she looked down at the red-faced, screaming infant cradled in her arms, which was flailing its little pink arms and legs about.

"Look you, my friends!" she cried as they approached. " 'Tis my wee son, Galen, just as I said! The sea has brought him safely back to his mother. Smile for your aunties, my darling," she cooed, gently bouncing the squalling, naked babe to soothe its cries, while she opened the neck of her tunic and bared a breast to nurse it.

Edan and Maida exchanged startled glances as the child— a little girl—latched her mouth eagerly onto Alaine's nipple and began to suckle, uttering little gasps and contented sucking sounds.

"Did she tell you she'd lost a child?" Edan whispered, husky-voiced with emotion.

Tears filling her own eyes, Maida nodded. "Aye, but only after a fashion. She told me she had a newborn son, and that she'd sent him to safety when the Vikings first attacked her hamlet. I thought—I thought she'd sent him to her kinsman, look you, but now!—"

"You think Thorvald's men . . . ?"

Maida nodded, unable to speak.

Edan swallowed. Tears smarted behind her eyes, as she silently marvelled at the diverse paths grief could take. Maida had lost her husband, Hugh, before her very eyes. She did not know the fate of her young son, the novitiate, Matthew, but she had gritted her teeth and gone on nonetheless, grimly determined to survive. Una had cast herself into the sea, rather than face the uncertainty of another tomorrow. As for herself, she had been numb at first, but was learning to carry on, to endure one day at a time, despite the terrible, bruising pain of her loss, thanks to Maida's timely intervention. And Alaine—well, Alaine had surely seen her infant son tossed into the sea and left to drown like an unwanted kitten. Unable to bear what she had seen, her grieving mind had supplied an explanation that was far less painful for a mother to bear. And now, "her" baby had returned to her by the sea that had taken it from her. "But, where *did* the child come from?" she whispered.

Maida shrugged. "Who knows? But my Hugh used t'say that Vikings threw their unwanted babes into the sea."

Edan looked down at the darling little girl cradled in Alaine's protective arms. Her pretty elfin face was capped with silky brown curls, her eyes were tightly closed as she nursed. *Dear God, to lose something so utterly perfect and priceless!*— How had Alaine managed to keep her hold on sanity, however tenuous? Had the child been her own, she thought with a pang of longing, she would have gone quite mad at its loss. . . .

"My lady, *look!*"

Jerked back to the moment with a rude jolt, Edan looked over her shoulder and saw dark figures with a cart on the rise above them, jabbering excitedly to each other and pointing in their direction.

Clearly, word of their escape had quickly circulated through the market town, reaching even those who had come here to bury their dead.

"Come on! We must hide!" Edan hissed. Taking Alaine by the elbow to chivvy her along, the three women hastened down the narrow, shingled beach.

In truth, there were few places to hide, now that dawn had broken. The shore was quite flat, save for clumps of tall grass that grew in the sandy soil above the water line and a few scattered rocks. The beach was likewise unbroken—save for a wrecked dragon-ship half-buried in the sand about a hundred tailor's lengths from where they were standing! It had been cast ashore, wrong-side up, then came to rest in the sand with its ribs partially exposed, like the carcass of a beached whale.

"In there?" Maida asked.

"What choice do with have? It's either the wreck, or back to the town! Come on! There's a slim chance they might think we got away by sea, somehow. We'll hide here till it gets dark, then try again. . . ."

But their former good fortune had abandoned them.

Some time later, huddled under the shattered timbers of the wreck, they heard the shouts of Thorvald, Gorm, Arne, and Oleg as they searched the dunes for them. The sounds of their loud, harsh voices grew louder and louder as they rode closer, filling the women with mounting terror.

"Keep very quiet. They are close," Edan whispered, peering through a chink in the wreck's bows.

Alaine seemed not to understand their position. She cuddled the babe against her, swathed in Gorm's stolen mantle, and crooned softly to it. Her little eyes were closed, tiny, tawny lashes curled against flushed cheeks, rosebud lips hungrily rooting for the lost nipple.

Thorvald and his sons reined in their horses only a short distance from their hiding place. Edan held her breath, too frightened to breathe. Fists on hips, the Danish chieftain looked up and down the beach. "The men were wrong. We are too late. They have gone."

"Gone! They are but women, sir! They cannot have run far. 'Tis but a short time since they were sighted."

"Mayhap the wreck, Father?" Gorm suggested. He looked, Edan thought—her heart thundering, beating so loudly and so violently, it seemed it would surely burst from her chest— decidedly unsteady on his feet. He was also markedly greenish about the gills. Surely his cracked skull must be paining him, as he added, " 'Tis the only place to hide hereabouts!"

"The wreck? Pagghh! Those crafty sluts are too clever for such an obvious trick!" Thorvald denied. "*Nej,* my sons! That black-haired vixen has thought of another way. . . ." he added thoughtfully, his tone one of grudging pride, as he stroked his bushy black beard.

Edan crossed her fingers and signalled for Maida to do likewise. Blessed God be thanked, the Danes were moving away, riding on, down the beach, their horses' hooves throwing huge clods of wet sand up behind them!—

They were almost out of earshot, when the baby awoke, opened her mouth very wide, and gave a loud and carrying wail. . . .

Chapter Twenty-One

The Hedeby market boasted traders from all four corners of the known world. The Scandinavian merchants who sold their wares there claimed that everything under the sun could be purchased in Hedeby for a price, whether a man's heart's desire was precious amber, coveted for its magical powers; or beeswax; exquisite silks and brocades; Rhennish wines; costly furs such as sables, martens and white squirrels; or even exotic beasts. By far the most valuable commodity to be found there, however, was slaves, in particular the golden-haired, blue-eyed, ivory-skinned females taken from the cold northern lands.

Such women were highly prized in the harems and brothels of Constantinople—Queen of the Bosporus, City of Mosques! —to the east. Indeed, Arab and Moorish slave masters had been known to pay a fortune in gold and jewels for a particularly lovely slave girl who could win them a sultan's favor. It was just such a slave master Thorvald the Black was hoping to attract with the live cargo he had stolen from Walas.

To that end, he sent his sons down to the breakwater early the following morning to welcome the vessels that had arrived with the morning tide.

Meanwhile, he and his *godi*, his house priest, sacrificed a young boar in Njord's name, for he brought riches to the sea-farer. Afterward, the carcass was hung from a pole outside his longhouse to attract good fortune.

Many other Danes had come to Hedeby to sell their cargoes of slaves and plunder, taken from the Loire and Seine valleys of Gaul. Thorvald wanted his slaves to be the first to catch the eye of the wealthiest Turk!

"Make way for the Great One! Make way for my Lord Kadar ibn Kalil, Exalted Slave Master of Istanbul. Step aside, you Danish dung beetles! Clear a path for the All Powerful, the Omnipotent One, Kadar ibn Kalil, favored of Allah!" bellowed a huge, clean-shaven older man. Dressed in a turban of deep blue silk and sporting a golden ring in one ear, the fellow was bare chested, save for a sleeveless waistcoat of brocade and baggy breeks tucked into boots of soft leather. The man strode before his master, staff in hand, clearing the street with his bellows and his imposing air.

"Thanks be to Odin! I smell gold coming down the street!" Thorvald chuckled, gleefully rubbing his hands together. "Stay here, watch and learn, but keep your mouths shut, my sons!" he ordered Arne, Oleg, and Gorm. To his steward, he murmured, "Have the slaves make ready!" Then, hands clasped over his great belly, the Viking swaggered forward to meet the splendidly robed Turkish flesh merchant, Kadar ibn Kalil, making a deep bow, as the exalted foreigner halted before his stall.

The merchant was robed in flowing midnight blue silk with borders of gold thread embroidery. The folds billowed about him in the morning breeze. A length of the same fabric was wound about the crown of his tall cap several times, like a turban. The free end had been draped across his lower face, hiding all but his burning eyes. Beneath the mantle, he wore an embroidered brocade caftan patterned in blood red and dark blue, shot through with gold threads. Full silken breeches of a burgundy hue were tucked into tall boots of supple black kid. At his side, thrust into a belt of embroidered leather, curved a gleaming scimitar with a jewelled hilt. The damascened blade shone like a silvery crescent of moonlight. Upon his gloved fist rode a pure white falcon, its dainty head hidden beneath a jewelled hood of soft crimson suede. Leather jesses finished with tiny, tinkling silver bells adorned its talons.

In startling contrast, the small woman who stood behind the Turkish lord was dowdy beyond belief—a veritable peahen compared to that glorious peacock!—for she was robed from head to foot in dusty black, like an aging raven. There was but a small opening left in the front of the tentlike garment, so that she could see just enough to walk. Although she was virtually invisible, she nevertheless kept her head modestly bowed.

Thorvald hid a snort of disgust. These Turks! He had yet to discover if their women were so lovely, they must be hidden from the sight of other men, for fear they would drive them mad with lust—or so hideously ugly, all men would weep in pity for the poor Turks who were forced to take them to their furs—or wherever it was the Turks mated their women!

"May the gods's blessings be upon ye, fine sir!" Thorvald declared.

"And may Allah smile upon thee, Dane," the man rejoined in accented Danish, touching his palm to his brow. He drew aside the cloth that covered his lower face, baring a square, black-bearded jaw and a silky black moustache. *"Salaam alei-kum.* Peace be unto you."

"And upon you, lord!" Thorvald greeted the merchant, beaming expansively. "And may I compliment you on your mastery of my tongue." The Turk inclined his head, graciously aloof. "Now, my good sir, what is your will? Exquisite crystal from the lands of the Rus? Jet brought from the misty isle of Britain? *Nej, nej,* I fancy 'tis something . . . softer, more pleasing to the touch, that you are after, *ja?"*

The Turk smiled, but the laughter never reached his dark eyes. "You are a clever fellow, Dane," he said softly. "You know the secrets of a man's heart."

Thorvald flashed his sons a smug glance and brayed like a donkey. "Pray, be seated, my lord. Enjoy some refreshment, while my steward brings out the slave girls. They are of the finest quality, sir, as you will see, and all but one is untouched, as pure as the driven snow. . . ."

"Do not lie to me, Dane," Kadar ibn Kalil murmured. "For

if you do, I shall slice the false tongue from your mouth and feed it to my falcon, bit by bit.''

"*Er. . . . Almost* untouched,'' Thorvald amended hastily, paling under the Turk's unwinking stare. The man was tall and of lean, wiry build. He was by far the bigger man, and yet . . . there was something about the merchant that struck fear even in Thorvald's cruel heart. "You, steward! The women!'' he roared.

The Turk reclined upon a low couch draped with furs that Thorvald's thralls set before him. He idly partook of the foaming goblet of warm milk served him by Marta the Tall, while his diminutive wife stood behind him on his right, unseated, ignored and unrefreshed, her hands clasped before her, her head bowed, as patient and silent as an ox.

One by one, both wrists fettered together by a short length of chain, the captive women were paraded before the slave master in turn. From time to time, the Turk would indicate that he wished a woman to turn. At others, he would stand and make a closer inspection for himself, examining a girl's teeth, running his hand down her legs to see if she was sound, or walking slowly around her. His inspection concluded, he would shake his head to the steward and resume his seat. Then, with a bored gesture, he would command the man to bring out the next girl.

When Maida was led out, a ripple of interest passed through the marketgoers. Many passersby stopped at Thorvald's stall to watch the proceedings, as the steward made the full-breasted, flaxen-haired wench turn, then tilted her chin and inspected her teeth. She made no attempt to resist his touch, but she did scowl at him, her brown eyes consigning him to the regions of Hel.

"How many summers have you, my fair one?'' the Turk asked, taking over the examination for himself.

Reluctantly, she told him.

"And how many little ones did you bear your husband, before your capture?''

"Three.''

"There! You see! A good breeder! And she is lovely, is she

not, my lord?'' Thorvald murmured ingratiatingly, hurrying forward. ''A golden beauty worth many mancuses! Would you like to see her naked? She has wonderful breasts—like pillows!''

Ignoring the chieftain as if he were vermin, unworthy of his notice, Kadar ibn Kalil swept past the man and returned to his couch. Resuming his seat, he indicated with a bored flourish that the steward should bring out the next girl.

''What!'' Thorvald blanched, unable to believe what he was seeing. The Turk was dismissing the golden-haired goddess! Odin had surely abandoned him, despite the generous sacrifice he had made in his name! Kalil had shown no interest whatsoever in the cream of his cargo!

But, as the steward was leading the girl away, the merchant's wife ducked her head and murmured something in her husband's ear.

Her husband sighed heavily, then lifted his hand, as if the effort was too much trouble. ''Wait, steward! My concubine is taken with the blond houri. She is too old for my master's harem, but . . . ! My little Barakah has set her heart upon having the golden-haired woman as a nursemaid for our little ones. How much, Dane?''

Thorvald named an optimistic price.

The merchant snorted. ''Surely you jest, Dane?''

''But . . . it is a fair price, my lord!''

''Fair? Thief! Rogue! It is robbery! You are a greedy fellow, Dane. A jackal in the guise of a man! The woman is lovely, but she is no longer young. Her flesh has lost the firmness of youth. Moreover, she has been well-used by her husband and has borne several children. You will not find a place for her in any harem in Constantinople, my friend. May Allah strike me if I do not speak truly! The best you can hope for is to sell her to one of the brothels in Istanbul. Next, steward!''

''Wait, my lord. Did you not say your woman was taken with the wench?''

Again the woman whispered in her lord's ear.

''She leaves the decision to me. I will pay thee . . .'' He named a price. ''Take it or leave it, 'tis my final offer.''

"By Loki, there is more than one robber at this market today, my lord Kadil!" sputtered Thorvald.

"And more than one fair-skinned wench, by Allah!" The Turk smiled thinly and rose. "Come, Barakah. We will look elsewhere—"

"Sold!" Thorvald bellowed in desperation. "By Odin, you strike a hard bargain, my lord—a very hard bargain, indeed! But, sold!"

The Turk inclined his head to seal the agreement, gesturing the steward to give the slave woman into the keeping of his bodyguard. "Have you no younger women in your cargo, Dane?" Kadil cut him off. "Or must I examine the cargo of another trader?"

Thorvald frowned. "There is a wench of high blood who might interest you, my lord, but . . ."

"But what?"

"I was thinking I might wed her to one of my sons."

"*Ja.* To me!" Gorm cut in, with an evil grin, rubbing the lumps on his head. "And I'll tame the spiteful witch, too, by Loki!" he snarled.

"Shut your mouth, you loose-lipped donkey!" Thorvald whispered hoarsely. "The Turk will want nothing to do with a slave who seeks to brain her master, however comely!"

"Is she then so fair, this deadly maiden?" the merchant asked, his dark eyes igniting with interest. He had clearly caught their aside.

"No maiden, alas, but a young widow of eighteen years. And she is not deadly at all, my lord! Merely a little . . . headstrong. And very proud! She is of royal blood, you see? A daughter of the house of Alaric, prince of Kent, from the isle of Britain."

"A princess, you say? But so they all claim! Tell me, her hair, is it golden?"

"Alas, *nej,* my lord. 'Tis glossy as jet and falls to her waist in coils of midnight. Her eyes are light—the color of spindrift, but!—" He frowned. "'Tis not her beauty alone that makes a man's root harden with lust for her."

"Nay? What is it, then, trader? Has she special knowledge of the erotic arts?"

"*Nej,* my lord—or at least, none that I know of! 'Tis her defiant spirit! She makes a man want to tame her, to make her his own, above all else! And, although a captive, she remains wilful and undaunted. Twice, she has fled my household," he exaggerated, "only to be brought back, fighting and spitting like a wild cat both times. I have threatened her with the lash, yet she is still not cowed, my lord! Aahh, what grandsons such a firebrand would give me! They would be warriors for the *skalds* to sing of, by Loki"

"Indeed? Then I would not dream of stealing such a treasure from thee, Dane."

"Then again, nothing has been decided upon as yet, my lord . . ." Thorvald cut in hurriedly. "The vixen will not come cheaply, but . . . she can be bought."

"Very well, then. I will see her. Who knows? She may serve my purpose. Have your steward bring her forth, Dane. My master, the caliph, grows old. At seventy winters, his root is slower to harden than it was in the days of his youth. Such a fiery beauty as you've described would heat his blood. And the battle to tame her would arouse his passions more than the costliest aphrodisiac!" The merchant smiled thinly, stroking the falcon's hooded head. The bird uttered little throaty noises of affection in return, before he handed it back to his bodyguard. "Of course, I would have been prepared to pay more, were she flaxen-haired, but . . ." He shrugged. "It costs nothing to look, eh, Dane?"

"*Nej,* my lord Kalil. Not a penny! I will have her brought out."

"You! On your feet."

She shot the guard a murderous glance, then swore at him in Saxon. Despite his command, she remained curled on the straw, hugging her knees, her head turned away. She refused to look at him, or rather, dare not, for she knew she would give way to the tears that were aching to burst free, if she did.

After they had been dragged back to Thorvald's longhouse the day before, they had been chained hand and foot, soundly cuffed, then thrown into the byre. Gorm had sulkily demanded that they be stripped and whipped within an inch of their lives for the hurts they had done him and for daring to escape, but Thorvald had refused to have his finest merchandise marked in any way.

Telling Gorm he was a fool and had only himself to blame for the ills that had befallen him, he'd ordered the women taken away. To her and Maida's surprise, he had allowed Alaine to keep the baby girl with her. At the time, they had not known why.

The explanation for his unexpected kindness had been obvious early the following morning, when an escort had arrived from further inland, along with the messenger he had sent.

"God has smiled upon thee, Alaine! You have been sold as wet-nurse for the only child of a powerful Danish lord," the olive-skinned slave girl, Leya, whispered when she brought them the bread and watered beer that was their only food.

Alaine had nodded dreamily, too wrapped up in the doings of the baby to care what the girl said, even had she understood it—which Edan doubted.

Leya had looked at her strangely, then cocked her brows at the women in inquiry.

"She lost her own child when we were captured," Edan had explained in a whisper. "She believes the baby girl she found on the beach yesterday is her son."

"Aaah. *Pobrecita.*" Leya shook her head sympathetically. "Still, your friend will be happy in Jarl Siegfried's household, I think. He is a kinder man than most. As for his woman, the lady Karen is a Christian. She is kindhearted, too. 'Tis said she had almost despaired of giving her husband a child. Then she visited a pagan standing stone in Jutland that was shaped like a man's root. For three days and nights, the lady Karen prayed there and begged the goddess Freya to answer her request. Miracle of miracles, within the year, she found herself growing large with child! She was delivered of a baby boy just two nights hence! Never fear, the lady Karen will be kind to her

new son's wet-nurse, for she has no milk of her own and no
new mothers in her household to suckle him. Mayhap she will
find your friend a husband, when the boy is weaned?''

They could only hope and pray that Leya was right.

''And what of my son, Matthew Stewardson. You said you
would ask after him?''

''I have. But no one by that name was brought here aboard
Arne Thorvaldson's *drakkar.* I am sorry.''

'' 'Tis not your fault,'' Maida had assured her, giving the
girl a smile, but Edan sensed that she was perilously close to
breaking down.

They had been granted only a few moments to make their
farewells, after that. Then Alaine was led away from them.
There had been no need for chains or bonds of any kind. She
had gone willingly with her escort, an older man, and had been
smiling when she left them, while the baby gurgled and cooed
in her arms. And, though they had hugged and kissed her and
wept, she had bid them only a distant farewell.

Afterwards, she and Maida had cried and sworn a pact to
remain together, come what may. But, now Maida was gone,
too. . . .

So it was that, when the guard had told her to stand, she'd
sworn at him—more from fear than anything else—like a desperate, cornered animal turning on its keeper.

Though the guard had not understand her words exactly, her
meaning was plain enough. He scowled blackly. ''You'll be
singing a different tune 'ere long, wench,'' he promised, with
a snicker. ''Off to the brothels of Constantinople you go, slut,
unless I miss my mark! You'll whore for them Turks—or fer
any man with the coin to pay yer master, you'll s—yoowwgh!''

The guard let out a yell, for as he'd bent down to grasp her
wrist and jerk her to her feet, Edan had grasped his nose and
twisted it as hard as she could, then raked her nails down his
cheek, drawing blood.

''Why, you!—'' So saying, he grasped the short length of
chain that was strung between the iron bands about her wrists
and dragged her to standing. ''Scratch me again, I'll have ye
myself before ye leave here—*ja,* and I'm no stupid Gorm

Thorvaldson ye can truss like a captured boar, your cursed Majesty! I promise, ye'll not get past me."

"I'll be sure to tell Gorm what ye said, slug," she purred, silkily. "Since it seems we are to be wed. Think on it, oaf! I might well be your mistress, before long—and then where will you be, hmm?"

The guard scowled, but wisely offered no comment. He had heard the chieftain and the Lady Marta discussing the possibility of Gorm taking the black-haired vixen to wife. Mayhap she knew more than he did? "Come on! Get going—and hurry it up," he growled. "The Turk's not a patient man."

Her face flamed, as the guard gave her over to the steward's care. A circle of spectators had gathered around the open area where Thorvald paraded his live cargo—everything from goats to human beings.

There were Vikings from the northern lands, as well as Danes, Swedes, Norwegians, and Finns. Merchants from Constantinople and Russia all crowded around to watch the goings-on. To watch *her*.

Meanwhile, the eastern merchant the guard had mentioned was reclining comfortably on a folding wooden couch spread with skins. He cut a striking figure in his tall turban headdress, a silk mantle billowing about him on the breeze. To one side of him, his powerful arms crossed over a muscular chest and a brocade jerkin, stood his bodyguard, or servant, a hunting falcon perched upon his wrist. At the servant's feet knelt Maida, while a strange little figure—male or female she could not have said!—stood with one hand resting possessively on her shoulder.

"Surely this woman has been starved," the Turk said softly, rising to his feet and walking slowly around Edan.

Her face burned, as she stood there. Her cheeks flamed crimson under his dark-eyed scrutiny. "I have not!" she retorted before Thorvald could protest.

"Nevertheless, she is too slender for the tastes of my land," the Turk continued, as if she had not spoken. "In my land, a woman is considered beautiful when her buttocks are round and full as a melon and her breasts large and firm as pomegranates."

"If 'tis fruit you want, heathen, then visit the fruit stalls!" Edan hissed.

"Yet, her face is fair, I grant you that much," the Turk continued, as if she had not spoken. "And her eyes and lips are not . . . displeasing."

"In truth, I am honored, lord!" she snapped, her eyes turning a smoldering, smoky hue that belied her words.

The Turk nodded, clearly amused by her angry response. "And so you should be, my dark jewel! Few women are chosen to grace my master's harem. How much, Dane?"

"I thought . . . fifty?"

"By Allah! I am plagued with vultures! Would you have the blood from my veins, too, merchant? The salt from my sweat? *Fifty!* Never! Twenty, no more."

"Forty."

"Attend your mistress, Ali. I will find what I seek elsewhere . . ."

"Wait!"

The Turk paused. "What is it, Dane?"

"Thirty-five and the falcon, and the wench is yours."

"The falcon? Truly, you are touched by madness, Dane! Such a falcon is worth two such scrawny women! Twenty-five."

"Twenty, then—*and* the falcon."

A resigned smile tugged at the merchant's lips. He nodded once, his lips compressed to a thin, emotionless line. "Very well, rogue! You shall have the falcon. Pay Jarl Thorvald's steward, Ali, then take the slaves to my ship."

"As you will, my lord Kadar." The man made his master a deep bow.

"Farewell, little one," the Turk murmured to the falcon, scratching its hooded head. Then his bodyguard handed the beautiful bird over to her new master. "Come, Barakah!" he urged the black-robed woman. "Now that our business is concluded, let us see what delights this Hed-e-by has to offer."

So saying, he made a lordly bow to Thorvald, touching palm to brow and thence to his heart, before striding away, one hand clamped over the hilt of his scimitar, as if the transaction had already been forgotten.

The short woman followed him. In her flowing black robes, she created the impression of a small tent slipping—legless and armless—over the paved street in her husband's wake.

"Well! At least we'll be together," Maida murmured, squeezing Edan's hand. "Are you not happy about that, my lady?"

"I am, very," she agreed, forcing a smile she did not feel. "But . . . I cannot help but wish it were otherwise. Oh, Maida, once we enter the harems of Constantinople, 'twill be as if we were dead! We will never be free again. . . !"

Chapter Twenty-Two

To Edan's surprise, the Turkish merchant's trading vessel was no eastern dhow, but a *drakkar* with a snarling dragon figurehead, very similar to Thorvald's own. Still, it was little wonder that he had chosen to sail the world in a vessel of foreign design, for the Vikings' skill at shipbuilding was well-known. Countless other vessels—both dragon-ships, and the heavier *knorrs,* or merchant boats—were moored alongside it at the breakwater, tall masts creating a leafless forest as they rocked at their moorings.

All manner of goods were heaped on the breakwater, either being loaded onto carts for transporting to the market, or else being unloaded from the carts onto the decks of the waiting vessels. There was fowl, clucking and quacking in wicker coops, and baled fleeces, barrels of Danish beer, spices and silks from the east, and countless other goods. Sailors—mostly Norsemen, who grinned appreciatively as the two lovely young women were hurried past them by their towering guard—were busy loading or unloading these cargoes.

The bodyguard herded them, their wrists still in fetters, up the gangplank, leading them to an awning that had been erected on the foredeck. Indicating that they should be seated, he ran another length of chain through their fetters and fastened it about the mainmast.

"You will stay beneath here, pretty ladies, till our master returns," the great lout said, with a lecherous grin for Maida. "My lord Kadar would have my head, if he found thee gone. Or if he learned that the eyes of other men had fallen upon thee in his absence. The crew will be returning soon. We sail on the evening tide. Meanwhile, do not lift the awning nor show yourselves." His eyes came to rest on Edan, who ignored him, her face stony, as he added, "and remember, my lady, that any slave who attempts to escape will be beaten. My master is not a patient man."

Maida scowled at him, tossed her cornsilk hair, and pointedly looked away.

Laughing, the rogue winked at her, dropped the side of the awning, and strode off.

Despite Edan's fears, it did not appear that they would be cruelly treated—or at least, not yet. The deck beneath the awning had been spread with blankets and furs to make a soft, comfortable resting place. The length of chain running through their fetters was generous, its links lightweight, and it did nothing to impede their movements. In the awning's gloom, Edan could see a basket, heaped with bread, fruit, and cheese. There was a skin of beer, too.

"Well, we may as well eat," she suggested, her chains rattling, as she reached for the basket. "This might be our last meal till we reach the Golden Horn."

"At least we were sold together, my lady. I'm glad about that."

Edan smiled. "So am I. Here. Have some cheese. It's delicious!"

They ate, then slept, for they'd had little sleep the night before. Their fear of what would befall them at the market this morning had kept them both sleepless and stolen their appetite for the bread and watered beer Leya brought them. Now, having had some of their questions answered, both hunger and weariness had returned.

When they had eaten their fill, they slept, deeply but—mercifully!—without dreams.

When she awoke, Edan saw that the light on the other side of the awning had faded. Afternoon had passed. Day had become evening. Soon, the vessel would set sail, if the bodyguard had known what he was talking about.

She sat up. She could hear men shouting back and forth as goods slammed down onto the decks made loud thumps. The crew, surely? They must be getting ready to cast off. She glanced down at Maida. She was still sound asleep, her cheek cradled on her arm.

Rocking forward onto her knees, Edan raised the awning a few inches and peeked beneath it.

As she'd thought, the crew had returned and was preparing to set sail. Men were everywhere, scurrying about, stowing painted wooden shields along the vessel's sides, coiling lines, or else loading provisions and stacking them on the deck. In the midst of all the activity stood the lordly Turk—God rot him!—one hand still clamped over the hilt of his scimitar, a booted foot propped on a carved chest, as he surveyed the goings-on with eagle-eyed disdain. But then he turned, suddenly, and glanced in her direction.

She dropped the awning, guiltily remembering his servant's admonition to remain hidden. Still, she could not shrug off the disquieting sensation that he had known she was spying on him, though of course, that was impossible.

Soon after, she heard the command to cast off, followed by the splash of the oars, then felt the deck moving beneath her, as the oarsmen rowed the ship away from the breakwater and out, into the open sea.

Resigned, she leaned back and, soon after, heard the crack and snap of the sails she'd grown accustomed to hearing aboard Thorvald's ship, as the wool sail unfurled and filled with wind. There would be no escape now—or at least, none until they reached their destination and dry land. For better or worse, they were on their way.

Lulled by the motion of the ship, her eyelids drooped. . . .

"Ladies?"

She opened her eyes what seemed like only a moment later to see that in the short while she'd slept, the awning had been raised. The bodyguard ducked down, looked in at her and grinned. "Ah! You are awake, my lady. Very good."

"Go away."

"I trust you enjoyed the victuals, my lady?" His eyes twinkled, for the basket of victuals was quite empty. Not so much as a crumb remained.

"Go away, I said, wretch!"

"Nothing would give me greater pleasure, my lady. However, my master commands you to come to him. It would be wise to obey."

She swallowed. Apprehension lay like a cold stone in her belly. Without a doubt, the Turk would not be put off as easily as that lout, Gorm, had been. But what would be the consequence of refusing his commands? More importantly, what did he want with her? "Tell him . . . tell him that I am sleeping. Nay, nay, tell him I am unwell, and will not—cannot!—see him!"

The bodyguard squatted briefly to unlock her chains, then struck her fetters with a small hammer. "My lord awaits you in the bows, my lady. 'Twould be best if ye told him yourself," he suggested, as she rubbed her chafed wrists. After freeing Maida, who slept on throughout his gentle manipulations, he bowed and went away.

"Maida! Maida, wake up!" She shook her shoulder. "Maida! We're at sea!"

"Whe-ere?"

"At sea! Bound for the Golden Horn!—And that . . . that savage Turk has demanded to speak with me—or so his servant claims! Oh, Maida, he's not even a Christian!" she wailed, as Maida sat up, yawning and rubbing her eyes.

Maida blinked and looked at her wrists, surprised to find she had been freed while she slept. "True, but talking to him cannot hurt, surely, lovie? He said he'd bought ye for his master, the caliph, remember? Not for himself!"

Edan scowled. "Nevertheless, I do not trust him. His eyes! He was lying, I know it!"

"But, there's nothing you can do about it, is there?" Maida pointed out, ever the practical Welshwoman. "We're at sea— and this vessel is his to command, heathen or nay, my lady, along with all upon her."

"True. But while you were asleep, I've been thinking. He— that savage!—might agree to ransom me to my father! My family would pay any sum to get me safely home, I just know they would! What say you?"

"Me? Why, I think you must do whatever you can to get free, my lady," Maida agreed levelly.

"Oh, dear Maida, do not sound so bereft! I meant that you should come, too! Truly, I would never leave you behind! Let that strange little creature in black find another nurse for her babes!"

Maida smiled, clearly relieved. "Why not ask the Turk, then? He can but tell thee nay. And there's every chance he'll see the advantages to such a plan, if he's greedy."

"He must! All merchants are greedy by nature, are they not?" Edan declared. "Come with me when I ask him, please?"

She ducked under the awning, Maida following.

Outside, the sun was setting, a great fire-colored shield poised on the horizon, just waiting to plunge into the indigo sea. A glittering golden path spread from it, stretching across the amethyst water to the vessel's sides. The little vessel rose and fell smoothly, as she sailed down that glittering path toward the fiery orange orb. The crimson sail was flapping, and the same wind tossed Edan's hair about her shoulders.

"You, girl. Come here."

He had not even turned to summon her, but remained as she had spied him earlier, gazing out to sea with one booted foot resting on the chest. With a grimace over her shoulder at Maida, she padded across the deck toward him. That ill-mannered oaf! Had he eyes in the back of his head, like a demon? He had not even deigned to turn and look at her!

"Closer!" he urged, when she paused two tailor's lengths from him, her hands clasped primly before her.

"This is close enough," she seethed, forcing the words

through clenched teeth, in her anger. "Aye, milord, more than enough!"

"*That* is for me to decide, wench. Not you. I am your master now. Come closer!"

Her eyes grew cold as ice, taking on a silvery pallor. "Nay, my lord," she refused, drawing herself up to her full height and tossing her mane of unruly midnight curls. "I acknowledge but one master. He who once was master of my heart!" Her voice broke as she said the words.

"*Ewellah!* And where is this. . . . master of hearts now?" the Turk asked softly.

She pressed her lips together. "He awaits me in Heaven." He drew his foot from the chest and turned slowly to face her. "Can this be Heaven, then, mavourneen?" he asked, drawing off the turban.

She swayed, as she gaped at him, for a few stunned seconds, unable to believe her eyes. The blood roared in her ears, for his hair was long and black, and fell in ebony waves to his shoulders. The fine, dark beard he had sported earlier was gone. And clean-shaven, the handsome Turkish merchant was the image of—

"Sure, and it's me, mavourneen. You've no call t'grow so pale. 'Tis no ghost ye're after seeing before ye!"

"*Kerrin? Oh, dear God, it is you!*" she whispered, her knees giving way.

"Sure, and who else would give his last coin t' buy such a scrawny wench! Come here!"

Standing, she ran to him, flung herself headlong into his arms, howling with delight. Her tears fell, as his arms went around her, holding her fiercely. He swung her high into the air, then whirled her around, full circle, both of them laughing and crying at the same time.

"I thought . . . oh, God, I thought Thorvald had killed you that night!" she blurted out, her eyes shining up at him through a veil of tears. "I thought . . . oh, Kerrin, I thought you'd thrown yourself on his sword, and that I'd never see you again—or at least, not in this world," she told him tremulously, her words muffled against his broad chest. "I—I wanted to kill him, I hated him so. Oh, Kerrin, my lord, my love, hold me! Hold me *tightly,* so I know you're truly here!''

He needed no second urging. Taking her in his arms, he held her, kissed her hungrily, tasting the salt of her tears on his lips. ''I am here, sure enough,'' he said, when he broke the kiss. ''We're aboard my ship, the *Storm Chaser,* bound for Eire, and Wulfskeep! Thanks be, she'd been repaired and was ready to sail when we reached St. Daffyd's, the morning after the Danes carried you off.''

''But, you were so convincing in the market!'' she cried, laughing through her tears, as she playfully punched his chest. ''Wretched man! I had no idea 'twas you! I imagined us walled up alive in a harem for the rest of our years!''

''And so ye shall be!'' he teased. ''In *my* harem. Serving *my* pleasure.''

''Rogue! But—oh, Kerrin, what of your falcon? You traded Yseult for—for me, and she was so—so very precious to thee!'' Her lips quivered. Tears trembled on her lashes like raindrops.

''Sssh. 'Tis naught to cry about, love. Nothing in this world is as precious to me as you are, little one,'' he murmured, cupping her face. His green eyes were tender, earnest, filled with love. ''And Thorvald will be kinder to Yseult than he is to his sons or his wife, I have little doubt of that.''

''You are right,'' she agreed, laughing through her tears. The old sea-wolf took better care of his belongings than he did his family. She lowered her voice to ask, ''But, who was it played your concubine? Old Myrla?'' The black robed figure was standing nearby. She could not tell for certain, but she thought the woman might be listening to their conversation.

He shook his head, grinning. ''Nay. Someone else. Someone Mistress Maida here will be happy to see, I wager. Show her, lad!'' he called in a louder voice.

Lad?

With that, the small, black robed creature flung off its robes, revealing a slender twig of a boy with vivid, sparkling blue eyes and a brace of large front teeth, like a hare's. These beauties were shown to fullest advantage by his broad grin. ''Hello, Mother!'' he chirped.

"Matthew!" Maida's shout could surely have been heard by those on the darkening shores off their port side! "My son!—"

In a rush, they ran to meet each other. Mother and son were reunited, laughing and weeping as they hugged each other.

"God bless thee, sir!" Maida whispered, turning to take Kerrin's hand in her own and kissing it. "I'll never be able to repay thee, but I'll try. Our heartfelt thanks, from the both of us!"

"Never was any lad more deserving, Mistress Maida. Matthew is small, aye, but he has the courage of a lion! Few lads would have gone with me into that den of sea-wolves for love of his mother, as Matt did! He's a son to be proud of."

"Lord love him, bless his little heart!" his mother murmured, ruffling her son's red head and casting him a look filled with pride. "My lady?"

"Yea, Maida?"

"About the awning . . ."

She frowned. "Aye. What of it?"

"Me and the boy . . . well, we have so much to talk about! Whereas you and your lord . . ." She blushed. "Well, I was thinking . . ."

Edan sighed, her gray eyes dreamy in the mellow sunlight of early evening. " 'My lord and I!'—How sweet that sounds! You're right, Maida. We all have much to talk about."

Kerrin smiled as he took Edan's elbow. "I doubt talking was what Maida had in mind for us, my wee wren. Mistress Maida, if ye have need of anything—food, garments, whatever—my man Niall will bring it for ye. Ye have but to ask. And if Niall cannot help ye, ye'll know where to find us!" He winked and Maida laughed and reddened.

"That I will, my lord!" she agreed, hugging Matthew about the shoulders.

"Niall is here?" Edan asked, as Kerrin swept her up, into his arms and carried her across the decks, past the row of grinning oarsmen who were seated on their boxes and resting, now that the wind had filled the sails and they no longer needed to row. Many of them touched their forelocks to her as she passed, for although she had never met them, she was their lord's bride.

"Did ye not know poor Niall, my love? But then, he makes a fine bodyguard with his whiskers shaved, does he not!"

Her dark brows winged skyward, as he set her down on the deck. "That was Niall?"

"It was," he admitted, as he lifted the awning. "After you, my lady."

Coccooned in velvety darkness, he took her in his arms and lay back upon the furs with her cradled in the crook of his arm. "Little love, how I've missed thee," he whispered, stroking her hair.

She felt a curious shyness, now that they were reunited. She wanted him, aye, but 'twas enough, for the moment, to simply lie in his arms, to be able to reassure herself over and over again, by just a touch, a word, that she was really here with him, and that they were both safe from harm. The rest would surely follow, soon enough. . . .

He dropped a kiss on her hair, remembering all the nights he had spent pacing the decks, restless and wakeful with fear for her safety. He had barked at the men and driven them to the limit, afraid by the time they reached Denmark and Hedeby, she would already be gone, sold off, and lost to him forever— Or dead—Aye, by the gods, it had been all too easy for him to imagine his fiery Edan defying some quick-tempered Dane. One who would rape, then slay her the moment she fought him, no thought given to her value on the slave block.

"Thorvald and his men, they did not harm ye?" he asked gently. If those bastards had touched her, he would go back and geld the lot of them, somehow, even if it cost him his own life!

But she shook her head. "They tried, my lord, but they were no match for Maida and myself." She grinned. "Gorm and a fellow named Nils have the lumps to prove it!"

He chuckled. "I pity the poor devils. Almost. . . ." To find her not only untouched, but as spirited as ever exceeded his wildest expectations!

Smiling, she sat up, grasped the ragged hems of her tunic

and pulled it off without further ado. "We will talk later, my husband. As I recall, there are far more pleasing ways to celebrate our reunion."

"My lovely wanton," he murmured, as she cast the crude garments aside. Raising one side of the awning, he gazed down at her, moved by her beauty in the moonlight. "My eyes had almost forgotten how lovely ye are," he murmured huskily, "though my heart never could, God help me."

The fading light heightened the creamy pallor of her skin and cast her inky tresses into darker contrast. Beneath the awnings' murky confines, she glowed with a pink and cream luminescence, like a freshwater pearl. *His pearl.*

"All of me, sir? Not just my 'pleasing mouth and eyes?' " she teased cheekily. Her eyes shone with mischief. A dimple appeared in her cheek, as she looked innocently up at him.

"All of ye, minx. Every blessed, luscious inch!" He pretended to bite her hip, growling like a bear.

"Even my . . . pomegranates?"

"Especially your pomegranates, aye, and your melons—all of ye! Ye gods, woman, I thought I'd never see ye again." His voice had cracked. It grew deeper with desire, as he ran his hands over her sleek little body. He cupped her cheek, then trailed his finger down her throat to the curve of her breast. "Lovely pomegranates," he murmured, and she giggled as he moved lower, to the tiny well of her navel, idly circling it with his fingertip.

Aroused, she drew a shaky breath—and held it until he caressed her again.

He laughed softly. "Breathe, my love. I won't stop. Ye've no need to hold your breath!"

"I must! If I don't, 'twill break the spell and you'll vanish!" She was smiling, as she said it, but the fear was there, in her voice and eyes, nonetheless.

Drawing her hand to his lips, he kissed it. "Never again, my love. I swear it!—"

"I just—oh, Kerrin, I cannot believe you're alive!" Framing his fine dark head between her hands, she drew his head down and kissed his lips, his cheeks, his chin, his brow, then wrapped her arms about him in a fierce embrace. How hard his body felt, compared to her own soft curves! Hard, powerful, and very, very dear . . .

"Nor I, love," he murmured, parting her thighs to kneel between them. Leaning forward, he gently kissed each breast in turn. Her nipples hardened into tight, hot buds, as his damp tongue caressed them, circled them, flicked across both exquisitely sensitive tips. Ducking his head still lower, he ran the tip of his tongue down the flat, velvety plateau of her stomach, before lapping and circling the tiny well of her navel, as he had done with his finger. When she moaned, he slipped his hands beneath her bottom and raised her hips to taste her honeyed essence on his tongue.

She closed her eyes and gasped, as the first thunderbolt of pleasure shuddered through her.

"Aah, love, just the taste of ye! Ye could drive a man to madness, mavourneen." Braced on his palms above her, their bodies touching their entire lengths, he murmured, "Edan. Open your eyes. Look at me, beloved."

Her gray-lavender eyes were large and liquid in the moonlight, as she looked up into his strong, handsome face. His expression was very intense, almost fierce, as she asked, "What is it, my dear one?"

"I love ye, Edan. Whatever comes, promise ye'll never forget that. Promise me!"

"I promise. Of course I do! Indeed, I *swear* it, for I love you, too, my husband!" With a cry, she took him inside her, arching her hips to deepen his possession as, with slow, deep thrusts, he began to show her with his body the love he carried in his heart.

Sometimes, he stroked the silky curves that rose up, off the furs, to meet his thrust. Or caressed the taut breasts she offered up, like sacrifices to his eager lips. Many times, he kissed her, their opened mouths fitting together as perfectly as their lower bodies. Time and time again, in countless different ways, he brought her to the brink, first building the liquid pulses that had returned to beat, slow and deep, inside her, then holding back till she had grown half-mad with wanting.

Tenderly, he postponed and prolonged her pleasure, like a master of the erotic arts, then plied her with slow deep strokes, with languid, melting strokes, before driving faster, harder, deeper, until her desire had built to a sweet, wild frenzy she could not contain.

It began with a single cry torn from deep in her throat: one that broke on the shadows like a violent storm. Shuddering gasps racked her, as her body pulsed around his, drawing him deeper with every spasm. Sobbing, she arched her head back, her fingers digging into his upper arms, as she sobbed his name: *"Kerrin, oh, Kerrin!"*

Her cries of ecstasy, the secret pulses of her body, were a catalyst for Kerrin's own climax. With a cry that was half-roar, half-shout—he found his own release in a shuddering, hot rush.

Afterwards, they lay with hands linked, legs intimately entwined. Fanned by cool breezes, scented with brine and kelp, that flowed beneath the raised awning, they gazed at the beautiful night.

Far above them, the moon scudded on high amidst a yawning canopy of stars, scattered over the sky, like sequins strewn across a wizard's mantle.

The sea, too, was truly lovely by night, each dark wavelet rimmed with silver, each splash of surf bleached to a blinding whiteness by the moon's ethereal light.

As the *Storm Chaser* carried them westward toward Eire, the vessel's swaying motion rocked the lovers to sleep. *They were together again at last!* Edan thought, drowsily, as she drifted off. The misfortunes Old Myrla had prophesied for them had come and gone. Nothing but happiness lay ahead for them now. . . .

Chapter Twenty-Three

Black hair and green plaid furling about her, Edan stood with Kerrin in the dragon prow of the *Storm Chaser*, gazing inland.

The crew had reefed the vessel's crimson sail when they first entered the river inlet. Now, manned by sailors hauling smoothly on the long oars to bring her alongside, the boat was skimming across the glassy harbor mouth to the stone jetty, like a bird winging home to its nest.

"There!" Kerrin exclaimed, pointing. There was excitement in his eyes and pride in his voice, as he added, *"Wulfskeep!"*

Following his pointing finger, Edan was struck speechless by the sight of her future home.

Framed by vivid blue sky, the stone keep soared skyward from a hilltop overlooking the river Suir and the harbor, flaunting her beauty and her power to all comers.

From the walks atop the keep fluttered standards of emerald silk, emblazoned with the black wolf's head that was the mac Torrins' badge. Seeing it, a thrill of pride ran through her. Squeezing her eyes tightly shut, she linked her fingers through Kerrin's and offered up a silent prayer: *Almighty God, let me serve you, my husband, and the people of Waterford, to the*

*very best of my abilities here. Grant that my lord and I may
live long, happy lives here together and never be parted again.
Let us always be at peace in this lovely land and call every
man friend or brother. Amen.*

The mound on which the keep stood was encircled by a
broad, deep moat filled with water on three sides. The fourth
side overlooked the river itself. Surrounding the keep was a
lofty palisade of logs and stone. These strong walls were rein-
forced by the addition of towers at regular intervals.

Within the palisade lay the keep proper: an impressive,
sprawling stronghold built of gray limestone and stout oak, she
saw, with yet another, taller, round tower facing seaward to St.
George's channel: a lookout point from which to scan the inlet
and the channel for raiders? She believed so. How ironic that
mighty Torrin, a sea-raider himself, had feared attack by others
of his kind!

A thrill ran through her, as she gazed at her new home. The
primitive, barbarian keep she'd imagined throughout the long,
overland journey from Kenley to Wales, and thence on the sea
voyage from Denmark to Eire, was nowhere to be found!

On many starlit nights aboard the *Storm Chaser,* she and
Kerrin had talked till dawn flushed the sky. In those intimate
moments, they had shared their hopes and dreams for the future,
the stories of their pasts.

Kerrin had told her that his father, Torrin the Red, had
planned to conquer all of Munster from the stronghold he had
built in Waterford, before drink and bitterness had dulled his
ambition. He had not exaggerated. Wulfskeep *was* worthy of
a conqueror!

The fortress commanded a magnificent view over its defensive wall to the rolling green countryside that surrounded it.
Shading her eyes against the brilliant summer light, she gazed
to the west of the harbor. There, she saw emerald hills, their
vivid color broken by craggy granite outcroppings and flocks
of woolly sheep. Lighter patches of green betrayed where the
treacherous peat bogs Kerrin had mentioned could be found,
waiting to entrap the unwary rider. And beyond the hills—

their peaks wreathed in billowing mist, like grubby fleeces this morn—loomed the mountains of Comeragh.

Once the *Storm Chaser* had been firmly secured to her moorings, Kerrin scooped her up, into his arms.

"Whoa! What are you doing? Put me down, do! In truth, you are quite mad, my lord!" she cried, laughing.

He grinned down at her. "Mad, is it? Enough o' your blatherin', wench. I'm getting ready t' carry ye over the threshold. Sure, an' we're *home,* darlin'!" Planting a smacking kiss on her lips, he stepped over the side of the dragonship and balanced on an oar, his bride in his arms.

"Kerrin, stop! Put me down, you brute!" she shrieked, as he tottered unsteadily. "You'll drop me!"

"Never, mavourneen!" he vowed. "Have a wee bit of faith in yer man, woman!"

Balancing gingerly, he swayed from side to side for a moment or two, before regaining his precarious balance. Then, with but a brief pause to recover himself, he leaped to the next oar, then the next and the next, carrying his shrieking bride with him.

"I pray our lady mistress can swim, Maida!" Niall observed, a broad grin breaking through his gray-streaked beard. "For if she can't, I wouldn't want ter be in his lordship's place after he fishes her out!" He squeezed Maida about the waist, then playfully rubbed his whiskers against her pink cheek.

"Rogue!" Maida scolded and pushed him away. But she was smiling as she did so.

In the weeks since they had left Hedeby, the two of them had become friends, if not quite the sweethearts Niall had hoped for. Maida had confided to Edan that she was ashamed of her burgeoning feelings for Niall, coming so hard on the heels of her Hugh's death. Was it not unseemly to have feelings for another man so soon? Did it mean that she had not loved the man she'd married, the father of young Matthew?

Edan had gently reminded her of her own counsel, when Edan was numbed by shock, that survival was what mattered. Life was short. Maida should take whatever happiness life handed her, she had urged her. Hugh was gone, after all, she'd reminded her gently, and Maida's grief could not bring him back, no matter how many tears she shed. Consequently, Maida had begun to turn to Niall for comfort, though she took pains not to appear too quickly wooed and won. Matthew was watching her and scowling, for, although he was glad to see his mother safe and well, he did not welcome the thought of another man replacing his father in her favor.

While Edan shrieked and clung fiercely to Kerrin's neck, threatening to topple them both into the calm gray waters of the inlet, her husband sprang from oar to oar, halting each time to recover his balance before going on.

His crew watched, placing bets on the outcome and offering encouragement, till their chieftain was close enough to spring from the gently bobbing vessel to the gangplank, carrying his lady in his arms.

"Sure, and you're not the slip of a colleen ye once were!" he panted. "Ye're growing plump as a wee piglet, mavourneen!"

"The devil I am, Kerrin mac Torrin," she denied, batting at his dark head. "How dare y—" She broke off, as she looked over her husband's shoulder to the smiling couple standing behind him. "Grania? *Grania!* Is it really you?"

"Aye, my lady! Oh, you're safe!" the other young woman cried, running to meet her. "I can't believe my eyes! I thought you dead and gone to Heaven, I did! Or the captive of some heathen sea-wolf!"

Edan laughed in delight. "And I thought you'd been killed at Kidwelly. Were you truly unharmed, as Kerrin told me?"

"Aye, mistress. Right as rain, thanks to you and my Tavish here. Well, maybe just a bit groggy," she amended. She cast an adoring look at the man standing behind her. "If it weren't for you attacking that great Norseman like a—like a raging lioness, and this rogue coming back t' find me after the North-man had knocked both of us senseless—why, I'd have shared your fate, I would! The Danes left me for dead, see?"

"Tavish, you rogue!" Kerrin bellowed, slapping his friend's shoulder. "I didn't recognize ye with those moustaches, man!"

"Who else were ye expecting, then, mac Torrin? St. Patricus himself?" Tavish asked, his merry face creasing with laughter.

Trading insults and uttering shouts that sounded like two

bull-walruses coming together in mortal combat, Tavish and Kerrin celebrated their reunion with bear hugs and much hearty backslapping.

"By Thor, I thought you dead, your pretty face forever lost to this world!" Kerrin declared, cuffing Tavish hard enough to burst an eardrum, then grinning even broader, as he squeezed his best friend's cheek.

"Sure, an' I thought the same—though the divil knows, being spared your ugly face would be a treat for the rest of us, aye?" Tavish came back, beaming.

Kerrin chuckled. "Yea, yea, but . . . what news?" he asked in a more serious tone. "What—what of my uncle, Torrin?"

"Dead, *min jarl.* The steward, Sullivan, says he died within hours of your departure for Britain in the spring, his lungs filled with water."

He could barely summon the voice to ask, "And?"

"On his deathbed, Torrin summoned everyone to the hall. There, he publicly acknowledged ye as his son and rightful heir."

"What!"

"You heard me. And then he put his mark on the documents to acknowledge his true will. Welcome home, *min jarl!* Welcome home to Wulfskeep, Jarl Padraic mac Torrin!"

Kerrin planted both palms on his friend's shoulders and squeezed. Their eyes met. Kerrin's own were moist. *"Takke,* my friend. And my heartfelt thanks for believing in me when others did not. I won't forget that your friendship was freely given, at a time when no other man would offer me his hand. *Takke."*

Their eyes met in silent communion. After a moment, Tavish coughed and looked away to hide his feelings.

"There is more?" Kerrin asked softly.

"Aye." Tavish hesitated, as if he did not know how best to go on. "Before he left this world, your father withdrew the accusations of adultery he had lodged against his brother, Rolf, and your mother, the Lady Deirdre. He—er—he exonerated them both of all wrongdoing, then made it known to the priest that he wanted Deirdre released from St. Brigit's and returned to the keep.''

Stunned, Kerrin sucked in a breath. ''Sweet Christ! And has she returned?''

''Not thus far, nay.'' Tavish's mouth quirked. ''Would you, sir, under the circumstances?''

He grimly shook his head. Who could blame Deirdre for shunning Wulfskeep and, with it, himself? She had spent her youth, the better part of her life, mewed up in St. Brigit's cold stone walls. A sixteen-year-old girl had suffered a lifetime's punishment for a sin she did not commit!

As for himself, he'd had not a single, gentle word for her . . . not a one. Rather, he had been cruel, cold, accusing. He swallowed, racked with guilt, her parting words coming back to haunt him then. *''I shall pray each day for God to open your eyes to the truth, Padraic mac Torrin! One day, you will regret your cruelty. And, when ye come to me on bended knee, I pray I'll yet have breath to forgive thee.''*

The Adam's apple bobbed in his throat. A lump that was impossible to swallow threatened to choke him. Damn Torrin's black soul! His father had believed Canute's jealous lies. And because of it, an innocent young man had died horribly and a beautiful young woman's youth and life had been wasted. ''What then?'' he growled, choked with emotion.

''Torrin accepted holy baptism, followed by the last rites. He died soon after, a Christian in a state of grace.''

''A Christian!'' Kerrin snorted in disgust. ''Forgive me if I find that hard to believe, friend Kerrin. A single drop o' holy water cannot work such miracles! Torrin was kinsman to the devil! Holy baptism could not change that.''

Tavish nodded, soberly. It would take Kerrin more than just hearing that Torrin had accepted Christian baptism at the hour of his death to erase the bitterness of a lifetime of harsh words, cruel treatment, and poisonous doctrines. It would take time, and—God willing!—the affection and love of his faithful lady, to bring about that miracle.

Tavish cleared his throat. ''We had word yesterday that the *Storm Chaser* had been sighted in the channel. I took the liberty of ordering a feast prepared, in the hope that you and your lady were aboard her.''

Kerrin nodded, swallowing over the lump in his throat. ''A homecoming feast, eh? My wife will thank you for it!'' He forced a grin. ''I fancy Edan imagined me chieftain of some crude long-house roofed with peat and peopled with swine and cattle. Will ye look at her now, man! She's all atwitter to discover she's wed an earl of some consequence—a prince of Eire, no less!'' Despite his disparaging expression, his tone was tender, proud.

His brows rose is surprise. ''Well, now! Something good has happened since last we were together. You have come to love the lady, aye?''

''With all my heart, I do.'' His green eyes looked bleak and distant for an instant, then he sighed and added, ''Aye, Tavish. God help us both, I do!''

Tavish gripped his friend's shoulder. ''Take heart, my lord. You and your lady have weathered much together and won. Why not that—why not that *other* trial, with the help of God?''

A thin smile played over Kerrin's lips. ''Because this is *not* of God, friend Tavish. 'Tis of the Otherworld! And neither priest nor physician can cure me. In truth, I despair of ever finding a solu—Ah! At last!!'' he added in a louder voice for the benefit of Edan and Grania. ''Our ladies come, friend Tavish!''

Arms linked, the two women were strolling along the little stone wharf to join their men. They made a pretty picture, Edan's dark head and Grania's fair one bent together in earnest conversation, their colorful skirts and mantles flapping about them in the breeze.

''They're bringing the horses ashore for us now, man. We'll discuss this matter anon. Meanwhile, my friend, attend your lady. She—er—she is still your lady, I trust?'' Kerrin cocked a questioning black brow in Tavish's direction and smiled. If Grania's radiant glow and gently rounded belly were aught to go by, the sweethearts had become far more than travelling companions since the night the Vikings had attacked Kidwelly Abbey!

"My lady and more, sir. I am proud to say that Grania is now my wife."

"Wife! Where and when did that happen?"

"Shortly after ye left the two of us at St. Daffyd's, sir." He shrugged. "My poor Grania was distraught after her mistress's abduction. She blamed herself for trysting with me that night, ye see? I offered her . . . consolation and a broad shoulder t'cry on, and!—" He grinned ruefully. "Well, one thing led to another. She's all I've ever wanted in a woman, she is, my Grania. Since I would not play false with her affections, we were wed."

Kerrin nodded. "My felicitations, man! And—judging by the bloom on your wee rose!—I'd say 'twas not a day too soon. . . ."

That night, the wild harp music of the *shanachies* rose to the smoke-blackened rafters of Wulfskeep's feasting hall. Both torches and fires cast ruddy light over the feasters' smiling faces, as the *skalds* sang their old, familiar songs: the wonderful *sagas* of the gods who had lived and loved when the world was young.

Taking up her harp, Calandra, which she had left in camp with Kerrin's crew at Kidwelly that fateful night, Edana left her husband's table. She went to sit on a three-legged stool by the hearth stones, so that she could play for the gathering.

With a shy smile for the faces fixed expectantly upon her, she ran her slim white fingers over Calandra's strings. A chord spilled from the harp's throat, a sound like a burst of rippling birdsong. With another, she began the moving tale of Balder the Beautiful, favorite of the Norse gods.

Balder was so very beloved, every living creature and plant swore oaths to do him no harm, she sang, except for the mistletoe. Another god, jealous Loki, took advantage of Balder's one weakness. Seeking Balder's death, Loki persuaded blind Hod to shoot a mistletoe arrow at Balder. Hod did so and Balder was pierced by it and died.

Edan sang:

> Then onto the great ship, Hringhorni
> Our beloved Balder was carried,
> Bright and vast was his ship-burning.
> Like an omen star falling
> Through the dark night
> Of our sorrow. . . ."

As she sang of the rivers of tears that were Hel the Hag's price for ransoming Balder from her dark realms, there were few in the hall whose eyes remained dry.

And, when Edan ran her fingers down over Calandra's strings and the harp gave ringing voice to a last, triumphant chord, the people of Wulfskeep went wild. They roared and howled, stamped and whistled, thumped their fists and their beakers upon the trestles in approval, applauding till the rafters rang.

Flushed with the warm reception she'd received from her new people, Edan stood to make them all a graceful bow and to say simply, "You have taken me into your hearts, good people of Wulfskeep. I thank you, one and all—and welcome you into mine."

"Let's drink to Edana of Wulfskeep! To the lady Edana, God bless her!"

"Aye, long life and good health to our lord and his lady!"

"Health, wealth—and a litter of babbies, too!"

"Amen!" yelled Little Hurleigh, stuffing a pillow beneath his tunic.

Soon after she had retired, Kerrin joined her in their bower. He found her seated before a silver looking glass, combing her long black hair with a jewelled comb. In the firelight, she was lovely indeed, a rosy flush of happiness riding high in her cheeks, a sparkle in her gray eyes.

He came up behind her and swept her hair aside, bending to touch his lips to the nape of her neck, as she sat. Then, plucking the comb from her hands, he combed her inky ringlets himself.

He ran the comb slowly, sensually through her springy curls, watching the strands part under the teeth, like dark, fertile earth furrowed by a score of tiny plows.

"Hmm, husband," she murmured huskily, reaching up behind him and catching his wrist. Their eyes met in the looking glass. "Your touch is most pleasing." She drew his hand around to her lips, pressed it to her cheek, then kissed his knuckles. "We will have a good life here together, will we not, my love?"

"The best," he vowed, raising her to standing and turning her to face him. "We will guide our people wisely and well. In time, God willing, they will forget my un—my father's cruelty."

Taking her hand, he led her to their bed, which was softened with a pallet of goosedown and bolsters of the same. Tall posts rose from each of its corners, boasting a carved head of one of the apostles.

He set her gently down upon the pallet and stretched out beside her, tracing the curves of her cheek and chin with his finger, down to the raven-dark tumble of curls that pooled upon the pallet.

With a sigh, she closed her eyes, thrilling to his gentle caresses, growing warm with desire, as his lips brushed her eyelids, her ear, the dark hollows at the base of her throat.

"My dear and perfect love," he murmured, inhaling her lily-of-the-valley fragrance. "My life was so empty before. A dark and bitter thing! You have brought sunshine and sweetness to it!"

"And you, my dearest lord, have made my life complete," she whispered, curling her arms about his neck.

Reaching between them, he unfastened the ties of her night kirtle and bared her for his kisses, brushing his lips over her throat and bosom.

Her blood raced; her breathing quickened and grew husky, as he caressed her, building the fire in her veins, drawing little moans from her parted lips.

When it seemed she must go mad with wanting, he lifted himself over her, entering her in one swift thrust that tore a loud, giddy shout of pleasure from her lips.

"Noisy wench," he teased, kissing the tip of her nose, as he settled himself comfortably between her thighs. "Would ye waken the dead, then?"

She grinned at him. "Why, now, I'll be damned if I care, mac Torrin, my love! Sure, and what are ye waiting for, man?"

"Impudent wench!"

They came together lustily, hungrily, enjoying each other to the fullest for the very first time in a real bed! There were no wet leaves, no splintery, shifting decks beneath her bottom here. Naught but a downy pallet of feathers—and her husband's loving arms . . .

They must have slept afterwards, for the next thing she knew, she was awake, and the fire burned low. Only a heap of gray ashes and a scattering of embers glowed on the hearthstones. Without a log to feed it, the fire would soon be out. And, for all that it was almost midsummer, the bower was chill.

Shivering, Edan lifted Kerrin's arm from across her and slipped from the bed, pulling on her discarded shift, as she went.

The fire seen to, she turned to the windeye, drawn by the brilliance of the moonlight, which was shining through the narrow opening. What she saw through it made her gasp.

"Kerrin! My lord, wake up! Look here!"

"Aye, what is it?" he demanded, springing from the bed and coming to stand behind her. "What did ye see?"

By way of answer, she pointed.

Below, on the river meadow, hares were dancing by the light of Lady Moon, bounding and leaping about like the long-eared celebrants of a pagan ritual. A thrill ran down Edan's spine, as she watched them, for the Dance of the Hares was a rare sight; one her own mother and father had been privileged to witness in their youth. Though they had told her of it many times, she had never seen it for herself till this moment.

"All my life, I have lived on the land, sleeping in ditch and hollow, yet never have I seen the likes o' this!'' Kerrin murmured in wonder, drawing her closer and resting his chin upon her head. ''What does it mean, do ye suppose?''

She turned a glowing face up to his. '' 'Tis an omen of good fortune, my love.''

Chapter Twenty-Four

Edan rose early the following morning and ran to peer from her bower windeye.

The hares were gone, yet a different magic remained: the magic that was Ireland! *Eire!* How very beautiful she was—a jewel of an island, wrought in brilliant greens of every shade. A place of mist, mountains, myths, and music!

Facing east, the slitted opening afforded a lovely, if narrow, view across the emerald hills to the distant gray sea. It was a fine, clear morn outside, she saw, and the sunbeams slanting through the windeye felt warm upon her face. She inhaled. What a wonderful new day to begin her fine new life!—A happy life, at that, if seeing the Dance of the Hares was truly a promise of good fortune!

After she had washed and dressed, she left her bower on the second floor of Wulfskeep and ventured down to the hall below in search of her husband. Although he had returned to their bed with her last night, he had later risen and left their bed. The pallet beside her had been cool when she awoke. She frowned. Had he gone roaming abroad last night, as had been his habit as they journeyed across Britain? Or had he risen very early to see to his estates? Aye, that was it, surely.

"A good morning to ye, my lady! What are ye doing up so soon? I had thought to let ye lie abed this morning, after your long journey," Grania scolded, by way of greeting, when she entered the hall. "Are ye not weary?"

"Not a whit," Edan denied. "In truth, I'm champing at the bit, eager to take over the running of my husband's household at last! Pray, where is the earl?"

"Lord Kerrin has gone riding over the estates with his steward, Master Sullivan, mistress," Grania supplied. "But here's your household, such as it is." She made an expansive, sweeping gesture at the gloomy, dusty hall.

By torch and firelight, Wulfskeep's hall had seemed warm and welcoming, both well-appointed and cared for. Shadows had concealed its shortcomings, however. In the light of day, she could see glaring faults.

Beautiful tapestries embroidered with religious scenes hung upon the walls, as in only the finest halls. However, they had been shamefully neglected. Their brilliant colors were darkened by soot, their fibers laden with dust. Nor were the rushes strewn over the stone-flagged floor as fresh as they might have been. The trestles, covered with freshly laundered cloths of white linen for the feast the evening before, were disgusting without them, the crusted remainders of long-ago meals firmly attached to their surfaces. The hounds lounging about the hearthstones were scratching.

Seeing the direction in which her mistress's disapproving gaze had fallen, Grania wrinkled her nose in disgust. "As ye can see, mistress, Wulfskeep—imposing though she may be from the outside—is no Kenley! Leastwise, not by the light of day!" She sighed. "I've done what I could to clean it up a bit since Tavish and I arrived, but from what the other wenches tell me, no one's been near the place since earl Torrin died and went to . . . Well, went to wherever it is that such terrible men go after they die! T'ell the truth, my heart wasn't truly in the task, my lady, not knowing what had befallen ye." Tears glimmered in her eyes. Impulsively, she caught both Edan's hands in her own and squeezed them tightly. "Oh, dearest lady,

I suppose 'tis the babe that makes me maudlin and weepy, but—I'm so glad you're safe, and that we're back together!''

"As am I, dearest Grania," Edan murmured.

The two old friends hugged one another warmly and exchanged kisses.

"Tell me, Grania, what happened to the old woman with the donkey?''

"Grandmother Myrla?'' Grania frowned, then shrugged. "The morn after ye were taken from Kidwelly, your lord husband marched the rest of us to St. Daffyd's, where his ship awaited him—like a man possessed! He told Myrla she was to return to Wulfskeep with Tavish and myself on a merchant vessel.'' Grania shook her head. "That channel crossing was a rough one, let me tell ye! I was sick as any dog, but the old woman was an even worse sailor. It nigh killed her t' cross water! Happen she's been sickly ever since. . . .'' Grania shrugged.

"But you did not go to enquire after her?''

Ashamed, Grania shook her head. "Nay, mistress. Besides,'' she added, a trifle defiantly, "Tavish said 'twas her custom t' keep to her cottage. He said no one was more surprised than your lord when the old woman said she was going to Britain with him to fetch his bride.''

"And you've not see her since your arrival?''

"Once, aye. Up on the headlands by the Maidens she was, gathering herbs with her donkey. She was gazing out to sea and muttering to herself. She was midwife to your lord's mother, did ye know that, mistress? According t' the folk hereabouts, Myrla had much of the raising of him, after his mother was sent to the convent.'' She shrugged. "I reckoned Myrla was watching the channel, waiting for the earl t' come back to her, but I did not want t' have to speak with her.''

"Why not?''

"Why not what?''

"Why did you not go and ask after her health, at least? The poor old soul had been deathly ill, had she not?''

Grania shuddered. "I dared not! With that long gray hair

blowing in the wind and that ragged mantle of hers flapping about her, she frightened me, she did.'' She hugged herself about the arms, yet eyed Edan defiantly. ''All bones and wrinkles and few teeth!—She puts me in mind of witches, that one does!''

''Witches? Nonsense, Grania! She is but old, toothless and bony—as we shall all be some day if, God willing, we live long enough.''

Grania nodded, but cast her eyes down, chastened by her mistress's sharp words. Edan had changed since they'd been separated, she sensed. She seemed more mature, more calm and in command of herself. In fact, more of what a mistress of a keep should be! Edan was right, though, she had to admit. She had nothing to fear from a poor old woman. ''Aye, mistress,'' she admitted without looking up, ashamed of herself.

''When was it you saw her?''

''Oh, it must be at least ten days ago, madam. Why do ye ask?''

''Has anyone been to visit her since then?'' She intentionally ignored Grania's question, wondering if the poor old woman could have died and hoping against hope that she had not.

''Not that I know of, nay.''

Her mistress frowned. ''Then I shall take a walk to her cottage myself this morning. Which way is it, pray?''

''Just follow the lake westward, my lady. If you'll wait while I fetch my shawl, I'll come with you.''

''Nay, Grania. I prefer to go alone this time. While I'm gone, find as many churls as ye can and put them to work. Have them take these old rushes out, then burn them. Afterwards, have the hall thoroughly swept and dusted and the tapestries taken out and beaten. When I return, we'll sprinkle the hall with pennyroyal to get rid of the fleas. I should be back in plenty of time to supervise the rest of the cleaning, all going well. By then, every last cobweb should be gone,'' she warned, wrinkling her nose in distaste, as she ran a finger down the nearest wall. It came away black with soot from the smoke of countless open fires. ''But first, have the cook prepare me a basket of victuals for Myrla, would you, Grania? Some cold broken meats. Milk. A newly laid egg or two.''

"Straightway, my lady.''

Myrla's mossy hut was carved from the underbelly of a low hill, hard by some woods. It proved more cave than true cottage, Edan discovered. Bowered about with oak and hazel trees, pungent yellow gorse and blackberry briers all but concealed its location. Wild roses and honeysuckle vines twined about the low doorway, perfuming the warm, summery air with their fragrances, while honeybees buzzed drowsily in the gorse and amongst the yellow-flowering shamrocks that carpeted the ground.

On a perch before the door sat a large raven. Its bright, beady black eyes watched her as she advanced.

Braying mournfully, Ahearn came trotting up, as Edan strode across the turf towards the cottage. When she halted to scratch between his long, velvety ears, he nuzzled at the fringes of her shawl in search of food, then nosed her basket, seeming ravenously hungry.

A glance at the beast's hollow sides confirmed her suspicions. He had once been a handsome—if wicked—beast. A veritable king amongst donkeys! Now, the poor creature's ribs were showing through a dull and dusty coat. Myrla must have been too sickly to care for him of late, she thought, and her anxiety deepened. She had doted on the little beast. . . ! Fishing an apple from her basket, she fed it to him, then shooed him away. "Go on, now, and let me see to your mistress.''

"*Cawk! Cawk!*'' The raven croaked and spread its night-black wings uneasily, as she beat upon Myrla's door, but there was no answer to her knocking. Pushing the door inwards on leather hinges, she stepped inside.

The bars of bright summer sunshine that fell across the threshold illuminated a single, gloomy room. On one side was a hearth circled with stones and, above it, a hole cut in the turf of the hillside, through which the smoke escaped. The fire had gone out long since, however. There were only cold ashes on the hearth now. The spit that reached between the hearthstones was empty, likewise the flesh-hook and the black kettle that hung over them.

A harsh coughing sound sent her whirling about. In the far corner of the hut was a heap of straw. Upon it, wrapped to her chin in a threadbare mantle, lay Myrla. She was shivering uncontrollably.

"Grandmother!" Edan exclaimed, removing her shawl and tucking it over the poor old crone. She dropped to her knees beside the pallet, overwhelmed with pity for the old woman. She must have huddled here, sick and suffering, the good Lord knew how many days. "You're burning with fever!"

It was no more than the obvious. In truth, the old woman seemed close to death. Still, she would do what she could for her and pray that little was enough. Touching Myrla's forehead, she found it warm, though her teeth chattered with cold. Her eyes were closed, deeply sunken above hollowed cheeks. Her seamed lips were gray and bloodless, drained of all color.

"Myrla! Mother Myrla! Can you hear me?"

". . . my poor lady Deirdre and fulfil their destinies. Blessed Goddess, help them, help them all . . ." Myrla muttered, tossing in the delirium of her fever. "So cold, so cold! Cold as my poor laddie's heart, all the love locked away, alas, alack. . . ."

Casting about her, Edan found an earthenware basin. She hurried outside and filled it with water from the lough. Pouring some into a smaller dish, she sniffed the contents of several dusty pouches and flasks on the rough shelf above the hearthstones. Selecting a pinch of herbs from one, she added it to the water and stirred. *Borage.* It lowered fevers and brought healing sleep. Then, once she had the fever firmly under control, she would do what she could for the chest ague that was hampering Myrla's breathing.

Sliding one arm beneath the old woman's head, she pressed the rim of the dish to her pale lips, forcing her to swallow a trickle of the tepid liquid at a time.

When the basin was all but empty, she tore two strips of linen from the hem of her underkirtle. With it, she set about bathing the old woman with the remaining cool water, into which she'd stirred soothing honeysuckle leaves.

When Myrla had been bathed from head to toe and gently patted dry, Edan dressed her in a fresh garment, then combed and neatly plaited her hair, before tucking a blanket, a mantle, and her own shawl over her once again.

Dropping to her knees beside the hearth, she made a small pyramid of the twigs she found there and worked with flint and wood shavings to coax a spark to fire.

Before long it caught, and she settled back, resigned to gazing into the flames and letting her thoughts wander where they would. There was nothing else she could do now but wait.

Within the hour, Myrla's fever began to break. Beads of sweat broke upon her withered brow and upper lip. Taking up a fresh basin of water, Edan gently bathed and dried her a second time. Myrla's breathing, though noisy from congestion, was regular now. The borage was working its magic.

"Are ye an angel, then?" her reedy voice asked, a short while later.

Edan rose from the three-legged stool by the hearth. She went to the bedside and touched Myrla's brow. Praise be, the fever had lessened! She was no longer either clammy and cold, or burning up. Her voice was raspy, true, and the breath yet whistled in and out of her lungs, but her color was less hectic than before. Her eyes were no longer unnaturally bright.

"Well? Am I gone t' the Otherworld, eh?"

"Nay," Edan reassured her gently. "You are far from dead, Grandmother—and I'm no angel, by certes! 'Tis Edan of Kenley, your lord's wife."

"Who?"

"Edan. Remember? You cast the runes for me in Britain?"

"Ah. I remember."

"You are ill, Grandmother. But you'll be better very soon, I promise thee."

"And Kerrin?"

"Gone to inspect his lands with Sullivan."

"Aah. Thank the Lady! But then, I knew ye'd both come home 't Wulfskeep. 'Twas in the runes that night. . . ."

There were tears in Edan's eyes, as she looked down at the old woman who had raised Kerrin from infancy. She was, to all intents and purposes, the only mother he'd ever really known.

Since she had seen her last in Kidwelly, Myrla had become little more than a bundle of bones encased in leathery, wrinkled skin, so thin and fragile had she grown. Edan bit her lip. She would have died here, forgotten and unloved, had they not returned in the nick of time. Aye, and might yet die, despite her very best efforts to heal her!—

Taking the old woman's gnarled, papery hand in her own, she could not help but recall her own paternal grandmother, poor mad Lady Wilone, who had rocked her and Beorn in their cradles and sung lullabies to them for hours on end, thinking they were her own "lost" twins, Farant and Alaric. Although she'd not been in her right mind for many years, Wilone had been loved and cared for tenderly by everyone at Kenley till the very hour of her death.

Edan blinked away a tear. It was not right for anyone, no matter their station in life, to die unloved and alone. The questions she had wanted to ask could wait, till Myrla was stronger.

"I'm going back to Wulfskeep for a cart, Grandmother. You will stay there with us till you're well again. I've given you borage to bring you sleep. Rest, and I'll be back as soon as may be."

With Myrla's slight nod of assent, she left the hut.

She stepped at a brisk clip across the springy turf, the wind tugging her hair and flapping her skirts about her legs. Seabirds were wheeling overhead, describing sweeping arcs against the blue sky, as she hurried around the glassy lake toward Wulfskeep.

There would be a fine view from above by the standing stones, she thought, pushing the hair from her eyes to see— one that reached across the rolling hills to misty St. George's Channel beyond. She'd not be surprised to see the coast of west Wales from up there on a clearer day. Small wonder the Irish had a settlement there, at St. Daffyd's in west Wales. 'Twas little more than a stone's throw away!

Shading her eyes, she saw Kerrin's horse cantering towards

the Gray Maidens and frowned, wishing he had taken her with him to explore the ring of ancient standing stones. Or . . . was he heading for the convent of St. Brigit's, beyond the henges?

Removing her veil, she waved it vigorously to attract his attention. To her relief, he saw her, waved back, and turned his mount in her direction. Obviously something of her urgency had communicated to him, for he dug his heels into Orion's sides and rode quickly around the sparkling lough to her side.

"It is Myrla, my lord. She is very sick—the lung ague, I think. She'd be better off at Wulfskeep, where I may nurse her day and night, than here."

His expression concerned, Kerrin dismounted and strode into the cottage. Lifting Myrla into his arms, as if she were a mannikin of straw, he took her up on his horse before him.

"Ye gods! She weighs next to nothing!" he exclaimed, his expression troubled. "What of you, love? Will you follow us on foot?"

"See to her. Don't worry about me."

Myrla was almost lost beneath blankets and mantles, yet she revived sufficiently to open rheumy blue eyes. And, despite her sickness, she recognized Kerrin. "Well, now, ye young divil. Came home t' me after all, did ye?" she murmured. "Aye, and ye took your sweet time to do it, too, did ye not?"

"Sure, an' I couldn't live without ye, could I, my old beauty?" he came back.

Myrla cackled with laughter, which dissolved into yet another dry, hacking cough.

"Make haste, before she catches another chill in this wind. Oh, and bid the churls boil kettles of water to make steam!" Edan called after him, as he quickly rode away.

She followed him on foot, but had not gone far, when she saw another woman coming toward her on the same narrow path that led around the lake to Myrla's cottage. She was robed in white and wore the full cowl of her white mantle pulled up, over her hair.

"Good day to thee," the woman greeted her, her accent that of the nobly born and the educated. Slender and of medium height for a woman, her face was framed by wisps of black hair that were liberally streaked with white.

"And to thee, lady," Edan murmured politely.

"If I may inquire, do you come from Myrla's cottage?"

"I do, aye."

The woman's expression was searching, as she asked, "How so? Is she not well?"

"Nay, madam. She has been stricken with lung ague. My lord husband has taken her to Wulfskeep."

"Your lord husband?"

Edan nodded. "Kerr—Padraic of Wulfskeep. I am his lady wife."

"Aah. And Myrla is ill, you say?" The woman frowned, her lips pursed with worry. "I had feared as much when she did not come to visit me. . . ."

"If she is your friend, then you are welcome to visit her at Wulfskeep, lady. At her great age, she has few friends left, I fear. Those she has must be doubly dear."

The woman reached out and, to Edan's surprise, touched her cheek. "You are kindhearted, daughter—and as lovely as your reputation! I am glad to have met you." With that, she smiled and went back the way she had come, leaving Edan staring after her.

With a shrug, she hurried on to Wulfskeep, preparing a mental checklist of the herbs she'd need, as she went; pine balsam to loosen the thick, lung-clogging secretions, surely?; hyssop tea to heal Myrla's lungs; horehound for the cough; aye, and a cordial of black currant to soothe her poor, dry throat. . . .

Chapter Twenty-Five

"Your amulet, child!"

The reedy voice, coming so suddenly, after so many hours of nothing but Myrla's raspy breathing and the pop and crackle of the logs in the fire, startled her. She had been gazing into the flames, wondering what her family was doing at that moment in distant Kent. Her thoughts had been leagues away. "What, Grandmother?" she murmured, going to Myrla's bedside. "Say again, pray. I did not hear thee."

"The amulet! The amulet!"

"Surely you are dreaming, my dear?" she told her gently. "There is no amulet here."

"Not here, hssst! The fishes amulet!"

"The silver amulet that was mine?" She could think of no other.

The old woman nodded weakly, her irritation spent. "Aye."

" 'Twas lost, Grandmother. I left it at Kidwelly Abbey when I went to find Grania that night. It burned when the abbey burned, I expect. Or else Thorvald and his fellows took it before they razed the church. Alas, I enjoy its protection no longer." She had grown accustomed to the weightiness of the amulet, to the feel of it resting against her belly, or swinging from its chain whenever she moved. Now, like an old friend, she missed it.

"Ah, but ye shall, girlie! 'Tis what I meant. The amulet is in my safekeeping!"

"Yours! How so?"

"I was rummaging about in the ashes after the fire. It called t' me, it did, girlie—and the sun striking its pretty face showed where it hid!" she hissed. " 'Twas powerful hot when I picked it up, but touched by neither flame nor smoke. 'Twas strong magic that protected it! *The strong magic of him who made it,*" she finished in a lower voice.

"My mother's uncle, Sven," Edan supplied, wringing out the cloth she'd dipped in rosewater. She patted Myrla's face. "Did it not melt, even a little?" she asked, curious.

"Not so much as a link, girlie! Whist, now, enough of that smelly water. Sure, and I must reek like a camp follower!"

Edan laughed. The old woman was fast recovering. Despite her frailty, these past few days she'd proven herself as feisty as an old hen—and a perfect tyrant when it came to ordering the churls about! In truth, they balked now when asked to attend her! "Be good, Grandmother, 'else I'll not play for thee," she threatened, teasingly, patting Myrla's face dry. "Where is the amulet now, pray?"

"Hidden safe in my cottage. I'll give it ye anon. Tell me. Did she come t' see me?"

"She?"

"My own dear lady. Your Kerrin's mother! Did she come whilst I was lost to the fever?"

"Nay," Edan gently denied, reluctant to disappoint the old woman.

"Ah, no matter. She will, fore long," Myrla said, with an air of conviction. With that, she fell to slurping down the bowl of mutton and barley broth that Edan placed before her, with noisy relish, moistening the heel of dark rye bread in the savory broth till it was soft enough to swallow. Her remaining teeth were too few to chew it.

Taking up Calandra, Edan sat by the windeye and played the harp for her patient, while she supped. Her sweet voice

accompanied Calandra's own rippling voice, as she sang of
Alfred, former high-king of Britain. The song she'd chosen
told how Alfred and her father had driven the Danes from
Wessex and defeated their leader, wily Guthrum, so that the
people of western Britain might live in peace.

> Now, in every shepherd's cottage,
> And in all the country round,
> The name of Alaric, Bear of Kent,
> Shall surely be renown,
> And history shall tell the tale
> Of battles fought and won,
> By Alfred, Great and noble king,
> And Alaric, Earldorman!''

"Lovely, lovely," Myrla murmured approvingly, when she
was done. "Your pretty voice could soothe the Divil, darlin'—
aye, and meself, too, no doubt," she added slyly, chuckling at
her own jest. "Homesick for Britain, are ye, chick?"

"Aye, Mother, that I am."

Myrla clicked her remaining teeth. "Alas and alack, there
will be naught but strife and bloodshed between your lovely
isle and this, 'ere long. Mark well my words, child! There will
come a time when the land of Eire will be divided, head from
body and body from head. Sure, and both parts will live in fear
of the other!"

"When?" Edan whispered, a trickle of foreboding slithering
down her spine. Was it an attack on Wulfskeep by Canute that
Myrla saw? She was pale, as she set the harp aside, for the old
woman's voice had taken on the eerie ring of prophecy. The
sunlit bower seemed no longer quite as bright, but cast over
by a dark and threatening cloud.

"Never fear, girlie! Small battles lay ahead—one very soon,
in which blood will war against blood for the lair of the wolf.
But the great battle will not be fought in your lifetime. Nor
during the lives of your great-grandchildren."

" 'Tis in the future?''

The old woman nodded, her eyes distant, as she gazed at a

tomorrow Edan would never see. " 'Twill be long in coming—and still longer in going!—but 'twill come, nonetheless. From the east. 'Twill be fought in the name of the White Christ!''

Edan swallowed, fascinated, yet somehow ashamed of her own lurid curiosity, as she pressed, "What else do you see?"

Myrla chuckled. "If I was t' tell ye, girlie, ye'd think me mad!"

"Tell me anyway," she whispered.

"Is my wee Ahearn fed and watered?" Myrla demanded suddenly.

The question disconcerted her. "What? Oh, aye. I sent a groom out to your pastures to bring him here. "But, will ye not tell me more of what you have seen? Please, Grandmother?"

Myrla nodded and closed her eyes. For several moments, she appeared to be sleeping, then of a sudden her breathing quickened; her bony chest rose and fell alarmingly. "I see a time coming when death will stalk the world," she uttered, "reaping a stinking harvest with his scythe! Thousands will swell up, blacken, and die from a sickness no herbs can cure. Bodies numbering in the tens of thousands will lie unburied, and the trees will turn black with carrion eaters, as if hung with a dark and bitter fruit."

"Jesu!" Edan exclaimed, crossing herself, yet there was still that ghoulish hunger for knowledge of the future, as she asked, "Is there . . . is there more?"

"I see great beasts that belch smoke from their nostrils," Myrla murmured.

She swallowed. "Like . . . dragons?"

"Like dragons, aye—yet with the jointed tails of serpents! They race the winds across the world, travelling paths of iron, belching fire and smoke. And—"

"Go on!"

"Their bellies are filled with . . . *people.*"

"People?" Edan asked, aghast.

"Aye," Myrla murmured solemnly. "People."

"Jesu protect us!" She leaned forward. "What else?"

"I have seen silver birds wrought of metal that can fly to the very stars! And towers of stone that scrape the belly of the sky. Staircases that move up and down, whilst the people upon them stand still!'' Myrla babbled excitedly. ''Ah, such visions I see!—Aiiee! My poor old head is cracking!''

''Staircases that move, ye say?''

''Aye, aye!''

''But, what of Kerrin and myself? What does the future hold for us?'' She held her breath. Time seemed to stand still.

''The time is coming wherein ye'll be forced t' take a life, if ye would give a life. *His* life, girlie.''

Myrla's words rang on the sudden hush, each one twanging like a broken harpstring.

''What?—'' Myrla's spell broken, Edan stood up, laughing at her own gullibility. For a moment—just a moment!—she'd almost believed Myrla had the gift of Sight, despite what Kerrin had told her, months ago. ''Oh, what nonsense! Mayhap you need another dose of borage, Mother? I fear the fever is rising again.''

''Fever! Paggh! Don't believe me, if it please ye. Call my visions 'nonsense,' if ye must! I know what I know, so there! Believe what ye will!'' Myrla grumbled, pulling the coverlet up, over her head. '' 'Twill all come to pass! You'll see,'' she added, in a muffled voice.

Laughing, Edan set about straightening the old woman's bed, carrying her basins and pouches of herbs to the scrivener's table she had set by the windeye. There, the northern light was strong and clear for the mixing of medicines.

''My lady?''

''Aye, what is it, Grania?'' she asked. Her expression was troubled. Despite what she had said, the old woman's prophecy had disturbed her. Could there be any truth in any of it, she wondered, turning to the doorway?

Grania stood there, lifting the curtain that kept out the draft to look in.

''There is a lady below. A—a holy sister. She has come from the convent and is asking to see the old woman—um—Grandmother Myrla.''

''Oh? What name did she give?''

''She says . . . she says she is the Lady Deirdre, mistress.''

Edan's mouth went dry. "Deirdre of Wulfskeep?"

"Aye, my lady."

"Ah ha! Told ye, wench!" Myrla exclaimed, with a triumphant cackle, throwing off the coverlet that had hidden her.

Grania shrieked with surprise and leaped a good six inches into the air, for the pallet had appeared empty till Myrla suddenly sat up, beaming gummily. Her malicious eyes were like tiny black currants stuck into a bun, glittering with cunning amidst a web of wrinkles.

"Pray, show her to me, Grania," Edan bade the young woman, nervously reaching up to neaten her hair. She smoothed down the simple kirtle of russet-dyed wool she wore for every day. Given a choice, she would have chosen to meet her lord's mother for the first time under better circumstances, robed in her best garments, with her hair perfectly coiffed and her finest jewels glittering at brow, throat, and finger. As it was, she must look a sight!—The lady would probably mistake her for a house churl, she thought, nervously straightening the bower she had set aside for Myrla's use.

"Welcome to Wulfskeep, my lady!" she greeted, sweeping a deep curtsey, as the woman, ushered in by Grania, entered the bower with the graceful bearing of a queen.

The stranger pushed back the cowl of her white mantle, baring a head of neatly plaited and coiled black hair, liberally threaded with gray. Startled, Edan saw that Myrla's visitor was the woman she'd met on the path to the cottage a few days earlier. " 'Tis you, my lady!"

Deirdre smiled. "Indeed it is. But come, Lady Edana. Do not look so frightened, child! Contrary to what your husband may have told you, I am no ogress!"

"Forgive me for being uncivil, milady, but my husband has said nothing of the sort. I never meant to imply that he—"

"Rest assured, you have not," the older woman assured her, coming to stand before her. "I should not have let my tongue run away with me." Framing Edan's face with her slender, elegant white hands, just as Kerrin was wont to do, she kissed her brow. "I bid you fond welcome to Waterford and to the isle of Eire, my daughter. Greetings!"

"Thank you, my lady," Edan whispered. "I am happy to be here."

"Praise be, child! You love him, do you not?" Deirdre exclaimed wonderingly, watching the young woman's face.

"Aye, madam, I do. With all my heart!" she confirmed.

"And what of my son? Does Padraic—does Kerrin return your love?"

"He does, madam, aye."

"Then I pray that you can help him. Who knows? Perhaps your love is the answer to what ails my son . . . ? What say you, my poor old dear?" Deirdre asked, turning from Edan to Myrla's bedside.

"Don't ye 'old dear' me in that tone, Dierdre mac Murragh! I'm old, aye, but I'm not senile yet! Whissst! Ye took your sweet time in coming to see me, did ye not? But, no doubt, ye've more important things t'do than visit a sick old woman, now that that old sot, Torrin is dead, and you're free to go where ye will, eh . . . ?"

Deirdre turned to Edan, who was standing by the windeye, watching the pair. The older woman's eyes were twinkling, she saw, and laughter tugged at the corners of her mouth. "Thanks be! She is all salt and vinegar again! I do believe she's well on her way to recovery—and she has you to thank for it, my dear!"

Edan smiled uncertainly. "I pray you are right, my lady. And now, would you care for some refreshment?"

"Where is my lady wife?" Kerrin demanded, striding into the hall with a brace of shaggy wolfhounds padding at his heels.

Few people were there at this time of day. There was a house churl, strewing fragrant dried lavender and rosemary over the clean rushes, while another raked cold ashes from the hearth, tasks he did not recall seeing done while Torrin—while his father was still alive. Otherwise, the hall was empty. The fast-breaking over and done with, the people of Wulfskeep had dispersed to the kitchens, the stables, the dairy, and their various labors.

"Lady Edana is in the west bower, my lord. And sir, the Lady Deirdre is come here, an' all!" the wench with the basket of lavender pods blurted out excitedly, her eyes shining. She clearly expected some evidence of pleasure from her master.

"She's here? Where?" he barked, scowling.

"She visits the old woman in the west bower, sir, with your lady wife."

He muttered a curse and turned away. He still had not the courage to face his mother, let alone make his apologies. He snorted. How *did* a man apologize for a lifetime's misjudgment of a woman, anyway? What could he possibly say that would mean a damned thing? Joining them was out of the question!

With a snort, he strode from the hall, going back outside into the bailey, where some of his men were still drilling under Niall and Tavish's eagle eyes.

Ordering the hounds to stay, he bellowed for a groom to bring out his horse.

He'd hoped to spend more time in the company of his lady once they reached Wulfskeep, but the wretched fates were conspiring against him in that regard!

For the past few days since their arrival, Edan had been kept busy either in setting the household to rights, or in nursing Grandmother Myrla. For his own part, he'd discovered the steward and reeve, Master Sullivan's accounting records either missing or inaccurate, and the keep's small garrison stale and in dire need of vigorous drilling and practice at swordplay to restore its former superior fighting skills.

Accordingly, he had set about correcting both problems, resigned to seeing little of his lady until Myrla was well again and gone home to her own cottage. And now, just when the old dear was recovering, the Lady Deirdre had come to Wulfskeep!

Consequently, he was eager to be gone from his keep, for the while. He had been driven out, forsooth!

"How, now! Do I detect a storm brewing?"

"Aye, ye do. And I'm warnin' ye, Tavish, I'm in foul temper. Ye'd best leave well enough alone, till it's blown itself out."

Tavish grinned. "Your lady left your bed nights whilst she tended the old one, did she, now?"

"Damme ye, Tavish, I!—" He broke off, as the groom brought out his horse. The spirited roan stallion had been Torrin's own mount. However, Torrin's hard hand and cruelty had made the beautiful beast fearful of men. Still, Kerrin had high hopes it would respond to his gentleness in time. Meanwhile, the groom was having difficulty in holding the snorting, curvetting animal.

"Down, ye great brute! Down!" The man raised his fist to strike the horse, yet before he could do so, Kerrin caught his arm in a grip of iron.

"Nay, blast ye! 'Tis your sort that have made the beast fearful. Mend your ways, else be off with ye!"

"Your pardon, my lord. It won't happen again, sir. I swear it," the groom promised, hastily.

"See that it doesn't."

"Going riding, are ye? I pity the poor creature beneath ye today! Where are ye bound, man?"

"To the upland meadows to speak with the shepherds," Kerrin confided, still scowling, as he stroked the stallion's arched neck. "My reeve's accounting leaves much to be desired. I would learn from the shepherds how much wool my flocks gave last summer."

"Last year's wool yields?" Tavish snorted. "The shepherds are busy with the lambing. They'll have little time for that. Come hunting with me, instead."

Kerrin shot him a dark look. "I know what the shepherds are about. Was I not born to this land, like yourself, man?"

Tavish threw up his hands in mock surrender. "Tsk. Tsk. You're like a bad tooth this mornin', mac Torrin. Just a little poke at ye, and ye wince! Shall I ride along with ye, my friend? Keep ye out of trouble?"

"I'd sooner go alone," Kerrin refused with a growl, and swung himself up into the saddle. Turning his horse's head, he rode from the bailey without looking back.

Tavish had been right, he saw, as his horse crested a low hill. Below, in the little valley, the lambing was well underway. Two or three ewes were down on their sides, giving birth to their young. As he rode across grassy fields, starred with white daisies and golden buttercups, frisky little lambs gambolled about, whisking long, woolly tails, or else tottered after their mothers on tiny cloven hooves. The remainder of the flock was crowded together, far to one side of the meadow, in the fashion of silly sheep.

He found the shepherds gathered around an enormous ewe, shaking their heads in consternation.

"Why, welcome home, Kerrin, me boyo—er, I mean, milord!" the oldest shepherd greeted him, respectfully tugging his forelock. " 'Tis glad we are t'see ye home, and lord of Wulfskeep, moreover!"

"And 'tis glad I am to be back, Colin. What have you here? A difficult birthing?" He nodded at the laboring ewe.

"Twins, milord. The first was quickly born. The second, aye, 'tis a harder one, longer in coming. She's a young ewe, but I reckon as how this birthing will kill her, lord."

Just then, one of the younger shepherds gave a shout. He and the others hastily stepped back, away from the laboring ewe. Muttering amongst themselves, they made the horned sign against the evil eye with their fingers . . .

"What's wrong with them?"

Colin pushed the younger shepherds aside and knelt on the grass. Kerrin followed suit.

On the bloodied grass, still attached to the afterbirth by its cord, lay the second newborn lamb. But, instead of being white-fleeced, like his brother, who was already struggling to stand, this lamb was black.

"The lads think 'tis the work of the devil when lambs are born black like this," Colin murmured.

"And you? What do you think?" The old man was unlettered, but wise for all that. Kerrin had known Colin since he was a boy, and respected him.

"I think the ewe was cursed, right enough, milord. And that cursed ewes oftimes beget cursed lambkins."

Kerrin stiffened. With Colin's words, 'twas as if something he'd been trying to evade had found him and lain hold upon his heart. Like a cold hand, it squeezed. "Cursed by who? Why do you think this?" he demanded hoarsely.

Colin shrugged bony shoulders beneath his smock. "I have
seen it happen many times in my lifetime, lord. And me father
and grandsire spoke of it happening in theirs, too. A cursed
ewe will birth both white and black lambs in her lifetime, ye
understand? Yet even perfect lambs throw imperfect young,
when they be grown and mated. There's nothing for it but to
slaughter the lot of them. To destroy their bloodline forever."

The same cold hand danced icy fingers down his spine now.
"And what of that little fellow?" he asked, nodding to the
tottering black newborn lamb, which was trying to suckle from
his dead mother. "Will he be slaughtered, too?"

"Aye, milord. Ye can depend upon it," Colin promised,
misreading his master's concerns.

"Then give it to me, instead. My lady enjoys cossetting
small, sickly creatures," he murmured. He added silently, *And
I shall let her cosset this one, since she will have no babes of
her own. By certes, I shall see to that, henceforth!*

"As ye will, my lord, but . . . him should not be mated, when
'tis grown." Colin's warning was marked by a frown.

"I understand, man. Give it here!"

The little black lamb was bleating piteously, as he tucked
him under his mantle to keep him warm. It continued to bleat,
as he discussed the wool yields with Colin and was still bleating
loudly when, with a nod to him and the other shepherds, he
turned and rode back the way he'd come.

With any luck, his mother would have left Wulfskeep for
the convent by the time he returned, and he would find Edan
alone at last. He clenched his jaw.

In but the blink of an eye, in just a few casual words, his
life had been changed forever. He'd left Wulfskeep disgruntled
at being unable to have his wife to himself, let alone able to
satisfy his desire for her. Now, alas, the prospect of being alone
with Edan was no longer the pleasing prospect it had been
earlier. . . .

Colin's words kept coming back to him as he rode down
into the river valley of the Suir. *Destroy their bloodline forever,*
the shepherd had said. He swallowed. His father, Torrin, had

been cursed, had he not? Now it was his turn. But he would see to it he sired no sons or daughters to carry on his tainted bloodline. When he died, the mac Torrins would cease to exist!

Digging his heels into his horse's sides, he raced with the wind, trying desperately to exorcise the demons from his heart.

Chapter Twenty-Six

"Well, now. To where are you bound this morn, my love?" Kerrin asked the following Monday morning. His lady wife, sporting her shabbiest kirtle, yet so lovely that she stole his breath away, had come to the high table where he sat, breaking the night's fast.

"Now that Myrla's gone, my women and I are free to go gathering herbs. I need fresh ones to replace my stores, or the summer flux will take me unawares. Will you not come with us, sir?" she implored, casting him a look that promised all manner of naughty diversions to be had outdoors.

"Alas, I cannot. I told Sullivan that I would hold court this morning, to hear the claims of my people. My . . . er . . . my father had grown lax about such matters of justice fore he died. It must be done, and done soon. There are many whose complaints have gone unheard for over a year."

"Then another day would not hurt, would it, my lord?" she wheedled, placing a hand upon each of his shoulders. "Please? For me, sir?"

Her beauty, her warmth and scent, were dizzying, heady as a fine vintage wine from southern Gaul. He felt himself grow lightheaded, then harden like a green boy as the minx—standing between his legs while he sat—drew his dark head against her bosom. She lazily stroked his hair and neck, her hand flowing like water over the noble shape of his skull, the sturdy, powerful column of his neck and the bulk of his shoulders.

"Come now, what say you, sir? Hard work—or play?" She uttered the last word in a breathy purr that played havoc with his senses, then blew gently in his ear. Her hot breath raised the fine hairs down his arms and increased the ache in his groin. She had learned much since that first time in the hut. . . .

"Vixen!" He grasped both her wrists and pulled her down onto his thigh. "I want to—God! More than you know! But, alas . . . I have duties I must attend to. As, my sweet, do you," he reminded her, nodding at the basket she'd placed upon the rushes. "I have justice to dispense, while you have your healing herbs to gather. If we neglect our duties, sweet, the people will suffer in some way."

"I know it. But . . . oh, Kerrin, it's been long since you . . . since we. . . . were close. I have missed you, my husband," she confessed shyly. Her lower lip pouty, ripe, just begging for his kiss. "I want it to be as it was between us aboard the *Storm Chaser*." Ashamed of her wanton admission, she mumbled the words against his shoulder. "You remember, don't you?"

"How could I forget?" he assured her, stroking her hair, fondling the soft mound of her breast. The nipple hardened beneath the stuff of her kirtle and his shaft bucked in response.

"Tonight, then?" she asked hopefully. Leaning back, she searched his face, the rounded curve of her hip pressed snugly against his aching groin.

"I . . . will . . . try." His eyes slid away and would not meet her own.

"Kerrin? Love? Promise me!"

"Nay, Edana. I make no promises I cannot—in good conscience —swear to keep. I say again, I will try," he repeated, hating himself for the lie.

"Good enough, then, my lord!" She forced a carefree smile. "Now, I must away! Maida and the others are waiting."

"Will you not stay and break the fast with me?" What harm

could there be in the two of them enjoying a meal together? He had missed her company. Missed her laughter, her ready smiles, her clever wit. Her affectionate ways.

She hesitated, wanting to be with him, to erase those dark shadows from beneath his eyes with her kisses, but . . . Maida and Grania had both suggested she spend as little time as possible in his company for a few days. Avoid him! Shun him like the plague! Force him to pursue his quarry before he conquers it! That was the way to woo him back to her bed—or so they'd claimed!

"Grania has a basket of victuals we're planning to share on the banks of the river," she explained gaily. "Food tastes much better eaten outside! 'Tis such a fine morning, mac Torrin, is it not?"

"Indeed it is!" he agreed. Reluctantly, he sent her on her way with a kiss he wished might last forever. The fragrant scent of her hair lingered to torment him, long after she was gone.

"Sullivan!" he bellowed when she had left the hall, taking the sunshine with her. "Sullivan, damn ye! To me!"

"Aye, milord?" Sullivan panted, coming at a run.

"Make ready your inks and scrolls. I go to administer justice to my people. We shall hold court outside, on the river meadow." He gritted his teeth. " 'Tis a fine morn to be out, is it not?"

Sullivan eyed his master's dark, scowling face askance. Fine morn be damned! He would not want the mac Torrin to pass judgement upon *him* today, even were he innocent, not with that ominous, brooding look about him. Nay, not for all the shamrocks in Ireland!—

"What have you got there, Mary?" Edan asked, as one of her women emptied the contents of her skirts onto the grass beside her. "Ah. Nasturtiums!" she exclaimed, selecting a plant and carefully examining it before adding it to those already in her basket. "Boiled as a tea, these are excellent for ridding the stomach of worms. And this is cress, of course. Cresses rid the complexion of pustules and improve the digestion. You've done well, Mary. The people of Wulfskeep will thank you.''

''Thank ye, mistress,'' Mary murmured, blushing to the roots of her hair. ''I'll fetch ye some more.'' With that, she ran off to join the other young women of Wulfskeep, who were gathering herbs along the banks of the Suir with their young mistress.

The remnants of a small feast were scattered about on the grass: a crock of hard-boiled eggs—brown and speckled—taken warm from beneath the hens that very morn; cold broken meats; fruit tartlets, bread, and a skin of mead. The only person still eating, however, was Grania. Tavish had laughingly vowed she was becoming a glutton with the babe growing inside her.

''I've some herbs for ye, lady!''

''Put them down here, Pegeen. Let's see what you have. Ah. This one here, see? 'Tis monkshood.''

''Nay, mum. That 'un be wolfbane,'' Pegeen corrected her boldly. A spry red-haired wench with a golden complexion that was liberally sprinkled with freckles, her impudence was engaging, Edan thought.

''They call it wolfbane here, my lady. Aconite in other places. Three names, but 'tis the same plant, for all that. Or so Edythe was wont t'say. 'Tis just as deadly, by whatever name it's known!'' Grania supplied, between mouthfuls of fruit tart.

''And this one, here?''

''Adder's tongue,'' Pegeen murmured, touching a plant with arrow-shaped leaves. ''And this 'un be pond lily. Me gran's a healing woman. She says water lilies is for curing, too.''

''Adder's tongue? I've not heard it called that before,'' Edan murmured, examining the little plant. The verse etched upon her amulet had mentioned the adder's tongue—or rather, employing the *silver* adder's tongue. She frowned. Had the verse referred to a whitish variety of the same plant—or to a silver arrow-shaped object? *A silver arrow?*

''What do ye call it in Britain, my lady?''

''What? Oh. 'Tis known as the dogtoothed violet.''

''Shall we go into the woods now, mistress?'' Mary asked, flinging herself down onto the riverbanks alongside them. ''I seen some mistletoe there just yesterd'y. Mistletoe protects ye from the evil eye an' from sorcery, mum.''

Pegeen snorted. ''Ye'd best not ask what our Mary was after doing in the deep woods yesterd'y, though, my lady,'' she volunteered with a knowing grin.

''Peg, whist ye! Hush!'' Mary pleaded, tugging at her friend's elbow.

Pegeen giggled, but ignored her pleas, adding in a hoarse whisper, ''I seen the two o' ye, I did, Mary o'Comeragh! Ye were with Brendan Dungarven's brother, Donn. Courting something fierce, ye were, too.'' She rolled bright blue eyes heavenward.

''I was not!'' Mary denied, her cheeks flaming.

Pegeen grinned. ''Ye were, too! Come on, my lady! Mary here will show us where the best herbs are after hidin'. I reckon she knows all the best places, do ye not, our Mary?''

''I hate ye, Pegeen! Sure, and I'll tear yer red hair out for telling on me!''

The two youngest serving wenches scampered off towards the woods, hair flying on the breeze. Their skirts were hitched up before them to form a pouch in which to carry the plants they gathered, revealing slender ankles and dirty bare feet.

Edan laughed. In the not-so-distant past, she and her sisters had run wild, as the pair were doing—she and Danica racing on ahead, while poor little Gayla huffed and puffed, trying to catch up with them on her short, sturdy legs.

''Mayhap we should follow, my lady, before those two scratch each other's eyes out!'' Maida suggested, laughing and shaking her head.

''You're right. Come on, Grania, you glutton! On your feet! In truth, the babe will be bigger than Baa-Baa before it's born, if you keep eating so much!'' Baa-Baa was the name she had given the noisy little black lamb that Kerrin had brought her, now much heavier than he had weighed at birth.

''I'm done!'' Grania declared, with a sigh of satisfaction, licking sticky red juice from her fingers. She scrambled to her feet, brushing crumbs from her skirts.

Watching her, Edan felt a pang of envy, for she had noted the gentle rounding to Grania's belly.

Grania caught her eye and smiled, reaching out to squeeze her hand. "Don't look so glum, my lady. 'Twill be your belly swelling with child 'ere long. You'll see!"

"I hope and pray so," she came back, but in her heart, she was far from sure that Grania was right. How could she get with child unless her husband shared her bed? Of late, Kerrin seemed bent on avoiding her, though she did not know why. Despite his denials, had he a leman he was visiting? Some lovely Irish colleen he'd left behind, when he sailed to Britain?

With a sigh, she hastened after the others, leaving the riverbanks for the woods.

It was lovely amongst the trees that morning. Sunlight fell through the leafy boughs to dapple their faces with green-gold light. The grass smelled sweet as hay, and the birds were singing in the branches. In the distance, the Comeragh mountains slumbered beneath a bluish haze, their peaks crowned with streamers of fluffy white cloud.

The serving wenches and Edan's women separated, each going off in a different direction to search about the boles of the trees and through dense hawthorn thickets and oak groves for the herbs, grasses, and plants that would make the medicines Edan needed for her healing: yarrow for toothache; rue for easing the complaints of women; raspberry leaves to prevent miscarriage and the pangs of birthing; primrose for headaches and sleeplessness; mistletoe and wolfbane for charms against sorcery.

She strayed some distance from the others in search of the mistletoe Mary had mentioned seeing, but found a tall foxglove plant instead, covered with purple bells. The leaves made a wondrous tonic for the heart. As she crouched down to pluck some, she found her thoughts returning to their conversation on the riverbanks. Something Pegeen had mentioned had struck a note of alarm in her memory. It worried at her like a hound worrying a bone. What was it Peg had said? What on earth could it have been?

She straightened up, plants falling forgotten to the ground as she remembered. "Pegeen!"

"Aye, mum?" Peg answered, poking her bright red head up from behind a nearby clump of hawthorn bushes.

"Who was it ye said Mary was courting?"

The girl grinned. "Why, 'twas that sullen Donn o'Dungarvan, mum, Brendan o'Dungarvan's brother. Aye, and a sly wretch he is, if ever I've seen one! He'll get a babe in Mary's belly, then he'll go running off t' sea, just like . . ."

Edan did not hear the rest of what she was saying. Her thoughts were pursuing different quarry. *Donn o'Dungarvan.* The name of the traitor who'd left their numbers near Winchester to join Canute's ranks! The man who'd slain Kerrin's horse. She swallowed, suddenly dry mouthed with fear. And if Dungarvan was here, in County Waterford, surely there was every chance Canute was also here? And if that were true, then what had been Donn's purpose in returning in secret to Waterford and courting little Mary in the woods . . . ?

To learn their numbers! screamed a voice in her head. Why else? And what point would there be in knowing their numbers or what defenses Kerrin had readied, unless his master, Canute planned to attack?

"My ladies! Girls! Make haste!" she called. "Gather up your baskets. We must return to the keep—quickly! Oh, make haste! Run!" Even as she spoke, Canute could be advancing upon the keep, he and his pack planning to fall like wolves upon unsuspecting Wulfskeep.

"Why, my lady? What's wrong? Are ye ill?"

"Nay, nay, just . . . just make haste, Grania. Here, give me that basket, I'll tell ye as we go! Pegeen! Mary! Grace! Bridget—hurry!"

"Did Dungarvan tell ye where he was lodged, girl?" Tavish demanded, pacing around Mary. He was wearing a ferocious scowl.

"Nay, sir. I swear it!" she sobbed. "I thought he'd come

back with yerself and his lordship from Britain, I did! I didn't know!''

Tavish nodded, still unsmiling. ''And when he left ye, which way did he go?''

''D—deeper into the woods, sir,'' Mary whispered.

''Did he say anything—anything at all!—that might help us here?''

''Nothing, sir.'' Mary drew a long, shuddering breath. ''He—he asked how many men his lordship had come home with. An'—an' how many fighting men were in the new lord's garrison.''

''He put his questions just that way?''

''Well, nay, sir. It—it were a jest, like.''

''A jest? How so?'' Tavish demanded, rounding on the frightened wench. ''Tell me!''

A furious blush filled little Mary's cheeks. ''He said . . . he said that I were comely, sir. And that all the men o' Wulfskeep must be wanting t' court me. He laughed, then he said, ''Exactly how many lads are buzzing like bees around ye, my pretty Mary?'' Then he chucked me 'neath the chin. Well, I thought he were just funnin' me, so I told him. Oh, may I go now, please, sir?''

Tavish exchanged glances with Kerrin, who was seated in his lord's carved chair.

He looked every inch a chieftain that nooning, stern of face, black hair scraped back into a leather thong, a mantle of the mac Torrin plaid pinned at his right shoulder with a bronze wolf's head brooch. The jewelled hilt of his sword, Widow-Maker, jutted from the scabbard at his side. With a dismissing gesture of his hand, he nodded. ''Be gone, lass.''

Mary needed no second urging. Picking up her skirts, she fled the hall at a run, weeping noisily, as she went. Pegeen, Bridget, and the others were waiting at the doorway to console her. They bore her off to the kitchens for their own interrogation.

''So. What do you think?'' Tavish asked, when the wenches were gone.

''The same as I thought the first time I heard Dungarvan

was back in Waterford: that Canute will attack Wulfskeep,'' Kerrin said, grim-faced.

Tavish shrugged. ''Then we must prepare for the worst. You know him better than any of us—''

''Aye, more's the pity. I do!''

''—Then what's your best guess? How and when will your uncle attack?''

''How and when, I know not. But ye can rest assured, my friend, an attack will come by foul means, never fair. 'Tis his very nature to be underhanded, aye? Lies, half-truths, cowardly deceit—these are my uncle's stock-in-trade, as well you know.'' *Nevertheless, let him come!* he added silently. He would give his life before he let Canute lay claim to one iota of what was his. Because of the lies his uncle had told his father—the charges of adultery Canute had made against his mother—he had been robbed not only of both parents, but of his upbringing as a chieftain's son and heir. Canute would not rob him of Edan and Wulfskeep, too.

Chapter Twenty-Seven

Canute came, as Kerrin had foreseen, on the next dark-moon night, launching his attack—not from the direction of the woods, as might have been expected—but from the river itself, in true Viking fashion.

Dropping anchor in the mouth of the Suir, Canute and his men waded ashore from their vessel, their weapons borne aloft to keep them dry.

On the motte above the river, Wulfskeep slumbered—to all intents and purposes, their unsuspecting victim. The keep rose, dark and silent, from swirling river mist that was as thick as any mantle.

"Here they come!" Tavish hissed to the fighting men, concealed in the bushes all about him. "Steady, lads! Not yet! Steady!" He tightened his grip on the hilt of his sword. "Await my signal!"

"How many would ye say, Niall?" Kerrin asked softly.

"Thirty-five, forty at most, sir."

"Good. Our numbers are well-matched. Return to your men, captain. Bid them make ready."

As Niall scrambled back to his position along Wulfskeep's northeast wall, the first Viking attacker encountered one of

Kerrin's hidden men. Unable to see his footing in the darkness and the mist, he had trod upon Little Hurleigh's hand!

With a yelp, Hurleigh sprang up from the ground with his dagger in hand. *"For Wulfskeep, ye spalpeen!"* he roared, and threw himself upon the Viking with a banshee's howl. Wild-eyed, he slashed at the invader's throat, left, then right.

Blood gushed from the man's mortal wounds. He dropped to his knees, dead before he ever hit the ground.

Lunging forward, Hurleigh used the darkness for cover and thrust his blade deep into the next man's belly.

"Odiiiin!" the injured Viking roared. Despite his wound, he swung his two-headed axe in a sweeping curve, felling Hurleigh with a deep cut to his left side.

"Naaay!" screamed Hurleigh's boon companion, Brendan Dungarvan, whirling his broadsword over his head single-handed. With a single, sweeping cut, he lopped the attacker's head from his body. "And a good riddance to ye, brother Donn! Ye'll betray us no more, by God!"

"For Wulfskeep!" Tavish roared. "Forward!"

All along the riverbanks, men sprang up from the darkness and mist, as if the night had suddenly sprouted a human harvest! Blade crashed against blade. Groans, screams, and the thuds of flesh meeting flesh rang out over the river, carried into the misty darkness and the damp night air.

"Lothar and Canute. Do ye see them, Tavish?" Kerrin panted, slamming the flat of his blade across the skull of one man. The blow crushed the back of his attacker's skull like an eggshell.

"Nay, sir. I do not," Tavish came back, flicking runnels of sweat from his eyes. Planting a boot on the chest of the man he'd run through, he withdrew his bloody blade.

"Then where the devil are they, man? Blessed Jesu, *where are they?"* But it was only a rhetorical question. Kerrin suddenly knew exactly where they were, where they *must* be. Yet, he had no time to act upon that knowledge. Even as he turned, another attacker fell upon him. "Fall back!" he roared. "Fall back t' defend the keep!"

* * *

"What was that?" Edan sat up. Head cocked, she held her breath to listen. She had tried to stay awake last night, as she had for the past three nights, but had failed once again, falling into an exhausted, uneasy slumber that lasted till she awoke with the dawn. The hall was still dark this time, however, lit only by a solitary torch and the flicker of the fire, about which they'd congregated,

"Hmm? I heard nothing, my lady," Grania mumbled sleepily, yawning and only half awake. In an instinctively protective gesture, she pressed her palm to her belly, as she struggled to sit up, rubbing bleary eyes on her knuckles.

"I heard it too, my lady," Maida volunteered, casting aside the blanket that covered her so she could sit up. " 'Twas a scream!"

"Aye," Edan agreed, unhappily. "I thought so, too."

All around them on the rushes, the women of Wulfskeep were coming awake, stirring, yawning, stretching cramped limbs. Alarm and fear filled their pale faces, as Edan and Maida explained what they had heard.

"You, Pegeen, come with mistress Maida and myself. The rest of you, stay here. Remain calm, but be ready for anything. Matthew, Mistress Sullivan, and you, Mary, turn the trestles over against the wall. Have the children hide behind them. The rest of you, go to the kitchens and arm yourselves with whatever comes to hand. Ladles, fleshhooks, pitchforks, brooms—any weapon is better than your bare fists. But hurry!"

"I will come with ye, my lady," Matthew demanded. Having been torn from the care of the monks and the church, he had since decided he was better suited to the life of a warrior than a novitiate. When he was not in Kerrin or Tavish's shadow, he hung about the men of the garrison, doing as they did, speaking as they did, aping their swaggering gait, their rough-and-ready soldiers' manners. Consequently, it had not pleased him when Kerrin had sternly ordered him to remain behind with the women, children, and old ones. He had begged to be allowed to take part in the defense of his new home.

''Nay, Matthew,'' Kerrin had told him sternly, a heavy hand clamped over the boy's shoulder. ''You're all your mother has left now. And if ye've a mind to disobey me, remember that a warrior never refuses the order of his lord. Besides, the women and children will need a man to defend them, should the enemy break through our ranks. 'Tis an honor I do ye, boy! I'm entrusting ye with my own lady's care.''

Matthew had scowled, but said nothing more. Now, with Kerrin gone, he was far more vocal. ''I can defend ye, my lady!'' he vowed, brandishing the light, short sword that Niall had fashioned for him from a full-sized, broken weapon.

''Very well. My thanks,'' Edan accepted solemnly, and Matthew's blue eyes shone in the gloom.

''Do ye think the Vikings will get through the men, my lady?'' Mary asked shakily. Her blue eyes were dilated with terror. Tales of Torrin's attack upon Waterford many years ago had fueled the nightmares of her childhood.

''I hope and pray not,'' she came back. ''But whilst I am gone, all of you, pray. Pray very hard, and ask God to protect us all this night!''

''We will. Take care, my lady,'' Grania murmured, stepping forward to kiss her cheek. ''May God be with you.''

''And with you.'' Giving Grania a kiss and a quick hug, she took up her sword, crossed herself, and was gone.

Matthew, Pegeen, and Maida, armed with wooden staffs, followed her out into the darkened bailey. The men Kerrin had left behind to defend the keep proper were ranged behind slits in the walls, or else stationed in the watchtowers along them. They were armed with bows and arrows, as well as broadswords and daggers, but the overcast night would make all but hand to hand combat virtually impossible.

What little they could see confirmed Edan's suspicions, however, and the captain of the guard gave gruff orders to her and her ladies to go back to the hall.

Shouts, screams, and the clang and crash of metal against metal were readily heard from up here. The cries were chilling to the listening women and the lad, though they only seemed to fuel the excitement of the seasoned warriors, who—like old warhorses—were eager to be a part of the battle. The occasional wink through the mist, of moon and star on blade and helm, confirmed that a fierce battle was indeed taking place below. Moreover, they could see the prow of a single dragon-ship anchored in the river mouth, its serpent figurehead silhouetted against the water.

As if to underscore the danger, at that moment, a hunting horn sounded three long blasts in succession. It was the signal the men had agreed upon! The garrison captain answered it with three blasts of his own.

"Those blasts mean his lordship's falling back t' defend the keep," Matthew explained importantly, pleased to contribute something.

"Very well. We had best return to the hall. I want to make sure our women are armed and the children well hidden, should Canute break through our walls. Come on!"

But the instant Edan reentered the hall, she sensed that something was terribly awry.

The air in the hall crackled, charged with fear and with something more—something that turned the blood in her veins to ice.

The children were hidden behind the overturned trestles, wailing and sobbing loudly. But it was not their crying that raised the hackles on the back of her neck, but the behavior of their mothers. Whitefaced, the women awkwardly sat or stood about the hall, their eyes enormous with terror. They were staring straight ahead, unnaturally stiff and still. Tears glistened on Mary's ashen cheeks in the torchlight, while Bridget seemed close to swooning.

"What is it?" she asked hoarsely. "For the love of God, tell me! What has happened here?"

"*We* have happened, my lady. Or should I call you, 'niece?' Lothar, ye whoreson! Did you not hear your lady cousin? Show her what you've been about!" a scornful voice demanded.

"*Ja,* min Father." A hideous giant with lank brown hair and massive shoulders stepped from the shadows, a woman held erect before him like a mannikin. Her head was lolling on her chest, while her long, fair hair swept forward, covering her face like a veil. From the angle of her head, Edan knew, with a sickening jolt, that her neck was broken.

The giant grasped a fistful of the woman's hair and pulled it back, so that her head was raised, her face exposed. "Pretty!" he said thickly, lovingly, looking first at the woman, then grinning down at Edan.

The blood drained from her lips. Her knees buckled.

It was Grania.

"My uncle has outdone himself in this foul murder," Kerrin said bitterly, heartsick, as Tavish, stone-faced, gently lifted his wife's limp body into his arms and bore her slowly from the hall. "Damme Canute's black soul! He shall pay for this senseless murder with his life! Niall!"

"Sir!"

"Have the wounded carried to the hall for the women to tend. Then pick a score of men—your best! We're going after Canute."

"I'm going with you," Tavish said softly, a terrible fury in his eyes, as he strode back into the hall.

Kerrin nodded. Tavish's need for vengeance was one he understood, all too well.

" 'Tis Wulfskeep he's after, sir," Niall pointed out softly, noting the tightening of his lord's jaw. "Never fear, your lady will be safe, till she has served his purpose."

"And what purpose might that be, sir?" asked Lachlann.

"The same as when Jarl Torrin lived, ye simpleton. Canute hopes to ransom our lady for this keep!" snarled Brendan.

"Enough, men! Waste no further time in talk!" Kerrin snapped. "To horse!"

"But, how shall we find them, lord? 'Tis dark as the bottom of a well out there!" Trevor pointed out. "And misty, besides."

"I'll show ye!" piped up a young voice, shrill with excitement, exhaustion, fear. His clothing wet with dew, his face streaked with mud, his bright hair tangled with twigs and leaves, Matthew staggered into their midst.

"Matthew!" his mother cried, overjoyed to see him back, safe.

But Matthew waved her away, stepping importantly past his mother and Niall to Kerrin.

"My lord, I know where they've taken the mistress! Ye told me t' guard her with my life, so I followed them!"

"Good man. Lead on!" his chieftain commanded. "By God, lead on!"

Chapter Twenty-Eight

Kerrin remained silent, deep in troubled thought, as they rode forth from Wulfskeep into the waking world.

When Thorvald had taken Edan, he had felt a deep and inconsolable sense of loss. Now that Canute had done so, he felt as if his very heart had been tore, beating, from his breast. He clenched his jaw, fighting the tide of emotion that rose through him, threatening to unman him.

In but the space of a few short months, she'd become more dear to him than life itself, he realized. In truth, he would give his own life for hers, were it asked of him, for he had come to fear death far less than he feared living without the woman he loved.

Matthew rode behind him on the roan's broad rump, clinging to his sides like a limpet. To his right rode Tavish, his usually merry face carved with the fresh, deep wounds of grief. Though he kept his feelings under brutal rein, Kerrin could guess the self-recriminations that filled his head. *"If only I'd not done such and such!"* Or, *"I might have saved Grania, had I done this or that."*

He was harboring the same thoughts himself, blaming himself for Edan's abduction. Had he not said that everything

Canute did was devious or underhanded? He should have known he would not content himself with a simple attack on Wulfskeep! He should never have assigned so few of his garrison to defend the women and children left behind in his keep. He should have . . .

"Are ye sure this is the way, boyo?" he heard Tavish softly ask young Matthew.

"Aye, sir. I am."

"That sly bastard! D'ye see what he's done, Kerrin? Canute's circled back. He's taking your lady to his *drakkar!*" Tavish suddenly exclaimed. "Where did you see them last, lad?" he demanded of the boy.

"Up there, sir!" Matthew indicated a point just above the river, where a small copse of trees would offer concealment to a handful of men trying to reach the river. In the meager dawn light, however, they could see very little.

Kerrin rose in his stirrups, not looking inland, but toward the dragon-ship anchored in the river. *Tavish was right!* His guess also explained why Canute's men had fallen back so soon after launching their attack. They'd been needed to man the *drakkar's* oars when Canute and Lothar returned with the hostage!

Sure enough—though it was too far for him to see details of faces—the bright glitter of water, streaming off many oars in the dawn light, showed that oarsmen were indeed in place, pulling hard to row Canute's dragon-ship, *The Serpent,* downriver to the sea.

"To the dragon-ship!" Kerrin cried, turning the roan's head to the landing where his vessel had been beached.

As one man, the riders turned their mounts toward the river after Kerrin, riding down to the shingle banks at suicide pace.

The first long fingers of a saffron sunrise were stretching over the land, as Kerrin and his men sprang down from their lathered horses. They hefted the *Storm Chaser* up, onto their shoulders and bore her down to the water at a run. In another moment, they had scrambled aboard her.

Though only two-thirds the number needed to properly propel the vessel, they took the rowers' seats and bent their backs to the oars to move the *drakkar* smoothly out into the center of the river.

"*Pull!*" Kerrin roared, punching the air with his fist to give weight to his command. "*Pull!*" He stood in the bows with his booted feet braced apart on the decks, his dark hair furling on the wind. The *Storm Chaser* rose and fell, riding the river in swift pursuit of the other vessel, her prow lifting like the nose of a greyhound scenting the wind.

As the distance between them closed, Kerrin saw his uncle standing in the bows and was struck as never before by his resemblance to his hated father, Torrin.

Hatred boiled inside him. Like Torrin, Canute had a long red-gold beard and long, shaggy locks beneath his winged helmet. And, like Torrin, Canute was a merciless predator: one who preyed upon those weaker than himself. He was a cold, heartless killer, a man to whom power and riches were everything. In Canute's life, neither love nor kinship played any part.

At the moment, Canute's red-lipped mouth was parted in a jeering, challenging shout.

"What does the old divil say?" Tavish asked, coming to stand beside him.

Kerrin clenched his jaw. A muscle ticked in his temple. "He said, 'Your keep or your woman! Choose, nephew!' "

"Whoreson dog! Get me close enough, Kerrin! But give me the chance, I'll tear the whoreson limb from limb!" Tavish seethed, his fists clenched, his brown eyes burning. "The blood eagle will flap its wings upon Canute's back, 'ere this day dies, I swear it on my love for Grania!"

It was no idle threat.

"I can hit him from here, sir!" Brendan claimed, nocking an arrow against his bowstring.

"Good man! Ready your weapon, but stay low and await my signal," he murmured.

In a voice that carried clearly across the water, he shouted, "If ye would bargain, Uncle, ye must prove my lady yet lives!"

In answer, Canute turned from them. When he turned back, Edan stood beside him, both fragile wrists held fast in Lothar's cruel grip. A length of chain connected her hands. Her face was pale, yet furious.

"Edaaaan!" Kerrin roared, the cry ripped from him.

"Stay back!" she screamed. Despite her pallor, her voice was strong, as she added, "His promises are empty! He will kill me, no matter what you do! Stay back!"

" 'Tis a chance ye must take, is it not, Kerrin Torrinson!" Canute jeered, using the Viking form of Kerrin's name. He forced Edan to stand directly before Lothar, destroying Brendan's chance of picking off the giant with an arrow. "Choose, nephew! Which will it be? Your woman, or Wulfskeep?"

"Ram them, sir!" Niall murmured, joining them. "Let the bastards swim for it!"

Tavish and Kerrin exchanged quick glances. Niall's plan was a good one. Besides, their options were damnably few. If Canute escaped down the river to the sea, Kerrin might never see Edan again. At least with Niall's way, there was a chance . . .

"Prepare to ram!" he barked. "You heard your captain, lads! *Pull! Pull! Puuull!*"

The *Chaser* shot forward, true to her name. Her dragon prow lanced through the water like a stooping hawk falling upon its prey, as she closed the distance between herself and the other vessel.

Realizing what Kerrin was about, Canute threw back his head and roared with mocking laughter. "Try to ram me, would ye, ye young whelp? Come on, then! Do it, damme ye! Let's see whose blood is stronger: your Viking sire's or your Irish dam's!"

From her position in the stern, Edan had guessed what Kerrin was about to try. The *Chaser* was fast bearing down upon them, rapidly gaining speed, although her crew was incomplete. Should Kerrin succeed in ramming Canute's vessel—as he very well might!—everyone aboard the *Serpent* would be thrown into the river! And with her hands chained, there was a good chance she would be drowned in the confusion. Or that Kerrin would risk his own life to save hers, unless . . .

In the instant before the two vessels collided, she jabbed viciously backwards with first one elbow, then the other, then stepped hard on both the enormous boots behind her. She heard Lothar's startled grunt, but flung herself forward before he had time to recover his wind, twisting like an eel to escape the dimwit's outstretched paws.

"After her, oaf!" Canute roared.

But in three strides, she'd reached the *Serpent's* sides and had flung herself over, plunging feet first into the chill river with a mighty splash.

Lothar's massive fists closed on air, just missing her flying hair, as he lunged after her. His great size had worked against him, just as she'd hoped. His weight had also made him slow and clumsy—and unable to stop.

Thrown off balance, he followed Edan over the side.

Seconds later, the prow of the *Chaser* plowed into the stern of Canute's vessel. There was a terrible grinding of wood upon wood. A shriek sounded that was uncannily alive, as timbers splintered and shattered. Then both vessels gave a great shudder—the death rattle of two great sea monsters, locked in their death throes.

Kerrin leaped up onto the gunwales. He poised there for an instant or two, frantically searching the churning water, then arched over the side.

Moments later, the *Chaser* heeled violently and began sinking. All aboard her either slithered from her decks, or were flung headlong into the river. The crew of the *Serpent* were likewise cast overboard.

The river churned with movement, as though it were boiling, as both lurching vessels took on water and rapidly sank. Over fifty men struck out frantically to gain the nearest shore, some screaming that they could not swim. Provisions and belongings bobbed about.

In all the confusion, Kerrin could not find the beloved dark head he'd sighted before he dived. He surfaced once again, spewing water and flicking his dark head to see, scanning the river all about him. *Where was she? To where had she vanished?*

He dived again, thrusting aside a body that he recognized: Canute's drowned corpse. He fought his way through choking water weeds and clouds of river mud in search of Edan. Lungs exploding, he bobbed up again like a cork. And, as his streaming head broke the surface, he heard her frantic cry.

"Kerr-*agggh!*"

Sweet Jesu! Lothar had her! While Kerrin had thought her still trapped under water, the giant had dragged her from the river and up onto the banks. Both massive arms wound about her. He held her before him as he had held Grania, while he paused to catch his breath.

Kerrin swallowed. If Lothar was startled, frightened in any way, he might tighten his hold and crush every bone in her body. . . .

"Pretty!" Lothar gurgled thickly. Water streamed from his hair and clothing, as he leered down at Edan.

Like a man possessed, Kerrin struck out for the shore, yet it was like some terrible nightmare in which the water had turned to a thick, dragging ooze that kept him from gaining the banks. Time seemed to stand still as he swam, and he knew, with a terrible certainty, that he could not hope to reach her in time.

And then, as he crawled out onto the opposite banks at last, his lungs afire and breathing heavily, he heard Tavish shout: "*Lothar!*"

He heard, rather than saw, Tavish's arrow. The air of its passage kissed his cheek, whining like the high-pitched song of the wind through the strings of a harp.

The arrowhead found its target in Lothar's jutting brow, striking him between the eyes and killing him instantly.

The giant's eyes opened very wide, as if he could not comprehend what had befallen him. Then he threw up his arms and toppled backwards, releasing his precious hostage, as he fell.

"Christ, man! An inch or two lower, ye'd have killed my bride!" Kerrin growled, as Edan ran into his arms.

Tavish permitted himself a thin, mirthless smile. Tears glistened in his eyes, as he murmured softly. "Never, milord. Sure, and I had an angel guiding me, don't ye know . . . ?"

Chapter Twenty-Nine

In the weeks following Grania's death, Edan tried time and time again to draw comfort from the closeness of the marriage bed. Yet, though Kerrin would hold her, kiss her, offer his comfort in any other fashion, he would not lie with her.

Most nights, she fell asleep weeping, mourning Grania, then mourning the closeness she'd lost with her husband by turns. And, when her spirits were at their lowest ebb, she blamed herself for both.

But summer came at last to Waterford—although it was winter in her heart—spilling golden sunshine over the land and ripening the crops that stood tall in the fields.

The glorious light lasted well into the evening, while the harvest was gathered in, flooding the hills with liquid gold, before day melted into starlit, sultry night. Kerrin went out into the fields and worked alongside the reapers, driven by some inner demon she could not comprehend.

The corncrake's harsh cry replaced the spring call of the cuckoo. The thrush and blackbird warbled all day long, yet Edan could take no pleasure in their soaring song.

"What has changed between us? What have I done, that you will not share my bed, sir?" she demanded, rounding on Kerrin one evening. Once again, he'd made some poor excuse for not retiring with her, and she was done with pretending it did not matter. "Do you find me ugly? Repulsive?"

"You know full well that I find thee lovely, my treasure," he gently admonished her, tweaking her chin. "Had I not, sure, and I would have left ye in Hedeby!"

But she did not smile at his gentle teasing, nor soften at his endearments.

"How would I know how you feel about me, milord? You have not lain with me in many weeks, sir! What else should I think, pray, but that I'm abhorrent to ye?"

The quiver of her lower lip, the break in her voice, cut him to the quick, yet she bravely lifted her chin and glared at him, demanding an answer.

"Edan—love—the fault is not in you."

"Oh? Where is it, then, pray? Do you—do you have a leman, sir? Some other wench who pleases you, since I do not?"

"Edan, don't!" he growled. "There is no woman but you, I swear it. You are my life, my heart. Never think so!"

"Then what am I to think?" She rounded on him, furiously pacing their bower. "You swear that you love me—and yet you will not hold me. You say that you desire me—and yet you will not share my bed! Forgive me if I doubt your claims of love, sir!" she flung at him. Her voice was husky with emotion, her eyes the muddy hue of pewter in her hurt.

"It is *because* I love you that I will not—cannot!—share your bed," he explained heavily at some length. He stood with his hands clasped behind his back, his broad shoulders rigid, as he stared into the fire.

"But, why? If you would have me understand, explain yourself, pray! Are you . . . are you ill in some way?"

He grimaced. "In a manner of speaking, aye. Soul sick, some call it."

"Soul sick? I do not understand, sir."

A nerve danced at his temple. "I have been cursed."

"What!—" She snorted in disbelief. Her first reaction to his bald statement was an overwhelming desire to laugh, but Kerrin's grave expression forbade such frivolous response on her part. He was graver, more serious than she had ever seen him. Furthermore, the admission had clearly been torn from him, judging by the anguish in his face.

"Cursed? But by whom, sir?" she began, gently. "When did it happen? Why and how?"

"The mac Torrin bloodline was cursed by my grandfather, Earl Murragh, before my birth. With his dying breath, he condemned all of Torrin's seed. It happened to Torrin, and now, it is happening to me! I can feel the power of that curse inside me, Edan! It gnaws at me, devouring all that is good and just and right!"

"I—I see," she said slowly, though she did not, not really. How could she? "But what has Murragh's curse to do with sharing our marriage bed?"

"Do you not see?" he demanded hoarsely. "A child conceived of my seed would be tainted by the same foul curse!"

Understanding dawned. "Sweet Jesu!" she whispered, crossing herself.

"This, my love, is why I've shunned your bed. The *only* reason."

"But there must be a way to counter such a curse? We must think!"

"I *have* thought—long and hard," Kerrin insisted, his face stern, although the touching way she said 'we,' rather than 'you,' had not gone unnoticed. "Night after night, I have lain awake, seeking a solution."

"And you have found one?" she whispered hopefully, reading something in his face that made her suddenly breathless.

"I have." A sad smile curved his lips at the eager way her eyes lit up, but it was quickly gone. "I have decided the truest measure of my love would be for me to . . . to leave you."

"Leave me?" she echoed, the words choked from her. Eyes smoking, she shook her head from side to side in furious denial. Her lip curled in scorn. "*Ha!* That is no 'solution' at all, my lord! 'Tis but a—a craven's retreat!"

His green eyes darkened. His jaw tightened. "Call me coward if you will, but 'tis true. Better were you my widow, than my wife."

"Never say so!" she cried, furious, her voice cracking. Running to him, she beat at his chest with her fists. *"Never, never, never!"*

He stood there, tight-lipped, hard jawed, his hands clenched at his sides making no effort to ward off her blows as her fists rained over him. When the storm of hurt and angry frustration had finally spent itself, she uttered a strangled sob and wrapped her arms about him, instead, holding him lovingly, fiercely. "I love you! I won't abandon you, not for some wretched curse, not for anything! How dare you think I could give thee up because of this! Or love thee any less?"

Dear God, the thud of his heart was so loud beneath her cheek. How could she go on, were that great heart stilled? If the warm, vital body in her arms were grown stiff and cold in death? She gritted her teeth. Giving up was not her way. She would not surrender him to any power—be it of this world or of some other—not without a fight.

There was a catch in her throat as she looked up. Kerrin's tormented expression tore at her heart. Going up on tiptoe, she pressed trembling fingertips across his lips and commanded, "Hush. Speak no more of dying! There *is* an antidote. There must be! If it can be found, I will find it!"

"Not for this poison, my love. You know it, too, in your heart. Why else would you weep?" He traced the glistening snail trail of a tear down her cheek, then brought that finger to his lips, tasting the salt of her sorrow upon it.

Edana. His lady wife, the Queen of his heart. He loved her more than life itself, but—

But despite his love, it was becoming harder to fight his other, inner self. To keep at bay that savage side of his nature, which stirred with every rising of the moon and the promise that night was imminent. The same insistent voice that urged him now to turn from the woman—turn, and answer the call!

Unable to ignore the siren song, he slowly shifted his gaze from Edan to stare through the narrow windeye. There was longing and a reluctant fascination in his gaze. After a few moments, he added softly, as if speaking to himself, "This thing is of the Otherworld, do you not see, my sweet? Not even the power of love can destroy it.''

And, if he were ruthlessly honest, there was a part of him that no longer wanted to destroy it! A growing part of him that yearned to embrace the life of the man-wolf, to run with the pack, to lose himself in the deep woods with others who were unworthy of being loved.

He licked his chops. Beyond Wulfskeep, the darkened hillsides clambered up from the banks of the gleaming Suir to meet the charcoal underbelly of the sky. Shadowy forests lay beyond them, leafy treetops bathed in gray-white light. The huge August moon was as full as a gold mancuse. Its reflection swam in the indigo channel, a silvery path of shimmering light that reached from the murky horizon to the foot of the granite cliffs.

A full midsummer moon, and the wolfsbane was blooming. . . .

A part of him longed to be abroad on this moon-drenched Lamas' Eve, so rich with promise and magic. The night shimmered with the sharp scents of danger, of excitement, and of those secrets known only to the brethren of man-wolves.

The slow evolution taking place within him—its seeds sown, when he was but a child—was almost complete, he sensed. Soon, he would be one of them. Would become one *with* them forever! He need no longer fear for his immortal soul, for he would have no soul. Rather, he would live forever, craving the flesh and warm blood of mortals, as he ran with the pack.

An involuntary quiver moved through him. He twitched, flexing his spine and hindquarters. A silent howl coalesced in his throat, straining to burst forth. His nostrils flared, while cords stood out down his throat with the effort it took to maintain his human form. A delicious shudder of anticipation began at the nape of his neck. It rippled down his spine, making his hackles lift, stirring the fine hairs down his forearms, so that they stood on end. They were calling him to the hunt. . . .

''Kerrin? *Kerrin, nay!*'' Edan cried. ''You are wrong! Our love can conquer anything. Aye, even this!'' Cupping his chin, she made him look at her, praying her hold upon him was strong enough to bring him back from that other, shadowy realm his spirit longed to enter.

Thank God, it was. For now.

Slowly, he turned and looked at her, over his shoulder.

She flinched, despite herself, for as their eyes met, his glowed green. They were ringed with sulphur, brimming with gold— And there was more: In just those few moments, she fancied the bones of his skull had subtly begun to alter, too, flattening in some places, elongating in others, so that there was a savage cast—a blurring of his chiselled features—that had not been there a short while before. The shadow of his beard seemed darker, heavier, too, as if he was shifting form and shape, becoming—becoming—

Nay! She would not say it, would not even think it! To give her fears a name would make them *real*. She was afraid, yet she stood her ground. She must have courage, if she was to help her husband. Still, the tiny, yet telling, signs of his metamorphosis filled her with dread. ''I love you, Kerrin!'' she reminded him, hoarsely. ''For my sake, if not to save your soul, I beg you, *fight it!* Don't go to them! Stay here with me, and with our people!''

For what seemed an eternity, he gave no answer. Nor did he give any sign that he had heard her. He seemed instead to be listening, ears pricked, to some other, inner voice she could not hear.

A low, warning sound rumbled in his throat. A threatening growl? His eyes glowed in the firelit gloom of their bower.

''Kerrin! For the love of God, heed me!''

God's name succeeded, where her own had not.

As if waking from a dream, Kerrin flicked his head. The glowing sulphur in his eyes dimmed, as he looked down at her, then vanished completely. His unnatural alertness softened.

''Edan, I!—Forgive me.'' Taking her icy hand between his own, he drew it to his lips. It was soft and smooth as the moss on a tree, yet warmer, richly alive. He could sense her blood pulsing, flowing just beneath the fragile surface of her skin. He inhaled her scent. Its vital, lovely fragrance filled him with shame, as much as it did pleasure, for it was the smell of innocence, of virtue and goodness.

The scent of all that he was not, and never could be.

"Edan. Fairest Edan," he murmured. Spanning her slender waist, he drew her closer. "You must accept that there can be no escape from this. Not for me. Nor can there be any future for the two of us, unless Murragh's curse is lifted." He paused. "You and I, we are worlds apart, my love. As different as night and day, or good and evil. That is why I have decided to—to set you free."

Free? She wetted her lips and was filled with slow burning anger, as his meaning sank home. What was he trying to tell her? That he meant to send her back to her father's household like . . . like some unwanted hound? Or, did he speak in riddles in which "free" meant death? His own death and, with it, her freedom?

Fresh, furious tears welled anew behind her eyelids. She swallowed over the aching lump in her throat, refusing to yield to useless tears. "Nay, my lord! There is yet hope! If curses can be placed, they can be lifted!"

He ran a troubled hand through his long dark hair. "Once, perhaps, aye. But, now—"

"Tell me! What is so different now, pray?"

"It has been too long. For years now, this . . . thing . . . has continued to grow in me like a poisonous weed. It has flourished unchecked, feasting itself upon the hatred and coldness my father instilled in me. Man-wolf . . . shapeshifter . . . call it what you will, the beast has become a part of me now. *The greater part!* Soon, there will be nothing of Padraic mac Torrin—nor of Kerrin—left to love!"

"Even were there but the smallest part remaining, I would yet love you!" She hardened her jaw. "But, you are right. If you choose to run, rather than fight this thing—then *ja*, the beast will win!" she flung back at him, her speech and her aggressive hands-on-hips stance an unconscious imitation of her fiery mother at the height of an angry outburst. She tossed her midnight hair over her shoulders and glared at him, her gray eyes smoldering. "Well? Have you no answer? Tell me, what else are you becoming, husband?'' she demanded. ''Some lily-livered whelp? A white-spleened coward who flinches at shadows? Beloved . . . Kerrin. . . . hear me!'' she begged in a gentler, yet no less determined, tone. '' 'Tis too soon to yield. I have not come to love you just to give you up! We must—we *shall*—find another way!''

Her voice had risen at the last. It was laced with fear, despite her ringing vows. *Perhaps he was right? Perhaps it really was too late?* Already she could sense him leaving her, withdrawing. Could sense that he was turning from the love they had so newly found. Abandoning the trust and passion they had only begun to share.

A part of him was eager to be gone, she sensed. To become one with the night. To join the slender gray shadows who called to him from the forest's edge. *Jesu!* She could hardly bear to look at him this way! Every fiber of his being strained towards the door. His ears were pricked. His fine dark head was raised and cocked, alert as any mastiff's. Even his nostrils were flared to capture the night scents that streamed through the windeye!

The man within him was dwindling. Soon, only the wolf would hold sway. . . .

She swallowed, denial beginning its silent screaming in her head. His howling brethren of man-wolves would not have him. She would not let them.

She and Kerrin had been joined twice over—once by the holy vows they'd taken, a second time by those forged in their hearts. They belonged together now. Dark Death would not come between them, nay, not yet. She was the daughter of Prince Alaric, Bear of Kent. The daughter of Freya, Lady of Danehof. Above all, she was Edana, Lady of Wulfskeep, wife to Padraic Kerrin mac Torrin, her lord, her love, her very heart. And she would risk anything to save him!—

''What of Old Myrla,'' she demanded suddenly, pacing back and forth over the rushes. ''Can she do naught?''

He frowned. ''She is but a country midwife. A charm woman and reader of runes. She owns no powers beyond these. Sure, and had she possessed such knowledge, she'd have used it long since," he told her, gently. "After all, 'twas she who brought me into this world."

He offered no further explanations. After all, what could he say? Instead, he drew her against him and held her tight, flattening her small, round breasts against his abdomen. Burying his face in her hair, he inhaled her elusive scent, as if he would drown in its bouquet. God help him, even if this was the last night he ever held her, he wanted her as never before!

"Edan," he breathed. "My precious wee colleen. . . ." He swept aside her fragrant hair to kiss the soft hollow where her throat met her shoulder. "You are all that is gentle and good in my life." It was no lie. Before Edan, he'd had little contact with her like, he reflected.

Summoned to Torrin's hall while yet a small boy, he had been wrenched from Myrla's stern yet gentle care, given over to Torrin's cruelty and vindictiveness, and the vicious spite of his whores.

Even now, he could remember, all too well, the frightened, lonely little lad he'd been, hiding his broken, battered heart behind so many thorny walls that no one could ever hope to scale them—not old Myrla, and certainly not his mother. Only among the wild things had he felt acceptance and ease. It was from hound, horse, and hawk that had learned how to care and to be cared for—till Edan came into his life.

"Love, oh, dearest love," she whispered, turning to him. He lowered his head and she tilted her flower face up to his, like a sunflower lifting its face to the morning sun. As they kissed, her hands wormed their way beneath the soft linen folds of his tunic. She murmured against his lips, as she ran her hands over the lean, hard body beneath it. Her lips parted beneath his on a breathy sigh, yielding a clover sweetness. "Hmmm, how strong you feel."

The muscles of his belly clenched beneath the fairy brush of her fingers. His groin tightened with desire. Reaching around her, he cupped her buttocks and drew her closer. His manhood rose hard against her soft belly, as he pressed her against him, chest to chest, hard flank to curving hip. "Edan, ah, my own

colleen,'' he breathed thickly. ''Sure, woman, I need ye t'
night.''

''As I need you,'' she responded, trembling at the impassioned timbre of his voice. ''But . . . not here, in this airless
bower. 'Tis Lamas' Eve, my lord! Did you forget? And, though
your lawful bride, I have yet to be properly bedded. . . .''

''You said otherwise the first time I had ye, as I recall!'' he
reminded her, pointedly. A reluctant grin tugged at the corners
of his sensual mouth, as he recalled the fisherman's cobwebby
hovel they'd shared, the drumming rain that had fallen all
that night—and her cries of passion fulfilled. ''Not properly
bedded,'' indeed!

She smiled, remembering. ''Enough of your teasing, mac
Torrin. Will ye follow me?''

''To the ends of the blessed earth, if you but say the word!''

Her gray eyes turned silvery in the meager light. Her teeth
became pearly, as she laughed. ''Never fear, 'tis not so far as
that!''

''Where, then?''

''Sure, and you'll see, soon enough, boyo,'' she came back
cheekily, flashing him a mysterious, bewitching smile.

Tonight, they would consummate their marriage all over
again, she promised herself, just as the god, Lugh, had consummated his marriage to a mortal bride that first eve of Lamas.

And in that special place, she would ask the Gray Maidens
to lift the curse from Kerrin. 'Twas said that fire was best
fought with fire, was it not? Perhaps curses from the Otherworld
were best battled with forces from the same? . . .

Taking his hand, she led him away from the smoky, airless
keep, into the sultry hush of the summer's eve.

Chapter Thirty

In serene silence, broken only by the whisper of the breeze through the grass and the faint hooting of a white owl, as it drifted over the hills, she led him from the marshes about the river's mouth, toward the Comeragh foothills.

The countryside was brightly lit by the light of the August moon. Following a rough sheep track that circled the silent lough, before turning toward the headlands, they clambered up amidst ragged slabs and craggy outcroppings of dark granite that made angry wounds in the coarse turf and came finally to a place of cliffs. From there, they could look down over the sleeping hamlet of Waterford, or follow the gleaming black and silver snake of the Suir to its outpouring in the moon washed channel of St. George, beyond.

On nearby hillsides, both to the east and the west, the bonfires of those who'd come to County Waterford for the Lamas' fair glowed red against the night. Indeed, on this eve, folk all over Eire—and those across the water, on the isle of Britain—would be congregating in fields near large hamlets such as this one. They met on the first day of August to celebrate the old pagan feast day of Lugnasadh, converted to the Christian harvest feast of Lamas, which coincided with the gathering in of the sheaves.

The festivities would begin early tomorrow morn at Wulfs-keep's chapel, when the priest gave his traditional blessing to the harvest's first loaves. Then the celebration would continue in earnest with horse races, sword fights, wrestling contests, and so on. There would be strolling jugglers and acrobats to delight the crowds. Bards playing harps and flutes, as well as merchants and tinkers with stalls offering gaily colored ribands, feathered caps, mantles, purses, leather pattens, and such. Smiths, artisans, and farmers would be selling their various wares.

Traditionally, parents arranged marriages for their sons and daughters on Lamas' Day, too, and signed the betrothal contracts on this same date. In pagan times, those weddings were celebrated before the setting of the sun on the following eve.

And, like her's and Kerrin's, after moonrise, those weddings would be consummated in bower, bush, or briar. . . .

Breathing hard, they reached the grassy cliffs upon which the Gray Maidens stood. The standing stones cast long moon shadows across the silent turf.

Edan could feel the ancient power of the henges thrumming within the stones, when she touched her fingertips to their cool, pitted surfaces. The same life thrummed within her veins, hummed in the earth and sod beneath her feet, yet she sensed no sinister threat emanating from the ancient monoliths. Whatever spirits dwelled within them were surely benign, rather than malevolent, so what had she to fear?

These stones were not like the forbidding horseshoe of henges that stood upon the windswept plains of Old Sarum in Britain. Nor were these soaked in the sacrificial blood of the ages.

The Maidens seemed friendly monuments—protective almost—like stout spinster aunts, robed in fraying stone! The image of aunts pleased her, for she had no aunts amongst her kinsmen.

"Gentle Aunts, hear me this Lamas' Eve! I beg thee, answer my prayer!" she implored silently, her eyes tightly closed. *"Lift Murragh's curse from my lord and love. Return him to*

me!'' Then, shaking out her mantle of midnight hair, she went to find Kerrin.

He had left the circle of ancient stones and was standing on the highest part of the cliff. Booted feet braced apart, black hair furling in the wind, he was gazing out across the gleaming dark mouth of the Suir to the moonlit, whitecapped channel of St. George beyond.

He had never looked so sternly handsome nor so alone as he did then. Her loving heart went out to him.

Stepping into the bright moonlight, she softly called his name.

He sucked in a breath, as she came toward him, for she was naked, but for her raven hair. She had woven a handful of pale wild flowers through its curling strands, like a Lamas bride. In the moonlight, her bare skin held the lustre of freshwater pearls. Her arms were slender and graceful, her belly and thighs ivory pale, in sharp contrast to the dark cluster of curls at their joining.

Though she could not be certain at such a distance, she thought Kerrin's features softened when he saw her, and her hopes soared. Smiling, she held out her arms to him. ''Come, my husband! 'Tis said the Maidens will grant a new bride any wish on Lamas' Eve. Let us pledge our love here, upon the grass. Then after, we will kneel and ask the spirits of the stones to bless us and remove the curse.''

The prayers of the Viking noblewoman, who had taken Alaine as her wetnurse, had been answered by standing stones such as these. Mayhap the Maidens would answer their prayers, too?

But to her dismay, Kerrin angrily shook his head. Scowling, his black brows crashed together in disapproval. ''Such beliefs are for children! Cover yourself, Edana. We can never be together that way again.'' His voice was thick and unsteady, as if he'd drunk too deep of the water o' life. ''Ah, my poor lady-lass! I should have left ye long before it came t' this pass,'' he added, despairingly.

''But my lord, we are husband and wife,'' she reminded him gently. ''And husbands and wives share a marriage bed.''

''Ordinary men, perhaps. But not this man,'' he denied vehe-

mently. "And not this woman. I shall bequeath this curse to
no innocent babe—nor put your life at risk a moment longer.
Go home, my sweet," he coaxed more gently. "Here. Wrap
my mantle about ye and go home." His hands were knotted
over the dark plaid. His grip was so fierce, his knuckles were
bled white. A muscle worked in his jaw, as he added, huskily,
"Forget me."

She bristled. Forget him, indeed! Wretched man, beloved
man, she'd as soon cut off her head than begin to forget him!
"Truly, there is nothing to fear. I have taken Edythe's herbs,"
she explained, gently, turning him to face her. "Believe me,
there can be no child from our coupling."

His brows lifted. "What is this?"

"My word upon it," she added, squirming at the patent
doubt in his piercing emerald eyes. "My lady mother swore
by Edythe's herbs and by her vinegar douches."

"The lady Marissa?" His dark brows rose.

She nodded. "After my little sister, Gayla was born, the
midwives warned that if she was brought to childbed again,
her life could be forfeit." She shrugged. "Sooner than banish
my father from her bed, my mother turned to Edythe's remedies
to prevent conception. That was almost five *childless* years
ago. So you see, there is naught to fear. Such methods work."
Hands on her swaying hips, she came towards him. "Now,
come ye here to me, my pretty young sir. Ye've naught to fear
from your Edana the Lusty. Green lad or nay, I shall deal with
thee gently, good master."

"Ye're mad, woman," he growled. Yet a reluctant grin
tugged at his lips. She sounded like some bawdy slattern, eager
to be tumbled in a ditch for a kiss and a mite. And God knew,
he wanted her tonight!—

"Mad, is it?" Laughing, she reached up and twined her arms
about his throat. Gently tugging his dark head down to hers
and whispered, "With you, pretty sir, Lusty Edana cannot help
herself!"

Her lashes dropped to veil her eyes, as she ran her fingers
up, up his muscled thigh, to cover the hard ridge at his groin.

Running the tip of her tongue across her swollen lower lip, she squeezed.

"Blessed Frey!" he groaned. "Stay your hand, my lovely witch!" There was a desperate light in his eyes now. His expression was that of a man brought dangerously close to the brink. "Have done, will ye, woman? It won't work, I say. I love ye too much!"

His words made her heart sing. "Do ye? Honestly and truly?"

"Aye!"

Grasping fistfuls of his black mane, she roughly tugged his head down to hers, silencing his sharp yelp of pain by sealing her lips to his. And then, when he was firmly anchored to her mouth, she drew his hands up to cover her bared breasts, sighing blissfully, as he caressed her.

"Mavourneen, my treasure!" he groaned against her open mouth. "Ye taste like ambrosia." Despite his protests, his mouth was greedy. Hungrily, he deepened their kiss, his tongue warring with her own small, pointed one.

His breath was wild and sweet, spiced with mint and with mead. It mingled with her own, as he cupped her chin, then angled his head to fit his lips to hers. His kisses melted her bones. She felt warm, lazy, and langorous with desire, as she dreamily leaned against him. . . .

Lust streaked through his loins, as her warm curves pressed against him. She deliberately rode against the straining ridge yet hidden by his breeks. Uttering a curse under his breath, he dragged her against him, savoring the silky texture of her skin on his, delighting in the honeyed secrets of her body. It was as if she were a delicious sweetmeat to be savored before devouring.

With a sob, she shouted his name to the stars that wheeled above. His gentle, enflaming caresses gave her such exquisite pleasure, they all but brought her to her knees. Yet her body, so long denied, demanded more than kisses, more than caresses. *Oh, so much more!*

"Make haste, oh, love, make haste!" she whispered, her

breath rising warm and urgent against his lips. "Love, hurry, do!"

Her hands fumbled to untie the lacings of his breeks; to put that which was inside them where it more properly belonged—inside her.

"Wait! What about the—"

"I—will—have—thee," she insisted, dropping to her knees on the thick turf. Reclining, she held out her arms.

By Loki, how could any man resist her, 'lest he were carved from ice and stone? And she had sworn. . . .

He dropped to his knees beside her.

The green and earthy scent of crushed wild flowers was heady on the night air, mingled with the delicate scent of her musk. He was hot to take her, hungry to master her creamy, smooth curves beneath his harder, rougher body. To join with her, while the wheel of life spun on. . . .

Uttering a low growl deep in his throat, he pressed her down into the lush summer grasses that grew all about the crumbling standing stones. Pulling his tunic over his head, he shrugged off his breeks and knelt between her thighs.

She gasped as he mounted her, her gray eyes widening in dizzy pleasure, as he loomed above her. His powerful torso was swarthy and shadowed, his shoulders muscular. Oh, and his arms!—His arms were oak saplings, building a fortress of love all about her!

From his chest hair rose two dark rose nubbins, firm as little berries. Edan licked her lips like a cat over a basin of fresh cream, then fastened her mouth over one nubbin as it hovered above her, and greedily nuzzled it.

He groaned and gritted his teeth His fingers tightened in her hair. "Edan! Whist, woman, how I love ye!"

And how I love thee, my dark, mysterious lord, she thought, turning her attentions to the other nubbin, as she guided his rearing manhood home.

She gasped, as he thrust strongly forward, sheathed to the hilt inside her. Her arms enfolded him. Her legs held him fast. She was his, body, heart, and—yea, her very soul!—Her immortal soul. *His soul.*

His imperiled soul.

Something bright stirred on the edges of her memory, but quickly fled, as he began to move, thrusting deep and hard between her thighs. All but Kerrin was forgotten then, for his thrusts quickened the river of fire in her belly, fueled the inferno in her loins.

''Aah!'' With a lusty groan, he quickly ducked his head to kiss her snowy breasts, cupped in his hands. As his mouth brushed her skin, his dark hair pooled like scrivener's ink across the creamy vellum of her bosom. His hands, his nostrils, his every sense, were filled to overflowing with her!

Instinctively, she moved with him, matching the rhythm of her hips to the driving of his flanks, till they were moving together, rising and falling on the grass as one, locked in the ancient rite of creation.

Sweat rolled down his brow as he slipped his hands beneath her buttocks, lifting her higher, higher!

Oh, wondrous sweet!—

Of a sudden, the stars pulsed, wheeled, then ran together in comets of molten silver, trailing tails of fire. The moon spun, slowly at first, then faster and still faster, till the fireball shattered, giving birth to a galaxy of white-hot stars.

She soared, wingless!

When the moment of exquisite pleasure receded, Edan sighed and opened her eyes. Through a fringe of fluttering long lashes, she saw Kerrin smiling down at her. His lambent gaze, so full of love, caressed her like an emerald flame. His naked gaze touched her in hidden, secret places, like an intimate caress.

Breathing shallowly, she watched the play of emotions cross his face. There was tenderness. And love. And what else? Aye, sadness! A terrible sadness.

''Why do you scowl at me so, my love? Do I not please thee?'' she asked lightly, stroking his cheek to divert him from whatever had caused those axewounds in his brow.

What could he say? That he felt as though he'd made love to a goddess here, surrounded by fairy rings of blossoms that glowed like fallen stars in the moon's ashy light? That in truth, she had pleased him far too well and that knowing what must come 'twas torment...?

Words that were half curses, half endearments escaped Kerrin's lips as he gathered her into his arms and held her tightly to him, rubbing her long silky curls between his fingers.

Edana. Her very name spoke of heaven! Yet, what was he? A beast. A shapeshifter. A creature of the Otherworld.

A man-wolf.

He flung his head back and howled at the golden Lamas moon, spilling his seed to the turf as he rolled off her. He loved her, trusted her with his very life—but he dare not risk that she had been lying, not in this. Edythe and her potions be damned! No child would bear his curse.

Pulling his mantle over them both, he held her, whispering that he loved her, would love her till the end of time.

He continued his lullaby of soothing words and tender caresses, till she grew quiet and still in his embrace, holding her long after the even rise and fall of her bosom told him she had fallen asleep.

When she awoke, a rose and saffron dawn was breaking. Birds were singing matins in the trees, but Kerrin was gone.

He ran until his lungs felt close to bursting, the rasp of his own breathing like the panting of a wild animal on the morning. On every side, the land was cloaked in summer, yet he was blind to its green and golden beauty, deaf to its buzzing bees and warbling birdsong, immune to the warmth of summer's breath and summer's taste on his tongue.

Instead, he ran.

Ran as the wild ones of forest and meadow ran when they were pursued by the hounds.

Ran as an outlaw flees from the just.

Yet, his pursuers would grant him no respite, give him no quarter. Rather, they rowelled him with their hateful spurs, slashed at him with their keenest blades, pricked him with their sharpest daggers—*memories.*

"Why, now! That ragged lad has your looks, ja, milord?"

A sly, female voice. One of Torrin's sluts? He could not recall. "Is he then your son?"

"Son? I have no sons, as yet. You, whelp! Get out of my sight! Be gone from here—else feed the wolves, like your cursed father!"

"Ho, lads, what have we here? The wolf-boy's crying like a snot-nosed wench! Look at him! Look at him! He wears a chain about his throat! Woof! Woof! Let's put him down the well!"

"Leave me alone!" His own voice. Leaden. Weary.

"Me mother's told me all about you! Your mother was a Viking's whore!" came the taunting voice. "Your father was—"

"My mother's dead, damn ye!" he'd denied, his temper finally flaring. "Leave off, else I'll clout ye!"

"Come on! Try it, ye whoreson bastard!"

"Leave off, all of ye!" That was Tavish. "He's done ye no harm!"

"He doesn't belong, Tavish. He's not wanted here. Nobody wants him . . . nobody . . . nobody."

His lungs were pumping like bellows now, his breathing agonized, noisy, as he plunged into the woods, fleeing desperately from his past.

Within the forest's secret heart lay peace and blessed sanctuary. . . .

Chapter Thirty-One

"Did you not hear me, Grandmother?" Edan cried, rounding on the old woman in her mossy cave. "Kerrin has left me!"

Half mad with grief, she took Myrla by her bony shoulders and shook her. "He has gone, and I cannot bring him back! I have no magic, no counterspell, no antidote to break this wretched curse! And without one, there can be no help for us!"

"Untrue, Daughter! Untrue!" Irritably clicking her teeth, Myrla shrugged off the young woman's bruising fingers and hobbled across the cottage to feed the fire with peat and twigs. Her grizzled gray hair and her withered-apple face lent her a frightening cast, as she poked at the glowing embers with a flesh-hook.

"All bones and wrinkles and few teeth!—She puts me in mind of witches, that one does!" Grania had once said. Edan sighed, very close to giving way to tears. Poor, dear Grania. She had missed her very badly, but now, with Kerrin gone, too. . . .

With a low roar, the flames suddenly leaped higher, spewing a handful of sparks over the hearthstones that drew her thoughts back to the moment at hand.

"You have the answer at your fingertips!" Myrla was saying in a scolding tone.

"I do?" She wetted her lips. "Where?"

" 'Tis in the amulet, child, hanging there, from the peg! Look upon its shining face. It bears the image of Pisces, the Fishes, does it not? 'Tis the Sign ruled by Neptune, lord of the Seas! Is this the sign under which you were born, daughter?"

She frowned. "Nay. I was born while Taurus ruled the heavens. In the month of May."

"Aye, girlie. Pisces is the constellation that governed *Kerrin's* birth, the night I dragged him, blue and bloodied, from my lady's body. Too large for an easy birthing, he was. A great strapping lad, cast in the mold of his Viking sire!" Her rheumy eyes gleamed.

"Viking? Are you saying Rolf Yellow Locks was—"

Myrla spat into the fire and muttered a disgusted string of Gaelic oaths. "Rolf?—Never! Rolf Yellow Hair was no stallion, to steal Torrin's mare from under him! Nor was my lady Deirdre one to cuckold her husband, for she had come to love Torrin by the time their babe was ready to be born. Nay, colleen. Kerrin was truly Torrin's son, although the bastard denied it for over a score of years."

"And Kerrin carries earl Murragh's curse because he is of Torrin's seed."

"So he believes, aye." Myrla's lips pursed.

"You don't?"

Myrla spat into the fire. "Curses of themselves have no power, girlie. 'Tis the *believing in them* that harms ye, not the words themselves! Believing is the strongest magic of all, for it makes all things possible!" Planting her bony rump squarely on a three-legged stool, her knees spread wide beneath her homespun skirts, she tugged her shawl about her shoulders.

Edan fidgeted. It was stifling in this cave, tucked deep within the hill, aye, and musty-smelling, to boot. Basins, jars, and earthen pots of herb charms, along with pestles and mortars, added to the clutter. Sweet, rank, and spicy herbal odors gave the sensation of stifling closeness.

Myrla bit into a morsel of coarse dark bread to test its freshness, then offered it to Edan, who impatiently refused.

Chewing gummily for a bit before answering, the old woman at last began to explain: "Earl Murragh cursed his murderer as he lay dying. *"A curse upon you—yea, and upon your seed, Torrin the Red!"* he said. I was the lady Deirdre's nurse back then, ye see? I heard him cry out, while we were waiting for those butchering brutes to come for her. *"Man-wolves! Unholy curs! You shall rue the day you sailed your dragon-ships to Waterford!"* That's what Lord Murragh said."

Caught up in the story, Edan scarce dared to breathe, let alone speak. But when a moment's pause stretched into several minutes, Edan gave her a verbal nudge to go on with the tale. "Aye, Grandmother? Go on! What did Earl Torrin do then?"

"Hmm? Well, Torrin was taken aback, at first, aye? But then he laughed, God rot him. He scoffed and said that Murragh's curse was a dying man's last chance—his final bid to leave behind something of himself to torment his enemy. Torrin swore to name his new stronghold Wulfskeep—Keep of the Wolves!—in defiance of Earl Murragh's curse. Yet, before too many moons had passed, he had come to believe the old earl's curse had indeed survived the grave. He fancied he was changing, becoming a 'man-wolf,' an 'unholy cur'—a shape-shifter!—just as Murragh had sworn!

"As the years passed, Torrin began to doubt the lies Canute had told him, for he could see himself in the boy. He knew then he had wronged my lady—and murdered his younger brother, Rolf, for naught!" Myrla shook her grizzled head, remembering. "But, rather than admit his guilt and make retribution, he sought escape in mead and beer, instead. Guilt, denial, strong drink—these were his true curse, girlie! At the last, as he lay dying, he named Kerrin to succeed him. It was all he could do to make amends for his injustice and cruelty, heartless bastard that he was."

"Cruelty?"

Myrla nodded. "Powerful cruel, he was, was Torrin!" Her eyes filled with tears. "Sure, and many's the time I've seen my poor wee lad chained to Jarl Torrin's chair like a flea-bitten hound, allowed neither blanket nor crust for his comfort—and him not seven winters' old, if he'd a day! Whipped, he was, too—always the scapegoat for his father's drunken outbursts. Every word he flung at the boy was shaped and twisted, so that the blame for all his hurts would fall upon Deirdre, his mother. There's Kerrin's true curse, girlie. His past!''

"But, if he didn't believe Kerrin was his son, why did Torrin agree to our betrothal?" she whispered.

Myrla chuckled mirthlessly. "Torrin thought it a fine jest t' play upon the high-king of Britain, betrothing a boy who was not his true son to the daughter of a fine Saxon prince."

"I see." She swallowed. "Rolf Ericksen—how did he die?"

Myrla's faded eyes filled with fresh horror, as she remembered. " 'Twas February, child, and bitter cold, both outdoors and in. Eire had suffered a bad harvest that year, followed by a harder winter. The wild ones of forest and meadow were starving. The deer were stripping the bark from the trees to stay alive. The people had fared little better.

"Jarl Torrin had several wolves trapped and lowered into a dried-up well. He had both of Rolf's legs broken, then put the poor laddie down in the pit with the starving beasts." She chewed gummily, her expression bleak. " 'Twas neither quick, nor pretty. Rolf's screams haunted Torrin 'til his death.''

"Sweet Jesu!" Edan whispered, crossing herself. She uttered a silent prayer for Rolf—whose only sin had been to befriend Padraic's lonely mother—and another for her dear, lost lord, wherever he might be. Life had not been kind to him. Small wonder he had seemed so cold, so incapable of affection, at the first! Having been shown so little love in his life, he had not known how to express what he felt for her—nor how to accept the affection of others. "But, my amulet, Grandmother? What has that to do with lifting the curse?"

"Ye told me 'twas a gift, aye? Given ye by one who had the Sight?''

"My uncle Sven. He was my mother's uncle. He died when I was a just a little girl."

Myrla nodded. Taking up a ladle, she skimmed greasy broth from the bubbling kettle and tasted it, slurping and smacking her chops in satisfaction. "Oh, 'tis a tasty drop o' mutton stew, it is. Aye, very tasty. Sup, child!"

"Nay, Mother. I cannot. My thanks, but I have not the belly for it, not now."

"Tsk. Ye'll fade away, sure, if ye won't eat, girlie—and where will my Kerrin's babe be then, aye?"

"His babe?" She was taken aback. "What . . . what babe?"

Myrla cackled. "Sure, and I saw ye last night. The two of ye, up on the headlands by the Maidens. 'Twas the two-headed beast ye were making, an' all—and there's but one reason a woman takes her man t' the stones: to get his babe in her belly! Mark my words. There'll be a Beltane birth from your Lamas mating!" The old hag grinned toothily, her rheumy eyes gleaming.

Edan flushed. " 'Twill be a babe without a father, then, I fear!"

"Not if ye can decipher the runes, girl! Take heart. 'Twas for just this purpose your amulet was made, I know it. Your Uncle Sven was wise. He had the Gift, which gave him knowledge of this day, though 'twas yet to come. Do you know what the runes say?"

She nodded. "I know them by heart."

"Then, come. Tell old Myrla what is written there."

With a shrug, Edan turned the silver talisman over. She could not read the mysterious markings for herself, for they were written in an old runic script of which she had no knowledge. And so, she chanted from memory:

> *Employ the silver adder's tongue*
> *If his imperiled soul you'd win.*
> *With courage slay the monstrous beast*
> *Set free the love that lies within.*

She frowned, a dull throb beginning at her temple. " 'Slay the monstrous beast?' " A flutter of excitement stirred in her belly. Could Myrla be right? Was the solution truly hidden in the runes? "Could the—is the 'monstrous beast' the man-wolf, Old Mother?"

Myrla smiled. "It might be, aye," she acknowledged, nodding sagely. She hesitated for a moment before adding in a thoughtful tone, "Or rather, *that part* of your lord that he believes is the man-wolf."

"A part, you say? But, how could that be?" Edan whispered. "One part of my lord could not exist, were the other slai . . . *Nay!*" Shocked, she would not finish the thought. By the campfire long ago in Kidwelly, then again while Myrla had been recovering at Wulfskeep, had the old woman not prophesied that she would slay her husband? . . . *"The time is coming wherein ye'll be forced t'take a life, if ye would give a life."* Take Kerrin's life? Nay! 'Twas a deed too abhorrent to contemplate.

"Tsk, tsk. Did I say I had all the answers, child?" Myrla grumbled, sucking on her gums. "Ye must have patience. Pray. Ask the gods t' help ye. When the Lady wills it—*if* she wills it—your answers will come." Scowling, she spat into the flames. They hissed and fell back for a moment, like chastened hounds. Smoke billowed, then slowly drifted upwards in a column, drawn through a small opening in the cave's roof to the outside world.

Myrla regarded the young women's distraught face through the smoke clouds, then added in a gentler tone, "Have courage, bless ye, child!" She cackled with laughter. "Mayhap old Myrla will visit the headlands for herself and seek the Maidens's help, aye? Come, now. Sup, then sleep, my lady-lass. On the morrow, we'll begin unravelling the tangled skeins of your mystery."

"I pray that there's still time!" she said vehemently, crossing herself.

"Amen and so be it," old Myrla muttered, piously. Adding another prayer to her own Lady of the Moon under her breath for good measure, she hobbled back to the fire, and began ladling broth into wooden bowls for herself and the girl.

The runes had whispered to her that Samhain would bring about an ending of some sort for the young couple. She frowned. The old pagan celebration fell on the last day of October, the Christian feast of Allhallows's Eve. 'Twas a fitting time for endings, for that same date had once been the last day of the old Celtic year. Would Samhain bring about an ending to her laddie's woes, she wondered? Or, an ending to his life? She sighed. The Sight, aided by the rune stones, pointed the way to much, but did not always reveal what she most wanted to see!

Like the girl, she could only wait and hope—and pray.

Chapter Thirty-Two

In the days that followed, golden August shimmered into mild, lovely September, then September drifted into the month of October, with falling leaves of russet and gold carpeting the woods, and amethyst evenings that were damp and chill with mist. They could as easily have been April and May, or June and July, for all Edan cared. One day had become much the same as any other for her. Lonely. Empty. Filled with despair.

She passed her time in searching for Kerrin, either combing the caves that riddled the cliffs along the seashore or roaming the mountain foothills and the woods. When inclement weather forced her indoors, she sat by the fire, trying to read some other meaning into the amulet's cryptic message than the one she had come to, or spent long days in nursing the sick. Ah, yes, the sick! There were so many of them stricken that autumn!

As she had feared, the summer flux had come to Waterford, yet it had come late. Still, it spared no one, from the smallest child to the oldest graybeard. Indeed, so many of Wulfskeep's people had fallen ill that by the third week of the month, her stores of herbs were almost depleted.

Sick cottagers kept to their huts, shivering and shaking with fever and chills, and growing gaunter by the day, as the sickness gnawed the flesh from their bones.

She, Myrla, and her ladies visited them tirelessly, portioning out what medicines they had, along with broth and bread and a hefty measure of prayer. Even so, many died: little ones scarce out of swaddling, graybeards, ruddy-cheeked farmers, dairymaids in the full flush of rosy youth—in truth, the flux showed no favorites.

"Here, madam, a seat. You are grown so very pale," Tavish observed one afternoon, as she tottered into the hall. Since Grania's death and Kerrin's disappearance, he had made the lady Edan his main concern. "Are you unwell, my lady?"

Edan closed her eyes and considered his question. She had spent yet another day going amongst the sick of the county. With Myrla's help, and Maida, Pegeen and Mary to attend her, she had made her rounds to one cottage after another, dosing each family with her herbal remedies: tea brewed from the bark of the myrtle or dried basil for loose bowels; boiled oak bark and oak leaves to halt vomiting; borage for fever; horehound for coughs. . . . "Naay, I am well enough, thank thee. Just a little weary," she decided, giving him a wan smile of reassurance, as she sank down onto a trestle by the hearth. Baa-Baa trotted over to her, baaing loudly and butting his black nose into her hand for attention, but she ignored the woolly little creature. Her eyelids felt so heavy. Heat burned behind them. Jesu, nay! She could not afford to fall sick herself, not when so many needed her. . . . She sighed. An exhausted tear leaked from behind her closed eyelids and trickled down her cheek. "We lost Colin Shepherd's wife this morn, Tavish. Then Grannie Dungarven this nooning. Aileen Wat's little daughter died during the night—so many good people, lost! Oh, Tavish, I miss my lord husband and my—your—Grania so very much!" She swallowed. Her lower lip quivered. "I—I'm trying not to let them down, but—oh, Tavish, there's so much to do here! Our people are dying, and there's nothing I can do to stop it. Nothing!"

Tavish tried to swallow over the lump choking his own throat. He opened his mouth to offer the mistress of Wulfskeep some words of comfort, but found he could not speak. He was yet too filled with grief of his own. "No one could ask more than what ye've done for the people, my lady," he murmured huskily. "I—"

"It's all right, Master Tavish, sir. You go on, now. I'll see to Lady Edana, never fear," Maida promised Tavish, gently. "Some good hot victuals and a drop of mulled cider will work wonders for the lady's spirits. Sit you down, do, lovie."

As Tavish beat a relieved retreat, the Welshwoman bustled about, fussing over Edan like a mother hen, alternately scolding and coaxing her, as she felt necessary.

In short order, Edan's sodden mantle had been taken from about her shoulders and a dry one, warmed by the fire, snugly tucked about her. Her boots had been removed and replaced with warm woolen hose and warm suede slippers. Mary briskly dried her mistress's damp hair with a linen cloth, while Pegeen chafed her hands to warm them. A smiling kitchen churl set a tray before her, bearing a bowl of her favorite mutton broth, a generous slice of thickly buttered, freshly baked bread, a small wedge of cheese, a pot of clover honey, and a sun-ripened pear. Mulled cider steamed in a goblet. Its delicious aroma made her mouth water.

But just a single spoonful of the savory broth, rich with barley, leeks, and turnips, set her stomach to heaving. Hastily clapping a hand over her mouth, she ran from the hall to the midden in the bailey. There, she vomited, feeling immeasurably better afterwards, although embarrassed by her treacherous innards!

Maida was waiting with a damp cloth to wipe her face and cold well water to rinse out her mouth when she returned to the hall.

"Well, well, now, *fach*. How far along are ye?" she asked sympathetically, her voice low.

"How far? . . . "

"The babe. When will it be born?" Noting her perplexed expression, Maida added, "Your courses, lovie. How many have ye missed?"

Edan frowned, slowly understanding what Maida was

implying. "Oh . . . two . . . almost three, I suppose. But I never thought! . . ." Nay. Despite what Myrla had said, she'd never imagined she could be carrying Kerrin's babe! Indeed, she had not realized that the nausea she'd been having late in the afternoons could mean the same as the morning sickness so common to women who were breeding. The knowledge filled her with joy. *A baby!*

She placed her fingertips on her queasy belly. It was flat as yet, only slightly hard. She blinked back tears. As yet unseen and unfelt, a wonderful, new life was enfolding deep within her womb—a life she refused to believe could be cursed in any way, but would instead, she vowed, be blessed. Blessed and filled with as much love as she could *possibly* give it! With as much love as she and Kerrin had poured—albeit unwittingly—into its creation. This little one would not be unwanted and uncared for, as its father had been. It would not be alone and unloved in a cruel world, denied both parents' love, as he had been. She would love it with every fiber of her being, with every beat of her heart and every breath that she drew! "When will the child be born?" she asked, the wonder filling her face with a radiant glow.

Maida laughed. It was the first time since that terrible night when Canute attacked Wulfskeep that she had seen Edan smile. The good Lord knew, she'd had precious little to smile about, poor lamb, what with losing first Grania, then her husband vanishing, in swift succession. . . . "That depends, my dear. On the answer to my question," she added. Seeing the confusion in Edan's face, she chuckled and repeated, "When were your last courses?" When Edan told her, she counted on her fingers. "Ten cycles of the moon. 'Twill be born in May or early June, lovie."

A Beltane babe from a Lamas mating, just as Myrla had foretold. However, Edan believed this particular prophecy owed more to the old woman's keen powers of observation than her gift of the Sight!

For the first time since Kerrin's disappearance, there was a little sunshine in her life.

* * *

One morning in the last week of October, Edan and her ladies left Wulfskeep to gather salt from the tide pools along the shore.

Over the last two weeks, the weather had grown cold, for summer had left Waterford at last. Mercifully, she had taken the flux with her, or so it seemed. The culling of the herds for the winter would begin on the first of November, as it did each and every year. Vast quantities of salt were needed to preserve the winter's meat, which would be salted in barrels to preserve it. Because of the sickness, however, the salt gathering had been postponed. They could afford to delay it no longer.

While a party from Wulfskeep's garrison went deer hunting for winter venison, Edan and her ladies went down to the shore.

They passed the chill, blustery morning scraping coarse white crystals into sacks, their chapped, cracked hands smarting from the salty harvest. The damp wind off the gray sea had whipped color into their cheeks and dried their lips. Edan had just decided it was high time to return to Wulfskeep, when she spotted Niall riding down the narrow beach toward them.

"My lady!" he greeted her excitedly, ignoring the other women—including his beloved Maida—with unusual rudeness.

"Aye, what is it, Niall?"

"I have seen Lord Kerrin, my lady!"

Her heart skipped a beat. Her hand flew to her breast. "Where?" she whispered.

"We were hunting when we spotted him, madam! His lordship is living in the deep woods about the Comeragh foothills like a—like a hermit, my lady."

He had meant to say "like a wild animal," she knew.

"God be thanked, my lord is alive! How did he look?" she demanded eagerly.

Niall frowned. "Not well, my lady. Not well at all. His mantle and breeks were ragged, and his hair and beard are grown long and unkempt as any beggar's. But—"

"Aye, go on," she urged quickly, when he paused.

"It was his eyes that troubled me! They—" He broke off, again reluctant to continue.

"What, what? Go on, sir! Spare no thought for my feelings, but tell me all. What was it about his eyes?" she urged, gently.

"They were filled with such torment, my lady! He stood there, still as one of the trees, and his eyes implored me t'— t'slay him, madam. God help me, I'd nocked an arrow and made ready to let it fly, before I came to my senses!" Niall shook his head, his kindly face grave and deeply troubled. 'Twould have been a kindness, in truth, my lady," he added in a defensive tone. "My poor lord was like a wounded animal, he was, begging to be put out of its misery."

Edan bit her lip, filled with shame. Niall had been prepared to offer her husband what she, coward that she was, could not: merciful release from a tormented life. Surely this was what the amulet had intended all along? "With courage, slay the monstrous beast," and, by so doing, "set free the love" that Kerrin carried within himself?

She swallowed, tears smarting behind her eyes. It seemed she could hear Kerrin's voice, after he had granted his beloved stallion, Conn, a quick and merciful end. *"Once life has stretched you on her rack a time or two, you will realize there are worse things than dying."* he had said. *"Living on, in pain and torment, is but one of them. I hope and pray that if I'm ever brought to such a pass, a friend will do the same for me, in the name of love."*

In the name of love, he'd said. The words seemed oddly prophetic now.

And she loved Kerrin with all her heart, did she not? . . .

Chapter Thirty-Three

The bow she selected for the task was the same bow she had employed at the archery contest in Winchester. Hewn from supple ash, its hardwood had been taken from an ancient tree that had begun its life in the forests near Kenley long ago, when the world was young. The wood had been carefully chosen, then lovingly shaped and carved for her reach alone by Dewey the Welshman, her father's master fletcher—the same Dewey who had given her a doeskin quiver of arrows and an arrowhead mold, when she left Kenley. She doubted the shy fletcher had ever imagined his best student using his weapons on such "prey" as this, however!

At first, it had taken all her strength to bend that bow, she remembered. The muscles in her shoulders and chest had protested the torture, screaming with pain. What few arrows she had managed to nock and let fly had fallen miserably short of their target. On more than one occasion, she had fled the practice butts in frustrated, angry tears, determined never to return. Yet, at Dewey's insistence—and with much bullying and cajoling—she had. And in due time—though only after much hard work, diligence, and patience—she had become proficient. More times than not, her arrows struck their target, as Queen Aefflaed's archery contest at Winchester had proven.

Three arrows. Three chances. She would have only the three! Would they be enough?

"Sharpen my eyes, I beg thee, Lord. Guide my hands! Do not let me fail in this!" she murmured, fervently. Overwhelmed by the sudden fear that something might go terribly wrong, she reached over her shoulder, needing to touch the three silver-headed arrows that jutted from the doeskin quiver, slung over her back.

The three shining arrowheads had been cast for her by Wulfskeep's fletcher from the melted-down silver of her fish amulet. Each silver arrowhead was shaped like the "adder's tongue"— the arrowhead-shaped leaves of the ferny plant that Pegeen had picked that fateful day along the river. There would be no second chances, not in this. It would be all or naught this Samhain night!

Colored autumn leaves rustled underfoot, as she followed the huge paw prints of a massive wolf along a bridle path. *Kerrin's tracks,* she wondered? Was his transformation completed, then? Had he truly become a man-wolf? Or, as Myrla had suggested, was it memories of his monstrous past that had driven him into the woods? . . .

The path she followed wove in and out among leafless trees, pines, and firs, leading her ever deeper into the forest and farther from both the comforts of Wulfskeep and the small camp on the forest's outskirts, where she'd left Niall, Tavish, and the horses. Kerrin's two loyal followers and friends had insisted on accompanying her that far.

A wind lifted and stirred through the woods. It soughed and moaned among the somber pines, creating a chill damp current that raised goosebumps down her arms and spine, despite her heavy garments. Daylight was fading. Night was fast approaching. Soon, it would be full dark. Then the moon would rise and the wolves would leave their dens to hunt.

She shivered. *Would Kerrin be among them?*

Upon leaving Wulfskeep, with her persistent escorts, she had ridden through the small hamlet of Waterford and seen hollowed-out turnips and pumpkins set by the wayside, leering faces carved into their sides. Each turnip candle had been lit by a tallow candle, set carefully inside it, in the hopes that the little goblin lights would scare away ghosts and evil spirits.

Allhallows Eve. She sighed. She would give a queen's ransom for a light—any light!—at this moment!

As she wound her way deeper into the forest, twilight became true dusk. Long shadows stretched themselves between the trees, like charcoal cats. With the gloaming, small sounds and movements sounded louder, seeming more threatening than they had by the light of day. Bushes that had been leafy, yet harmless, before, were magically transformed into monstrous shapes. They became hairy ogres—a hundred Lothars with daggers in their hands, or dragons lashing spiky tails.

"With courage . . . " *"With courage . . . "* The same two words from the amulet repeated over and over in her head, partnering the thunder of her heart. She wanted to be brave, to do what was right for Kerrin, but!—Dear Lord, she had so little courage for this!

The Samhain moon rose, ascending into the heavens like a floating crystal ball. It drenched the woods below in silver and painted every leaf and grassy blade with gilt. Errant breezes shivered through the treetops: cowled druids, whispering magic to each other. Indeed, all of a sudden, the air seemed charged with magic. Crackling. . . .

Closing her eyes, she offered up a silent prayer—not to the Lady of the Moon, but to her own dear God, beseeching Him to help her. A second prayer she made to Sven, who was in heaven now, looking down upon her. She asked him to guide her eyes, her hand, her heart, her aim.

When she opened her eyes again, Kerrin was standing across the broad clearing, watching her.

Clothed now in only a ragged tunic and breeks, he stood there like a wraith. His face was gaunt and hollow-eyed as, arms at his side, he waited.

Waited for her to free him.

Waited for her to . . .

She swallowed, unable to still the trembling in her knees,

certain they would fail her. *She could not do this—she could not! She loved him so! Then how, in God's Name, could she possibly slay him?*

But then again, if she loved him, how could she not?

Reaching behind her, she slowly drew an arrow from the doeskin quiver. She carefully nocked it against the bow string. Hands shaking, she raised the bow and sighted down the shaft.

Moonlight flashed off the gleaming silver arrowhead, like a streak of lightning.

Kerrin stood there, unmoving. His fists were clenched at his sides, as he stared directly at her. It was only then, as their eyes met, that she saw the tracks upon his cheeks, glistening in the moonlight. *"Do it!"* his gaze commanded her, silently. *"Do it now, Edana! If you love me—if you ever loved me— set me free!"*

Summoning all her courage, she slowly drew back, then let the first silver arrow fly.

Tavish and Niall found her, still kneeling on the same spot, at sunrise the following morning, her quiver empty. She was shivering with the night's chill, soaked to the bone with mist and rain. Almost incoherent with shock, she implored them to find her lord's body. Worse than any physical discomfort was the terrible pain in her heart. Had she gone mad? *She had killed him!* She must have, for she had seen her third arrow lodge deep in his chest. Had heard the terrible howl of pain torn from him, as it struck him. Blessed Jesu, she was a murderess! Kerrin's blood was on her hands! Surely she had been taken by a fit, to do such a thing? *Oh, what had she done?*

Despite an exhaustive search of the woods by both hunters and woodsmen of Wulfskeep, Kerrin's body could not be found, though her first two arrows and several drops of blood were found on the frosty grass where he had stood.

Edan suspected that the men of Wulfskeep privately believed Kerrin had been mortally wounded and, like a wild animal, had crawled off to die in hiding elsewhere. It was, she supposed—sick to her very heart—as fitting an explanation as any.

"My lady, think of the babe!—There is nothing more you can do here," Tavish remonstrated with her later that same day. "Come back to Wulfskeep."

When the search parties had returned to the camp, she had run to each man in turn.

"Have you seen my lord . . . ?"

"My husband, sir? Have you news of him? . . . "

"In what part of the woods did you search, sir? . . . "

"You are certain you did not see him? . . . "

She'd asked each man a barrage of questions, demanding answers, growing more wild-eyed and desperate with every answer she received in the negative.

Finally, Tavish could bear it no longer. Bidding Niall dismiss the search parties, he took his mistress by the elbow and drew her away. He was deeply concerned by his lady's waxy pallor, the trembling of her hands, the bloodless quality to her lips.

"You think I was wrong, don't you?" she demanded of him, wild-eyed. "You think I murdered him for my own ends!"

"I think, my lady, that you are cold," Tavish murmured, placing his own mantle about her shoulders. Her hands were icy, despite the roaring fire Niall had built for her. Offering her his arm, he would have raised her to her feet, yet she was so weakened, she could not stand unaided.

"Wha-aat?" She looked up at him, frowning in confusion. Tavish was growing taller and taller, somehow. His merry features ran together, like dyes in a vat! A soft moan escaped her, as she swayed, light-headed and dizzy, then sky and earth abruptly switched places, as she swooned—

Catching her before she could fall, Tavish carried her to his own horse and placed her before him on the saddle.

By the time they reached Wulfskeep, she was burning with fever and mumbling in delirium.

The flux had claimed its final victim.

Chapter Thirty-Three

The next month passed like a bad dream from which Edan could summon neither the strength nor the will to waken. Hour after hour, she tossed in a restless sleep, consumed by a fever that, like a sticky web, would not loose its hold upon her, but, instead, left her weaker by the hour.

She tried to break through those sticky strands, knowing there was something . . . someone . . . she had to find. But she could not escape.

At times, she glimpsed lights and heard the murmur of voices through the fog that enveloped her. She tried to call out to whoever was there, just beyond her field of vision, begging them to help her. But whoever it was—if anyone was ever truly there at all!—just drifted away, ignoring her cries.

At other times, she dreamed she was being pursued across rolling hills that were mantled with powdery snow. Running . . . running . . . running, as if through a sucking quagmire, she tried desperately to escape the pack of golden-eyed wolves who snapped at her heels, awakening with a jolt to find herself still in her bed, and screaming for Kerrin to help her.

Instead, she would find Maida looking down at her, her pretty face blurred, yet filled with compassion and concern.

"Here, pet. Drink this down. 'Twill help the nightmares go away," she said, pressing the hard, cold rim of a basin to Edan's lips. Her voice seemed to come from a great distance away.

With Maida's support, she would lift her aching head from the pallet, take a few sips, then sink back down into yet another fitful sleep, till the next awakening.

She made no effort to fight the weakness or the lethargy. Rather, she surrendered to it utterly. In her heart, she didn't want to wake up—or to get well—for then she would be forced to acknowledge that Kerrin was really gone, that slaying him had not been just some terrible dream. And that she could not bring herself to do.

And so, since she could escape the truth only in sleep, she slept.

As the days wore on, her caretakers changed. Sometimes it was still Maida who gave her sips of herbal tea, or spooned gruel and broth between her lips, but at others, Pegeen or little Mary, or even old Myrla tended her. She saw tears streaming down their faces and absently wondered if their weeping meant she was going to die. But she could not find the energy to care, even if that was so.

On other days, she was convinced that Grania was alive again. In her dreams, they laughed, quarrelled, and talked together, as they had always done. There was also another face—a vaguely familiar, lovely face that looked down at her and smiled when she opened her eyes. But though she tried to put a name to the woman, in her muddled condition the memory evaded her.

Cruellest by far, however, were the times when it seemed Kerrin himself was with her, when she thought she heard his lilting brogue, crooning to her, as if she were one of his wild creatures.

"Come now. Take a weep sip o' the broth, mavourneen. 'Twill give ye strength. . . . "

Or, "Will ye look how thin you're grown!—Sure, you're as scrawny as an old hen, sweet! Will ye not take a bite, just for me? Or if not for me, then for our precious babe?"

At such moments, her heart sang. She would awaken from

those wondrous dreams strengthened by hope, restored by the certainty that she would find him at her bedside when she opened her eyes. But alas, that hope proved yet another dream.

It was best not to think or hope or feel at all, she decided. To remain here forever, drifting safe in her dreamworld where all the harsh edges of reality were softened, blunted, and hurtful truth had lost its power to gouge or to wound. . . .

"Lady Edan don't want to get well, mum," Pegeen observed sadly, sniffing back her tears. "And so she won't! Me granny says ye must want to be healed when ye're sick. Just herbs and such in't enough."

"You're granny's a wise woman, *fach*," Maida said thoughtfully, looking down at Edan.

In the past three weeks, the flesh had fallen from her bones till she'd become so slender, a light breeze could have bowled her over. She had a delicate, almost ethereal beauty now, with her pale, heart-shaped face framed by a mass of ebony hair that was black as soot. Lavender smudges ringed her eyes, while her lips were shell pink, almost bloodless. Indeed, at times, her breathing was so light, so shallow, Maida feared she had passed from this world to the next, with no more than a sigh. She had to press her fingers to the pulse in her throat to discover if she yet lived. . . .

"I wonder what would give her back the will to live?" Maida murmured aloud. She and Pegeen exchanged meaningful glances.

They both knew the answer to that question.

Bundled warmly into a fur-lined mantle, the coweled hood pulled up to cover her hair, Edan was lifted up onto the saddle before Tavish again. His horse plodded up the bridle path towards the headlands where the Gray Maidens stood, silently waiting.

Lifting her head, Edan saw the standing stones and frowned.

What were they doing here? Why had they come to the Maidens?

But the standing stones were not their final destination, she realized, for Tavish rode on and past them, leaving the somber monoliths behind. They were, she realized dully, heading for the convent of St. Brigit's, yet she was too exhausted by the effort of dressing and staying upright before her gentle escort to care why he had brought her here.

After a brief exchange through the grilled window in a huge wooden gateway, a novice robed in white unbarred the convent gates and allowed them entry.

Inside the convent's little courtyard, Tavish dismounted and lifted the Lady Edan down after him. She was as weak as a kitten—so very frail that, fearful she would fall and hurt herself, he was reluctant to let her walk unaided. Yet, she vehemently refused his offer to carry her. And so, giving her his strong arm to lean upon, instead, he assisted her at a snail's pace to one of the cells belonging to the holy sisters.

"Praise be, you are come, Daughter!" an older woman declared, smiling in welcome, as she entered. Seeing the confusion in Edan's expression, she gently explained, "I am the Lady Deirdre, my dear. Do you not remember me?"

"I—I remember, aye. Of course," she murmured. Her legs were trembling uncontrollably. "By your leave, madam, a chair . . . ?"

"Of course. Forgive me." Gentle, elegant hands helped her to seat herself comfortably upon a small wooden bench of spartan design placed along one wall. A younger sister came and pressed a beaker of mulled wine into her icy hands, folding her numbed fingers around the cup. "Drink, my lady," the young nun urged, smiling down at her. "By God's good grace, 'twill fortify thee."

"Why am I here?" she whispered, after taking a sip of the heated red wine. Its warmth spread through her, returning the flow of blood and feeling to her fingers and toes, as the nun had promised. "Why have the others left?" Both the Lady Deirdre and her faithful Tavish had abandoned her. She and the young novice were quite alone now. Had they condemned her to a living death, mewed up within the convent's walls, for taking Kerrin's life? "Am I . . . am I to stay here, then?" she asked, in a small voice.

"God love ye, nay, madam!" the novice denied, merrily. Her plump, pretty face was wreathed in a broad smile beneath her severe wimple. "The lady Deirdre will return very soon. Just a moment more, you'll see."

True to the novice's words, the lady Deirdre returned soon after. "Sister Kathleen, that will be all here, my dear. Run along, now. Mother Superior is calling ye."

The young nun bobbed the lady a sketchy curtsey, flashed her a smile, and made a hasty exit.

"Well, now, Edana. Do you feel sufficiently rested to walk a short distance with me?"

"I will try, madam," she promised, uncertainly.

"Lean upon my arm, Daughter," Deirdre murmured, as she led the way from the cell. "Ah, you poor, dear child! How pale and thin you've grown!"

"Forgive me, madam, but I am confused. Why was I brought here, to the convent?"

Deirdre halted before yet another cell, the doorway to which stood slightly ajar. "Go inside, Edana. I think you'll find your answer there, my dear."

Frowning, Edan tottered inside. Her eyes took in the stone chamber in a single sweep. The cell was stark, spartan in the simplicity of it furnishings. There was a small stool, a little writing table with a rushlight upon it, a tiny slitted window that let in the bright, wintry light, and on one wall, a wooden crucifix. Her gaze came to rest upon a narrow cot, in which lay a dark-haired man.

Her heart skipped a beat.

Nay. It could not be.

She would not allow herself that hope.

And yet . . . and yet . . .

Her heart began to race erratically. Her hands flew to her throat.

"Have ye no greeting for me, colleen?"

That voice, dear God! *His voice!* —

An involuntary cry escaped her, a cry that was shock, disbelief, joy, at one and the same time. Her weakness was forgotten, as she flung herself across the cell and into Kerrin's open arms.

"You're alive!" she whispered, tears streaming down her face, as he tenderly embraced her. She touched his hollowed cheek, his brow, his midnight hair—in which a single streak had turned pure white—with a sense of wonder. 'Twas as if she could not believe what her eyes were telling her, and only by touching him could she make it real. Smiling through her tears, she tentatively stroked his cheek. "The men of Wulfskeep searched the forest high and low, but they could find no sign of you, my love. I thought—dear God!—I feared I had killed you!"

Smiling, he took her hand in his own and drew it to his lips. He kissed her knuckles. "Not so. In doing what ye did, ye gave me back my life, Edan. Ye set me free! I thank ye for your courage, with all my heart," he added huskily. Drawing her into his arms, he kissed her, then rocked her against his chest. "Colleen, colleen, I've so much to make up to ye."

"Don't dwell upon the past," she urged, laughing through happy tears. "Put it where it belongs, my love—behind us. We have a future to look forward to now, and a wonderful life for the three of us."

"Three?" His dark brows rose. His gaze locked on hers, he slipped his hand beneath her mantle to her belly. He pressed his palm to the unmistakable swelling there, and wonder filled his handsome face. "Our child?"

"Aye!" she admitted, laughing at his stunned expression. The baby moved, then. Feeling its vigorous fluttering, they both smiled in wonder " 'Twill be born in the spring."

He cradled her head, stroking the dark ringlets that spilled across her chest. "Thank you, mavourneen."

"But, tell me. How is it you are here?" she asked, leaning back to look up at him.

He shook his head. "Some instinct drove me to the convent, when I was wounded by your arrow. They found me the next morning, outside the convent gates. I—I was frozen and half out of my mind, demanding to see her."

"Your mother?"

"Aye." He paused, wondering how he could explain what had brought him to the convent. "All my life, I'd held her to account for the ills I had suffered, Edan: my bastardy; the cruelties Torrin rained upon me as a child. All my life, I hated her for what she had done, when, in truth, she was innocent, blameless. As much the victim of Canute's lies and my father's jealousy as was I! The knowledge that I had wronged her wracked me with guilt and shame. I came here to ask—nay, to beg!—her forgiveness, mavourneen."

"And did she give it?"

"Aye, verily. And along with it, a mother's love."

She blinked back tears, moved by the wonder in his face— wonder that anyone should love him. "Had you—had you lost much blood?"

"Very little. 'Twas naught but a flesh wound. Look," he murmured. Drawing aside the neck of his tunic, she saw the purple knot of a newly healed wound, high on his left chest, just below the shoulder. "Nevertheless, within a day or two, I was out of my mind with fever." Reading her thoughts, he explained, "It was not the arrow wound that laid me low, my love, but a far deeper, inner wound that had festered over the years. In truth, it was a sickness of the soul, in need of cautery! For days, I lay like one dead, not caring if I lived or died. And then. . . ."

"Aye, go on," she breathed.

"And then I dreamed of you. I heard you call to me. You said you loved me. And that you . . . that you needed me. . . ."

"I did, oh, love, I did!"

". . . and I wanted to get well. To go to you. My lady mother says 'twas at that moment I began to recover," he finished simply. " 'Twas your love, not your arrow, that freed me, Edana! By loving me, when all my life, I'd believed myself unworthy of being loved, you gave me back the will to live. It is thanks to you that I am here, and well."

She searched his face. Despite his pallor, she sensed a serenity, an acceptance in his expression that had not been there before. "Praise be! You have made your peace with both the Lady Deirdre, and with your past, have you not, my lord?"

"I have, and more. My love, I have made peace within myself!"

She looked up into his shining green eyes, fringed with long, sooty lashes that any wench would envy, and saw that they were clear, now. As green, clear, and unmuddied as a woodland pool. His spirit was no longer in peril or in turmoil, but strong, whole, and well. Soon, his body would also be healed. Her lips quivered. She blinked back tears. "I love you, Padraic mac Torrin. Never forget it, never doubt it! I have loved you from the moment I set eyes upon thee! I will always love thee."

With a sigh of happiness, she went into his arms.

Epilogue

As Myrla had prophesied, Edan gave birth the following spring, soon after the feast of Beltane—though not to one babe, but two!

Her waters broke at the feast Kerrin gave in mid-May to celebrate the wedding of Maida to his captain, Niall. Edan's lengthy labor all that night was followed by a surprisingly easy double birth the following spring morn that Myrla, bless her, did much to ease.

Although twins, in appearance little Brianna and her brother, Donovan—who was younger than she by only a few moments—were as different as chalk and cheese. Brianna's hair was the hue of polished horse chestnuts, a darker shade of her grandmother Marissa's red-gold locks, soft auburn curls clinging to her little head like a fitted cap. Baby Donovan, on the other hand, favored his parents' coloring, and had a mop of hair as black as a raven's glossy wing. It was soon apparent that the infants were very much alike in temperament, however, for they would both set up a loud, impatient squalling when denied their mother's breasts!

''They remind me of their lady mother when she was carrying

them,'' Kerrin observed, slyly, one summer morning. ''Always hungry!''

Edan shot him an indignant scowl and rudely stuck out her tongue, as she lifted Brianna to her swollen breast. ''I shall ignore your insults, my lord, if you will quiet your son. Like his lord father, he is loud of voice and of a bullying nature.''

Chuckling good-naturedly, Kerrin lifted his small son over his shoulder and patted his tiny, squirming bottom. Straightway, the squalling miraculously ceased, fading into hiccups, then contented silence that was broken only by small, satisfied sucking sounds, as the babe gnawed on his tiny fist.

Edan smiled. Kerrin's way with the wild creatures was equally successful with their babes! Both Brianna and Donovan would cease their crying the very moment he picked them up.

''Clever lad,'' Kerrin praised his son. ''Do ye see, mavourneen, my treasure? Our wee Donovan's ready to abandon his mother's milk for meat! This week, his fingers. The next, 'twill be a meaty leg o' lamb he's after gnawing on!''

Edan laughed as she bubbled their little daughter, who had fallen asleep with her wobbly little head resting upon her mother's breast. A dribble of milk had escaped the corner of her mouth. It dampened the exquisite, lace-edged gown her Grandmother mac Torrin had sewn for her, with love in every perfect stitch.

The Lady Deirdre had taken up residence with them at Wulfskeep since last Yuletide. She had since become a much cherished and respected dowager of the household, as well as Edan's friend and ally. Indeed, Deirdre's gentle counsel and affectionate manner had done much to fill the void left by Edan's boisterous, loving family's absence.

''Did you hear your Papa, Brianna, my darling? He is quite mad, is he not?'' she murmured. She nuzzled the baby's warm neck, inhaling the sweet baby scent of her.

As if in answer, the baby burped loudly. Her parents laughed. Startled, Brianna's eyes flew open again. Her rosebud mouth turned downwards in a heartrending whimper. Her lower lip jutted. Her chin quivered, tremulously.

"Pray, rock our daughter to sleep, milord, so that I may nurse our son."

They carefully made the exchange, Kerrin taking his tiny daughter into his arms with the same tender care that he had carried his infant son. He smiled down at his little girl, who had wrapped her tiny fingers about his own, just as readily as she had wrapped them about his heart. His expression was filled with love. "Each time I look at our children, I see the future, Edan. Do you remember telling me that to see the Dance of the Hares was an omen of good fortune?"

"I do, aye."

"At the time, it seemed impossible. I couldn't bring myself t'believe it, but I was wrong. Sure, and we'll have a good life together, Edan. I know it. A long, wonderful life filled with love and happiness!"

"God willing, and Amen," she murmured, flashing him a radiant smile.

Leaning down, their little daughter in his arms, their son in hers, they embraced and shared a long and tender kiss.

Beauty had been won. The Beast had been slain. Love had conquered all.

It was time to live happily ever after.

DANGEROUS GAMES   (0-7860-0270-0, $4.99)
by Amanda Scott

When Nicholas Barrington, eldest son of the Earl of Ul-
combe, first met Melissa Seacort, the desperation he
sensed beneath her well-bred beauty haunted him. He
didn't realize how desperate Melissa really was . . . until
he found her again at a Newmarket gambling club—being auctioned off by her father to the highest bidder. So,
Nick bought himself a wife. With a villain hot on their
heels, and a fortune and their lives at stake, they would
gamble everything on the most dangerous game of all:
love.

A TOUCH OF PARADISE   (0-7860-0271-9, $4.99)
by Alexa Smart

As a confidence man and scam runner in 1880s America,
Malcolm Northrup has amassed a fortune. Now, posing
as the eminent Sir John Abbot—scholar, and possible
discoverer of the lost continent of Atlantis—he's taking
his act on the road with a lecture tour, seeking funds for
a scientific experiment he has no intention of making.
But scholar Halia Davenport is determined to accompany
Malcolm on his "expedition" . . . even if she must kidnap
him!